ALSO BY IVAN DOIG

FICTION

Prairie Nocturne
Mountain Time
Bucking the Sun
Ride with Me, Mariah Montana
Dancing at the Rascal Fair
English Creek
The Sea Runners

NONFICTION

Heart Earth
Winter Brothers
This House of Sky

ENGLISH CREEK

IVAN DOIG

SCRIBNER

New York · London · Toronto · Sydney

Again for Carol

SCRIBNER
1230 Avenue of the Americas
New York, NY 10020

First Scribner trade paperback edition 2005

SCRIBNER and design are trademarks of Macmillan Library Reference USA, Inc., used under license by Simon & Schuster, the publisher of this work.

For information about special discounts for bulk purchases, please contact Simon & Schuster Special Sales: 1-800-456-6798 or business@simonandschuster.com

DESIGNED BY LAUREN SIMONETTI

Manufactured in the United States of America

13 15 17 19 20 18 16 14

Library of Congress Control Number: 2005046550

ISBN 978-0-689-11478-6
ISBN 978-0-7432-7127-1 (Pbk)

"You got to make your way in this old pig iron world."

Miss Rose Gordon (1885–1968)

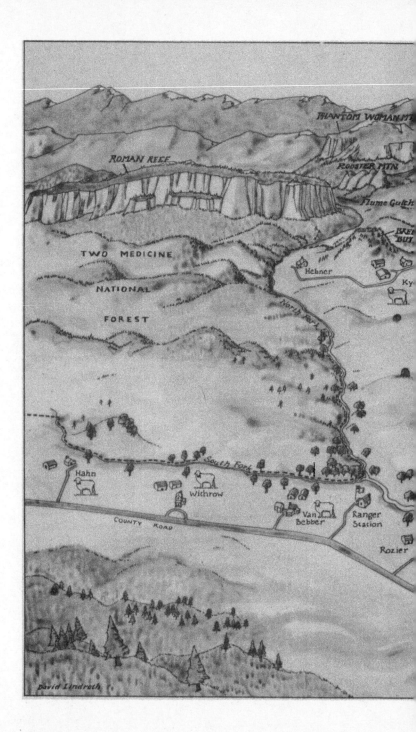

PHANTOM WOMAN MT.

ROOSTER PT'N

ROMAN REEF

Flume Gulch

BRE—
BUT.

TWO MEDICINE

Hebner

Ky—

NATIONAL

North Fork

FOREST

South Fork

Hahn

Withrow

Van
Bebber

Ranger
Station

COUNTY ROAD

Rozier

David Lindreth

ENGLISH CREEK

Distance from Gros Ventre to the
Ranger Station is nine miles.

Dashed line (---) indicates boundary of
Two Medicine National Forest.

Sheep ranches   Cattle ranches

JERICHO REEF

Reese

Egan

Noon Creek

COUNTY ROAD

Double W

TO Glacier Park

English Creek

Frew

Busby   Hill   Finletter

COUNTY ROAD

GROS VENTRE

ONE

This time of year, the report from the dust counties in the northeastern part of the state customarily has it that Lady Godiva could ride through the streets there without even the horse seeing her. But this spring's rains are said to have thinned the air sufficiently to give the steed a glimpse.

—*GROS VENTRE WEEKLY GLEANER, JUNE 1*

THAT MONTH OF JUNE swam into the Two Medicine country. In my life until then I had never seen the sidehills come so green, the coulees stay so spongy with runoff. A right amount of wet evidently could sweeten the universe. Already my father on his first high patrols had encountered cow elk drifting up and across the Continental Divide to their calving grounds on the west side. They, and the grass and the wild hay meadows and the benchland alfalfa, all were a good three weeks ahead of season. Which of course accounted for the fresh mood everywhere across the Two. As is always said, spring rain in range country is as if halves of ten-dollar bills are being handed around, with the other halves promised at shipping time. And so in the English Creek sheepmen, what few cowmen were left along Noon Creek and elsewhere, the out-east farmers, the storekeepers of Gros Ventre, our Forest Service people, in just everyone that start of June, hope was up and would stay strong as long as the grass did.

Talk could even be heard that Montana maybe at last had seen the bottom of the Depression. After all, the practitioners of this bottomed-out notion went around pointing out, last year was a bit more prosperous, or anyway a bit less desperate, than the year before. A nice near point of measurement which managed to overlook that for the several years before last the situation of people on the land out here had been godawful. I suppose I ought not to dwell on dollar matters when actually our family was scraping along better than a good many. Even though during the worst years the Forest Service did lay off some people—Hoovered them, the saying went—my father, ranger Varick McCaskill, was never among them. True, his salary was jacked down a couple of times, and Christ only knew if the same wasn't going to start happening again. But we were getting by. Nothing extra, just getting by.

It gravels me every time I read a version of those times that makes it sound as if the Depression set in on the day Wall Street tripped over itself in 1929. Talk about nearsighted. By 1929 Montana already had been on rocky sledding for ten years. The winter of 1919—men my father's age and older still just called it "that sonofabitch of a winter"— was the one that delivered hard times. Wholesale. As Dode Withrow, who had the ranch farthest up the south fork of English Creek, used to tell: "I went into that '19 winter with four thousand head of ewes and by spring they'd evaporated to five hundred." Trouble never travels lonesome, so about that same time livestock and crop prices nosedived because of the end of the war in Europe. And right along with that, drought and grasshoppers showed up to take over the dry-land farming. "It began to be just a hell of a situation," my father always said of those years when he and my mother were trying to get a start in life. "Anyplace you looked you saw people who had put twenty years into this country and all they had to show for it was a pile of old calendars." Then when drought circled back again at the start of the thirties and joined forces with Herbert Hoover, bad progressed to worse. That is within my own remembering, those dry bitter years. Autumn upon autumn the exodus stories kept coming out of the High Line grain country to the north and east of us, and right down here on the highway which runs through the town of Gros Ventre anybody who looked could see for himself the truth of those tales, the furniture-loaded jitney trucks with farewells to Montana painted across their boxboards in big crooked letters: GOODBY OLD DRY and AS FOR HAVRE YOU CAN HAVE 'ER. The Two country did have the saving grace that the price for lambs and wool recovered somewhat while other livestock and crops stayed sunk. But anybody on Two land who didn't scrape through the early thirties with sheep likely didn't scrape through at all. Cattle rancher after cattle rancher and farmer after farmer got in deep with the banks. Gang plow and ditcher, work horses and harness, haymow and cream separator: everything on those places was mortgaged except the air. And then foreclosure, and the auctioneer's hammer. At those hammer sales we saw men weep, women as stricken as if they were looking on death, and their children bewildered.

So it was time hope showed up.

"Jick! Set your mouth for it!"

Supper, and my mother. It is indelible in me that all this began there right at the very outset of June, because I was working over my saddle and lengthening the stirrups again, to account for how much I was growing that year, for the ride up with my father on the counting trip the next morning. I can even safely say what the weather was, one of those brockled late afternoons under the Rockies when tag ends of storm cling in the mountains and sun is reaching through wherever it can between the cloud piles. Tell me why it is that details like that, saddle stirrups a notch longer or sunshine dabbed around on the foothills some certain way, seem to be the allowance of memory while the bigger points of life hang back. At least I have found it so, particularly now that I am at the time where I try to think what my life might have been like had I not been born in the Two Medicine country and into the McCaskill family. Oh, I know what's said. How home ground and kin together lay their touch along us as unalterably as the banks of a stream direct its water. But that doesn't mean you can't wonder. Whether substantially the same person would meet you in the mirror if your birth certificate didn't read as it does. Or whether some other place of growing up might have turned you wiser or dumber, more contented or less. Here in my own instance, some mornings I will catch myself with a full cup of coffee yet in my hand, gone cold while I have sat here stewing about whether my threescore years would be pretty much as they are by now had I happened into existence in, say, China or California instead of northern Montana.

Any of this of course goes against what my mother forever tried to tell the other three of us. That the past is a taker, not a giver. It was a warning she felt she had to put out, in that particular tone of voice with punctuation all through it, fairly often in our family. When we could start hearing her commas and capital letters we knew the topic had become Facing Facts, Not Going Around with Our Heads Stuck in Yesterday. Provocation for it, I will say, came from my father as reliably as a dusk wind out of a canyon. Half a night at a time he might spend listening to Toussaint Rennie tell of the roundup of 1882, when the cowmen fanned their crews north from the elbow of the Teton River to the Canadian line and brought in a hundred thousand head. Or the tale even bigger and earlier than that, the last great buffalo hunt, Toussaint having ridden up into the Sweetgrass Hills to see down onto a prairie that looked burnt, so dark with buffalo, the herd pinned into place by the plains tribes. Strange, but I can still recite the tribes and where they pitched their camps to surround those miles of buffalo, just as Toussaint passed the lore of it to my father: Crows on the southeast, Gros Ventres and Assiniboines on the northeast, Piegans on the west, Crees along the north, and Flatheads here to the south. "Something to see, that must've been," my father would say in his recounting to the rest of us at supper. "Mac, somebody already saw it," my mother would come right back at him. "What you'd better Put Your Mind To is the Forest Supervisor's Visit Tomorrow." Or if she didn't have to work on my father for the moment, there was Alec when he began wearing a neck hanky and considering himself a cowboy. That my own particular knack for remembering, which could tuck away entire grocery lists or whatever someone had told me in innocence a couple of weeks before, made me seem likely to round out a houseful of men tilted to the past must have been the final stem on my mother's load. "Jick," I can hear her yet, "there isn't any law that says a McCaskill can't be as forward-looking as anybody else. Just because your father and your brother—"

Yet I don't know. What we say isn't always what we can do. In the time after, it was her more than anyone who would return and return her thoughts to where all four of our lives made their bend. "The summer when . . ." she would start in, and as if the three-note signal of a chickadee had been sung, it told me she was turning to some happening of that last English Creek summer. She and I are alike at least in that, the understanding that such a season of life provides more than enough to wonder back at, even for a McCaskill.

"JICK! Are you coming, or do the chickens get your share?" I know with all certainty too that that call to supper was double, because I was there at the age where I had to be called twice for anything. Anyway, that second summons of hers brought me out of the barn just as the pair of them, Alec and Leona, topped into view at the eastern rise of the county road. That is, I knew my brother as far as I could see him by that head-up way he rode, as if trying to see beyond a ridge-line in front of him. Leona would need to be somewhat nearer before I could verify her by her blouseful. But those days if you saw Alec you were pretty sure to be seeing Leona too.

Although there were few things more certain to hold my eyes than a rider cresting that rise of road, with all the level eastern horizon under him as if he was traveling out of the sky and then the outline of him and his horse in gait down and down and down the steady slow slant toward the forks of English Creek, I did my watching of Alec and Leona as I crossed the yard to our house behind the ranger station. I knew better than to have my mother call me time number three.

I went on in to wash up and I suppose was a little more deliberately offhand than I had to be by waiting until I'd dippered water into the basin and added hot from the kettle before announcing, "Company."

The word always will draw an audience. My father looked up from where he was going over paperwork about the grazers' permits, and my mother's eyebrows drew into that alignment that let you know you had all of her attention and had better be worth it.

"Alec and Leona," I reported through a face rinse. "Riding like the prettiest one of them gets to kiss the other one."

"You seem to know a remarkable lot about it," my mother said. Actually, that sort of thing was starting to occur to me. I was fourteen and just three months shy of my next birthday. Fourteen, hard on to fifteen, as I once heard one of the beerhounds around the Medicine Lodge saloon in Gros Ventre describe that complicated age. But there wasn't any of this I was about to confide to my mother, who now instructed: "When you're done there you'd better bring in that spare chair from your bedroom." She cast the pots and pans atop the stove a calculating look, then as if having reminded herself turned toward me and added: "Please." When I left the room she already had rattled a fresh stick of wood into the kitchen range and was starting in on whatever it is cooks like her do to connive food for three into a supper for five.

"Remind me in the morning, Bet," I could overhear my father say, "to do the rest of this Uncle Sam paper."

"I'll serve it to you with breakfast," promised my mother.

"Fried," he said. "Done to a cinder would suit me, particularly Van

Bebber's permit. It'd save me arguing the Section Twenty grass with him one goddamn more time."

"You wouldn't know how to begin a summer without that argument with Ed," she answered. "Are you washed?"

By the time I came back into the kitchen with the spare chair which had been serving as my nightstand Alec and Leona were arriving through the doorway, him inquiring "Is this the McCaskill short-order house?" and her beaming up at him as if he'd just recited Shakespeare.

They were a pair to look on, Alec and Leona. By now Alec was even taller than my father, and had the same rich red head of hair; a blood-bay flame which several hundred years of kilts and skirts being flung off must have fanned into creation. Same lively blue eyes. Same straight keen McCaskill nose, and same tendency to freckle across it but nowhere else. Same deep upper lip, with the bottom of the face coming out to meet it in stubborn support; with mouth closed, both Alec and my father had that jaw-forward look which meets life like a plow. Resemblance isn't necessarily duplication, though, and I see in my mind's eye that there also was the message of that as promptly as my brother and my father were in the same room that evening. Where my father never seemed to take up as much space as his size might warrant, Alec somehow took up his share and then some. I noticed this now, how Alec had begun to stand in that shambly wishbone way a cowboy adopts, legs and knees spraddled farther apart than they need to be, as if hinting to the world that he's sure longing for a horse to trot in there between them. Alec was riding for the Double W ranch, his second summer as a hand there, and it had caused some family ruction; his going back to cowboying instead of taking a better-paying job, such as driving a truck for Adam Kerz as my mother particularly suggested. But the past year or so Alec had had to shut off his ears to a lot of opinions my parents held about this cowboy phase of his. Last Fourth of July, when Alec showed up in rodeo clothes which included a red bandanna, my father asked him: "What, is your Adam's apple cold?"

Not that you could ever dent Alec for long. I have told that he had a head-up, nothing-in-life-has-ever-slowed-me-up-yet way of riding. I maybe should amend that to say that on horseback Alec looked as if he was riding the world itself, and even afoot as he was here in the kitchen he seemed as if he was being carried to exactly where he wanted to go. Which, just then, I guess you would have to say he was. Everything was coming up aces for Alec that year. Beating Earl Zane's time with Leona.

Riding for the Double W in a green high-grass summer. And in the fall he would head for Bozeman, the first McCaskill to manage to go to college. Launching Alec to college from the canyon of the Depression was taking a mighty exertion by our whole family, but his knack for numbers plainly justified it; we none of us held a doubt that four years from now he would step out of Bozeman trained in mechanical engineering. Yes, Alec was a doer, as people said of him. My own earliest memory of this brother of mine was the time, I must have been four and him eight, when he took me into the pasture where the ranger station's saddle horses were grazing and said, "Here's how you mooch them, Jick." He eased over to the nearest horse, waited until it put its head down to eat grass, then straddled its neck. When the horse raised its head Alec was lifted, and slid down the neck into place on its back and simultaneously gripped the mane to hang on and steer by. "Now you mooch that mare," Alec called to me and I went beside the big chomping animal and flung my right leg over as he had, and was elevated into being a bareback rider the same as my brother.

"'Lo, Jicker," Alec said across the kitchen to me now after his greeting to my mother and father. "How's the world treating you?"

"Just right," I said back automatically. "'Lo, Leona."

Leona too was a horseperson, I guess you'd call it these days. When Tollie Zane held his auction of fresh-broke saddle horses in Gros Ventre every year he always enlisted Leona to ride them into the auction ring because there is nothing that enhances a saddle pony more than a good-looking girl up there on his back. Right now, though, as she entered my mother's kitchen Leona's role was to be milk and honey. Which she also was first-rate at. A kind of pause stepped in with Leona whenever she arrived somewhere, a long breath or two or maybe even three during which everyone seemed to weigh whether her hair could really be so gold, whether her figure actually lived up to all it advertised on first glance. I managed to notice once that her chin was pointier than I like, but by the time any male looked Leona over enough to reach that site, he was prepared to discount that and a lot more.

Anyhow, there in the kitchen we went through that pause period of letting Leona's looks bask over us all, and on into some nickel and dime gab between Alec and my father—

"Working hard?"

"Well, sure, Dad. Ever see me do anything different?"

"Just times I've seen you hardly working."

"The Double W makes sure against that. Y'know what they say. Nobody on the Double W ever gets a sunburn, we don't have time."

—and an old-as-womankind kitchen ritual between Leona and my mother—

"Can I help with anything, Mrs. McCaskill?"

"No, probably it's beyond help."

—until shortly my mother was satisfied that she had multiplied the food on the stove sufficiently and announced: "I expect you brought your appetites with you? Let's sit up."

I suppose every household needs some habited way to begin a meal. I have heard the Lord thanked in some of the unlikeliest of homes, and for some of the unholiest of food. And seen whole families not lift a fork until the patriarch at the head of the table had his plate full and his bread buttered. Ours, though, said grace only once every three hundred sixty-five days, and that one a joke—my father's New Year's Eve invocation in that Scotch-preacher burr he could put on: "We ask ye on this Hogmanay, gi' us a new yearrr o' white brread and nane o' yourrr grray."

Other than that, a McCaskill meal started at random, the only tradition to help yourself to what was closest and pass the food on clockwise.

"How's cow chousing?" My father was handing the mashed potatoes to Leona, but looking across at Alec.

"It's all right." Alec meanwhile was presenting the gravy to Leona, before he realized she didn't yet have spuds on her plate. He colored a little, but notched out his jaw and then asked back: "How's rangering?"

When my father was a boy a stick of kindling flew up from the ax and struck the corner of his left eye. The vision was saved, but ever after that eyelid would droop to about half shut whenever amusement made him squint a little. It descended now as he studied the meal traffic piling up around Leona. Then he made his reply to Alec: "It's all right."

I had the bright idea this conversation could benefit from my help, so I chimed in: "Counting starts tomorrow, Alec. Dode's sheep, and then Walter Kyle's, and then Fritz Hahn's. Dad and I'll be up there a couple, three days. Remember that time you and I were along with him and Fritz's herder's dog Moxie got after a skunk and we both—"

Alec gave me a grin that was tighter than it ought to have been from a brother. "Don't let all those sheep put you to sleep, sprout."

Sprout? Evidently there was no telling what might issue from a person's mouth when he had a blond girl to show off in front of, and the look I sent Alec told him so.

"Speaking of counting," Alec came up with next, "you got your beavers counted yet?" Here he was giving my father a little static. Every so often the Forest Service regional headquarters in Missoula—"Mazoola," all of us pronounced it my father's way, "emphasis on the zoo"—invented some new project for rangers to cope with, and the latest one we had been hearing about from my father was the inventory he was supposed to take of the beaver population on the national forest portion of English Creek. "Christamighty," he had grumped, "this creek is the beaver version of New York City."

Now, though, with Leona on hand—this was the first time Alec had brought her out for a meal; the rest of us in the family recognized it as an early phase, a sort of curtain-raiser, in the Alec style of courting—my father just passed off the beaver census with: "No, I'm waiting for policy guidance from the Mazoola inmates. They might want me to count only the tails and then multiply by one, you never know."

Alec didn't let it go, though. "Maybe if they like your beaver arithmetic, next summer they'll have you do fish."

"Maybe." My father was giving Alec more prancing room than he deserved, but I guess Leona justified it.

"Who's this week's cook at the Double W?" My mother, here. "Leona, take some more ham and pass it on to Jick. He goes through food like a one-man army these days." I might have protested that too if my plate hadn't been nearly empty, particularly of fried ham.

"A Mrs. Pennyman," Alec reported. "From over around Havre."

"By now it's Havre, is it. If Wendell Williamson keeps on, he'll have hired and fired every cook between here and Chicago." My mother paused for Alec's response to that, and got none. "So?" she prompted. "How does she feed?"

"It's—filling." The question seemed to put Alec a little off balance, and I noticed Leona provide him a little extra wattage in her next gaze at him.

"So is sawdust," said my mother, plainly awaiting considerably more report.

"Yeah, well," Alec fumbled. I was beginning to wonder whether cowboying had dimmed his wits, maybe driven his backbone up through the judgment part of his brain. "You know. It's usual ranch grub." He sought down into his plate for further description and finally proclaimed again: "Filling, is what I'd call it."

"How's the buttermilk business?" my father asked Leona, I suppose to steer matters off Alec's circular track. Her parents, the Tracys, ran the creamery in Gros Ventre.

"Just fine," Leona responded along with her flash of smile. She seemed to be on the brink of saying a lot more, but then just passed that smile around to the rest of us, a full share to my father and another to my mother and then one to me that made my throat tighten a little, then letting it rest last and coziest on Alec. She had a natural ability at that, producing some pleasantry and then lighting up the room so you thought the remark amounted to a whole hell of a lot more than it did. I do envy that knack in a person, though likely wouldn't have the patience to use it myself even if I had it.

We still were getting used to the idea of Leona, the three of us in the family besides Alec. His girls before her were from the ranch families in here under the mountains or from the farm folks east of Gros Ventre. Nor was Leona in circulation at all for the past few years, going with Tollie Zane's son Earl as she had been. But this past spring, Alec's last in high school and Leona's next-to-last, he somehow cut Earl Zane out of the picture. "Swap one cowboy for another, she might as well have stayed put," my mother said at the time, a bit perturbed with Alec anyway about his intention for the Double W summer job again.

—"All right, I guess," Alec was answering profoundly to some question of my father's about how successful the Double W's calving season had turned out.

How's this, how's that, fine, all right, you bet. If this was the level of sociability that was going to go on, I intended to damn promptly excuse myself to get back to working on my saddle, the scenic attractions of Leona notwithstanding. But then just as I was trying to estimate ahead to whether an early piece of butterscotch meringue pie could be coaxed from my mother or I'd do better to wait until later, Alec all at once put down his fork and came right out with:

"We got something to tell you. We're going to get married."

This kicked the conversation in the head entirely.

My father seemed to have forgotten about the mouthful of coffee he'd just drunk, while my mother looked as if Alec had announced he intended to take a pee in the middle of the table. Alec was trying to watch both of them at once, and Leona was favoring us all with one of her searchlight smiles.

"How come?"

Even yet I don't know why I said that. I mean, I was plenty old enough to know why people got married. There were times recently, seeing Alec and Leona mooning around together, when I seemed to savvy more than I actually had facts about, if that's possible.

Focused as he was on how our parents were going to respond, the philosophy question from my side of the table jangled Alec. "Because, because we're—we love each other, why the hell do you think?"

"Kind of soon in life to be so certain on that, isn't it?" suggested my father.

"We're old enough," Alec shot back. And meanwhile gave me a snake-killing look as if I was going to ask old enough for what, but I honestly didn't intend to.

"When's all this taking place?" my father got out next.

"This fall." Alec looked ready to say more, then held on to it, finally just delivered it in one dump: "Wendell Williamson'll let us have the house on the Nansen place to live in."

It was up to my mother to cleave matters entirely open. "You're saying you'll stay on at the Double W this fall?"

"Yeah," Alec said as if taking a vow. "It's what I want to do."

The unsaid part of this was huge, huger than anything I had ever felt come into our kitchen before. The financing to send Alec to Bozeman my parents had been gathering like quilt pieces: whatever savings the household managed to pinch aside, plus a loan from my mother's brother Pete Reese, plus a part-time job which my father had set up for Alec with a range-management professor at the college who knew us from having spent time up here studying the Two, plus of course Alec's own wages from this summer, which was another reason why his choice of the Double W riding job at thirty dollars a month again was less than popular—Christ-amighty, since my own haying wages later this summer would go into the general household kitty, even I felt I had a stake in the Bozeman plan. And now here was Alec choosing against college. Against all the expectation riding on him. Against—

"Alec, you will End Up as Nothing More Than a Gimped-Up Saddle Stiff, and I for one Will Not—"

More out of samaritan instinct than good sense my father headed my mother off with a next query to Alec: "How you going to support yourselves on a cow chouser's wages?"

"You two did, at first."

"We starved out at it, too."

"We ain't going to starve out." Alec's grammar seemed to be cow-boyifying, too. "Wendell'll let me draw ahead on my wages for a few heifers this fall, and winter them with the rest of the outfit's. It'll give us our start."

My father finally thought to set down his coffee cup. "Alec, let's keep our shirts on here"—language can be odd; I had the vision just then of us all sitting around the table with our shirts off, Leona across from me in full double-barreled display—"and try see what's what."

"I don't see there's any what's what about it," Alec declared. "People get married every day."

"So does the sun rise," my mother told him, "without particular participation by you."

"Mom, now damn it, listen—"

"We all better listen," my father tried again. "Leona, we got nothing against you. You know that." Which was a bit short of true in both its parts, and Leona responded with a lower beam of smile. "It's just that, Godamighty, Alec, cattle have gone bust time after time these last years. That way of life just has changed. Even the Double W would be on hard times if Wendell Williamson's daddy hadn't left him such deep pockets. Whether anybody'll ever be able to start off from scratch in the cow business and make a go of it, I don't see how."

Alec was like any of us, he resisted having an idea pulled from under him. "Rather have me running sheep up on one of your allotments, is that it? There'd be something substantial to look forward to, I suppose you think, sheepherding."

My father seemed to consider. "No, most probably not, in your case. It takes a trace of common sense to herd sheep." He said it lightly enough that Alec would have to take it as a joke, but there was a poking edge to the lightness. "Alec, I just think that whatever the hell you do, you need to bring an education to it these days. That old stuff of banging a living out of this country by sheer force of behavior doesn't work. Hasn't for almost twenty years. This country can outbang any man. Look at them along the creek here, even these sheepmen. Hahn, Ed Van Bebber, Pres Rozier, the Busbys, Dode Withrow, Finletter, Hill. They've all just managed to hang on, and they're as good a set of stockmen as you'll find in the whole goddamn state of Montana. You think any of them could have got under way, in years like there've been?"

"Last year was better than the one before," Alec defended with that litany of the local optimists. "This one looks better yet."

I saw my father glance at my mother, to see if she wanted to swat down this part of Alec's argument or whether he should go ahead. Even I could tell from the held-in look of her that once she got started there'd be no stopping, so he soldiered on. "And if about five more come good back to back, everybody'll be almost to where they were fifteen or twenty years ago. Alec, trying to build a living on a few head of stock is a dead end these days."

"Dad—Dad, listen. We ain't starting from fifteen or twenty years ago. We're starting from now, and we got to go by that, not whatever the hell happened to—to anybody else."

"You'll be starting in a hole," my father warned. "And an everlasting climb out."

I say warned. What rang through to me was an alarm different from the one in my father's words; an iron tone of anger such as I had never heard out of him before.

"That's as maybe." Alec's timbre was an echo of the anger, the iron. "But we got to start." Now Alec was looking at Leona as if he was storing up for the next thousand years. "And we're going to do it married. Not going to wait our life away."

If I ever get old enough to have brains, I will work on the question of man and woman.

All those years ago, the topic rode with me into the next morning as my father and I set off from the ranger station toward the mountains. Cool but cloudless, the day was a decent enough one, except for wind. I ought to have been in a topnotch mood, elevated by the anticipation that always began with my father's annual words, "Put on your mountain clothes in the morning."

Going along on one of these start-of-June rides with my father as he took a count of the sheep summering on the various ranchers' range allotments in the national forest was one of the awaited episodes of life. Better country to look ahead to could not be asked for. Kootenai, Lolo, Flathead, Absaroka, Bitterroot, Beaverhead, Deerlodge, Gallatin, Cabinet, Helena, Lewis and Clark, Custer, Two Medicine—those were the national forests of Montana, totaling dozens of ranger districts, but to our estimation the Two Medicine was head and shoulders above the other forests, and my father's English Creek district the topknot of the Two. Anybody with eyes could see this at once, for our ride this morning led up the North Fork of English Creek, which actually angles mostly west and northwest to thread between Roman Reef and Rooster Mountain to its source, and where the coulee of the North Fork opened ahead of us, there the first summits of the Rockies sat on the horizon like stupendous sharp boulders. Only when our first hour or so of riding carried us above that west edge of the coulee would we see the mountains in total, their broad bases of timber and rockfall gripping into the foothills. And the reefs. Roman Reef ahead of us, a rimrock half a mile high and more than three long. Grizzly Reef even bigger to the south of it, smaller Jericho Reef to the north. I don't know, are mountain reefs general knowledge in the world? I suppose they get their name because they stand as outcroppings do at the edge of an ocean, steady level ridges of stone, as if to give a calm example to the waves beyond them. Except that in this case the blue-gray billow up there is not waves but the Continental Divide against the sky. The name aside, though, sections of a fortress wall were what the three reefs reminded me of, spaced as they were with canyons between them and the higher jagged crags penned up behind. As if the whole horizon of the west had once been barricaded with slabs of rock and these were the mighty traces still standing. I must not have been the only onlooker this occurred to, as an even longer barrier of cliff farther south in the national forest was named the Chinese Wall.

The skyline of the Two. Even here at the outset the hover of it all always caused my father to turn and appreciatively call over his shoulder to Alec and me something like "Nothing the matter with that." And always Alec and I would chorus "Not one thing" both because we were expected to and because we too savored those waiting mountains.

Always was not in operation this year, however. My father did not pause to pronounce on the scenery, I had no chance to echo him, and Alec—Alec this year was on our minds instead of riding between us.

So our first stint on the road up the North Fork was broken only by the sound of our horses' hooves or one or the other of us muttering a horse name and urging a little more step-along in the pace. Even those blurts of sound were pretty pallid, because where horse nomenclature was concerned my father's imagination took a vacation. A black horse he invariably named Coaly, a white one always Snowball. Currently he was riding a big mouse-colored gelding who, depend on it, bore the title of Mouse. I was on a short-legged mare called Pony. Frankly, high among my hopes about the business of growing up was that I would get a considerably more substantial horse out of it. If and when I did, I vowed to give the creature as much name as it could carry, such as Rimfire or Chief Joseph or Calabash.

Whether I was sorting through my horse hopes or the outset of this counting trip without Alec weighed more heavily on me than I realized, I don't know. But in either case I was so deep into myself that I was surprised to glance ahead and learn that Mouse and my father were halted, and my father was gandering back to see what had become of me.

I rode on up and found that we had arrived to where a set of rutted tracks—in flattery, it could have been called almost a road—left the North Fork roadbed and crossed the coulee and creek and traced on up the side of Breed Butte to where a few log buildings could be seen.

Normally I would have been met with some joke from my father about sunburning my eyeballs if I went around asleep with my eyes open like that. But this day he was looking businesslike, which was the way he looked only when he couldn't find any better mood. "How about you taking a squint at Walter's place," he proposed. "You can cut around the butte and meet me at the road into the Hebner tribe."

"All right," I of course agreed and turned Pony to follow the ruts down and across the North Fork swale. Walter Kyle always summered in the mountains as herder of his own sheep, and so my father whenever he rode past veered in to see that everything was okay at the empty ranch. This was the first time he had delegated me, which verified just how much his mind was burdened—also with that question of man and woman? at least as it pertained to Alec McCaskill and Leona Tracy?—and that he wanted to saunter alone awhile as he sorted through it all.

As soon as my father had gone his way and I was starting up Breed Butte, I turned myself west in my saddle to face Roman Reef, tapped the brim of my hat in greeting, and spoke in the slow and distinct way you talk to a deaf person: "'Lo, Walter. How's everything up on the reef?"

What was involved here was that from Walter Kyle's summer range up there in the mountains, on top of Roman Reef a good five miles from where I was, his actual house and outbuildings here on Breed Butte could be seen through Walter's spyglass. Tiny, but seen. Walter had shown Alec and me this stunt of vision when we took some mail up to him during last year's counting trip. "There ye go," he congratulated as each of us in turn managed to extend the telescope tube just so and sight the building specks. "Ye can see for as long as your eye holds out, in this country." Walter's enthusiasm for the Two was that of a person newly smitten, for although he was the most elderly of all the English Creek ranchers—at the time he seemed to me downright ancient, I suppose partly because he was one of those dried-up little guys who look eternal—he also was much the most recent to the area. Only three or four years ago Walter had moved here from down in the Ingomar country in the southeastern part of the state, where he ran several bands of sheep. I have never heard of a setup like it before or since, but Walter and a number of other Scotch sheepmen, dedicated bachelors all, lived there in the hotel in Ingomar and operated their sheep outfits out of their back pocket and hat, you might say. Not one of them possessed a real ranch, just grazing land they'd finagled one way or another, plus wagons for their herders, and of course sheep and more sheep. Away each of those old Scotchies would go once a week, out from that hotel with boxes of groceries in the back of a Model T to tend camp. For whatever reason, Walter pulled out of hotel sheep tycooning—my father speculated that one morning he turned to the Scotchman beside him at the table and burred, "Jock, for thirrty yearrs ye've been eating yourrr oatmeal aye too loud," got up, and left for good—and bought the old Barclay place here on Breed Butte for next to nothing.

Pony was trudging up the butte in her steady uninspired way, and I had nothing to do but continue my long-distance conversation with Walter. Not that I figured there was any real chance that Walter would be studying down here exactly then, and even if he was I would be only a gnat in the spyglass lens and certainly not a conversationalist on whom he could perform any lip reading. But I went ahead and queried in the direction of the distant reef: "Walter, how the hell do people get so crosswise with one another?"

For last night's rumpus continued to bedevil me from whatever angle I could find to view it. The slant at which Alec and my parents suddenly were diverging from each other, first of all. In hindsight it may not seem such an earthquake of an issue, whether Alec was going to choose college or the wedding band/riding job combination. But hindsight is always through bifocals; it peers specifically instead of seeing whole. And the entirety here was that my father and my mother rested great hopes on my brother, especially given all that they and others of their generation had endured in the years past, the Depression years they had gotten through by constantly saying within themselves "Our children will know better times. They've got to." Hopes of that sort only parents can know. That Alec seemed not to want to step up in life, now that the chance at last was here, went against my parents' thinking as much as if he'd declared he was going to go out on the prairie and dig a hole and live a gopher's existence.

Walter Kyle had seen a lot of life; his mustache, which must have been sandy in his youth, now was as yellow-white as if he'd been drinking cream from a jar. "What about that, Walter? From your experience, has Alec gone as goofy as my folks think?" And got back instead of Walter's long Scotch view of life my father's briefer Scotch one, his last night's reasoning to Alec: "Why not give college a year and then see? You got the ability, it's a crime not to use it. And Bozeman isn't the moon. You'll be back and forth some times during the year. The two of you can see how the marriage notion holds up after that." But Alec wasn't about to have time bought from him. "We're not waiting our life away," ran his constant response. "Our life": that convergence of Alec and Leona and the headlong enthusiasm which none of the rest of us had quite realized they were bringing to their romance. Well, it will happen. Two people who have been around each other for years and all of a sudden find that nobody else in history has ever been in love before, they're inventing it themselves. Yet apply my mind to it in all the ways I could, my actual grasp of their mood wasn't firm, for to me then marriage seemed about as distant as death. Nor did I understand much more about the angle of Leona and—I was going to say, of Leona and my parents, but actually of Leona and the other three of us, as I somehow did feel included into the bask she aimed around our kitchen. Leona, Leona. "Now there is a topic I could really stand to talk to you about, Walter." Yet maybe a bachelor was not the soundest source either. Perhaps old Walter Kyle knew only enough about women, as the saying goes, to stay immune. Anyhow, with all care and good will I was trying to think through our family situation in a straight line, but Leona brought me to a blind curve. Not nearly the least of last evening's marvels was how much ground Leona had been able to hold with only a couple of honest-to-goodness sentences. When my father and mother were trying to argue delay into Alec and turned to her to test the result, she said just "We think we're ready enough." And then at the end of the fracas, going out the door Leona turned to bestow my mother one of her sunburst smiles and say, "Thank you for supper, Beth." And my mother saying back, just as literally, "Don't mention it."

The final line of thought from last night was the most disturbing of all. The breakage between my father and Alec. This one bothered me so much I couldn't even pretend to be confiding it to Walter up there on Roman Reef. Stony silence from that source was more than I could stand on this one. For if I'd had to forecast, say at about the point Alec was announcing marriage intentions, my mother was the natural choice to bring the house down on him. That would have been expected. It was her way. And she of course did make herself more than amply known on the college/marriage score. But the finale of that suppertime was all-male McCaskill: "You're done running my life," flung by Alec as he stomped out with Leona in tow, and "Nobody's running it, including you," from my father to Alec's departing back.

Done running my life. Nobody's running it, including you. Put that way, the words without the emotion, it may sound like something concluding itself; the moment of an argument breaking off into silence, a point at which contention has been expended. But I know now, and I somehow knew even then, that the fracture of a family is not a thing that happens clean and sharp, so that you at least can calculate that from here on it will begin to be over with. No, it is like one of those worst bone breaks, a shatter. You can mend the place, peg it and splint it and work to strengthen it, and while the surface maybe can be brought to look much as it did before, the deeper vicinity of shatter always remains a spot that has to be favored.

So if I didn't grasp much of what abruptly was happening within our family, I at least held the realization that last night's rift was nowhere near over.

Thinking heavily that way somehow speeds up time, and before I quite knew it Pony was stopping at the barbwire gate into Walter Kyle's yard. I tied her to the fence on a long rein so she could graze a little and slid myself between the top and second strands.

Walter's place looked hunky-dory. But I did a circle of the tool shed and low log barn and the three-quarter shed sheltering Walter's old Reo Flying Cloud coupe, just to be sure, and then went to the front of the house and took out the key from behind the loose piece of chinking which hid it.

The house too was undisturbed. Not that there was all that much in it to invite disturbance. The sparse habits of hotel living apparently still were in Walter. Besides the furniture—damn little of that beyond the kitchen table and its chairs of several stiff-back varieties—and the open shelves of provisions and cookery, the only touches of habitation were a drugstore calendar, and a series of coats hung on nails, and one framed studio photograph of a young, young Walter in a tunic and a fur cap: after Scotland and before Montana, he had been a Mountie for a few years up in Alberta.

All in all, except for the stale feel that unlived-in rooms give off, Walter might just have stepped out to go down there on the North Fork and fish a beaver dam. A good glance around was all the place required. Yet I stood and inventoried for some minutes. I don't know why, but an empty house holds me. As if it was an opened book about the person living there. Peruse this log-and-chinking room and Walter Kyle could be read as thrifty, tidy to the verge of fussy, and alone.

At last, just to stir the air in the place with some words, I said aloud the conclusion of my one-way conversation with the mustached little sheepman up on the Reef: "Walter, you'd have made somebody a good wife."

Pony and I now cut west along the flank of Breed Butte, which would angle us through Walter's field to where we would rejoin the North Fork road and my father. Up here above the North Fork coulee the outlook roughened, the mountains now in full rumpled view and the foothills bumping up below them and Roman Reef making its wide stockade of bare stone between the two. On this part of our route the land steadily grew more beautiful, which in Montana also means more hostile to settlement. From where I rode along this high ground, Walter Kyle's was the lone surviving ranch to be looked back on between here and the English Creek ranger station.

The wind seemed to think that was one too many, for it had come up from the west and was pummeling everything on Walter's property, including me. I rode now holding on to my hat with one hand lest it skitter down to the North Fork and set sail for St. Louis. Of all of the number of matters about the Two country that I never have nor will be able to savvy—one life is not nearly enough to do so—a main one is why in a landscape with hills and buttes and benchlands everywhere a person is so seldom sheltered from the everlasting damn wind. I mean, having the wind of the Two forever trying to blow harmonica tunes through your rib cage just naturally wears on the nerves.

The Two, I have been saying. I ought to clarify that to us the term meant both the landscape to all the horizons around—that is pretty much what a Montanan means by a "country"—and the national forest that my father's district was part of. In those days the six hundred square miles of the Two Medicine National Forest were divvied into only three ranger districts: English Creek; Indian Head, west of Choteau; and Blacktail Gulch, down by Sun River at the south end of the forest. Actually only my father's northmost portion of the Two Medicine National Forest had anything at all to do with the Two Medicine River or Two Medicine Lake: the vicinity where the forest joins onto the south boundary of Glacier National Park and fits in there, as a map shows it, like a long straight-sided peninsula between the park and the Continental Divide and the Blackfeet Indian Reservation. So the Two Medicine itself, the river that is, honestly is in sight to hardly any of the Two country. Like all the major flows of this region the river has its source up in the Rockies, but then the Two Medicine promptly cuts a sizable canyon east through the plains as it pushes to meet the Marias River and eventually the Missouri. Burrows its way through the prairie, you might almost say. It is just the ring of the words, Two Medicine, that has carried the name all the way south along the mountains some thirty miles to our English Creek area. The derivation as I've heard it is that in distant times the Blackfeet built their medicine lodge, their place for sacred ceremony, two years in a row at a favorite spot on the river where buffalo could be stampeded over nearby cliffs, and the name lasted from that pair of lodges. By whatever way Two Medicine came to be, it is an interesting piece of language, I have always thought.

My father was waiting at another rutty offshoot from the North Fork road. This one had so many cuts of track, some of them dating from the era of wagon wheels, that it looked like a kind of huge braid across the grassland. My father turned his gaze from the twined ruts to me and asked: "Everything under control at Walter's?"

"Uh huh," I affirmed.

"All right." His businesslike expression had declined into what I think is called dolor. "Let's go do it." And we set off into the weave of tracks toward the Hebner place.

No matter what time of day you approached it, the Hebner place looked as if demolition was being done and the demolishers were just now taking a smoke break. An armada of abandoned wagons and car chassis and decrepit farm equipment—even though Good Help Hebner farmed not so much as a vegetable garden—lay around and between the brown old buildings. A root cellar was caved in, a tool shop had only half a roof left, the barn looked distinctly teetery. In short, not much ever functioned on the Hebner place except gravity.

Out front of the barn now as we rode in stood a resigned-looking bay mare with two of the littler Hebner boys astraddle her swayed back. The pair on the horse must have been Roy and Will, or possibly Will and Enoch, or maybe even Enoch and Curtis. So frequent a bunch were they, there was no keeping track of which size Hebner boy was who unless you were around them every day.

I take that back. Even seeing them on a constant basis wouldn't necessarily have been a foolproof guide to who was who, because all the faces in that Hebner family rhymed. I don't know how else to put it. Every Hebner forehead was a copy of Good Help's wide crimped-in-the-middle version, a pale bony expanse centered with a kind of tiny gully which widened as it went down, as if the nose had avalanched out of there. Across most of the left side of this divided forehead a hank of hair flopped at a crooked angle. The effect was as if every male Hebner wore one of those eye patches shown in pictures of pirates, only pushed up higher. Then from that forehead any Hebner face simply sort of dwindled down, a quick skid of nose and a tight mouth and a small ball of chin.

The tandem horsebackers stared us the length of the yard. It was another Hebner quality to gawp at you as if you were some new species on earth. My father had a not entirely ironic theory to explain that: "They've all eaten so goddamn much venison their eyes have grown big as deers'." For it was a fact of life that somewhere up there in the jack-pines beyond the Hebner buildings would be a woolsack hanging from a top limb. The bottom of the sack would rest in a washtub of water, and within the sack, being cooled nicely by the moisture as it went wicking up through the burlap, would be a hindquarter or two of venison. Good Help Hebner liked his deer the same way he preferred his eggs—poached.

"Actually, I don't mind Good Help snitching a deer every so often," my father put it. "Those kids have got to eat. But when the lazy SOB starts in on that goddamn oughtobiography of his—how he ought to have been this, ought to have done that—"

"Morning, Ranger! Hello there, Jick!"

I don't know about my father, but that out-of-nowhere gust of words startled me just a little. The greeting hadn't issued from the staring boys on the mare but from behind the screen door of the log house. "Ought to have been paying attention to the world so I'd seen you coming and got some coffee going."

"Thanks anyway, Garland," said my father, who had heard years of Good Help Hebner protocol and never yet seen a cup of coffee out of any of it. "We're just dropping off some baking Beth came out long on."

"We'll do what we can to put it to good—" Commotion in front of the barn interrupted the voice of Good Help. The front boy atop the old horse was whacking her alongside the neck with the reins while the boy behind him was kicking the mount heartily in the ribs and piping, "Giddyup, goddamn you horse, giddyup!"

"Giddyup, hell!" Good Help's yell exploded across the yard. It was always said of him that Good Help could talk at a volume which would blow a crowbar out of your hand. "The pair of you giddy off and giddy over to that goshdamn woodpile!"

We all watched for the effect of this on the would-be jockeys, and when there was none except increased exertion on the dilapidated mare, Good Help addressed my father through the screen door again: "Ought to have taken that pair out and drowned them with the last batch of kittens, way they behave. I don't know what's got into kids any more."

With the profundity of that, Good Help materialized from behind the screening and out onto the decaying railroad tie which served as the front step to the Hebner house. Like his place, Good Help Hebner himself was more than a little ramshackle. A tall yet potbellied man with one bib of his overalls usually frayed loose and dangling, his sloping face made even more pale by a gray-white chevron of grizzle which mysteriously never matured into a real mustache. Garland Hebner: nicknamed Good Help ever since the time, years back, when he volunteered to join the Noon Creek cattlemen when they branded their calves and thereby get in on a free supper afterward. In Dill Egan's round corral, the branding crew at one point looked up to see Hebner, for no reason that ever became clear, hoisting himself onto Dill's skittish iron-gray stud. Almost before Hebner was truly aboard, the gray slung him off and then tried to pound him apart while everybody else bailed out of the corral. Hebner proved to be a moving target; time and again the hooves of the outraged horse missed the rolling ball of man, until finally Dill managed to reach in, grab hold of a Hebner ankle, and snake him out under the corral poles. Hebner wobbled up, blinked around at the crowd, then sent his gaze on to the sky and declared as if piety was natural to him: "Well, I had some Good Help getting out of that, didn't I?"

Some extra stickum was added to the nickname, of course, by the fact that Good Help had never been found to be of any use whatsoever on any task anybody had been able to think up for him. "He has a pernicious case of the slows," Dode Withrow reported after he once made the error of hiring Good Help for a few days of fencing haystacks.

"Ranger, I been meaning to ask if it mightn't be possible to cut a few poles to fix that corral up with," Good Help was blaring now. The Hebner corral looked as if a buffalo stampede had passed through it, and translated out of Hebnerese, Good Help's question was whether he could help himself to some national forest pine without paying for it. "Ought to have got at it before now, but my back . . ."

His allergy to work was the one characteristic in which the rest of the family did not emulate Good Help. They didn't dare. Survival depended on whatever wages the squadron of Hebner kids could earn by hiring out at lambing time or through haying season. Then at some point in their late teens each Hebner youngster somehow would come up with a more serious job and use it as an escape ladder out of that family.

Alec and I had accidentally been witnesses to the departure of Sanford, the second oldest Hebner boy. It occurred a couple of springs before when Ed Van Bebber came by the ranger station one Friday night and asked if Alec and I could help out with the lambing chores that weekend. Neither of us much wanted to do it, because Ed Van Bebber is nobody's favorite person except Ed Van Bebber's. But you can't turn down a person who's in a pinch, either. When the pair of us rode into Ed's place early the next morning we saw that Sanford Hebner was driving the gutwagon, even though he was only seventeen or so, not all that much older than Alec at the time. And that lambing season at Van Bebber's had been a rugged one; the hay was used up getting through the winter and the ewes thin as shadows and not particularly ready to become mothers. Ed had thrown the drop band clear up onto the south side of Wolf Butte to provide any grass for them at all, which meant a tough mile and a half drive for Sanford to the lambing shed with each gutwagon load of ewes and their fresh lambs, and a played-out team of horses by the time he got there. With the ewes dropping eighty and ninety lambs a day out there and the need to harness new horses for every trip, Sanford was performing about two men's work and doing it damn well. The day this happened, dark had almost fallen, Alec and I were up on the hillside above the lambing shed helping Ed corral a bunch of mother ewes and their week-old lambs, and we meanwhile could see Sanford driving in with his last load of lambs of the day. We actually had our bunch under control just fine, the three of us and a dog or two. But Ed always had to have a tendency toward hurry. So he cupped his hands to his mouth and yelled down the hill:

"HEY THERE YOU HEBNER! COME UP HERE AND HELP US CORRAL THESE EWES AND LAMBS!"

I still think if Ed had asked properly Sanford probably would have been fool enough to have climbed up and joined us, even though he already had put in his workday and then some. But after the season of man's labor he had done, to be yelled at to come up and help a couple of milk-tooth kids like us chase lambs: worse than that, to not be awarded even his first name, just be shouted to the world as a Hebner— I still can see Sanford perched on the seat of that gutwagon, looking up the slope to us, and then cupping his hands to his mouth the same way Ed had, and hear yet his words carry up the hill:

"YOU GO PLUMB TO HELL YOU OLD SON OF A BITCH!"

And he slapped his reins on the rumps of the gutwagon team and drove on to the lambing shed. At the supper table that night, Sanford's check was in his plate.

Sanford and that money, though, did not travel back up the North Fork to this Hebner household. When Alec and I headed home that night Sanford rode double behind me, and when we dismounted at the ranger station he trudged into the dark straight down the English Creek road, asking at every ranch on the way whether a job of any sort could be had. "Anything. I'll clean the chicken house." The Busby brothers happened to need a bunch herder, and Sanford had been with them ever since; this very moment, was herding one of their bands of sheep up in the mountains of the Two. To me, the realization of Sanford's situation that evening when Ed Van Bebber canned him, Sanford knock-ing at any door rather than return home, having a family, a father that he would even clean chicken houses to be free of; to me, the news that life could deal such a hell of a situation to someone about the age of Alec and me came as a sobering gospel.

"Missus!" Having failed to cajole my father out of free timber, Good Help evidently had decided to settle for the manna we'd come to deliver. "Got something out here."

The screen door opened and closed again, producing Florene Heb-ner and leaving a couple of the very littlest Hebners—Garlena and Jonas? Jonas and Maybella?—gawping behind the mesh. Since the baked goods were tied in a dish towel on my saddle, I did the courte-ous thing and got off and took the bundle up to Florene. Florene was, or had been, a fairly good-looking woman, particularly among a family population minted with the face of Good Help. But what was most immediately noticeable about her was how worn she looked. As if she'd been sanded down repeatedly. You'd never have guessed the fact by comparing the two, but Florene and my mother went through grade school at Noon Creek together. Florene, though, never made it beyond the second year of high school in Gros Ventre because she already had met Garland Hebner and promptly was pregnant by him and, a little less promptly on Garland's part, was married to him.

She gave a small downcast smile as I handed her the bundle, said to me, "Thank your ma again, Jick," and retreated back inside.

"Funny to see Alec not with you," Good Help was declaiming to my father as I returned from the doorway to Pony. "But they do grow and go."

"So they do," my father agreed without enthusiasm. "Garland, we got sheep waiting for us up the mountain. You ready, Jick?" My father touched Mouse into motion, then uttered to Good Help in parting, purely poker-faced: "Take it easy."

The route we rode out of the Hebner place was a sort of topsy-turvy L, the long climbing stem of ruts and then the brief northwestward leg of the North Fork trail where it tops onto the English Creek–Noon Creek divide. Coming onto that crest, we now would be in view of the land-marks that are the familiar sentries of the Two country. Chief Moun-tain; even though it is a full seventy miles to the north and almost into

Canada, standing distinct as a mooring peg at the end of the long chain of mountains. Also north but nearer, Heart Butte; no great piece of geography, yet it too poses separate enough from the mountain horizon that its dark pyramid form can be constantly seen and identified. And just to our east the full timber-topped profile of Breed Butte, a junior landmark but plainly enough the summit of our English Creek area.

With all this offered into sight I nonetheless kept my eyes on my father, watching for what I knew would happen, what always happened after he paid a visit to the Hebner place.

There at the top of the rise he halted his horse, and instead of giving his regard to the distant wonders of Chief Mountain and Heart Butte, he turned for a last slow look at the Hebner hodgepodge. Then shook his head, said, "Jesus H. Christ," and reined away. For in that woebegone log house down there, and amid those buildings before neglect had done its handiwork on them, my father was born and brought up.

Of course then the place was the McCaskill homestead. And the North Fork known by the nickname of Scotch Heaven on account of the several burr-on-the-tongue-and-thistle-up-the-kilt families who had come over and settled. Duffs, Barclays, Frews, Findlaters, Erskines, and my McCaskill grandparents, they lit in here sometime in the 1880s and all were dead or defeated or departed by the time the flu epidemic of 1918 and the winter of '19 got done with them. I possessed no first-hand information on my father's parents. Both of them were under the North Fork soil by the time I was born. And despite my father's ear to the past, there did not seem to be anything known or at least fit to report about what the McCaskills came from in Scotland. Except for a single scrap of lore: the story that a McCaskill had been one of the stonemasons of Arbroath who worked for the Stevensons—as I savvy it, the Stevensons must have been a family of engineers before Robert Louis cropped into the lineage and picked up a pen—when they were putting the lighthouses all around the coast of Scotland. The thought that an ancestor of ours helped fight the sea with stone meant more to my father than he liked to let on. As far as I know, the only halfway sizable body of water my father himself had ever seen was Flathead Lake right here in Montana, let alone an ocean and its beacons. Yet when the fire lookout towers he had fought for were finally being built on the Two Medicine forest during these years it was noticeable that he called them "Franklin Delano's lighthouses."

Looking back from now at that matter of my McCaskill grandparents I question, frankly, whether my mother and father would or could have kept close with that side of the family even if it had still been extant. No marriage is strong enough to bear two loads of in-laws. Early on the choice might as well be made, that one family will be seen as much as can be stood and the other, probably the husband's, shunted off to rare visits. That's theory, of course. But theory and my mother together—in any case, all I grew up knowing of the McCaskills of Scotch Heaven was that thirty or so years of homestead effort proved to be the extent of their lifetimes and that my father emerged from the homestead, for good, in the war year of 1917.

"Yeah, I went off to Wilson's war. Fought in blood up to my knees." As I have told, the one crack in how solemn my father could be in announcing something like this was that lowered left eyelid of his, and I liked to watch for it to dip down and introduce this next part. "Fact is, you could get yourself a fight just about any time of day or night in those saloons outside Camp Lewis." That my father's combat had been limited to fists against chins in the state of Washington seemed not to bother him a whit, although I myself wished he had some tales of the actual war. Rather, I wished his knack with a story could have illuminated that war experience of his generation, as an alternative to so many guys' plain refrain that I-served-my-time-over-in-Frogland-and-you-by-God-can-have-the-whole-bedamned-place. But you settle for what family lore you can.

My father's history resumes that when he came back from conducting the war against the Camp Lewis saloonhounds, he was hired on by the Noon Creek cattle ranchers as their association rider. "Generally some older hand got the job, but I was single and broke, just the kind ranchers love to whittle their wages down to fit"—by then, too, the wartime livestock prices were on their toboggan ride down—"and they took me on."

That association job of course was only a summer one, the combined Noon Creek cattle, except those of the big Double W ranch, trailing up onto the national forest grass in June and down out again in September, and so in winters my father fed hay at one cow ranch or another and then when spring came and brought lambing time with it he would hire on with one of the English Creek sheepmen. I suppose that runs against the usual notion of the West, of cow chousers and mutton conductors forever at odds with each other. But anybody who grew up around stock in our part of Montana knew no qualm about working with either cattle or sheep. Range wars simply never were much the Montana style, and most particularly not the Two Medicine fashion. Oh, somewhere in history there had been an early ruckus south toward the Sun River, some cowman kiyiing over to try kill off a neighboring band of sheep. And probably in any town along these mountains, Browning or Gros Ventre or Choteau or Augusta, you could go into a bar and still find an occasional old hammerhead who proclaimed himself nothing but a cowboy and never capable of drawing breath as anything else, especially not as a mutton puncher. (Which isn't to say that most sheepherders weren't equally irreversibly sheepherders, but somehow that point never seemed to need constant general announcement as it did with cowboys.) By and large, though, the Montana philosophy of make-do as practiced by our sizable ranching proportion of Scotchmen, Germans, Norwegians, and Missourians meant that ranch people simply tried to figure out which species did best at the moment, sheep or cows, and chose accordingly. It all came down, so far as I could see, to the doctrine my father expressed whenever someone asked him how he was doing: "Just trying to stay level."

In that time when young Varick McCaskill became their association rider there still would have been several Noon Creek cattle ranchers, guys getting along nicely on a hundred or so head of cows apiece. Now nearly all of those places either were bought up by Wendell Williamson's Double W or under lease to it. "The Williamsons of life always do try to latch on to all the land that touches theirs" was my father's view on that. What I am aiming at, though, is that among those Noon Creek stockmen when my father was hired on was Isaac Reese, mostly a horse raiser but under the inspiration of wartime prices also running cattle just then. It was when my father rode in to pick up those Reese cattle for the drive into the mountains that he first saw my mother. Saw her as a woman, that is. "Oh, I had known she had some promise. Lisabeth Reese. The name alone made you keep her somewhere in mind."

Long-range opportunities seemed to elude my father, but he could be nimble enough in the short run. "I wasn't without some practice at girling. And Beth was worth some extra effort."

The McCaskill-Reese matrimony ensued, and a year or so after that, Alec ensued. Which then meant that my father and mother were supporting themselves and a youngster by a job that my father had been given because he was single and didn't need much wage. This is the brand of situation you can find yourself in without much effort in Montana, but that it is common does not make it one damn bit more acceptable. I am sure as anything that the memory of that predicament at the start of my parents' married life lay large behind their qualms about what Alec now was intending. My father especially wanted no repeat, in any son of his, of that season by season scrabble for livelihood. I know our family ruckus was more complicated than just that. Anything ever is. But if amid the previous evening's contention my father and Alec could have been put under oath, each Bibled to the deepest of the truths in him, my father would have had to say something like: "I don't want you making my mistakes over again." And Alec to him: "Your mistakes were yours, they've got nothing to do with me."

My brother and my father. I am hard put to know how to describe them as they seemed to me then, in that time when I was looking up at them from fourteen years of age. How to lay each onto paper, for a map is never the country itself, only some ink suggesting the way to get there.

Funny, what memory does. I have only a few beginning recollections of the four or so years we spent at the Indian Head ranger station down there at the middle of the Two Medicine National Forest, where my father started in the Forest Service. A windstorm one night that we thought was going to take the roof off the house. And Alec teaching me to mooch my way onto the back of a grazing horse, as I have told about. But clearest of all to me is a time Alec and I rode double into the mountains with our father, for he took us along on little chore trips as soon as we were big enough to perch on a horse. How can it be that a day of straddling behind the saddle where my brother sat—my nose inches from the collar of Alec's jacket, and I can tell you as well as anything that the jacket was green corduroy, Alec a greener green than the forest around us—is so alive, even yet? Anyway, after Indian Head came our move to English Creek and my father's rangering of the north end of the Two ever since. Now that I think on all this, that onset of our English Creek life was at the start of Alec's third school year, for I recall how damn irked I was that, new home or not, here Alec was again riding off to school every morning while I still had a whole year to wait.

Next year did come and there we both were, going to school to Miss

Thorkelson at the South Fork schoolhouse, along with the children of the ranch families on the upper end of English Creek, the Hahn boys, a number of Busbys and Roziers, the Finletter twins, the Withrow girls, and then of course the Hebner kids, who made up about half the school by themselves. Alec always stood well in his studies. Yet I can't help but believe the South Fork school did me more good than it did him. You know how those one-room schools are, all eight grades there in one clump for the teacher to have to handle. By a fluke of Hebner reproductive history Marcella Withrow and I were the only ones our age at South Fork, so as a class totaling two we didn't take up much of Miss Thorkelson's lesson time and she always let us read extra or just sit and partake of what she was doing with the older grades. By the time Marcella and I reached the sixth grade we already had listened through the older kids' geography and reading and history and grammar five times. I still know what the capital of Bulgaria is, and not too many people I meet do.

Stuff of that sort I always could remember like nobody's business. Numbers, less so. But there Alec shined. Shined in spite of himself, if such is possible.

It surprised the hell out of all of us in the family. I can tell you the exact night we got this new view of Alec.

It had been paper day for my father, the one he set aside each month to wrestle paperwork asked for by the Two Medicine National Forest headquarters down in Great Falls, and more than likely another batch wanted by the Region One office over in Missoula as well. The author of his sorrow this particular time was Missoula, which had directed him to prepare and forward—that was the way Forest Service offices talked—a report on the average acreage of all present and potential grazing allotments in his English Creek ranger district. "Potential" was the nettle in this, for it meant that my father had to dope out from his maps every bit of terrain which fit the grazing regulations of the time and translate those map splotches into acreage. So acres had been in the air that day in our household, and it was at supper that Alec asked how many acres there were in the Two Medicine National Forest altogether.

Alec was twelve at the time. Which would have made me eight, since there were four years between us. Three years and forty-nine weeks, I preferred to count it, my birthday being on September fourth and Alec's the twenty-fifth of that same month. But the point here is that we were both down there in the grade school years and my father didn't particularly care to be carrying on a conversation about any more acreage, so he just answered: "Quite a bunch. I don't know the figure, exactly."

Alec was never easy to swerve. "Well, how many sections does it have?" You likely know that a section is a square mile, in the survey system used in this country.

"Pretty close to 600," my father knew offhand.

"Then that's 384,000 acres," imparted Alec.

"That sounds high, to me," my father responded, going on with his meal. "Better get a pencil and paper and work it out."

Alec shook his head against the pencil and paper notion. "384,000," he said again. "Bet you a milkshake."

At this juncture my mother was heard from. "There'll be no betting at the supper table, young man." But she then got up and went to the sideboard where the mail was put and returned with an envelope. On the back of it she did the pencil work—600 times 640, the number of acres in a section—and in a moment reported:

"384,000."

"Are you sure?" my father asked her.

My mother in her younger days had done a little schoolteaching, so here my father simply was getting deeper into the arithmetic bog. "Do you want to owe both Alec and me milkshakes?" she challenged him back.

"No, I can do without that," my father said. He turned to Alec again and studied him a bit. Then: "All right, Mister Smart Guy. How much is 365 times 12?"

This too took Alec only an instant. "4,380," he declared. "Why? What's that?"

"It's about how many days a twelve-year-old like you has been on this earth," my father said. "Which is to say it's about how long it's taken us to discover what it is you've got in that head of yours."

That, then, was what might be called the school year portion of Alec. An ability he couldn't really account for—"I don't know, Jicker, I just can," was all the answer I could ever get when I pestered him about how he could handle figures in his head like that—and maybe didn't absolutely want or at least welcome. The Alec of summer was another matter entirely. What he didn't display the happy knack of, in terms of ranch or forest work that went on in the Two country at that season of year, hadn't yet been invented. Fixing fences, figuring how to splice in barbwire and set new braceposts, Alec was a genius at; anytime an English Creek rancher got money enough ahead for fence work, here he came to ask Alec to ride his lines and fix where needed. When Alec, at age thirteen, came to his first haying season and was to drive the scatter rake for our uncle Pete Reese, after the first few days Pete put him onto regular windrow raking for a while instead. As a scatter raker Alec was working the job for more than it was worth, trotting his team of horses anywhere in the hayfield a stray scrap of hay might be found; the regularity of making windrows, Pete said, slowed him down to within reason. That same headlong skill popped out whenever Alec set foot into the mountains. On our counting trips before this year, he perpetually was the first to see deer or elk or a red-tailed hawk or whatever, before I did and often before our father did.

The combination of all this in Alec, I am sure as anything, was what inspired my father and mother to champion college and engineering for him. They never put it in so bald a way, but Alec's mathematical side and his knacky nature and his general go-to-it approach seemed to them fitted for an engineer. A builder, a doer. Maybe even an engineer for the Forest Service itself, for in those New Deal times there were projects under way everywhere a place could be found for them, it seemed like. The idea even rang right with Alec, at first. All through that winter of his last year in high school Alec kept saying he wished he could go right now, go to the college at Bozeman and get started. But then Leona happened, and the Double W summer job again, and the supper ruckus about marriage over college.

Well, that was a year's worth of Alec, so to speak. His partner in ruckus, my father up there on the horse in front of me, can't be calendared in the strictly regular fashion either. Despite the order of months printed and hung on our wall at the English Creek ranger station, a Varick McCaskill year began with autumn. With Indian summer, actually, which in our part of Montana arrives after a customary stormy turn of weather around Labor Day. Of course every ranger is supposed to inspect the conditions of his forest there at the end of the grazing season. My father all but X-rayed his portion of the Two Medicine National Forest. South Fork and North Fork, up under the reefs, in beyond Heart Butte, day after day he delved the Two almost as if making sure to himself that he still had all of that zone of geography. And somehow when the bands of sheep trailed down and streamed toward the railroad chutes at Blackfoot or Pendroy, he was on hand there too to look them over, gossip with the herders, the ranchers, the lamb buyers, join in the jackpot bets about how much the lambs would weigh. It was the time of year when he could assess his job, see right there on the land and on the hoof the results of his rangering and give thought to how to adjust it. A necessary inventory season, autumn.

He never wintered well. Came down with colds, sieges of hacking and sniffing, like someone you would think was a permanent pneumonia candidate. Strange, for a man of his lengthy strength and one otherwise so in tune with the Two country. "Are you *sure* you were born and raised up there on the North Fork?" my mother would ask, along with about the third mustard plaster she applied onto him every winter. "Maybe a traveling circus left you."

More than likely, all of my father's winter ailments really were symptoms of just one, indoorness. For stepping out a door somehow seemed to extend him, actually tip his head higher and brace his shoulders straighter, and the farther he went from a house the more he looked like he knew what he was doing.

Does that sound harsh? It's not meant to. All I am trying to work into words here is that my father was a man born to the land, in a job that sometimes harnessed him to a desk, an Oliver typewriter, a book of regulations. A man caught between, in a number of ways. I have since come to see that he was of a generation that this particularly happens to. The ones who are firstborn in a new land. My belief is that it will be the same when there are births out on the moon or the other planets. Those firstborn always, always will live in a straddle between the ancestral path of life and the route of the new land. In my father's case the old country of the McCaskills, Scotland, was as distant and blank as the North Pole, and the fresh one, America, still was making itself. Especially a rough-edged part of America such as the Montana he was born into and grew up in. All my father's sessions with old Toussaint Rennie, hearing whatever he could about the past days of the Two Medicine country, I think were due to this; to a need for some footing, some groundwork of the time and place he found himself in.

The Forest Service itself was an in-between thing, for that matter. Keeper of the national forests, their timber, grass, water, yet merchant of those resources, too. Anybody local like my father who "turned green" by joining the USFS now sided against the thinking of a lot of people he had known all his life, people who considered that the country should be wide open, or at least wider open than it was, for using.

And even within all this, ranger Varick McCaskill was of a betwixt variety. A good many of the guys more veteran than my father dated back to the early time of the Forest Service, maybe even to when it originated in 1905; they tended to be reformed cowboys or loggers or some such, old hands who had been wrestling the West since before my father was born. Meanwhile the men younger than my father were showing up with college degrees in forestry and the New Deal alphabet on their tongues.

So there my father was, between and between and between. My notion in all this is that winter, that season of house time and waiting, simply was one more between than he could stand.

When spring let him out and around, my father seemed to green up with the country. In the Two, even spring travels in on the wind; chinooks which can cause you to lean into them like a drunk against a lamppost while they melt away the snowbanks of winter. The first roar of a chinook beginning to sweep down off the top of the Rockies signaled newness, promise, to my father. "The wind from Eden," he called the chinook, for he must have read that somewhere. Paperwork chores he had put off and off now got tackled and disposed of. He and his assistant ranger gave the gear of the English Creek ranger district a going-over; saddles, bridles, pack saddles, fire equipment, lookout phone lines, all of it. With his dispatcher he planned the work of trail crews, and the projects the Civilian Conservation Corps boys would be put to, and the deployment of fire guards and smokechasers when the fire season heated up.

And from the first moment that charitably might be classified as spring, my father read the mountains. Watched the snow hem along the peaks, judging how fast the drifts were melting. Cast a glance to English Creek various times of each day, to see how high it was running. Kept mental tally of the wildlife; when the deer started back up into the mountains, when the fur of the weasel turned from white to brown, how soon the first pile of coal-black droppings in the middle of a trail showed that bears were out of hibernation. To my father, and through him to the rest of us in the family, the mountains now were their own calendar, you might say.

And finally, spring's offspring. Summer. The high season, the one the rest of my father's ranger year led up to. Summer was going to tell itself, for my father and I were embarking into it now with this counting trip.

—

"—a gander. Don't you think?"

My father had halted Mouse and was swiveled around looking at me in curiosity. Sometimes I think if I endure in life long enough to get senile nobody will be able to tell the difference, given how my mind has always drifted anyway.

"Uh, come again?" I mustered. "I didn't quite catch that."

"Anybody home there, under your hat? I was saying, it's about time you checked on your packslinging. Better hop off and take a gander."

Back there on the subject of our horses I should have told too that we were leading one pack horse with us. Tomorrow, after we finished the counting of the Kyle and Hahn bands of sheep, we were going on up to Billygoat Peak where Paul Eliason, the junior forester who was my father's assistant ranger, and a couple of trail men were building a fire lookout. They had gone in the previous week with the pre-cut framework and by now likely had the lookout erected and shingled, but the guywire had been late in coming from Missoula. That was our packload now, the roll of half-inch galvanized cable and some eyebolts and turnbuckles to tie down the new lookout tower. You may think the wind blows in the lower areas of the Two, but up there on top it really huffs.

This third horse, bearer of the load whose lash rope and diamond hitch knot I now was testing for tautness, was an elderly solemn sorrel whom my father addressed as Brownie but the rest of us called by the name he'd been given before the Forest Service deposited him at the English Creek station: Homer. Having Brownie né Homer along was cause for mixed emotions. One more horse is always a nuisance to contend with, yet the presence of a pack animal also made a journey seem more substantial; testified that you weren't just jaunting off to somewhere, you were transporting.

Since the lookout gear and our food only amounted to a load for one horse it hadn't been necessary to call on my father's packer, Isidor Pronovost, and his eight-mule packstring for this counting trip of ours. But even absent he had his influence that morning as I arranged the packs on Brownie/Homer under my father's scrutiny, both of us total converts to Isidor's perpetual preachment that in packing a horse or a mule, balance is everything. One of the best things that was ever said to me was Isidor's opinion that I was getting to be a "pretty daggone good cargodier" in learning how to fit cargo onto a pack animal. These particular Billy Peak packs took some extra contriving, to make a roll of heavy guywire on one side of the pack saddle equivalent to some canned goods on the other side of it and then some light awkward stuff such as our cooking utensils in a top pack, but finally my father had proclaimed: "There, looks to me like you got it Isidored."

Evidently I had indeed, for I didn't find that the packs or ropes had shifted appreciably on our ride thus far. But I went ahead and reefed down on the lash rope anyway, snugging my diamond hitch even further to justify the report to my father: "All tight as a fiddle string."

While I was cross-examining the lash rope my father had been looking out over the country all around. Roman Reef predominated above us, of course. But just across the gorge of the North Fork from it another landmark, Rooster Mountain, was starting to stand over us, too. Its broad open face of slope was topped with an abrupt upshoot of rock like a rooster's comb, which gave it the name.

"Since we're this far along," my father decided, "maybe we might as well eat some lunch."

The view rather than his stomach guided him in that choice, I believe.

By now, late morning, we were so well started into the mountains above the English Creek–Noon Creek divide that we could see down onto both drainages and their various ranches, and on out to where the farm patterns began, east of the town of Gros Ventre. To be precise, on a map our lunch spot was about where the east-pointing panhandle of the Two Medicine National Forest joins onto the pan—the pan being the seventy-five-mile extent of the forest along the front of the Rockies, from East Glacier at the north to Sun River at the south. Somehow when the forest boundary was drawn the English Creek corridor, the panhandle route we had just ridden, got included, and that is why our English Creek ranger station was situated out there with ranches on three sides of it. That location like a nest at the end of a limb bothered some of the map gazers at Region One headquarters over in Missoula. They'd have denied it, but they seemed to hold the theory that the deeper a ranger station was buried into preposterous terrain, the better. Another strike was that English Creek sat nearly at the southern end of my father's district, nothing central or tidy about the location either. But the Mazoola inmates had never figured out anything to do about English Creek, and while the valley-bottom site added some riding miles to my father's job, the convenience of being amid the English Creek ranch families—his constituents, so to speak—was more than worth it.

My mother had put up sandwiches for us; slices of fried ham between slabs of homemade bread daubed with fresh yellow butter. You can't beat that combination. Eating those sandwiches and gazing out over the Two country mended our dispositions a lot.

If a person can take time to reflect on such a reach of land other matters will dim out. An area the size of the Two is like a small nation. Big enough to have several geographies and an assortment of climates and an appreciable population, yet compact enough that people know each other from one end of the Two to the other.

A hawk went by below us, sailing on an air current. A mark of progress into the mountains I always watched for, hawks and even eagles now on routes lower than our own.

Mostly, however, as my father and I worked our way through sandwiches and a shared can of plums, I simply tried to store away the look of the land this lush June. Who knew if it would ever be this green again? The experience of recent years sure as hell didn't suggest so. For right out there in that green of farmland and prairie where my father and I were gazing, a part of the history of the Depression began to brew on a day of early May in 1934. Nobody here in the Two could have identified it as more than an ordinary wind. Stiff, but that is never news in the Two country. As that wind continued east, however, it met a weather front angling down out of Canada, and the combined velocity set to work on the plowed fields along the High Line. An open winter and a spring of almost no rain had left those fields dry; brown talcum waiting to be puffed. And so a cloud of wind and topsoil was born and grew. By the time the dirt storm reached Plentywood in the northeastern corner of the state the grit of it was scouring paint off farmhouses. All across the Dakotas further dry fields were waiting to become dust. The brown storm rolled into the Twin Cities, and on to Chicago, where it shut down plane flights and caused streetlights to be turned on in the middle of the day. I don't understand the science of it, but that storm continued to grow and widen and darken the more it traveled, Montana dirt and Dakota dirt and Minnesota dirt in the skies and eyes of Illinois, Indiana, Ohio. And on and on the storm swept, into New York City and Washington, D.C., the dust of the West fogging out the pinnacle of the Empire State building and powdering the shiny tabletops within the White House. At last the dirt cloud expended itself into the Atlantic. Of course thereafter came years of dust, particularly in the Great Plains and the Southwest. But that Montana-born blow was the Depression's great nightmare storm; the one that told the nation that matters were worse than anyone knew, the soil itself was fraying loose and flying away.

In a way, wherever I scrutinized from the lunch perch of that day I was peering down into some local neighborhood of the Depression. As if, say, a spyglass such as Walter Kyle's could be adapted to pick out items through time instead of distance. The farmers of all those fields hemming the eastern horizon. They were veterans of years of scrabbling. Before WPA relief jobs and other New Deal help began to take hold, many a farm family got by only on egg money or cream checks. Or any damn thing they could come up with. Time upon time we were called on at the ranger station by one overalled farmer or another from near Gros Ventre or Valier or even Conrad, traveling from house to house offering a dressed hog he had in the trunk of his jalopy for three cents a pound. Believe it or not, though, those farmers of the Two country were better off than the ones who neighbored them on the east. That great dust storm followed a path across northern Montana already blazed by drought, grasshoppers, army worms, you name it. Around the time the CCC, the Civilian Conservation Corps, was being set up, my father and other rangers and county agents and maybe government men of other kinds were called to a session over at Plentywood. It was the idea of some government thinker—the hunch was that it came down all the way from Tugwell or one of those—that everybody working along any lines of conservation ought to see Montana's worst-hit area of drought. My father grumbled about it costing him three or four days of work from the Two, but he had no choice but to go. I especially remember this because when he got back he said scarcely anything for about a day and a half, and that was not at all like him. Then at supper the second night he suddenly looked across at my mother and burst out, "Bet, there're people over there who're trying to live on just potatoes. They feed Russian thistles to their stock. Call it Hoover hay. It— I just never saw such things. Never even dreamed of them. Fencelines pulled loose by the wind piling tumbleweeds against them. When a guy goes to drive a fencepost, he first has to punch holes in the ground with a crowbar and pour water to soften the soil. And out in the fields, what the dust doesn't cover, the goddamn grasshoppers get. I tell you, Bet, it's a crime against life, what's happening."

So that was the past that came to mind from the horizon of green farms. And closer below us, along the willowed path of Noon Creek, the

ENGLISH CREEK · 39

Depression history of the cattlemen was no happier memory. Noon Creek is the next drainage north of English Creek, swale country without as much cottonwood and aspen along its stream banks. Original cattle country, the best cow-grazing land anywhere in the Two. But what had been a series of about ten good ranches spaced along Noon Creek was dwindled to three. Farthest west, nearest our lunch perch, the Reese family place now run by my mother's brother Pete, who long ago converted to sheep. Just east from there Dill Egan's cow outfit with its historic round corral. And everywhere east of Dill the miles of Double W swales and benchland and the eventual cluster of buildings that was the Double W home ranch. Dill Egan was one of those leery types who steered clear of banks, and so had managed to hold his land. The Williamsons of the Double W owned a bank and property in San Francisco or Los Angeles, one of those places, and as my father put it, "When the end of the world comes, the last sound will be a nickel falling from someplace a Williamson had it hid." Every Noon Creek cowman between the extremes of Dill Egan and Wendell Williamson, though, got wiped out when the nation's plunge flattened the cattle market. Places were foreclosed on, families shattered. The worst happened at a piece of Noon Creek I could not help but look down onto from our lunch site; the double bend of the stream, an S of water and willows like a giant brand onto the Noon Creek valley. The place there had belonged to a rancher who, on the day before foreclosure, told his wife he had some things to do, he'd be a while in the barn. Where he tacked up in plain sight on one of the stalls an envelope on which he had written I CANT TAKE ANY MORE. I WONT HAVE MY EARS KNOCKED DOWN BY LIFE ANY MORE. And then hung himself with a halter rope.

The name of the rancher was Carl Nansen, and that Nansen land was bought up by the Double W. "Wendell Williamson'll let us have the house on the Nansen place to live in" had been Alec's words about the domestic plan after he and Leona became Mr. and Mrs. this fall.

The thought of this and the sight of that creek S were as if wires had connected in me, for suddenly I wanted to turn to my father and ask him everything about Alec. What my brother was getting himself into, sashaying off into the Depression with a saddle and a bridle and a bride. Whether there was any least chance Alec could be headed off from cowboying, or maybe from Leona, since the two somehow seemed to go together. How my father and my mother were going to be able to reason in any way with him, given last night's family explosion. Where we stood as a family. Divided for all time? Or yet the unit of four we had always been? Ask and ask and ask; the impulse rose in me as if coming to percolation.

My father was onto his feet, had pulled out his pocket watch and was kidding me that my stomach was about half an hour fast as usual, it was only now noon, and I got up too and went with him to our horses. But still felt the asking everywhere in me.

No, I put that wrong. About the ask, ask, ask. I did not want to put to my father those infinite questions about my brother. What I wanted, in the way that a person sometimes feels hungry, half-starved, but doesn't know exactly what it is that he'd like to eat, was for my father to be answering them. Volunteering, saying "I see how to bring Alec out of it," or "It'll pass, give him a couple of weeks and he'll cool off about Leona and then . . ."

But Varick McCaskill wasn't being voluntary; he was climbing onto his horse and readying to go be a ranger. And to my own considerable surprise, I let him.

We tell ourselves whatever is needed to go from one scene of life to the next. Tonight in camp, I told myself, as we ended that June lunchtime above the English Creek–Noon Creek divide. Tonight would be early enough to muster the asking about Alec. What I was temporarily choosing, with silence, was that my father and I needed this trail day, the rhythm or ritual or whatever it was, of beginning a counting trip, of again fitting ourselves to the groove of the task and the travel and the mountains. Of entering another Two summer together, I might as well say.

Dode Withrow's sheep were nowhere in evidence when we arrived at the counting vee an hour or so after our lunch stop. A late start by the herder might account for their absence, or maybe it just was one of those mornings when sheep are poky. In either case, I had learned from my father to expect delay, because if you try to follow some exact time when you work with sheep you will rapidly drive yourself loony.

"I might as well go up over here and have a look at that winter kill," my father decided. A stand of pine about a mile to the north was showing the rusty color of death. "How about you hanging on here in case the sheep show up. I won't be gone long." He forced a grin. "Think about how to grow up saner than that brother of yours."

"This whole family's sanity could stand some thinking about" crossed my mind in reply but didn't come out. My father climbed on Mouse and went to worry over winter kill on his forest.

I took out my jackknife and started putting my initials into the bare fallen log I was sitting on. This I did whenever I had time to pass in the forest of the Two, and I suppose even yet up there some logs and stumps announce *J McC* to the silent universe.

The wind finally had gone down, I had no tug at my attention except for the jackknife in my hand. Carving initials as elaborate as mine does take some concentration. The *J* never was too bad to make and the *M* big and easy, but the curves of the *C*s needed to be carefully cut. Thanks to the tardy Withrow sheep I had ample leisure to do so. I suppose sheep have caused more time to be whiled away than any other creatures in the world. Even yet on any number of Montana ridgelines there can be seen stone cairns about the height of a man. Sheepherders' monuments they are called and what they are monuments to is monotony. Just to be doing something a herder would start piling stones, but because he hated to admit he was out there hefting rocks for no real reason, he'd stack up a shape that he could tell himself would serve as a landmark or a boundary marker for his allotment. Fighting back somehow against loneliness. That was a perpetual part of being a sheepherder. In the wagons of a lot of them you would find a stack of old magazines, creased and crumpled from being carried in a hip pocket. An occasional prosperous herder would have a battery radio to keep him company in the evenings. Once in a while you came across a carver or a braider. Quite a few, though, the ones who give the herding profession a reputation for skewed behavior, figured they couldn't be bothered with pastimes. They just lived in their heads, and that can get to be cramped quarters. Those religions which feature years of solitude and silence I have grave doubts about. I believe you are better off doing anything rather than nothing. Even if it is only piling stones or fashioning initials.

In any event, that jackknife work absorbed me for I don't know how long, but to the point where I was startled by the first blats of the Withrow sheep.

I headed on down through the timber on foot to help bring them to the counting vee. A sheepman could have the whole Seventh Cavalry pushing his band along and he'd still seem glad of further help.

Dode Withrow spotted me and called, "Afternoon, Jick. That father of yours come to his senses and turn his job over to you?"

"He's patrolling to a winter kill. Said he'd be back by the time we get up to the vee."

"At the rate these sonsabitches want to move along today he's got time to patrol the whole Rocky Mountains."

This was remarked loud enough by Dode that I figured it was not for my benefit alone. Sure enough, an answer shot out of the timber to our left.

"You might just remember the sonsabitches ARE sheep instead of racehorses."

Into view over there between some trees came Dode's herder, Pat Hoy. For as long as I had been accompanying my father on counting trips, and I imagine for years before, Dode and Pat Hoy had been wrangling with each other as much as they wrangled their sheep. "How do, Jick. Don't get too close to Dode, he's on the prod this morning. Wants the job done before it gets started."

"I'm told you can tell the liveliness of a herder by how his sheep move," Dode suggested. "Maybe you better lay down, Pat, while we send for the undertaker."

"If I'm slow it's because I'm starved down, trying to live on the grub you furnish. Jick, Dode is finally gonna get out of the sheep business. He's gonna set up a stinginess school for you Scotchmen."

That set all three of us laughing as we pushed the band along, for an anthem of the Two was Dode Withrow's lament of staying on and on in the sheep business. "In that '19 winter, I remember coming into the house and standing over the stove, I'd been out all day skinning froze-to-death sheep. Standing there trying to thaw the goose bumps off myself and saying, 'This is it. This does it. I am going to get out of the sonofabitching sheep business.' Then in '32 when the price of lambs went down to four cents a pound and might just as well have gone all the way to nothing, I told myself, 'This is really it. No more of the sonofabitching sheep business for me. I've had it.' And yet here I am, still in the sonofabitching sheep business. God, what a man puts himself through."

That was Dode for you. Poet laureate of the woes of sheep, and a sheepman to the pith of his soul. On up the mountain slope he and Pat Hoy and I now shoved the band. It took a while, because up is not a direction sheep particularly care to go, at least at someone else's suggestion. Sheep seem perpetually leery of what's over the hill, which I suppose makes them either notably dumb or notably smart.

Myself, I liked sheep. Or rather I didn't mind sheep as such, which is the best a person can do towards creatures whose wool begins in their brain, and I liked the idea of sheep. True, sheep had to be troubled with more than cattle did, but the troubling was on a smaller scale. Pulling a lamb from a ewe's womb is nothing to untangling a leggy calf from the inside of a heifer. And a sheep you can brand by dabbing a splot of paint on her back, not needing to invite half the county in to maul your livestock around in the dust of a branding corral. Twelve times out of a dozen, in the debate of cow and ewe I will choose sheep.

For a person partial to the idea of sheep I was in the right time and place. With the encouragement of what the Depression had done to cattle prices the Two Medicine country then was a kind of vast garden of wool and lambs. Beginning in late May, for a month solid a band of sheep a day passed through the town of Gros Ventre on the way north to the Blackfeet Reservation, band after band trailing from all the way down by Choteau, and other sheep ranchers bringing theirs from around Bynum and Pendroy. (Not without some cost to the civic tidiness of Gros Ventre, for the passage of a band of a thousand ewes and their lambs through a town cannot happen without evidence being left on the street, and occasionally the sidewalks. Sheep are nervous enough as it is, and being routed through a canyon of buildings does not improve their bathroom manners any. Once, Carnelia Muntz, wife of the First National banker, showed up in the bank and said something about all the sheep muss on the streets. I give Ed Van Bebber his full due. Ed happened to be in there cashing a check, and he looked her up and down and advised: "Don't think of them as sheep turds, Carnelia. Think of them as berries off the money tree.") This was a time on the reservation when you could see a herder's wagon on top of practically every rise: a fleet of white wagons anchored across the land. Roy Cleary's outfit up around Browning in itself ran fifteen thousand head of ewes or more. And off to the east, just out of view beyond the bench ridges, the big sheep outfits from over in Washington were running their tens of thousands, too. And of course in here to the west where we were working Dode Withrow's sheep to the counting vee, my father's forest pastured the English Creek bands. Sheep and their owners were the chorus in our lives at the English Creek ranger station, the theme of every season and most conversation.

At the counting vee my father was waiting for us. After greetings had been said all around among him and Dode and Pat, Dode handed my father a gunny sack with a couple of double handfuls of cottoncake in it, said, "Start 'em, Mac," and stepped around to his side of the counting gate.

Here on the spread-out English Creek range the tally on each grazing allotment was done through a vee made of poles spiked onto trees, the sheep funneling past while my father and the rancher stood alongside the opening of the narrow end and counted.

Now my father went through the narrow gate into the vee, toward the leery multitude of ewes and lambs. He shook the sack in front of him where the sheep could see it and let a few cottonseed pellets trickle to the ground.

Then it came, that sound not even close to any other in this world, my father's coax to the sheep: the tongue-made *prrrrr prrrrr prrrrr,* remotely a cross between an enormous cat's purr and the cooing of a dove. Maybe it was all the R's built into a Scotch tongue, but for whatever reason my father could croon that luring call better than any sheepman of the Two.

Dode and Pat and I watched now as a first cluster of ewes, attentive to the source of the *prrrrrs,* caught the smell of the cottoncake. They scuffled, did some ewely butting of each other, as usual to no conclusion, then forgot rivalry and swarmed after the cottoncake. As they snooped forward on the trail of more, they led other sheep out the gate and started the count. You could put sheep through the eye of a needle if you once got the first ones going so that the others could turn off their brains and follow.

My job was at the rear of the sheep with the herder, to keep the band pushing through the counting hole and to see that none circled around after they'd been through the vee and got tallied twice—or, had this been Ed Van Bebber's band, I would have been back there to see that his herder, on instructions from Ed, didn't spill some sheep around the wing of the corral while the count was going on, so that they missed being tallied.

But since these were Dode's sheep with Pat Hoy on hand at the back of them I had little to add to the enterprise of the moment and was there mostly for show. I always watched Pat all I could without seeming to stare, to try to learn how he mastered these woolies as he did.

Some way, he was able just to *look* ewes into behaving better than they had in mind. One old independent biddy or another would step out, size up her chance of breaking past Pat, figure out who she was facing, and then shy off back into the rest of the bunch. This of course didn't work with lambs, who have no more predictability to them than hens in a hurricane. But in their case all Pat had to do was say "Round 'em, Taffy" and his caramel-colored shepherd dog would be sluicing them back to where they belonged. A sheep dog as good as Taffy was worth his weight in shoe leather. And a herder as savvy as Pat knew how to be a diplomat toward his dog, rewarding him every now and then with praise and ear rubbing but not babying him so much that the dog hung around waiting to be complimented rather than performing his work. That was one of my father's basic instructions when I first began going into the mountains with him on counting trips, not to get too affectionate with any herder's dog. Simply stroke them a time or two if they nuzzled me and let it go at that.

Taffy came over now to see if I had any stray praise to offer, and I just said, "You're a dog and half, Taffy."

"Grass gets much higher up here, Jick, I'm liable to lose Taffy in it," Pat called over to me. "You ever see such a jungle of a year?"

"No," I confessed, and we made conversation for a bit about the summer's prospects. Pat Hoy looked like any of a thousand geezers you could find in the hiring bars of First Avenue South in Great Falls, but he was a true grassaroo; knew how to graze sheep as if the grass was his own sustenance as well as theirs. No herder in all of the Two country was more highly prized than Pat the ten months of the year when he stayed sober and behind the sheep, and because this was so, Dode put up with what was necessary to hang on to him. That is, put up with the fact that some random number of times a year Pat proclaimed: "I quit, by damn, you can herd these old nellies your own self. Take me to town." Dode knew that only two of those quitting proclamations ever meant anything: "The sonofagun has to have a binge after the lambs are shipped and then another one just before lambing time, go down to Great Falls and get all bent out of shape. He's got his pattern down like linoleum, Pat has. For the first week he drinks whiskey and his women are pretty good lookers. The next week or so he's mostly on beer and his women are getting a little shabby. Then for about two weeks after that he's on straight wine and First Avenue squaws. That gets it out of his system, and I go collect him and we start all over."

You can see how being around Dode and Pat lifted our dispositions. When the count was done and we had helped Pat start the sheep on up toward the range he would summer them on—the ewes and lambs already browsing, taking their first of however many million nibbles of grass on the Two between then and September—Dode stayed on with us awhile to swap talk. "What's new with Uncle Sam?" he inquired.

"Roosevelt doesn't tell me quite everything, understand," my father responded. "We are going modern, though. It has only taken half of my goddamn life, but the Billy Peak lookout is about built. Paul will have her done in the next couple days. This forest is finally going to have a goddamn fire tower everyplace it ought to have one. Naturally it's happening during a summer when the forest is more apt to float away than burn down, but anyway." Dode was a compact rugged-faced guy whose listening grin featured a gap where the sharp tooth just to the left of his front teeth was missing, knocked out in some adventure or another. A Dode tale was that when he and Midge were about to be married he told her that he intended to really dude up for the wedding, even planned to stick a navy bean in the tooth gap. But if Dode looked and acted as if he always was ready to take on life headfirst, he also was one of those rare ones who could listen as earnestly as he could talk.

"Alec still keeping a saddle warm at the Double W?" Dode was asking next.

"Still is," my father had to confirm.

Dode caught the gist behind the tight pair of words, for he went on to relate: "That goddamn Williamson. He can be an overbearing sonofabitch without half trying, I'll say that for him. A while back I ran into him in the Medicine Lodge and we sopped up a few drinks together, then he got to razzing me about cattle being a higher class of animal than sheep. Finally I told him, 'Wendell, answer me this. Whenever you see a picture of Jesus Christ, which is it he's holding in his arms? Always a LAMB, never a goddamn calf.'"

We hooted over that. For the first time all day my father didn't look as if he'd eaten nails for breakfast.

"Anyway," Dode assured us, "Alec'll pretty soon figure out there are other people to work for in the world than Wendell goddamn Williamson. Life is wide, there's room to take a new run at it."

My father wagged his head as if he hoped so but was dubious. "How about you, you see a nickel in sight anywhere this year?" So now it was

Dode's turn to report, and my father just as keenly welcomed in his information that down on the Musselshell a wool consignment of thirty thousand fleeces had gone for twenty-two cents a pound, highest in years, encouragement that could "goddamn near make a man think about staying in the sheep business," and that Dode himself didn't intend to shear until around the end of the month "unless the weather turns christly hot," and that—

I put myself against a tree and enjoyed the sight and sound of the two of them. All the English Creek sheepmen and my father generally got along like hand and glove, but Dode was special beyond that. I suppose it could be said that he and my father were out of the same bin. At least it doesn't stretch my imagination much to think that if circumstances had changed sides when the pair of them were young, it now could have been Dode standing there in the employ of the U.S. Forest Service and my father in possession of a sheep ranch. Their friendship actually went back to before either of them had what could be called a career, to when they both were bronc punks, youngsters riding in the Egans' big round corral at Noon Creek every summer Sunday. My father loved to tell how Dode, who could be a snazzy dresser whenever there was any occasion, would show up to do his bronc-riding in a fancy pair of corduroy pants with leather trim. "To look at him, it was hard to know how much was Dode and how much was dude. But he was the best damn rider you'd ever see, too."

By this time of afternoon a few clouds had concocted themselves above the crest of the mountains and were drifting one after another out over the foothills below us. Small fleecy puffs, the kind which during the dry years made people joke in a disgusted way, "Those are empties from Seattle going over." This fine green year it did not matter that they weren't rainbringers, and with the backdrop of my father and Dode's conversation I lost myself in watching each cloud shadow cover a hill or a portion of a ridgeline and then flow down across the coulee toward the next, as if the shadow was a slow mock flood sent by the cloud.

"I hear nature calling," Dode now was excusing himself. He headed off not toward the timber, though, but to a rock outcropping about forty yards away, roughly as big and high as a one-story house. When Dode climbed up onto that I figured I had misunderstood his mission; he evidently was clambering up there to look along the mountain and check on Pat's progress with the sheep.

But no, he proceeded to do that and the other too, gazing off up the mountain slope as he unbuttoned and peed.

Do you know, even as I say this I again see Dode in every particular. His left hand resting on his hip and the arm and elbow kinked out like the handle on a coffee cup. His hat tilted back at an inquiring angle. He looked composed as a statue up there, if you can imagine stone spraddled out in commemoration of that particular human function.

My father and I grinned until our faces almost split. "There is only one Dode," he said. Then he cupped his hands and called out in a concerned tone: "Dode, I hope you've got a good foothold up there. Because you sure don't have all that much of a handhold."

By the time Dode declared he had to head down the mountain toward home, pronto, or face consequences from Midge, I actually was almost in the mood that a counting trip deserved. For I knew that traveling to tomorrow's sheep, those of Walter Kyle and Fritz Hahn, would take us up onto Roman Reef, always topnotch country, and after that would come the interesting prospect of the new Billy Peak lookout tower. It had not escaped me either that on our way to that pair of attractions we would spend tonight at a camping spot along the North Fork under Rooster Mountain, which my father and I—and, yes, Alec in years past—considered our favorite in the entire Two. Flume Gulch, the locale was called, because an odd high gully with steep sides veered in from the south and poured a trickle of water down the gorge wall into the North Fork. If you had to walk any of that Flume Gulch side of the creek, you would declare the terrain had tried to stand itself on end and prop itself up with thick timber and a crisscross of windfalls. But go on the opposite side of the creek and up onto the facing and equally steep slope of Rooster Mountain and you would turn around and say you'd never been in a grassier mountain meadow. That is the pattern the seasons make in this part of the Two, a north-facing slope bursting with trees and brush because snow stays longest there and provides moisture, while a south-facing slope is timberless but grassy because of all the sun it gets. Anyway, wild and tumbled country, Flume Gulch, but as pretty as you could ask for.

By just before dusk my father and I were there, and Mouse and Pony and Homer were unsaddled and tethered on the good grass of the Rooster Mountain slope, and camp was established.

"You know where supper is," my father advised. By which he meant that it was in the creek, waiting to be caught.

This far up the North Fork, English Creek didn't amount to much. Most places you could cross it in a running jump. But the stream was headed down out of the mountains in a hurry and so had some pretty riffles and every now and again a pool like a big wide stairstep of glass. If fish weren't in one of those waters, they were in the other.

Each of us took his hat off and unwound the fishline and hook wrapped around the hatband. On our way up, we had cut a pair of willows of decent length and now notched the wood about an inch from the small end, tied each fishline snug into each notch so it couldn't pull off, and were ready to talk business with those fish.

"Hide behind a tree to bait your hook," my father warned with an almost straight face, "or they'll swarm right out of the water after you."

My father still had a reputation in the Forest Service from the time some Region One headquarters muckymuck who was quite a dry-fly fisherman asked him what these English Creek trout took best. Those guys of course have a whole catechism of hackles and muddlers and goofus bugs and stone flies and nymphs and midges. "Chicken guts," my father informed him.

We didn't happen to have any of those along with us, but just before leaving home we'd gone to the old haystack bottom near the barn and dug ourselves each a tobacco can of angleworms. Why in holy hell anyone thinks a fish would prefer a dab of hair to something as plump as a stack-bottom worm I never have understood the reasoning of.

The fish in fact began to prove that, right then. I do make the concession to sportsmanship that I'll fish a riffle once in a while, even though it demands some attention to casting instead of just plunking into the stream, and so it pleased me a little that in the next half hour or so I pulled my ten fish out of bumpy water, while at the pool he'd chosen to work over my father still was short of his supper quota.

"I can about taste that milkshake," I warned him as I headed downstream a little to clean my catch. Theoretically there was a standing bet in our family, that anybody who fished and didn't catch ten owed the others a milkshake. My father had thought this up some summers ago to interest Alec, who didn't care anything for fishing but always was keen to compete. But after the tally mounted through the years to where Alec owed my father and me eight milkshakes each, during last year's counting trip Alec declared himself out and left the fishing to us.

And the two of us were currently even-stephen, each having failed to hook ten just once, all of last summer.

"I'm just corraling them first," my father explained as he dabbed a fresh worm to the pool. "What I intend is to get fish so thick in here they'll run into each other and knock theirselves out."

The fish must have heard and taken pity, because by the time I'd gutted mine here he came with his on a willow stringer.

"What?" I inquired as innocently as I could manage. "Did you decide to forfeit?"

"Like hell, mister. Ten brookies, right before your very eyes. Since you're so advanced in all this, go dig out the frying pan."

Even yet I could live and thrive on that Flume Gulch meal procedure: fry up both catches of fish, eat as many for supper as we could hold, resume on the rest at breakfast. Those little brookies, Eastern brook trout about eight inches long, are among the best eating there can be. You begin to taste them as quick as they hit the frying pan and go into their curl. Brown them up and take them in your fingers and eat them like corn on the cob, and you wish you had the capacity for a hundred of them.

When we'd devoured four or so brookies apiece we slowed down enough to share out a can of pork and beans and some buttered slices of my mother's bread, then resumed on the last stint of our fish supper.

"That hold you?" my father asked when we each had made seven or eight trout vanish.

I bobbed that I guessed it would, and while he went to the creek to rinse off our tin plates and scour the frying pan with gravel, I set to work composing his day's diary entry.

That the U.S. Forest Service wanted to know, in writing, what he'd done with his day constituted my father's single most chronic bother about being a ranger. Early on, someone told him the story of another rider-turned-ranger down on the Shoshone National Forest in Wyoming. "Trimmed my horse's tail and the wind blew all day," read the fellow's first diary try. Then with further thought he managed to conclude: "From the northeast." My father could swallow advice if he had to, and so he did what he could with the perpetual nag of having to jot his activities into the diary. When he did it was entirely another matter. Two or three weeks he would stay dutiful, then came a Saturday morning when he had seven little yellow blank pages to show for his week, and the filling in had to start:

"Bet, what'd I do on Tuesday? That the day it rained and I worked on Mazoola paperwork?"

"That was Wednesday. Tuesday you rode up to look over the range above Noon Creek."

"I thought that was Thursday."

"You can think so if you like, but you'd be wrong." My mother was careful to seem half-exasperated about these scriving sessions, but I think she looked forward to the chance to set my father straight on history, even if it was only the past week's. "Thursday I baked, and you took a rhubarb pie for the Bowens when you went to the Indian Head station. Not that Louise Bowen is capable of recognizing a pie."

"Well, then, when I rode to the Guthrie Peak lookout, that was—only yesterday? Friday?"

"Today is Saturday, yesterday most likely was Friday," my mother was glad to confirm for him.

When I became old enough to go into the mountains with him on counting trips my father perceived relief for his diary situation. Previously he had tried Alec, but Alec had the same catch-up-on-it-later proclivity as his. I think we had not gone a mile along the trail that very first morning when he reined up, said as if it had just occurred to him out of nowhere, "Jick, whyn't you kind of keep track of today for me?" and presented me a fresh-sharpened stub pencil and a pocket notebook.

It did take a little doing to catch on to my father's style. But after those first days of my reporting into my notebook in the manner of "We met up with Dill Egan on the south side of Noon Creek and talked with him about whether he can get a bigger permit to run ten more steers on" and my father squashing it down in his diary to "Saw D. Egan about steer proposition," I adjusted.

By now I was veteran enough that the day came readily to the tip of my pencil. "Patroled"—another principle some early ranger had imparted to my father was that if you so much as left the station to go to the outhouse, you had patroled—"Patroled the n. fork of English Creek. Counted D. Withrow's sheep onto allotment. Commenced packing bolts and turnbuckles and cable to Billy Peak lookout site."

My father read it over and nodded. "Change that 'bolts and turnbuckles and cable' just to 'gear.' You don't want to be any more definite than necessary in any love note to Uncle Sam. But otherwise it reads like the very Bible."

So the day was summed and we had dined on trout and the campfire was putting warmth and light between us and the night, and we had nothing that needed doing except to contemplate until sleep overcame us. My father was lying back against his saddle, hands behind his head and his hat tipped forward over his forehead. Ever since a porcupine attracted by the salt of horse sweat had chewed hell out of Alec's saddle on the counting trip a couple or three years ago, we made it a policy to keep our saddles by us.

He could make himself more comfortable beside a campfire than anybody else I ever knew, my father could. Right now he looked like he could spend till dawn talking over the Two country and everything in it, if Toussaint Rennie or Dode Withrow had been on hand to do it with.

My thoughts, though, still circled around Alec—well, sure, somewhat onto Leona too—and what had erupted at supper last night. But again the reluctance lodged itself in me, against outright asking my father what he thought the prospect was where Alec was concerned. I suppose there are times a person doesn't want to hear pure truth. Instead, I brought out something else that had been dogging my mind.

"Dad? Do you ever wonder about being somebody else?"

"Such as who? John D. Rockefeller?"

"What I mean, I got to thinking from watching you and Dode together there at the counting vee. Just, you know, whether you'd ever thought about how he could be in your place and you in his."

"Which would give me three daughters instead of you and Alec, do you mean? Maybe I'll saddle up Mouse and go trade him right now."

"No, not that. I mean life generally. Him being the ranger and you being the sheepman is what I had in mind. If things had gone a little different back when you guys were, uh, younger." Were my age, was of course what was hiding behind that.

"Dode jaw to jaw with the Major? Now I know I'm going to head down the mountain and swap straight across, for the sake of seeing that." In that time the regional forester, the boss of everybody in the national forests of Montana and northern Idaho, was Evan Kelley. Major Kelley, for he was like a lot of guys who got a big army rank during the war, hung on to the title ever afterward as if it was sainthood. The Major's style of leadership was basic. When he said frog, everybody better jump. I wish I had a nickel for every time my father opened his USFS mail and muttered: "Oh, Jesus, another kelleygram. When does he ever sleep?" Everybody did admit, the Major at least made clear the gospel in his messages to his Forest Service men. What he prescribed from his rangers was no big forest fires and no guff. So far, my father's slate was clean of both. In those years I didn't give the matter particular thought, but my father's long stint in charge of the English Creek district of the Two Medicine National Forest could only have happened with the blessing of the Major himself. The Pope in Missoula, so to speak. Nobody lower could have shielded ranger Varick McCaskill from the transfers that ordinarily happened every few years or so in the Forest Service. No, the Major wanted that tricky northmost portion of the Two, surrounded as so much of it was by other government domains, to be rangered in a way that wouldn't draw the Forest Service any bow-wow from the neighboring Glacier Park staff or the Blackfeet Reservation people; and in a way that would keep the sheepmen content and the revenue they paid for summer grazing permits flowing in; and in a way that would not repeat the awful fires of 1910 or the later Phantom Woman Mountain burn, right in here above the North Fork. And that was how my father was rangering it. So far.

"I guess I know what you're driving at, though." My father sat up enough to put his boot against a pine piece of squaw wood and shove it farther into the fire, then lay back against his saddle again. "How come we do what we do in life, instead of something else. But I don't know. I do not know. All I've ever been able to figure out, Jick, is that no job fits as well as a person would like it to, but some of us fit the job better than others do. That sorts matters out a little."

"Yeah, well, I guess. But how do you get in the job in the first place to find out whether you're going to fit it?"

"You watch for a chance to try it, is all. Sometimes the chance comes looking for you. Sometimes you got to look for it. Myself, I had my taste of the army because of the war. And it took goddamn little of army life to tell me huh uh, not for me. Then when I landed back here I got to be association rider for Noon Creek by setting out to get it, I guess you'd say. What I did, I went around to Dill Egan and old Thad Wainwright and your granddad Isaac and the other Noon Creekers and asked if they'd keep me in mind when it came time to summer their cows up here. Of course, it maybe didn't particularly hurt that I mentioned how happy I'd be to keep Double W cows from slopping over onto the Noon Creek guys' allotments, as had been going on. Anyway, the job got to be mine."

"What, the Double W was running cattle up here then?"

"Were they ever. They held a permit, in the early days. A hellish big one. Back then the Williamsons didn't have hold of all that Noon Creek country to graze. So, yeah, they had forest range, and sneaked cows onto anybody else's whenever they could. The number one belief of old Warren Williamson, you know, was that other people's grass might just as well be his." I didn't know. Warren Williamson, father of the present Double W honcho, was before my time; or at least died in California before I was old enough for it to mean anything to me.

"I'll say this one thing for Wendell," my father went on, "he at least buys or rents the country. Old Warren figured he could just take it." He gave the pine piece another shove with his boot. "The everlasting damn Double W. The Gobble Gobble You, as the gent who was ranger when I was association rider used to call it."

"Is that—" I had it in mind to ask if that was why he and my mother were so dead set against Alec staying on at the Double W, those old contentions between the Williamsons' ranch and the rest of the Two country. But no, the McCaskill next to me here in the fireshine was a readier topic than my absent brother. "Is that how you got to be the ranger here? Setting out to get the job?"

He went still for a moment, lying there in that sloped position against the saddle, feet toward the fire. Then shook his head. "The Forest Service generally doesn't work that way, and the Major sure as hell doesn't. Point yourself at the Two and they're liable to plunk you down on the Beaverhead or over onto the Bitterroot. Or doghouse you in the Selway, back when there still was a Selway. No, I didn't aim myself at English Creek. It happened."

I was readying to point out to him that "it happened" wasn't a real full explanation of job history when he sat up and moved his hat back so as to send his attention toward me. "What about you, on all this if-I-was-him-and-he-was-me stuff? Somebody you think you'd rather be, is there?"

There he had me. My turn to be less than complete. I answered: "Not rather, really. Just might have been, is all."

An answer that didn't even start toward truth, that one was. And not the one I would have resorted to anytime up until supper of the night before. For until then if I was to imagine myself happening to be anybody else, who could the first candidate have been but Alec? Wasn't all the basic outline already there? Same bloodline, same place of growing up, same schooling, maybe even the same body frame if I kept growing at my recent pace. Both of us September arrivals into the world, even; only the years needed swapping. The remarkable thing to me was that our interests in life were as different as they were, and I suppose I had more or less assumed that time was going to bring mine around to about where Alec's were. But now, precisely this possibility was what was unsettling me. That previous night at the supper table when Alec made his announcement about him and Leona and I asked "How come?" what I intended maybe was something similar to what my parents were asking of Alec. Something like "Already?" What was the rush? How could marriage and all be happening this soon, to my own brother? Yes, maybe put it this way: what I felt or at least sensed and was trying to draw into focus was the suggestion that Alec's recent course of behavior in some way foreshadowed my own. It was like looking through the Toggery window in Gros Ventre at a fancy suit of clothes and saying, by the Christ, they'll never catch me dead in *those*. But at the same time noticing that they seem to be your exact fit.

"Like who?" my father was asking in a tone which signaled me that he was asking it for the second time.

"Who?" I echoed, trying to think of anything more.

"Country seems to be full of owls tonight," he observed. Yet he was still attentive enough in my direction that I knew I had to come up with something that resembled an answer.

"Oh. Yeah. Who." I looked at the fire for some chunk that needed kicking farther in, and although none really did, I kicked one anyway. "Well, like Ray. That's all I had in mind, was Ray and me." Ray Heaney was my best friend at high school in Gros Ventre. "Us being the same age and all, like you and Dode."

This brought curiosity into my father's regard of me. "Now that takes some imagination," he said. "Dode and me are Siamese twins compared to you and Ray."

Then he rose, dusting twigs and pine needles off the back of him from where he had lain. "But I guess imagination isn't a struggle with you. You maybe could supply the rest of us as well, huh? Anyway, let's give some thought to turning in. We got a day ahead of us tomorrow."

If I was a believer in omens, the start of that next morning ought to have told me something.

The rigamarole of untangling out of our bedrolls and getting the campfire going and making sure the horses hadn't quit the country during the night, all that went usual enough.

Then, though, my father glanced around at me from where he had the coffeepot heating over a corner of the fire and asked: "Ready for a cup, Alec?"

Well, that will happen in a family. A passing shadow of absentmindedness, or the tongue just slipping a cog from what was intended. Ordinarily, being miscalled wouldn't have riled me. But all this recent commotion about Alec, and my own wondering about where anybody in this family stood anymore, and that fireside spell of brooding I'd done on my brother and myself, and I don't know what the hell all else—it now brought a response which scraped out of me like flint:

"I'm the other one."

Surprise passed over my father. Then I guess what is called contrition.

"You sure as hell are," he agreed in a low voice. "Unmistakably Jick."

About my name. John Angus McCaskill, I was christened. As soon as I began at the South Fork school, though, and gained a comprehension of what had been done to me, I put away that Angus for good. I have thought ever since that using a middle name is like having a third nostril.

I hadn't considered this before, but by then the John must already have been amended out of all recognition, too. At least I can find no memory of ever being called that, so the change must have happened pretty early in life. According to my mother it next became plain that "Johnnie" didn't fit the boy I was, either. "Somehow it just seemed like calling rhubarb vanilla," and she may or may not have been making a joke. With her you couldn't always tell. Anyhow, the family story goes on that she and my father were trying me out as "Jack" when some visitor, noticing that I had the McCaskill red hair but gray eyes instead of everybody else's blue, and more freckles than Alec and my father combined, and not such a pronouncement of jaw as theirs, said something like: "He looks to me more like the jick of this family."

So I got dubbed for the off card. For the jack that shares only the color of the jack of trumps. That is to say, in a card game such as pitch, if spades are led the jack of clubs becomes the jick, and in the taking of tricks the abiding rule is that jack takes jick but jick takes joker. I explain this a bit because I am constantly dumbfounded by how many people, even here in Montana, no longer can play a decent hand of cards. I believe television has got just a hell of a lot to answer for.

Anyway, Jick I became, and have ever been. An odd tag, put on me out of nowhere like that. This is part of the pondering I find myself doing now. Whether some other name would have shifted my life any. Yet, of what I might change, I keep deciding that that would not be among the first.

This breakfast incident rankled a little even after my father and I saddled up and resumed the ride toward the Roman Reef counting vee where we were to meet Walter Kyle's sheep at around noon. Nor did the weather help any. Clouds closed off the peaks of the mountains, and while it wasn't raining yet, the air promised that it intended to. One of those days too clammy to go without a slicker coat and too muggy to wear one in comfort.

To top it all off, we now were on the one stretch of the trail I never liked, with the Phantom Woman Mountain burn on the slope coming into sight ahead of us. Everywhere over there, acre upon acre upon acre, a gray cemetery of snags and stumps. Of death by fire, for the Phantom Woman forest fire had been the one big one in the Two's history except for the blazing summer of 1910.

Ahead of me, my father was studying across at the burn in the gloomy way he always did here. Both of us now moping along, like sorrow's orphans. If I didn't like the Phantom Woman neighborhood, my father downright despised it. Plainly he considered this gray dead mountainside the blot on his forest. In those times, when firefighting was done mainly by hand, a runaway blaze was the bane of the Forest Service. My father's slate was as clean as could be; except for unavoidable smudges before lightning strikes could be snuffed out, timber and grass everywhere else on his English Creek ranger district were intact, even much of the 1910-burnt country restoring itself by now. But the awful scar here was unhealed yet. Not that the Phantom Woman fire was in any way my father's own responsibility, for it happened before this district was his, while he still was the ranger at Indian Head rather than here. He was called in as part of the fire crew—this was a blaze that did run wild for a while, a whole hell of a bunch of men ended up fighting Phantom Woman before they controlled it—but that was all. You couldn't tell my father that, though, and this morning I wasn't in a humor to even try.

When time has the weight of a mood such as ours on it, it slows to a creep. Evidently my father figured both the day and I could stand some brightening. Anyway it was considerably short of noon—we were about two thirds of our way up Roman Reef, where the North Fork hides itself in a timber canyon below and the trail bends away from the face of Phantom Woman to the other mountains beyond—when he turned atop Mouse and called to me:

"How's an early lunch sound to you?"

"Suits me," I of course assured him.

Out like this, my father tended to survive on whatever jumped out of the food pack first. He did have the principle that supper needed to be a cooked meal, especially if it could be trout. But as for the rest of the day, if leftover trout weren't available he was likely to offer up as breakfast a couple of slices of headcheese and a can of tomatoes or green beans, and if you didn't watch him he might do the exact same again for lunch. My mother consequently always made us up enough slab sandwiches for three days' worth of lunches. Of course, by the second noon in that high air the bread was about dry enough to strike a match on, but still a better bet than whatever my father was apt to concoct.

We had eaten an applebutter sandwich and a half apiece and were sharing a can of peaches for dessert, harpooning the slices out with our jackknives to save groping into the pack for utensils, when Mouse suddenly snorted.

"Stand still a minute," my father instructed, which I already was embarked on. Meanwhile he stepped carefully backward the three or four paces until he was beside the scabbard on Mouse, with the .30-06 rifle in it. That time of year in the Two, the thought was automatic in anybody who at all knew what he was doing: look around for bears, for they are coming out of hibernation cantankerous.

What Mouse was signaling, however, proved to be a rider appearing at the bend of the trail downhill from us. He was on a blaze-face sorrel, who in turn snorted at the sight of us. A black pack mare followed into sight, then a light gray pack horse with spots on his nose and his neck stretched out and his lead rope taut.

"Somebody's new camptender, must be," my father said and resumed on our peaches.

The rider sat in his saddle that permanent way a lot of those old-timers did, as if he lived up there and couldn't imagine sufficient reason to venture down off the back of a horse. Not much of his face showed between the buttoned-up slicker and the pulled-down brown Stetson. But thinking back on it now, I am fairly sure that my father at once recognized both the horseman and the situation.

The brief packstring climbed steadily to us, the ears of the horses sharp in interest at us and Pony and Homer and Mouse. The rider showed no attention until he was right up to my father and me. Then, though I didn't see him do anything with the reins, the sorrel stopped and the Stetson veered half out over the slickered shoulder nearest us.

"Hullo, Mac."

"I had half a hunch it might be you, Stanley. How the hell are you?"

"Still able to sit up and take nourishment. Hullo, Alec or Jick, as the case may be."

I had not seen him since I was, what? four years old, five? Yet right then I could have tolled off to you a number of matters about Stanley Meixell. That he was taller than he looked on tat sorrel, built in the riderly way of length mostly from his hips down. That he had once been an occasional presence at our meals, stooping first over the washbasin for a cleanse that included the back of his neck, and then slicking back his hair—I could have said too that it was crow-black and started from a widow's peak—before he came to the table. That unlike a lot of people he did not talk down to children, never delivered them phony guff such as "Think you'll ever amount to anything?" That, instead, he once set Alec and me to giggling to the point where my mother threatened to send us from the table, when he told us with a straight face that where he came from they called milk moo juice and eggs cackleberries and molasses long-tailed sugar. Yet of his ten or so years since we had last seen him I couldn't have told you anything whatsoever. So it was odd how much immediately arrived to mind about this unexpected man.

"Jick," I clarified. "'Lo, Stanley."

It was my father's turn to pick up the conversation. "Thought I recognized that black pack mare. Back up in this country to be campjack for the Busby boys, are you?"

"Yeah." Stanley's yeah was that Missourian slowed-down kind, almost in two parts: yeh-uh. And his voice sounded huskier than it ought to, as if a rasp had been used across the top of it. "Yeah, these times, I guess being campjack is better than no jack at all." Protocol was back to him now. He asked my father, "Counting them onto the range, are you?"

"Withrow's band yesterday, and Kyle's and Hahn's today."

"Quite a year for feed up here. This's been a million dollar rain, ain't it? Brought the grass up ass-high to a tall Indian. Though I'm getting to where I could stand a little sunshine to thaw out with, myself."

"Probably have enough to melt you," my father predicted, "soon enough."

"Could be." Stanley looked ahead up the trail, as if just noticing that it continued on from where we stood. "Could be," he repeated.

Nothing followed that, either from Stanley or my father, and it began to come through to me that this conversation was seriously kinked in some way. These two men had not seen each other for the larger part of ten years. So why didn't they have anything to say to one another besides this small-change talk about weather and grass? And already were running low on that? And both were wearing a careful look, as if the trail suddenly was a slippery place?

Finally my father offered: "Want some peaches? A few in here we haven't stabbed dead yet."

"Naw, thanks. I got to head on up the mountain or I'll have sheepherders after my hide." Yet Stanley did not quite go into motion; seemed, somehow, to be storing up an impression of the pair of us to take with him.

My father fished out another peach slice and handed me the can to finish. Along with it came his casual question: "What was it you did to your hand?"

It took me a blink or two to realize that although he said it in my direction, the query was intended for Stanley. I saw then that a handkerchief was wrapped around the back of Stanley's right hand, and that he was resting that hand on the saddle horn with his left hand atop it, the reverse of usual procedure there. Also, as much of the handkerchief as I could see had started off white but now showed stains like dark rust.

"You know how it is, that Bubbles cayuse"—Stanley tossed a look over his shoulder to the gray pack horse—"was kind of snaky this morning. Tried to kick me into next week. Took some skin off, is all."

We contemplated Bubbles. As horses go, he looked capable not just of assault but maybe pillage and plunder and probably arson, too. He was ewe-necked, and accented that feature by stretching back stubbornly against the lead rope even now that he was standing still. "A dragger," the Forest Service packer Isidor Pronovost called such a creature. "You sometimes wonder if the sunnabitch mightn't tow easier if you was to tip him over onto his back." The constellation of dark nose spots which must have given Bubbles his name—at least I couldn't see anything else nameable about him—drew a person's attention, but if you happened to glance beyond those markings, you saw that Bubbles was peering back at you as if he'd like to be standing on your spine. How such creatures get into packstrings I just don't know. I suppose the same way Good Help Hebners and Ed Van Bebbers get into the human race.

"I don't remember you as having much hide to spare," my father said then to Stanley. During the viewing of Bubbles, the expression on my father's face had shifted from careful. He now looked as if he'd made up his mind about something. "Suppose you could stand some company?" Awful casual, as if the idea had just strolled up to him out of the trees. "Probably it's no special fun running a packstring one-handed."

Now this was a prince of an offer, but of course just wasn't possible. Evidently my father had gone absent-minded again, this time about the counting obligation he'd mentioned not ten sentences earlier. I was just set to remind him of our appointment with Walter's and Fritz's sheep when he added on: "Jick here could maybe ride along with you."

I hope I didn't show the total of astonishment I felt.

Some must have lopped over, though, because Stanley promptly enough was saying: "Aw, no, Mac. Jick's got better things to do than haze me along."

"Think about morning," my father came back at him. "Those packs and knots are gonna be several kinds of hell, unless you're more lefthanded than you've ever shown."

"Aw, no. I'll be out a couple or three days, you know. Longer if any of those herders have got trouble."

"Jick's been out that long with me any number of times. And your cooking's bound to be better for him than mine."

"Well," Stanley began, and stopped. Christamighty, he seemed to be considering. Matters were passing me by before I could even see them coming.

I will always credit Stanley Meixell for putting the next two questions in the order he did.

"It ought to be up to Jick." Stanley looked directly down at me. "How do you feel about playing nursemaid to somebody so goddamn dumb as to get hisself kicked?"

The corner of my eye told me my father suggested a pretty enthusiastic response to any of this.

"Oh, I feel fine about—I mean, sure, Stanley. I could, uh, ride along. If you really want. Yeah."

Stanley looked down at my father now. "Mac, you double sure it'd be okay?"

Even I was able to translate that. What was my father going to face from my mother for sending me off camptending into the mountains with Stanley for a number of days?

"Sure," my father stated, as if doubt wasn't worth wrinkling the brain for. "Bring him back when he's dried out behind the ears."

"Well, then." The brown Stetson tipped up maybe two inches, and Stanley swung a slow look around at the pines and the trail and the mountainslope as if this was a site he might want to remember. More of his face showed. Dark eyes, blue-black. Into the corners of them, a lot of routes of squint wrinkles. Thin thrifty nose. Thrift of line at the mouth and chin, too. A face with no waste to it. In fact, a little worn down by use was the impression it gave. "I guess we ought to be getting," Stanley proposed. "Got everything you need, Jick?"

I had no idea in hell what I needed for going off into the Rocky Mountains with a one-handed campjack. I mean, I was wearing my slicker coat, my bedroll was behind my saddle, my head was more or less on my shoulders despite the jolt of surprise that all of this had sent through me, but were those nearly enough? Anyway, I managed to blurt:

"I guess so."

Stanley delivered my father the longest gaze he had yet. "See you in church, Mac," he said, then nudged the sorrel into motion.

The black pack horse and the light gray ugly one had passed us by the time I swung onto Pony, and my father was standing with his thumbs in his pockets, looking at the series of three horse rumps and the back of Stanley Meixell, as I reined around onto the trail. I stopped beside my father long enough to see if he was going to offer any explanation, or instructions, or edification of any damn sort at all. His face, still full of that decision, said he wasn't. All I got from him was: "Jick, he's worth knowing."

"But I already know him."

No response to that. None in prospect. The hell with it. I rode past my father and muttered as I did: "Don't forget to do the diary."

"Thanks for reminding me," my father said, poker-faced. "I'll give it my utmost."

The Busby brothers, I knew, ran three bands of sheep on their forest allotment, which stretched beneath the cliff face of Roman Reef. Stanley had slowed beyond the first bend of the trail for me to catch up, or maybe to make sure I actually was coming along on this grand tour of sheepherders.

"Which camp do we head for first?" I called ahead to him.

"Canada Dan's, he's the closest. About under that promontory in the reef is where his wagon is. If we sift right along for the next couple hours or so we'll be there." Stanley and the sorrel were on the move again, in that easy style longtime riders and their accustomed horses have. One instant you see the pair of them standing and the next you see them in motion together, and there's been no rigamarole in between. Stopped and now going, that's all. But Stanley did leave behind for me the observation: "Quite a day to be going places, ain't it."

"Yeah, I guess."

It couldn't have been more than fifteen minutes after we left my father, though, when Stanley reined his horse off the trail into a little clearing and the pack horses followed. When I rode up alongside he said: "I got to go visit a tree. You keep on ahead, Jick. I'll catch right up."

I had the trail to myself for the next some minutes. Just when I was about to rein around and see what had become of Stanley, the white of the sorrel's blaze flashed into sight. "Be right there," Stanley called, motioning me to ride on.

But he caught up awfully gradually, and in fact must have made a second stop when I went out of sight around a switchback. And before long he was absent again. This time when he didn't show up and didn't show up, I halted Pony and waited. As I was about to go back and start a search, here Stanley came, calling out as before: "Be right there."

I began to wonder a bit. Not only had I been volunteered into this expedition by somebody other than myself, I sure as the devil had not signed on to lead it.

So the next time Stanley lagged from sight, I was determined to wait until he was up with me. And as I sat there on Pony, firmly paused, I began to hear him long before I could see him.

> *"My name, she is Pancho,*
> *I work on a rancho.*
> *I make a dollar a day."*

Stanley's singing voice surprised me, a clearer, younger tone than his raspy talk.

So did his song.

> *"I go to see Suzy,*
> *She's got a doozy.*
> *Suzy take my dollar away."*

When Stanley drew even with me, I still couldn't see much of his eyes under the brim of the pulled-down hat, although I was studying pretty hard this time.

"Yessir," Stanley announced as the sorrel stopped, "great day for the race, ain't it?"

"The race?" I gaped.

"The human race." Stanley pivoted in his saddle—a little unsteadily, I thought—enough to scan at the black pack mare and then the gray one. He got a white-eyed glower in return from the gray. "Bubbles there is still in kind of an owly mood. Mad because he managed to only kick my hand instead of my head, most likely. You're doing fine up ahead, Jick. I'll wander along behind while Bubbles works on being crabby."

There was nothing for it but head up the trail again. At least now I knew for sure what my situation was. If there lingered any last least iota of doubt, Stanley's continued disappearances and his ongoing croon dispatched it.

> *"My brother is Sancho,*
> *he try with a banjo*
> *to coax Suzy to woo."*

I have long thought that the two commonest afflictions in Montana—it may be true everywhere, but then I haven't been everywhere—

are drink and orneriness. True, my attitude has thawed somewhat since I have become old enough to indulge in the pair myself now and again. But back there on that mountain those years ago, all I could think was that I had on my hands the two worst of such representations, a behind-the-bush bottle tipper and a knot-headed pack horse.

> *"But she tell him no luck,*
> *the price is an extra buck,*
> *him and the banjo make two."*

I spent a strong hour or so in contemplation of my father and just what he had saddled me with here. All the while mad enough to bite sticks in two. Innocent as a goddamn daisy, I had let my father detour me up the trail with Stanley Meixell. And now to find that my trail compadre showed every sign of being a warbling boozehound. Couldn't I, for Christ's sake, be told the full extent of the situation before I was shoved into it? What was in the head of that father of mine? Anything?

After this siege of black mull, a new thought did break through. It occurred to me to wonder just how my father ought to have alerted me to Stanley's condition beforehand. Cleared his throat and announced, "Stanley, excuse us but Jick and I got something to discuss over here in the jackpines, we'll be right back"? Worked his way behind Stanley and pantomimed to me a swig from a bottle? Neither of those seemed what could be called etiquette, and that left me with the perturbing suggestion that maybe it'd been up to me to see the situation for myself.

Which gave me another hour or so of heavy chewing, trying to figure out how I was supposed to follow events that sprung themselves on me from nowhere. How do you brace for that, whatever age you are?

Canada Dan's sheep were bunched in a long thick line against a stand of lodgepole pine. When we rode up a lot of blatting was going on, as if there was an uneasiness among them. A sheepherder who knows what he is doing in timber probably is good in open country too, but vice versa is not necessarily the case, and I remembered my father mentioning that Canada Dan had been herding over by Cut Bank, plains country. A herder new to timber terrain and skittish about it will dog the bejesus out of his sheep, keep the band tight together for fear of losing some. Canada Dan's patch-marked sheepdog looked weary, panting, and I saw Stanley study considerably the way these sheep were crammed along the slope.

"Been looking for you since day before yesterday," Canada Dan greeted us. "I'm goddamn near out of canned milk."

"That so?" said Stanley. "Lucky thing near isn't the same as out."

Canada Dan was looking me up and down now. "You that ranger's kid?"

I didn't care for the way that was put, and just said back: "Jick McCaskill." Too, I was wondering how many more times that day I was going to need to identify myself to people I'd had no farthest intention of getting involved with.

Canada Dan targeted on Stanley again. "Got to bring a kid along to play nursemaid for you now, Stanley? Must be getting on in years."

"I bunged up my hand," Stanley responded shortly. "Jick's been generous enough to pitch in with me."

Canada Dan shook his head as if my sanity was at issue. "He's gonna regret charity when he sees the goddamn chore we got for ourselves up here."

"What would that be, Dan?"

"About fifteen head of goddamn dead ones, that's what. They got onto some deathcamas, maybe three days back. Poisoned theirselfs before you can say sic 'em." Canada Dan reported all this as if he was an accidental passerby instead of being responsible for these animals. Remains of animals, they were now.

"That's a bunch of casualties," Stanley agreed. "I didn't happen to notice the pelts anywhere there at the wag—"

"Happened right up over here," Canada Dan went on as if he hadn't heard, gesturing to the ridge close behind him. "Just glommed onto that deathcamas like it was goddamn candy. C'mon here, I'll show you." The herder shrugged out of his coat, tossed it down on the grass, pointed to it and instructed his dog: "Stay, Rags." The dog came and lay on the coat, facing the sheep, and Canada Dan trudged up the ridge without ever glancing back at the dog or us.

I began to dread the way this was trending.

The place Canada Dan led us to was a pocket meadow of bunch grass interspersed with cream-colored blossoms and with gray mounds here and there on it. The blossoms were deathcamas, and the mounds were the dead ewes. Even as cool as the weather had been they were bloated almost to bursting.

"That's them," the herder identified for our benefit. "It's sure convenient of you fellows to show up. All this goddamn skinning, I can stand all the help I can get."

Stanley did take the chance to get a shot in on him. "You been too occupied the past three days to get to them, I guess?" But it bounced off Canada Dan like a berry off a buffalo.

The three of us looked at the corpses for a while. There's not all that much conversation to be made about bloated sheep carcasses. After a bit, though, Canada Dan offered in a grim satisfied way: "That'll teach the goddamn buggers to eat deathcamas."

"Well," Stanley expounded next, "there's no such thing as one-handed skinning." Which doubled the sense of dread in me. I thought to myself, But there is one-handed tipping of a bottle, and one-handed dragging me into this campjack expedition, and one-handed weaseling out of what was impending here next and—

All this while, Stanley was looking off in some direction carefully away from me. "I can be unloading the grub into Dan's wagon while this goes on, then come back with the mare so's we can lug these pelts in. We got it to do." We? "Guess I better go get at my end of it."

Stanley reined away, leading the pack horses toward the sheep-wagon, and Canada Dan beaded on me. "Don't just stand there in your tracks, kid. Plenty of these goddamn pelters for both of us."

So for the next long while I was delving in ewe carcasses. Manhandling each rain-soaked corpse onto its back, steadying it there, then starting in with that big incision from tail to jaw, which, if your jackknife slips just a little deep there at the belly, brings the guts pouring out onto your project. Slice around above all four hooves and then down the legs to the big cut, then skin out the hind legs and keep on trimming and tugging at the pelt, like peeling long underwear off somebody dead. It grudges me even now to say so, but Stanley was accurate, it did have to be done, because the pelts at least would bring a dollar apiece for the Busby brothers and a dollar then was still worth holding in your hand. That it was necessary did not make it less snotty a job, though. I don't know whether you have ever skinned a sheep which has lain dead in the rain for a few days, but the clammy wet wool adds into the situation the possibility of the allergy known as wool poisoning, so that the dread of puffed painful hands accompanies all your handling of the pelt. That and a whole lot else on my mind, I slit and slit and slit, straddled in there over the bloated bellies and amid the stiffened legs. I started off careful not to work fast, in the hope that Canada Dan would slice right along and thereby skin the majority of the carcasses. It of course turned out that his strategy was identical and that Canada Dan had had countless more years of practice at being slow than I did. In other circumstances I might even have admired the drama in the way he would stop often, straighten up to ease what he told me several times was the world's worst goddamn crick in his back, and contemplate my scalpel technique skeptically before finally bending back to his own. Out of his experience my father always testified that he'd rather work any day with sheepherders than cowboys. "You might come across a herder that's loony now and then, but at least they aren't so apt to be such self-inflated sonsabitches." Right about now I wondered about that choice. If Canada Dan was anywhere near representative, sheepherders didn't seem to be bargains of companionship either.

Finally I gave up on trying to outslow Canada Dan and went at the skinning quick as I could, to get it over with.

Canada Dan's estimate of fifteen dead ewes proved to be eighteen. Also I noticed that six of the pelts were branded with a bar above the lamb number, signifying that the ewe was a mother of twins. Which summed out to the fact that besides the eighteen casualties, there were two dozen newly motherless lambs who would weigh light at shipping time.

This came to Stanley's attention too when he arrived back leading the black pack mare and we—or rather I, because Stanley of course didn't have the hand for it and Canada Dan made no move toward the task whatsoever—slung the first load of pelts onto the pack saddle. "Guess we know what all that lamb blatting's about, now," observed Stanley. Canada Dan didn't seem to hear this, either.

Instead he turned and was trudging rapidly across the slope toward his sheepwagon. He whistled the dog from his coat and sent him policing after a few ewes who had dared to stray out onto open grass, then yelled back over his shoulder to us: "It's about belly time. C'mon to the wagon when you get those goddamn pelts under control, I got us a meal fixed."

I looked down at my hands and forearms, so filthy with blood and other sheep stuff I didn't even want to think about that I hated to touch the reins and saddlehorn to climb onto Pony. But climb on I did, for it was inevitable as if Bible-written that now I had to ride in with Stanley to the sheepwagon, unload these wet slimy pelts because he wasn't able, ride back out with him for the second batch, load them, ride back in and unload—seeing it all unfold I abruptly spoke out: "Stanley!"

"Yeah, Jick?" The brown Stetson turned most of the way in my direction.

All the ways to say what I intended to competed in my mind. Stanley, this just isn't going to work out. . . . Stanley, this deal was my father's brainstorm and not mine; I'm heading down that trail for home. . . . Stanley, I'm not up to—to riding herd on you and doing the work of this wampus cat of a sheepherder and maybe getting wool poisoning and— But when my mouth did move I heard it mutter:

"Nothing, I guess."

After wrestling the second consignment of pelts into shelter under Canada Dan's sheepwagon I went up by the door to wash. Beside the basin on the chopping block lay a sliver of gray soap, which proved to be so coarse my skin nearly grated off along with the sheep blood and other mess. But I at least felt scoured fairly clean.

"Is there a towel?" I called into the sheepwagon with what I considered a fine tone of indignation in my voice.

The upper part of Canada Dan appeared at the dutch door. "Right there in front of your face." He pointed to a gunny sack hanging from a corner of the wagon. "Your eyes bad?"

I dried off as best I could on the burlap, feeling now as if I'd been rasped from elbow to fingertip, and swung on into the sheepwagon.

The table of this wagon was a square of wood about the size of a big checkerboard, which pulled out from under the bunk at the far end and then was supported by a gate leg which folded down, and Stanley had tucked himself onto the seat on one side of our dining site. Canada Dan as cook and host I knew would need to be nearest the stove and sit on a stool at the outside end of the table, so I slid into the seat opposite Stanley, going real careful because three people in a sheepwagon is about twice too many.

"KEEYIPE!" erupted from under my inmost foot, about the same instant my nose caught the distinctive smell of wet dog warming up.

"Here now, what the hell kind of manners is that, walking on my dog? He does that again, Rags, you want to bite the notion right out of him." This must have been Canada Dan's idea of hilarity, for he laughed a little now in what I considered an egg-sucking way.

Or it may simply have been his pleasure over the meal he had concocted. Onto the table the herder plunked a metal plate with a boiled chunk of meat on it, then followed that with a stained pan of what looked like small mothballs.

"Like I say, I figured you might finally show up today, so I fixed you a duke's choice of grub," he crowed. "Get yourselves started with that hominy." Then, picking up a hefty butcher knife, Canada Dan slabbed off a thickness of the grayish greasy meat and toppled it aside. "You even got your wide choice of meat. Here's mutton."

He sliced off another slab. "Or then again here's growed-up lamb."

The butcher knife produced a third plank-thick piece. "Or you can always have sheep meat."

Canada Dan divvied the slices onto our plates and concluded: "A menu you don't get just everywhere, ain't it?"

"Yeah," Stanley said slower than ever, and swallowed experimentally.

The report crossed my mind that I had just spent a couple of hours elbow deep in dead sheep and now I was being expected to eat some of one, but I tried to keep it traveling. Time, as it's said, was the essence here. The only resource a person has against mutton is to eat it fast, before it has a chance for the tallow in it to congeal. So I poked mine into me pretty rapidly, and even so the last several bites were greasy going. Stanley by then wasn't much more than getting started.

While Canada Dan forked steadily through his meal and Stanley mussed around with his I finished off the hominy on the theory that anything you mixed into the digestive process with mutton was probably all to the good. Then I gazed out the dutch door of the sheepwagon while waiting on Stanley. The afternoon was going darker, a look of coming rain. My father more than likely was done by now with the counting of Walter Kyle's and Fritz Hahn's bands. He would be on his way up to the Billy Peak lookout, and the big warm dry camp tent there, and the company of somebody other than Canada Dan or Stanley Meixell, and probably another supper of brookies. I hoped devoutly the rain already had started directly onto whatever piece of trail my father might be riding just now.

Canada Dan meanwhile had rolled himself a cigarette and was filling the wagon with blue smoke while Stanley worked himself toward the halfway point of his slab of mutton. "Staying the night, ain't you?" the herder said more as observation than question. "You can set up the tepee, regular goddamn canvas hotel. It only leaks a little where it's ripped in that one corner. Been meaning to sew the sumbitch up."

"Well, actually, no," said Stanley.

This perked me up more than anything had in hours. Maybe there existed some fingernail of hope for Stanley after all. "We got all that pack gear to keep dry, so we'll just go on over to that line cabin down on the school section. Fact is"—Stanley here took the chance to shove away his still-mutton-laden plate and climb onto his feet as if night was stampeding toward him—"we better be getting ourselves over there if we're gonna beat dark. You ready, Jick?"

Was I.

The line cabin stood just outside the eastern boundary of the Two forest, partway back down the mountain. We rode more than an hour to get there, the weather steadily heavier and grimmer all around us, and Stanley fairly grim himself, I guess from the mix of alcohol and mutton sludging around beneath his belt. Once when I glanced back to be sure I still had him I happened to see him make an awkward lob into the trees, that exaggerated high-armed way when you throw with your wrong hand. So he had finally run out of bottle, and at least I could look forward to an unpickled companion from here on. I hoped he wasn't the kind who came down with the DTs as he dried out.

Our route angled us down in such a back and forth way that Roman Reef steadily stood above us now on one side, now on our other. A half-mile-high stockade of gray-brown stone, claiming all the sky to the west. Even with Stanley and thunderclouds on my mind I made room in there to appreciate the might of Roman Reef. Of the peaks and buttresses of the Two generally, for as far as I'm concerned, Montana without its mountain ranges would just be Nebraska stretched north.

At last, ahead of us showed up an orphan outcropping, a formation like a crown of rock but about as big as a railroad roundhouse. Below it ran the boundary fence, and just outside the fence the line cabin. About time, too, because we were getting some first spits of rain, and thunder was telling of lightning not all that far off.

The whole way from Canada Dan's sheepwagon Stanley had said never a word nor even glanced ahead any farther than his horse's ears. Didn't even stir now as we reached the boundary fence of barbwire. In a hurry to get us into the cabin before the weather cut loose I hopped off Pony to open the gate.

My hand was just almost to the top wire hoop when there came a terrific yell:

"GODAMIGHTY, get AWAY from that!"

I jumped back as if flung, looking crazily around to see what had roused Stanley like this.

"Go find a club and knock the gatewire off with that," he instructed. "You happen to be touching that wire and lightning hits that fence, I'll have fried Jick for supper."

So I humored him, went off and found a sizable dead limb of jack-pine and tapped the hoop up off the top of the gate stick with it and then used it to fling the gate to one side the way you might flip a big snake. The hell of it was, I knew Stanley was out-and-out right. A time, lightning hit Ed Van Bebber's fence up the South Fork road from the English Creek ranger station and the whole top wire melted for about fifty yards in either direction, dropping off in little chunks as if it'd been minced up by fencing pliers. I knew as well as anything not to touch a wire fence in a storm. Why then had I damn near done it? All I can say in my own defense is that you just try going around with Stanley Meix-ell on your mind as much as he had been on mine since mid-morning and see if you don't do one or another thing dumb.

I was resigned by now to what was in store for me at the cabin, so started in on it right away, the unpacking of the mare and Bubbles. Already I had size, my father's long bones the example to mine, and could do the respected packer's trick of reaching all the way across the horse's back to lift those off-side packs from where I was standing, instead of trotting back and forth around the horse all the time. I did the mare and then carefully began uncargoing Bubbles, Stanley hanging on to the hal-ter and matter-of-factly promising Bubbles he would yank his goddamn spotty head off if the horse gave me any trouble. Then as I swung the last pack over and off, a hefty lift I managed to do without bumping the pack saddle and giving Bubbles an excuse for excitement, Stanley pronounced: "Oh, to be young and diddling twice a day again."

He took notice of the considerable impact of this on me. "'Scuse my French, Jick. It's just a saying us old coots have."

Nonetheless it echoed around in me as I lugged the packs through the cabin door and stashed them in a corner.

By now thunder was applauding lightning below us as well as above and the rain was arriving in earnest, my last couple of trips outside con-siderably damp. Stanley meanwhile was left-handedly trying to inspire a fire in the rickety stove.

The accumulated chill in the cabin had us both shivering as we lit a kerosene lantern and waited for the stove to produce some result.

"Feels in here like it's gonna frost," I muttered.

"Yeah," Stanley agreed. "About six inches deep."

That delivered me a thought I didn't particularly want. "What, ah, what if this turns to snow?" I could see myself blizzarded in here for a week with this reprobate.

"Aw, I don't imagine it will. Lightning like this, it's probably just a thunderstorm." Stanley contemplated the rain spatting onto the cabin window and evidently was reminded that his pronouncement came close to being good news. "Still," he amended, "you never know."

The cabin was not much of a layout. Simply a roofed-over bin of lodgepole logs, maybe fifteen feet long and ten wide and with a single window beside the door at the south end. But at least it'd be drier than outside. Outside in fact was showing every sign of anticipating a night-long bath. The face of the Rocky Mountains gets more weather than any other place I know of and a person just has to abide by that fact.

I considered the small stash of wood behind the stove, mostly kindling, and headed back out for enough armfuls for the night and morning. Off along the tree line I found plenty of squaw wood, which already looked soused from the rain but luckily snapped okay when I tromped it in half over a log.

With that provisioning done and a bucket of water lugged from a seep of spring about seventy yards out along the slope, I declared myself in for the evening and shed my wet slicker. Stanley through all this stayed half propped, half sitting on an end of the little plank table. Casual as a man waiting for eternity.

His stillness set me to wondering. Wondering just how much whiskey was in him. After all, he'd been like a mummy on the ride from Canada Dan's camp, too.

And so before too awful long I angled across the room, as if exercising the saddle hours out of my legs, for a closer peek at him.

At first I wasn't enlightened by what I saw. The crowfoot lines at the corners of Stanley's eyes were showing deep and sharp, as if he was squinched up to study closely at something, and he seemed washed out, whitish, across that part of his face, too. Like any Montana kid I had seen my share of swacked-up people, yet Stanley didn't really look liquored. No, he looked more like—

"How's that hand of yours?" I inquired, putting my suspicion as lightly as I knew how.

Stanley roused. "Feels like it's been places." He moved his gaze past me and around the cabin interior. "Not so bad quarters. Not much worse than I remember this pack rat palace, anyway."

"Maybe we ought to have a look," I persisted. "That wrapping's seen better times." Before he could waltz off onto some other topic I stepped over to him and began to untie the rust-colored wrapping.

When I unwound that fabric, the story was gore. The back of Stanley's hand between the first and last knuckles was skinned raw where the sharp calk of Bubbles' horseshoe had scraped off skin: raw and seepy and butchered-looking.

"Jesus H. Christ," I breathed.

"Aw, could be worse." Even as he said so, though, Stanley seemed more pale and eroded around the eyes. "I'll get it looked at when I get to town. There's some bag balm in my saddlebag there. Get the lid off that for me, would you, and I'll dab some on."

Stanley slathered the balm thick across the back of his hand and I stepped over again and began to rewrap it for him. He noticed that the wrapping was not the blood-stained handkerchief. "Where'd you come up with that?"

"The tail off my shirt."

"Your ma's gonna like to find that."

I shrugged. Trouble was lined up deep enough here in company with Stanley that my mother's turn at it seemed a long way off.

"Feels like new," Stanley tried to assure me, moving his bandaged hand with a flinch he didn't want to show and I didn't really want to see. What if he passed out on me? What if—I tried to think of anything I had ever heard about blood poisoning and gangrene. Supposedly those took a while to develop. But then, this stint of mine with Stanley was beginning to seem like a while.

I figured it was time to try to get Stanley's mind, not to say my own, off his wound, and to bring up what I considered was a natural topic. So I queried:

"What are we going to do about supper?"

Stanley peered at me a considerable time. Then said: "I seem to distinctly remember Canada Dan feeding us."

"That was a while back," I defended. "Sort of a second lunch."

Stanley shook his head a bit and voted himself out. "I don't just feel like anything, right now. You go ahead."

So now things had reached the point where I had lost out even on my father's scattershot version of cooking, and was going to have to invent my own. I held another considerable mental conversation with U.S. forest ranger Varick McCaskill about that, meanwhile fighting the stove to get any real heat from it. At last I managed to warm a can of provisions I dug out of one of the packs of groceries for the herders, and exploring further I came up with bread and some promising sandwich material.

An imminent meal is my notion of a snug fortune. I was even humming the Pancho and Sancho and Suzy tune when, ready to dine, I sat myself down across the table from Stanley.

He looked a little quizzical, then drew in a deep sniff. Then queried: "Is that menu of yours what I think it is?"

"Huh? Just pork and beans, and an onion sandwich. Why?"

"Never mind."

Canada Dan's cooking must have stuck with me more than I was aware, though, as I didn't even think to open any canned fruit for dessert.

Meanwhile the weather was growing steadily more rambunctious. Along those mountainsides thunder can roll and roll, and constant claps were arriving to us now like beer barrels tumbling down stairs.

Now, an electrical storm is not something I am fond of. And here along the east face of the Rockies, any of these big rock thrusts, such as that crown outcropping up the slope from the cabin, notoriously can draw down lightning bolts. In fact, the more I pondered that outcropping, the less comfortable I became with the fact that it neighbored us.

In my head I always counted the miles to how far away the lightning had hit—something I still find myself doing—so when the next bolt winked, somewhere out the south window, I began the formula:

One, a-mile-from-here-to-there.

Two, a-mile-from-here-to-there.

Three . . . The boom reached us then; the bolt had struck just more than two miles off. That could be worse, and likely would be. Meanwhile rain was raking the cabin. We could hear it drum against the west wall as well as on the board roof.

"Sounds like we got a dewy night ahead of us," Stanley offered. He looked a little perkier now, for whatever reason. Myself, I was beginning to droop, the day catching up with me. I did some more thunder-counting whenever I happened to glimpse a crackle of light out the window, but came up with pretty much the same mileage each time and so began to lose attention toward that. Putting this day out of its misery seemed a better and better idea.

The cabin didn't have any beds as such, just a cobbled-together double bunk arrangement with planks where you'd like a mattress to be. But anyplace to be prostrate looked welcome, and I got up from the table to untie my bedroll from behind my saddle and spread it onto the upper planks.

The sky split white outside the cabin. That crack of thunder I honestly felt as much as heard. A jolt through the air, as if a quake had leapt upward out of the earth.

I believe my hair was swept straight on end, from that blast of noise and light. I know I had trouble getting air into my body, past the blockade where my heart was trying to climb out my throat.

Stanley, though, didn't show any particular ruffle at all. "The quick hand of God, my ma used to say."

"Yeah, well," I informed him when I found the breath for it, "I'd just as soon it grabbed around someplace else."

I stood waiting for the next cataclysm, although what really was on my mind was the saying that you'll never hear the lightning bolt that hits you. The rain rattled constantly loud now.

At last there came a big crackling sound quite a way off, and while I knew nature is not that regular I told myself the lightning portion of the storm had moved beyond us—or if it hadn't, I might as well be dead in bed as anywhere else—and I announced to Stanley, "I'm turning in."

"What, already?"

"Yeah, already," a word which for some reason annoyed me as much as anything had all day.

Leaning over to unlace my forester boots, a high-topped old pair of my father's I had grown into, I fully felt how much the day had fagged me. The laces were a downright chore. But once my boots and socks were off I indulged in a promising yawn, pulled out what was left of my shirttail, and swung myself into the upper bunk.

"Guess I'm more foresighted than I knew," I heard Stanley go on, "to bring Doctor Hall along for company."

"Who?" I asked, my eyes open again at this. Gros Ventre's physician was Doc Spence, and I knew he was nowhere near our vicinity.

Stanley lanked himself up and casually went over to the packs. "Doctor Hall," he repeated as he brought out his good hand from a pack, a brown bottle of whiskey in it. "Doctor Al K. Hall."

The weather of the night I suppose continued in commotion. But at that age I could have slept through a piano tuners' convention. Came morning, I was up and around while Stanley still lay flopped in the lower bunk.

First thing, I made a beeline to the window. No snow. Not only was I saved from being wintered in with Stanley, but Roman Reef and all the peaks south beyond it stood in sun, as if the little square of window had been made into a summer picture of the Alps. It still floors me, how the mountains are not the same any two days in a row. As if hundreds of copies of those mountains exist and each dawn brings in a fresh one, of new color, new prominence of some feature over the others, a different wrapping of cloud or rinse of sun for this day's version.

I lit a fire and went out to check on the horses and brought in a pail of fresh water, and even then Stanley hadn't budged, just was breathing like he'd decided on hibernation. The bottle which had nursed him into that condition, I noticed, was down by about a third.

Telling myself Stanley could starve to death in bed for all I cared, I fashioned breakfast for myself, heating up a can of peas and more or less toasting some slices of bread by holding them over the open stove on a fork.

Eventually Stanley did join the day. As he worked at getting his boots on I gave him some secret scrutiny. I couldn't see, though, that he assayed much better or worse than the night before. Maybe he just looked that way, sort of absent-mindedly pained, all the time. I offered to heat up some breakfast peas for him but he said no, thanks anyway.

At last Stanley seemed ready for camptending again, and I figured it was time to broach what was heaviest on my mind. The calendar of our continued companionship.

"How long's this going to take, do you think?"

"Well, you seen what we got into yesterday with Canada Dan. Herders have always got their own quantities of trouble." Stanley could be seen to be calculating, either the trouble capacities of our next two sheepherders or the extent of my impatience. "I suppose we better figure it'll take most of a day apiece for this pair, too."

Two more days of messing with herders, then the big part of another day to ride back to English Creek. It loomed before me like a career.

"What about if we split up?" I suggested as if I was naturally businesslike. "Each tend one herder's camp today?"

Stanley considered some more. You would have thought he was doing it in Latin, the time it took him. But finally: "I don't see offhand why that wouldn't work. You know this piece of country pretty good. Take along the windchester," meaning his rifle. "If any bear starts eating on me he'll pretty soon give up on account of gristle." Stanley pondered some more to see whether anything further was going to visit his mind, but nothing did. "So, yeah. We got it to do, might as well get at it. Which yayhoo do you want, Gufferson or Sanford Hebner?"

I thought on that. Sanford was in his second or third summer in these mountains. Maybe he had entirely outgrown the high-country whimwhams of the sort Canada Dan was showing, and maybe he hadn't. Andy Gustafson on the other hand was a long-timer in the Two country and probably had been given the range between Canada Dan and Sanford for the reason that he was savvy enough not to let the bands of sheep get mixed. I was more than ready to be around somebody with savvy, for a change.

"I'll take Andy."

"Okey-doke. I guess you know where he is, in west of here, about under the middle of Roman Reef. Let's go see sheepherders."

Outside in the wet morning I discovered the possible drawback to my choice, which was that Andy Gustafson's camp supplies were in the pack rig that went on Bubbles. That bothered me some, but when I pictured Stanley and his hamburgered hand trying to cope with Bubbles for a day, I figured it fell to me to handle the knothead anyway. At least in my father's universe matters fell that way. So I worked the packs onto the black mare for Stanley—she was so tame she all but sang encouragement while the load was going on her—and then faced the spotty-nosed nemesis. But Bubbles seemed not particularly more snorty and treacherous than usual, and with Stanley taking a left-handed death grip on the halter again and addressing a steady stream of threats into the horse's ear and with me staying well clear of hooves while getting the packsacks roped on, we had Bubbles loaded in surprisingly good time.

"See you back here for beans," Stanley said, and as he reined toward

Sanford's camp Pony and I headed west up the mountain, Bubbles grudgingly behind us.

I suppose now hardly anybody knows that horseback way of life on a trail. I have always thought that horseback is the ideal way to see country, if you just didn't have to deal with the damn horse, and one thing to be said for Pony was that she was so gentle and steady you could almost forget she was down there. As for the trail itself; even in the situation I was in, this scene was one to store away. Pointed west as I was the horizon of the Rockies extended wider than any vision. To take in the total of peaks I had to move my head as far as I could to either side. It never could be said that this country of the Two didn't offer enough elbow room. For that matter, shinbone and cranium and all other kind, too. Try as you might to be casual about a ride up from English Creek into these mountains, you were doing something sizable. Climbing from the front porch of the planet into its attic, so to speak.

Before long I could look back out onto the plains and see the blue dab of Lake Frances, and the water tower of Valier on its east shore—what would that be, thirty miles away, thirty-five? About half as far off was the bulge of trees which marked where the town of Gros Ventre sat in the long procession of English Creek's bankside cottonwoods and willows. Gros Ventre: pronounced *Grove*-on, in that front-end way that town names of French origin get handled in Montana, making Choteau *Show*-toh and Havre *Hav*-er and Wibaux *Wee*-boh. Nothing entertained residents of Gros Ventre more than hearing some tourist or other outlander pop out with *Gross Ventree*. My father, though, figured that the joke was also on the town: "Not a whole hell of a lot of them know that Gros Ventre's the French for Big Belly." Of course, where all this started is that Gros Ventre is the name of an Indian tribe, although not what might be called a local one. The Gros Ventres originally, before reservation days, were up in the Milk River country near the Canadian line. Why a place down here picked up that tribe's name I didn't really know. Toussaint Rennie was the one who knew A to Why about the Two country. Sometime I would have to ask him this name question.

Distant yet familiar sites offering themselves above and below me, and a morning when I was on my own. Atop my own horse and leading a beast of burden, even if the one was short-legged and pudgy and the other one definitely justified the term of beast. Entrusted with a Winchester 30.30 carbine, not that I ever was one to look forward to shooting it out with a bear. A day to stand the others up against, this one. The twin feelings of aloneness and freedom seemed to lift and lift me, send me up over the landscape like a balloon. Of course I know it was the steady climb of the land itself that created that impression. But whatever was responsible, I was glad enough to accept such soaring.

Quite possibly I ought to think about this as a way of life, I by now was telling myself. By which I didn't mean chaperoning Stanley Meixell. One round of that likely was enough for a lifetime. But packing like this, running a packstring as Isidor Pronovost did for my father; that was worth spending some daydreams on. Yes, definitely a packer's career held appeal. Be your own boss out on the trail. Fresh air, exercise, scenery. Adventure. One of the stories my father told oftenest was of being with Isidor on one of the really high trails farthest back in these mountains of the Two, where a misstep by one horse or mule might pull all the rest into a tumble a few thousand feet down the slope, when Isidor turned in his saddle and conversationally said: "Mac, if we was to roll this packstring right about here, the buggers'd bounce till they stunk."

Maybe a quieter mountain job than packing. Forest fire lookout, up there in one of Franklin Delano's lighthouses. Serene as a hermit, a person could spend summers in a lookout cabin atop the Two. Peer around like a human hawk for smoke. Heroic work. Fresh air, scenery, some codger like Stanley to fetch your groceries up the mountainside to you. The new Billy Peak lookout might be the prime job. I'd be finding that out right now if my father hadn't detoured me into companioning damn old Stanley. Well, next year, next counting trip . . .

Up and up I and my horses and my dreams went, toward the angle of slope beneath the center of Roman Reef. Eventually a considerable sidehill of timber took the trail from sight, and before Pony and Bubbles and I entered the stand of trees, I whoaed us for a last gaze along all the mountains above and around. They were the sort of thing you would have if every cathedral in the world were lined up along the horizon.

Not much ensued for the first minutes of the forested trail, just a sharpening climb and the route beginning to kink into a series of switchbacks. Sunbeams were threaded down through the pine branches and with that dappled light I didn't even mind being in out of the view for the next little while.

A forest's look of being everlasting is an illusion. Trees too are mortal and they come down. I was about to face one such. In the middle of a straight tilt of trail between switchbacks, there lay a fresh downed lodgepole pine poking out over my route, just above the height of a horse.

On one of my father's doctrines of mountain travel I had a light little cruising ax along with me. But the steep hillside made an awkward place to try any chopping and what I didn't have was a saw of any sort. Besides, I was in no real mood to do trail maintenance for my father and the United States Forest Service.

I studied the toppled lodgepole. It barriered the trail to me in the saddle, but there was just room enough for a riderless horse to pass beneath. All I needed to do was get off and lead Pony and Bubbles through. But given the disposition of Bubbles, I knew I'd damn well better do it a horse at a time.

I tied Bubbles's lead rope to a middle-sized pine, doubling the square knot just to be sure, and led Pony up the trail beyond the windfall. "Be right back with that other crowbait," I assured her as I looped her reins around the leftover limb of a stump.

Bubbles was standing with his neck in the one position he seemed to know for it, stretched out like he was being towed, and I had to haul hard on his lead rope for enough slack to untie my knots.

"Come on, churnhead," I said as civilly as I could—Bubbles was not too popular with me anyway, because if he originally hadn't kicked Stanley I wouldn't have been in the camptending mess—and with some tugging persuaded him into motion.

Bubbles didn't like the prospect of the downed tree when we got there. I could see his eyes fixed on the shaggy crown limbs overhead, and his ears lay back a little. But one thing about Bubbles, he didn't lead much harder when he was being reluctant than when he wasn't.

I suppose it can be said that I flubbed the dub on all this. That the whole works came about as the result of my reluctance to clamber up that sidehill and do axwork. Yet answer me this, was I the first person not to do what I didn't want to? Nor was goddamn Bubbles blameless, now was he? After all, I had him most of the way past the windfall before he somehow managed to swing his hindquarters too close in against the hillside, where he inevitably brushed against a broken branch dangling down from the tree trunk. Even that wouldn't have set things off, except for the branch whisking in across the front of his left hip toward his crotch.

Bubbles went straight sideways off the mountain.

He of course took the lead rope with him, and me at the end of it like a kite on a string.

I can't say how far downslope I flew, but I was in the air long enough to get good and worried. Plummeting sideways as well as down is unnerving, your body trying to figure out how to travel in those two directions at once. And a surprising number of thoughts fan out in your mind, such as whether you are most likely to come down on top of or under the horse below you and which part of you you can best afford to have broken and how long before a search party and why you ever in the first place—

I landed more or less upright, though. Upright and being towed down the slope of the mountain in giant galloping strides, sinking about shin-deep every time, the dirt so softened by all the rain.

After maybe a dozen of those plowing footfalls, my journey ended. Horse nostrils could be heard working overtime nearby me, and I discovered the lead rope still was taut in my hands, as if the plunge off the trail had frozen it straight out like a long icicle. What I saw first, though, was not Bubbles but Pony. A horse's eyes are big anyway, but I swear Pony's were the size of Terraplane headlights as she peered down over the rim of the trail at Bubbles and me all the way below.

"Easy, girl!" I called up to her. All I needed next was for Pony to get excited, jerk her reins loose from that stump and quit the country, leaving me down here with this tangled-up pack horse. "Easy, Pony! Easy, there. Everything's gonna be—just goddamn dandy."

Sure it was. On my first individual outing I had rolled the packstring, even if it was only one inveterate jughead of a horse named Bubbles. Great wonderful work, campjack McCaskill. Keep on in this brilliant fashion and you maybe someday can hope to work your way up to moron.

Now I had to try to sort out the situation.

A little below me on the sidehill Bubbles was floundering around a little and snorting a series of alarms. The favorable part of that was that he was up on his feet. Not only up but showing a greater total of vigor than he had during the whole pack trip so far. So Bubbles was in one piece, I seemed to be intact, and the main damage I could see on the packs was a short gash in the canvas of the top pack where something snagged it on our way down. Sugar or salt was trickling from there, but it looked as if I could move a crossrope over enough to pinch the hole shut.

I delivered Bubbles a sound general cussing, meanwhile working along the lead rope until I could grab his halter and then reach his neck. From there I began to pat my way back, being sure to make my cussing sound a little more soothing, to get to the ruptured spot on the pack.

When I put my hand onto the crossrope of the diamond hitch to tug it across the gash, that top pack seemed to move a bit.

I tugged again in a testing way, and the summit of the load on Bubbles's back definitely moved, more than a bit.

"Son of a goddamn sonofabitch," I remember was all I managed to come out with to commemorate this discovery. That wasn't too bad under the circumstance, for the situation called for either hard language or hot tears, and maybe it could be pinpointed that right there I grew out of the bawling age into the cussing one.

Bubbles's downhill excursion had broken the last cinch, the one the lash rope ties into to hold the top pack into place on a horse's back. So I had a pack horse whole and healthy—and my emotions about Bubbles having survived in good fettle were now getting radically mixed— but no way to secure his load onto him. I was going to have to ride somewhere for a new cinch, or at the very least to get this one repaired.

Choices about like Canada Dan's menu of mutton or sheep meat, those. Stanley by now was miles away at Sanford Hebner's camp. Besides, with his hand and his thirst both the way they were, I wasn't sure how much of a repairer he would prove to be anyway. Or I could climb on Pony, head back down the trail all the way to the English Creek station, and tell that father of mine to come mend the fix he'd pitched me into.

This second notion held appeal of numerous kinds. I would be rid of Stanley and responsibility for him. I'd done all I could; in no way was it my fault that Bubbles had schottisched off a mountaintop. Most of all, delivering my predicament home to English Creek would serve my father right. He was the instigator of all this; who better to haul himself up here and contend with the mess?

Yet when I came right down to it I was bothered by the principle of anyone venturing to my rescue. I could offer all the alibis this side of Halifax, but the truth of it still stood. Somebody besides myself would be fishing me out of trouble. Here was yet another consequence of my damned in-between age. I totally did not want to be in the hell of a fix I was. Yet somehow I just as much did not relish resorting to anybody else to pluck me out of it. Have you ever been dead-centered that way?

Hung between two schools of thought, neither one of which you wanted to give in to? Why the human mind doesn't positively split in half in such a situation I don't know.

As I was pondering back and forth that way I happened to rub my forehead with the back of my free hand. It left moisture above my brow. Damn. One more sign of my predicament: real trouble always makes the backs of my hands sweat. I suppose nerves cause it. Whatever does, it spooks a person to have his hands sweating their own worry like that.

"That's just about enough of all this," I said out loud, apparently to Pony and Bubbles and maybe to my sweating hands and the mountainside and I suppose out across the air toward Stanley Meixell and Varick McCaskill as well. And to myself, too. For some part of my mind had spurned the back-and-forth debate of whether to go fetch Stanley or dump the situation in my father's lap, and instead got to wondering. There ought to be some way in this world to contrive that damn cinch back together. "If you're going to get by in the Forest Service you better be able to fix anything but the break of day," my father said every spring when he set in to refurbish the English Creek equipment. Not that I was keen on taking him as an example just then.

No hope came out of my search of Bubbles and the packs. Any kind of thong or spare leather was absent. The saddlestrings on my saddle up there where Pony was I did think of, but couldn't figure how to let go of the horse at hand while I went to get them. Bubbles having taken up mountaineering so passionately, there was no telling where he would crash off to if I wasn't here to hang on to him.

I started looking myself over for possibilities.

Hat, coat, shirt: no help.

Belt: though I hated to think of it, I maybe could cut that up into leather strips. Yet would they be long enough if I did.

No, better, down there: my forester boots, a bootlace; a bootlace just by God might do the trick.

By taking a wrap of Bubbles's lead rope around the palm of my left hand I was more or less able to use the thumb and fingers to grasp the lash cinch while I punched holes in it with my jackknife. All the while, of course, talking sweetly to Bubbles. When I had a set of holes accomplished on either side of the break, I threaded the bootlace back and forth, back and forth, and at last tied it to make a splice. Then, Bubbles's recent standard of behavior uppermost in my mind, I made one more set of holes farther along each part of the cinch and wove in the remainder of the bootlace as a second splice for insurance. In a situation like this, you had better do things the way you're supposed to do them.

I now had a boot gaping open like an unbuckled overshoe, but the lash cinch looked as if it ought to lift a boxcar. I did some more brow-wiping, and lectured Bubbles on the necessity of standing still so that I could retie his packs into place. I might as well have saved my breath. Even on level ground, contriving a forty-foot lash rope into a diamond hitch means going endlessly back and forth around the pack horse to do the loops and lashes and knots, and on a mountainside with Bubbles fidgeting and twitching every which way, the job was like trying to weave eels.

At last I got that done. Now there remained only the matter of negotiating Bubbles back up to where he had launched from. Talk about an uphill job. But as goddamn Stanley would've observed to me, I had it to do.

Probably the ensuing ruckus amounted to only about twenty minutes of fight and drag, though it seemed hours. Right then you could not have sold me all the pack horses on the planet for a nickel. Bubbles would take a step and balk. Balk and take a step. Fright or exasperation or obstinacy or whatever other mood can produce it had him dry-farting like the taster in a popcorn factory. Try to yank me back down the slope. Balk again, and let himself slide back down the slope a little. Sneeze, then fart another series. Shake the packs in hope the splice would let go. Start over on the balking.

I at last somehow worked his head up level with the trail and then simply leaned back on the lead rope until Bubbles exhausted his various acts and had to glance around at where he was. When the sight of the trail registered in his tiny mind, he pranced on up as if it was his own idea all along.

I sat for a while to recover my breath—after tying Bubbles to the biggest tree around, with a triple square knot—and to sort of take stock. The pulling contest definitely had taken all the jingle out of me.

There's this to be said for exertion, though. It does send your blood tickling through your brain. When I was through resting I directly went over to Bubbles, addressed him profanely, thrust an arm into the pack with the canned goods and pulled cans out until I found the ones of tomatoes. If I ever did manage to get this menagerie to Andy Gustafson's sheep camp I was going to be able to say truthfully that I'd had lunch and did not need feeding by one more sheepherder.

I sat back down, opened two cans with my jackknife, and imbibed tomatoes. "One thing about canned tomatoes," my father had the habit of saying during a trail meal, "if you're thirsty you can drink them and if you're hungry you can eat them." Maybe, I conceded, he was right about that one thing.

By the time I reached Andy Gustafson's camp my neck was thoroughly cricked from the constant looking back over my shoulder to see if the packs were staying on Bubbles. They never shifted, though. Thank God for whoever invented bootlaces.

Andy's band was spread in nice fashion along both sides of a timbered draw right under the cliff of Roman Reef. If you have the courage to let them—more of it, say, than was possessed by a certain bozo named Canada Dan—sheep will scatter themselves into a slow comfortable graze even in up-and-down country. But it takes a herder who is sure of himself and has a sort of sixth sense against coyotes and bear.

I was greeted by a little stampede of about a dozen lambs toward me. They are absent-minded creatures and sometimes will glance up and run to the first moving thing they see, which was the case with these now. When they figured out that Pony and Bubbles and I were not their mommas, they halted, peered at us a bit, then rampaged off in a new direction. Nothing is more likeable than a lamb bucking in fun. First will come that waggle of the tail, a spasm of wriggles faster than the eye can follow. Then a stiff-legged jump sideways, the current of joy hitting the little body so quick there isn't time to bend its knees. Probably a bleat, *byeahhh*, next, and then the romping run. Watching them you have to keep reminding yourself that lambs grow up, and what is pleasantly foolish in a lamb's brain is going to linger on to be just dumbness in the mind of a full-size ewe.

Andy Gustafson had no trove of dead camased ewes, nor any particular complaints, nor even much to say. He was wrinkled up in puzzlement for a while as to why it was me that was tending his camp, even after I explained as best I could, and I saw some speculation again when he noticed me slopping along with one boot unlaced. But once he'd checked through the groceries I'd brought to make sure that a big can of coffee and some tins of sardines were in there, and his weekly newspaper as well—Norwegian sheepherders seemed to come in two varieties, those whose acquaintance with the alphabet was confined to the

X they used for a signature and those who would quit you in an instant if you ever forgot to bring their mail copy of *Nordiske Tidende*—Andy seemed perfectly satisfied. He handed me his list of personals for the next camptending—razor blades, a pair of work socks, Copenhagen snoose—and away I went.

Where a day goes in the mountains I don't know, but by the time I reached the cabin again the afternoon was almost done. Stanley's saddle sorrel and the black pack horse were picketed a little way off, and Stanley emerged to offer me as usual whatever left-handed help he could manage in unsaddling Bubbles.

He noticed the spliced lash cinch. "See you had to use a little wild-wood glue on the outfit."

I grunted something or other to that, and Stanley seemed to divine that it was not a topic I cared to dwell on. He switched to a question: "How's old Gufferson?"

"He said about three words total. I wouldn't exactly call that belly-aching." This sounded pretty tart even to me, so I added: "And he had his sheep in a nice Wyoming scatter, there west of his wagon."

"Sanford's on top of things, too," Stanley reported. "Hasn't lost any, and his lambs are looking just real good." Plain as anything, then, there was one sore thumb up here on the Busbys' allotment and it went by the name of Canada Dan.

Stanley extended the thought aloud. "Looks like Dan's asking for a ticket to town."

This I didn't follow. In all the range ritual I knew, and even in the perpetual wrestle between Dode Withrow and Pat Hoy, the herder always was angling to provoke a reason for quitting, not to be fired. Being fired from any job was a taint, a never-sought smudge. True, Canada Dan was a prime example that even God gets careless, but—

The puzzle pursued me on into the cabin. As Stanley stepped to the stove to try rev the fire a little, I asked: "What, are you saying Canada Dan *wants* to get himself canned?"

"Looks like. It can happen that way. A man'll get into a situation and do what he can to make it worse so he'll get chucked out of it. My own guess is, Dan's feeling thirsty and is scared of this timber as well, but he don't want to admit either one to himself. Easier to lay blame onto somebody else." Stanley paused. "Question is whether to try disappoint him out of the idea or just go ahead and can him." Another season of thought. Then: "I will say that Canada Dan is not such a helluva human being that I want to put up with a whole summer of his guff."

This was a starchier Stanley than I had yet seen. This one you could imagine giving Canada Dan the reaming out he so richly deserved.

The flash of backbone didn't last long, though. "But I guess he's the Busby boys' decision, not mine."

Naturally the day was too far gone for us to ride home to English Creek, so I embarked on the chores of wood and water again, at least salving myself with the prospect that tomorrow I would be relieved of Stanley. We would rise in the morning—and I intended it would be an early rise indeed—and ride down out of here and I would resume my summer at the English Creek ranger station and Stanley would sashay on past to the Busby brothers' ranch and that would be that.

When I stumped in with the water pail, that unlaced left boot of mine all but flapping in the breeze, I saw Stanley study the situation. "Too bad we can't slice up Bubbles for bootlaces," he offered.

"That'd help," I answered shortly.

"I never like to tell anybody how to wear his boots. But if it was me, now . . ."

I waited while Stanley paused to speculate out the cabin window to where dusk was beginning to deepen the gray of the cliff of Roman Reef. But I wasn't in any mood for very damn much waiting.

"You were telling me all about boots," I prompted kind of sarcastically.

"Yeah. Well. If it was me now, I'd take that one shoestring you got there, and cut it in half, and lace up each boot with a piece as far as it'll go. Ought to keep them from slopping off your feet, anyhow."

Worth a try. Anything was. I went ahead and did the halving, and the boots then laced firm as far as my insteps. The high tops pooched out like funnels, but at least now I could get around without one boot always threatening to leave me.

One chore remained. I reached around and pulled my shirt up out of the back of my pants. The remainder of the tail of it I jackknifed off. Stanley's hand didn't look quite so hideous this time when I rewrapped it; in the high dry air of the Two, cuts heal faster than can be believed. But this paw of Stanley's still was no prizewinner.

"Well," Stanley announced now, "you got me nursed. Seems like the next thing ought to be a call on the doctor." And almost before he was through saying it, last night's bottle reappeared over the table, its neck tilted into Stanley's cup.

Before Stanley got too deep into his oil of joy, there was one more vital point I wanted tended to. Diplomatically I began, "Suppose maybe we ought to give some thought—"

"—to supper," Stanley finished for me as he dippered a little water into his prescription. "I had something when I got back from Sanford's camp. But you go ahead."

I at least knew by now I could be my own chef if I had to, and I stepped over to the packs to get started.

There a harsh new light dawned on me. Now that we had tended the camps the packs were empty of groceries, which meant that we— or at least I, because so far I had no evidence that Stanley ever required food—were at the mercy of whatever was on hand in Stanley's own small supply pack. Apprehensively I dug around in there, but all that I came up with that showed any promise was an aging loaf of bread and some Velveeta cheese. So I made myself a bunch of sandwiches out of those and mentally chalked up one more charge against my father.

When I'd finished, it still was only twilight, and Stanley just had applied the bottle and dipper to the cup for a second time. Oh, it looked like another exquisite evening ahead, all right. A regular night at the opera.

Right then, though, a major idea came to me.

I cleared my throat to make way for the words of it. Then:

"I believe maybe I'll have me one, too."

Stanley had put his cup down on the table but was resting his good hand over the top of it as if there was a chance it might hop away. "One what?"

"One of those—doctor visits. A swig."

This drew me a considerable look from Stanley. He let go of his cup and scratched an ear. "Just how old're you?"

"Fifteen," I maintained, borrowing the next few months.

Stanley did some more considering, but by now I was figuring out that if he didn't say no right off the bat, chances were he wouldn't get around to saying it at all. At last: "Got to wet your wick sometime, I guess. Can't see how a swallow or two can hurt you." He transferred the bottle to a place on the table nearer me.

Copying his style of pouring, I tilted the cup somewhat at the same time I was tipping the bottle. Just before I thought Stanley might open his mouth to say something I ended the flow. Then went over to the water bucket and dippered in a splash or so the way he had.

It is just remarkable how something you weren't aware of knowing can pop to your aid at the right moment. From times I had been in the Medicine Lodge saloon with my father, I was able to offer now in natural salute to Stanley:

"Here's how!"

"How," Stanley recited back automatically.

Evidently I swigged somewhat deeper than I intended. Or should have gone a little heavier on the splash of water. Or something. By the time I set my cup down on the board table, I was blinking hard.

While I was at this, Stanley meanwhile had got up to shove wood into the stove.

"So what do you think?" he inquired. "Will it ever replace water?"

I didn't know about that, but the elixir of Doctor Hall did draw a person's attention.

Stanley reseated himself and was gandering around the room again. "Who's our landlord, do you know?"

"Huh?"

"This cabin. Who's got this school section now?"

"Oh. The Double W."

"Jesus H. Christ." Accompanying this from Stanley was the strongest look he had yet given me. When scrutiny told him I was offering an innocent's truth, he let out: "Is there a blade of grass anywhere those sonuvabitches won't try to get their hands on?"

"I dunno. Did you have some run-in with the Double W too?"

"A run-in." Stanley considered the weight of the words. "You might call it that, I guess. I had the particular pleasure once of telling old Warren Williamson, Wendell's daddy, that that big belly of his was a tombstone for his dead ass. 'Scuse my French again. And some other stuff got said." Stanley sipped and reflected. "What did you mean, 'too'?"

"My brother Alec, he's riding for the Double W."

"The hell you say." Stanley waited for me to go on, and when I didn't he provided: "I wouldn't wish that onto nobody. But just how does it constitute a run-in?"

"My folks," I elaborated. "They're plenty piss—uh, peed off over it."

"Family feathers in a fluff. The old, old story." Stanley tipped a sip again, and I followed. Inspiration in a cup must have been the encouragement my tongue was seeking, for before long I heard myself asking: "You haven't been in the Two country the last while, have you?"

"Naw."

"Where you been?"

"Oh, just a lot of places." Stanley seemed to review them on the cabin wall. "Down in Colorado for a while. Talk about dry. Half that state was blowing around chasing after the other half. A little time in both Dakotas. Worked in the wheat harvest there, insofar as there was any wheat after the drouth and the grasshoppers. And Wyoming. I was an association rider in that Cody country a summer or two. Then Montana here again for a while, over in the Big Hole Basin. A couple of haying seasons there." He considered, summed: "Around." Which moved him to another drag from his cup.

I had one from mine, too. "What're you doing back up in this country?"

"Like I say, by now I been everyplace else, and they're no better. Came back to the everloving Two to take up a career in tending camp, as you can plainly see. They advertise in those big newspapers for one-handed raggedy-ass camptenders, don't you know. You bet they do."

He did seem a trifle sensitive on this topic. Well, there was always some other, such as the matter of who he had been before he became a wandering comet. "Are you from around here originally?"

"Not hardly. Not a Two Mediciner by birth." He glanced at me. "Like you are. No, I—"

Stanley Meixell originated in Missouri, on a farm east of St. Joe in Daviess County. As he told it, the summer he turned thirteen he encountered the down-row of corn: that tumbled line of cornstalks knocked over by the harvest wagon as it straddled its way through the field. Custom was that the youngest of the crew always had to be the picker of the down-row, and Stanley was the last of five Meixell boys. Ahead of him stretched a green gauntlet of down-row summers. Except that by the end of the first sweltering day of stooping and ferreting into the tangle of downed stalks for ears of corn, Stanley came to his decision about further Missouri life. "Within the week I was headed out to the Kansas high plains." If you're like me you think of Kansas as one eternal wheatfield, but actually western Kansas then was cattle country. Dodge City was out there, after all.

Four or five years of ranch jobs out there in jayhawk country ensued for Stanley. "I can tell you a little story on that, Jick. This once we were dehorning a bunch of Texas steers. There was this one ornery sonuvabitch of a buckskin steer we never could get corraled with the others. After enough of trying, the foreman said he'd pay five dollars to anybody who'd bring that sonuvabitching steer in. Well, don't you know, another snot-nose kid and me decided we'd just be the ones. Off we rode, and we come onto him about three miles away from the corral, all by hisself, and he wasn't about to be driven. Well, then we figured we'd just rope him and drag him in. We got to thinking, though—three miles is quite a drag, ain't it? So instead we each loosed out our lariat, about ten feet of it, and took turns to get out in front of him and pop him across the nose with that rope. When we done that he'd make a hell of a big run at us and we'd dodge ahead out of his way, and he choused us back toward the corral that way. We finally got him up within about a quarter of a mile of the dehorning. Then each of us roped an end and tied him down and went on into the ranch and hitched up a stoneboat and loaded him on and boated him in in high old style. The foreman was waiting for us with five silver dollars in his hand."

Cowboying in the high old style. Alec, I thought to myself, you're the one who ought to be hearing this.

As happens, something came along to dislodge Stanley from that cowboying life. It was a long bunkhouse winter, weather just bad enough to keep him cooped on the ranch. "I'd go give the cows a jag of hay two times a day and otherwise all there was to do was sit around and do hairwork." Each time Stanley was in the barn he would pluck strands from the horses' tails, then back he went beside the bunkhouse stove to braid horsehair quirts and bridles "and eventually even a whole damn lasso." By the end of that hairwork winter the tails of the horses had thinned drastically, and so had Stanley's patience with Kansas.

All this life history of Stanley's I found amazingly interesting. I suppose that part of my father was duplicated in me, the fascination about pawing over old times.

While Stanley was storying, my cup had drained itself without my really noticing. Thus when he stopped to tip another round into his, I followed suit. The whiskey was weaving a little bit of wooze around me, so I was particularly pleased that I was able to dredge back yet another Medicine Lodge toast. I offered it heartily:

"Here's lead in your pencil!"

That one made Stanley eye me sharply for a moment, but he said only as he had the first time, "How," and tipped his cup.

"Well, that's Missouri and Kansas accounted for," I chirped in encouragement. "How was it you got up here to Montana?"

"On the seventeenth of March of 1898, to be real exact," Stanley boarded the first train of his life. From someone he had heard about Montana and a go-ahead new town called Kalispell, which is over on the west side of the Rockies, about straight across from there in the cabin where Stanley was telling me all this. Two days and two nights on that train. "The shoebox full of fried chicken one of those Kansas girls fixed for me didn't quite last the trip through."

In Kalispell then, "you could hear hammers going all over town." For the next few years Stanley grew up with the community. He worked sawmill jobs, driving a sawdust cart, sawfiling, foremanning a lumber piling crew. "Went out on some jobs with the U.S. Geological Survey, for a while there." A winter, he worked as a teamster hauling lumber from Lake Blaine into Kalispell. Another spell, he even was a river pig, during one of the log drives on the north fork of the Flathead River. "It was a world of timber over there then. I tell you something, though, Jick. People kind of got spoiled by it. Take those fires—December of my first year in Kalispell. They burned along the whole damn mountains from Big Fork to Bad Rock Canyon and even farther north than that. Everybody went out on the hills east of town at night to see the fire. Running wild on the mountains, that way. Green kid I was, I asked why somebody didn't do something about it. 'That's public domain,' I got told. 'Belongs to the government, not nobody around here.' Damn it to hell, though, when I saw that forest being burned up it just never seemed right to me." Stanley here took stiff encouragement from his cup, as if quenching the distaste for forest fire.

"Damn fire anyhow," I seconded with a slurp of my own. "But what got you across the mountains, here to the Two?"

Stanley gave me quite a glance, I guess to estimate the state of my health under Dr. Al K. Hall's ministration. I felt first-rate, and blinked Stanley an earnest response that was meant to say so.

"Better go a little slow on how often you visit that cup," he advised. Then: "The Two Medicine country. Why did I ever kiss her hello. Good question. One of the best."

What ensued is somewhat difficult to reconstruct. The bald truth, I may as well say, is that as Stanley waxed forth, my sobriety waned. But even if I had stayed sharp-eared as a deacon, the headful of the past which Stanley now provided me simply was too much to keep straight.

Tale upon tale of the Two country; memories of how the range looked some certain year; people who passed away before I was born; English Creek, Noon Creek, Gros Ventre, the reservation; names of horses, habits of sheepherders and cowboys, appreciations of certain saloons and bartenders. I was accustomed to a broth of history from my father and Toussaint Rennie, some single topic at a time, but Stanley's version was a brimming mulligan stew. "I can tell you a time, Jick, I was riding along in here under the Reef and met an old Scotch sheepherder on his horse. White-bearded geezer, hadn't had a haircut since Christmas. 'Lad!' he calls out to me. 'Can ye tell me the elevation here where we are?' Not offhand, I say to him, why does he want to know? 'Ye see, I was right here when those surveyors of that Theological Survey come through years ago, and they told me the elevation, but I forgot. I'm pretty sure the number had a seven in it, though.'" The forest fires of 1910, which darkened daytime for weeks on end: Stanley helped combat the stubborn one in the Two mountains west of where Swift Dam now stood. The flu epidemic during the world war: he remembered death outrunning the hearse capacity, two and three coffins at a time in the back of a truck headed for the Gros Ventre town cemetery. The legendary winter of '19: "We really caught hell, that time. Particularly those 'steaders in Scotch Heaven. Poor snowed-in bastards." The banks going under in the early twenties, the tide of homesteaders reversing itself. "Another time I can tell. In honor of Canada Dan, you might say. Must of been the summer of '16, I was up in Browning when one of those big sheep outfits out in Washington shipped in five thousand ewes and lambs. Gonna graze them there on the north end of the Two. Those sheep came hungry from eighteen hours on the stock cars, and they hit the flats out there and got onto deathcamas and lupine. Started dying by the hundreds. We got hold of all the pinanginated potash and sulfate of aluminum there was in the drugstore at Browning, and sent guys to fetch all of it there was in Cut Bank and Valier and Gros Ventre too, and we started in mixing the stuff in washtubs and dosing those sheep. Most of the ones we dosed pulled through okay, but it was too late for about a thousand of them others. All there was to do was drag in the carcasses and set them afire with brush. We burned dead sheep all night on that prairie."

Those sheep pyres I believe were the story that made me check out of Stanley's companionship for the evening. At least, I seem to remember counseling myself not to think about deceased sheep in combination with the social juice I'd been imbibing, by now three cups' worth. Stanley on the other hand had hardly even sipped during this tale-telling spell.

"I've about had a day," I announced. The bunk bed was noticeably more distant than it'd been the night before, but I managed to trek to it.

"Adios till the rooster crows," Stanley's voice followed me.

"Or till the crow roosts," I imparted to myself, or maybe to a more general audience, for at the time it seemed to me an exceptionally clever comment.

While my tongue was wandering around that way, though, and my fingers were trying to solve the bootlace situation, which for some reason began halfway down my boots instead of at the top where I was sure they ought to be, my mind was not idle. Cowboying, teamstering, river pigging: all this history of Stanley's was unexpected to me. I'd sup-posed, from my distant memory of him having been in our lives when I was so small, that he was just another camptender or maybe even an association rider back when this range was occupied by mostly cattle instead of sheep. But riding along up here and being greeted by the ele-vation-minded sheepherder as an expert on the Two: that sounded like, what, he'd been one of the early ranchers of this country? Homesteader, maybe? Fighting that forest fire of '10: must have volunteered himself onto the fire crew, association rider would fit that. But dosing all those sheep: that sounded like camptender again.

Then something else peeped in a corner of my mind. One boot finally in hand, I could spare the concentration for the question. "Stan-ley, didn' you say you been to this cabin before? When we got here, didn' you say that?"

"Yessir. Been here just a lot of times. I go back farther than this cabin does. I seen it being built. We was sighting out that fenceline over there when old Bob Barclay started dragging in the logs for this."

Being built? Sighting the boundary fencelines? The history was skipping to the most ancient times of the Two forest now, and this turn and the whiskey together were compounding my confusion. Also, somebody had put another boot in my hand. Yet I persisted.

"What, were you up here with the Theologic—the Geologic—the survey crew?"

Stanley's eyes were sharp, as if a new set had been put in amid the webs of eyelines. And the look he fastened on me now was the levelest thing in that cabin.

"Jick, I was the ranger that set up the boundaries of the Two Medicine National Forest."

Surely my face hung open so far you could have trotted a cat through it.

In any Forest Service family such as ours, lore of setting up the national forests, of the boundary examiners who established them onto the maps of America as public preserves, was almost holy writ. I could remember time upon time of hearing my father and the other Forest Service men of his age mention those original rangers and supervisors, the ones who were sent out in the first years of the century with not much more than the legal description of a million or so acres and orders to transform them into a national forest. "The forest arrangers," the men of my father's generation nicknamed them. Elers Koch on the Gallatin National Forest, Coert duBois on the Lolo, other boundary men who sired the Beaverhead and the Custer and the Helena and so on; the tales of them still circulated, refreshed by the comments of the younger rangers wondering how they'd managed to do all they had. Famous, famous guys. Sort of combinations of Old Testament prophets and mountain men, rolled into one. Everybody in the Forest Service told forest arranger stories at any chance. But that Stanley Meixell, wrong-handed campjack and frequenter of Doctor Al K. Hall, had been the original ranger of the Two Medicine National Forest, I had never heard a breath of. And this was strange.

My sister is Mandy,
she's got a dandy.
At least so the boys say."

I woke with that in my ears and a dark brown taste in my mouth.

The serious symptoms set in when I sat up in my bunk. My eyes and temples and ears all seemed to have grown sharp points inward and were steadily stabbing each other. Life, the very air, seemed gritty, gray. Isn't there one hangover description that your tongue feels like you spent the night licking ashtrays? That's it.

"Morning there, Jick!" Stanley sang out. He was at the stove. "Here, better wash down your insides with this." Stepping over to the bunk, he handed me a tin cup of coffee turned tan with canned milk. Evidently he had heated the milk along with the coffee, because the contents of the cup were all but aflame. The heat went up my nose in search of my brain as I held the cup in front of my lips.

"No guarantee on this left-handed grub," Stanley called over his shoulder as he fussed at something on the stove top, "but how do you take your eggs?"

"Uh," I sought around in myself for the information. "Flipped, I guess."

Stanley hovered at the stove another minute or two while I made up my mind to try the death-defying trip to the table.

Then he turned and presented me a plate. Left-handed they may have been, but the eggs were fried to a crisp brown lace at the edges, while their pockets of yolk were not runny but not solidified either. Eggs that way are perfection. On the plate before me they were fenced in by wide tan strips of sidepork, and within a minute or so Stanley was providing me slices of bread fried in the pan grease.

I am my mother's son entirely in this respect: I believe good food never made any situation worse.

I dug in and by the time I'd eaten about half the plateful, things were tasting like they were supposed to. I even managed to sip some of the coffee, which I discovered was stout enough to float a kingbolt.

Indeed, I swarmed on to the last bite or so of the feast before it occurred to me to ask, "Where'd you get these eggs?"

"Aw, I always carry a couple small lard pails of oats for the horses, and the eggs ride okay in the oats."

Breakfast made me feel restored. "Speaking of riding," I began, "how soon—"

"—can we head down the mountain." Stanley inventoried me. And I took the chance to get in my first clear-eyed look of the day at him. Stanley seemed less in pain than he had when we arrived to this cabin but less in grasp of himself than he had during last night's recounting of lore of the Two. A man in wait, seeing which way he might turn; but unfortunately, I knew, the bottle habit soon would sway his decision. Of course, right then who was I to talk?

Now Stanley was saying: "Just any time now, Jick. We can head out as soon as you say ready."

On our ride down Stanley of course was into his musical repertoire again, one minute warbling about somebody who was wild and woolly and full of fleas and never'd been curried above her knees and the next crooning a hymnlike tune that went *"Oh sweet daughters of the Lord, grant me more than I can afford."*

My mind, though, was on a thing Stanley said as we were saddling the horses. In no way was it what I intended to think about, for I knew fully that I was heading back into the McCaskill family situation, that blowup between my parents and Alec. Godamighty, the supper that produced all that wasn't much more than a half a week ago. And in the meantime my father had introduced Stanley and Canada Dan and Bubbles, not to mention Dr. Al K. Hall, into my existence. There were words I intended to say to him about all this. If, that is, I could survive the matter of explaining to my mother why the tops of my boots gaped out like funnels and how come my pants legs looked like I'd wiped up a mountainside with them and where the tail of my shirt had gone. Thank the Lord, not even she could quite see into a person enough to count three tin cups of booze in him the night before. On that drinking score, I felt reasonably safe. Stanley didn't seem to me likely to trouble himself enough to advertise my behavior. On the other hand, Stanley himself was a logical topic for my mother. More than likely my father had heard, and I was due to hear, her full opinion of my having sashayed off on this campjacking expedition.

A sufficiency to dwell on, and none of it easy thinking. Against my intentions and better interests, though, I still found myself going back and forth over the last scene at the cabin.

I had just handed the lead rope for the black mare and ever-loving Bubbles up to Stanley and was turning away to go tighten the cinch on Pony's saddle. It was then that Stanley said he hoped I didn't mind too much about missing the rest of the counting trip with my father, to the Billy Peak lookout and all. "I couldn't of got along up here without you, Jick," he concluded, "and I hope you don't feel hard used."

Which of course was exactly how I had been feeling. You damn bet I was, ever since the instant my father volunteered me into Stanley's company. Skinning wet sheep corpses, contending with a pack horse who decides he's a mountain goat, nursing Stanley along, lightning, any number of self-cooked meals, the hangover I'd woke up with and still had more than a trace of—what sad sonofabitch wouldn't realize he was being used out of the ordinary?

Yet right then, eighteen-inch pincers would not have pulled such a confession from me. I wouldn't give the universe the satisfaction.

So, "No," I had answered Stanley, and gone on over to do my cinching. "No, it's all been an education."

Two

This will mark the fifteenth Fourth of July in a row that Gros Ventre has mustered a creek picnic, a rodeo and a dance. Regarding those festivities, ye editor's wife inquires whether somebody still has her big yellow potato-salad bowl from last year; the rodeo will feature $140 in prize money; and the dance music will again be by Nola Atkins, piano, and Jeff Swan, fiddle.

—*GROS VENTRE WEEKLY GLEANER, JUNE 29*

I HAVE TO HONESTLY say that the next few weeks of this remembered summer look somewhat pale in comparison with my Stanley episode.

Only in comparison, though.

You can believe that I arrived back to English Creek from the land of sheepherders and pack horses in no mood to take any further guff from that father of mine. What in Holy H. Hell was that all about, him and Stanley Meixell pussyfooting around each other the way they had when they met there on the mountain, then before it was over my father handing me over to Stanley like an orphan? Some counting trip, that one. I could spend the rest of the summer just trying to dope out why and what and who, if I let myself. Considering, then, that my bill of goods against my father was so long and fresh, life's next main development caught me by entire surprise. This same parent who had just lent me as a towing service for a whiskeyfield geezer trying to find his way up the Rocky Mountains—this identical father now announced that he would be off the English Creek premises for a week, and I hereby was elevated into being the man of the house.

"Your legs are long enough by now that they reach the ground," he provided by way of justification the suppertime this was unveiled, "so I guess that qualifies you to run this place, don't you think?"

Weather brought this about, as it did so much else that summer. The cool wet mood of June continued and about the middle of the month our part of Montana had its solidest rain in years, a toad-drowner that settled in around noon and poured on and on into the night. That storm delivered snow onto the mountains. Several inches fell in the Big Belts south beyond the Sun River, and that next morning here in the Two, along the high sharp parts of all the peaks a white skift shined, fresh-looking as a sugar sprinkle. You could bet, though, there were a bunch of perturbed sheepherders up there looking out their wagon doors at it and not thinking sugar. Anyway, since that storm was a straightforward douser without any lightning and left the forests so sopping that there was no fire danger for a while, the desk jockeys at the national forest office in Great Falls saw this as a chance to ship a couple of rangers from the Two over to Region headquarters for a refresher course. Send them back to school, as it was said. Both my father and Murray Tomlin of the Blacktail Gulch station down on the Sun River had been so assiduous about evading this in the past that the finger of selection now never wavered whatsoever: it pointed the pair of them to Missoula for a week of fire school.

The morning came when my father appeared in his Forest Service monkey suit—heather-green uniform, side-crimped dress Stetson, pine tree badge—and readied himself to collect Murray at the Blacktail Gulch station, from where they would drive over to Missoula together.

"Mazoola," he was still grumbling. "Why don't they send us to hell to study fire and be done with it? What I hear, the mileage is probably about the same."

My mother's sympathy was not rampant. "All that surprises me is that you've gotten by this long without having to go. Have you got your diary in some pocket of that rig?"

"Diary," my father muttered, "diary, diary, diary," patting various pockets. "I never budge without it." And went to try to find it.

I spectated with some anticipation. My mood toward my father hadn't uncurdled entirely, and some time on my own, some open space without him around to remind me I was half sore at him, looked just dandy to me. As did this first-ever designation of me as the man of the house. Of course, I was well aware my father hadn't literally meant that I was to run English Creek in his absence. Start with the basic that nobody ran my mother. As for station matters, my father's assistant ranger Paul Eliason was strawbossing a fire trail crew not far along the South Fork and the new dispatcher, Chet Barnouw, was up getting familiar with the lookout sectors and the telephone setup which connected them to the ranger station. Any vital forest business would be handled by one of those two. No, I had no grandiose illusions. I was to make the check on Walter Kyle's place sometime during the week and help Isidor Pronovost line out his packstring when he came to pack supplies up to the fire lookouts and do some barn cleaning and generally be on hand for anything my mother thought up. Nothing to get wild-eyed about.

Even so, I wasn't prepared for what lay ahead when my father came back from his diary hunt, looked across the kitchen at me, said, "Step right out here for some free entertainment," and led me around back of the ranger station.

There he went to the side of the outhouse, being a little gingerly about it because of his uniform. Turned. Stepped off sixteen paces— why exactly sixteen I don't know, but likely it was in Forest Service regulations somewhere. And announced: "It's time we moved Republican headquarters. How're your shovel muscles?"

So here was my major duty of "running" English Creek in my father's absence, Digging the new hole to site the toilet over.

Let me be clear. The job itself I didn't particularly mind. Shovel work is honest sweat. Even yet I would sooner do something manual than to diddle around with some temperamental damn piece of machinery. No, my grouse was of a different feather than that. I purely was perturbed that here was one more instance of my father blindsiding me with a task I hadn't even dreamt of. First Stanley, now this outhouse deal. Here was a summer, it was beginning to seem like, when every time I turned around some new and strange avenue of endeavor was already under my feet and my father was pointing me along it and chirping, "Right this way, Jick."

All this and I suppose more was on my mind as my father's pickup vanished over the rise of the Gros Ventre road and I contemplated my work site.

Moving an outhouse may not sound like the nicest occupation in the world. But neither is it as bad as you probably think. Here is the program: when my father got back from Missoula we would simply lever up each side of the outhouse high enough to slip a pole under to serve as a skid, then nail crosspieces to keep the pair of skids in place and, with a length of cable attached to the back of the pickup, snake the building over atop the new pit and let it down into place, ready for business.

So the actual moving doesn't amount to all that much. The new pit, though. There's the drawback. The pit, my responsibility, was going to take considerable doing. Or rather, considerable digging.

At the spot my father had paced to and marked, I pounded in four stakes with white kitchen string from one to another to represent the outhouse dimensions. Inasmuch as ours was a two-holer, as was considered good-mannered for a family, it made a considerable rectangle; I guess about half again bigger than a cemetery grave. And now all I faced was to excavate the stringed-in space to a depth of about seven feet.

Seven feet divided by, umm, parts of five days, what with the week's other jobs and general choring for my mother. I doped out that if I did a dab of steady digging each afternoon I could handily complete the hole by Saturday when my father was due back. Jobs which can be broken down into stints that way, where you know that if you put in a certain amount of daily effort you'll overcome the chore, I have always been able to handle. It's the more general errands of life that daunt me.

I don't mean to spout an entire sermon on this outhouse topic, but advancing into the earth does get your mind onto the ground, in more ways than one. That day when I started in on the outhouse rectangle I of course first had to cut through the sod, and once that's been shoveled out it leaves a depression about the size of a cellar door. A sort of entryway down into the planet, it looked like. Unearthing that sod was the one part of this task that made me uneasy, and it has taken me these years to realize why. A number of times since, I have been present when sod was broken to become a farmed field. And in each instance I felt the particular emotion of watching that land be cut into furrows for the first time ever—*ever;* can we even come close to grasping what that means?—and the native grass being tipped on its side and then folded under the brown wave of turned earth. Anticipation, fascination. Part of the feeling can be described with those words or ones close to them. It can be understood, watching the ripping plow cut the patterns that will become a grainfield, that the homesteaders who came to Montana in their thousands believed they were seeing a new life uncovered for them.

Yet there's a further portion of those feelings, at least in me. Uneasiness. The uneasy wondering of whether that ripping-plow is honestly the best idea. Smothering a natural crop, grass, to try to nurture an artificial one. Not that I, or probably anyone else with the least hint of a qualm, had any vote in the matter. Both before and after the Depression—which is to say, in times when farmers had money enough to pay wages—kids such as I was in this particular English Creek summer were merely what you might call hired arms; brought in to pick rocks off the newly broken field. And not only the newly broken, for more rocks kept appearing and appearing. In fact in our part of Montana, rock-picking was like sorting through a perpetual landslide. Anything bigger than a grapefruit—the heftiest rocks might rival a watermelon—was dropped onto a stoneboat pulled by a team of horses or tractor, and the eventual load was dumped alongside the field. No stone fences built as in New England or over in Ireland or someplace. Just raw heaps, the slag of the plowed prairie.

I cite all this because by my third afternoon shift of digging, I had confirmed for myself the Two country's reputation for being a toupee of grass on a cranium of rock. Gravel, more accurately, there so close to the bed of English Creek, which in its bottom was a hundred percent small stones. We had studied in school that glaciers bulldozed through this part of the world, but until you get to handling the evidence shovelful by shovelful the fact doesn't mean as much to you.

I am dead sure this happened on the third afternoon, a Wednesday, because that was the day of the month the English Creek ladies' club met. There were enough wives along the creek to play two tables of cards and so have a rare enough chance to visit without males cluttering up the scene. Club day always found my mother in a fresh dress right after our noon meal, ready to go. This day, Alice Van Bebber stopped by to pick her up. "My, Jick, you're growing like a weed," Alice crooned out the car window to me as my mother got in the other side. Alice always was flighty as a chicken looking in a mirror—living with Ed likely would do it to anybody—and away the car zoomed, up the South Fork road toward Withrows', as it was Midge's turn to be hostess.

I know too that when I went out for my comfort station shift, I began by doing some work with a pick. Now, I didn't absolutely have to swing a pick on this project. With a little effort the gravel and the dirt mixed with it were shovelable enough. But I simply liked to do occasional pickwork. Liked the different feel and rhythm of that tool, operated overhand as it is rather than the perpetual reach-down-and-heave of shoveling. Muscles too need some variety in life, I have always thought.

So I was loosening the gravelly earth at the bottom of the hole with swings of the pick, and on the basis of Alice Van Bebber's blab was wondering to myself why a grownup never seemed to say anything to me that I wanted to hear, and after some minutes of this I stopped for breath. And in looking up saw just starting down toward the ranger station from the rise of the county road a string of three horses.

Sorrel and black and ugly gray.

Or, reading back down the ladder of colors, Bubbles and the pack mare and the saddle horse that Stanley Meixell was atop.

I didn't think it through. I have no idea why I did it. But I ducked down and sat in the bottom of the hole.

The moment I did, of course, I began to realize what I had committed myself to. They say nine tenths of a person is above the ears, but I swear the proportion sometimes gets reversed in me. Not that I wasn't safely out of sight squatting down there; when I'd been standing up working, my excavation by now was about shoulder deep on me. No problem there. No problem so long as Stanley didn't get a direct look down into the hole. But what if that happened? What if Stanley stopped at the station, for some reason or other? And, say, being stopped anyway he decided to use the outhouse, and as he was headed out there decided to amble over to admire this pit of mine? What then? Would I pop up like a jack-in-the-box? I'd sure as the dickens look just as silly as one.

I was also learning that the position I had to squat in wasn't the world's most comfortable. And it was going to take a number of minutes for Stanley and company to saunter down from the rise and pass the station and go off up the North Fork road, before I could safely stand up. Just how many minutes began to interest me more than any-thing else. Of course I had no watch, and the only other way I knew to keep track of time was to count it off like each five-second interval between lightning and thunder: one a-mile-from-here-to-there— But the problem there, how much time did I have to count off? That I'd have to work out in my head, Alec style. Let's see: say Stanley and his horses were traveling 5 miles an hour, which was the figure Major Kel-ley was always raising hell with the Forest Service packers about, insist-ing they by God and by damn ought to be able to average that. But the Major had never encountered Bubbles. Bubbles surely would slow down any enterprise at least half a mile an hour, dragging back on his lead rope like a tug of war contestant the way he did. Okay, 4½ miles an hour considering Bubbles, and it was about a mile from the crest of the county road to down here at the ranger station; then from here to where Stanley would pass out of sight beyond the North Fork brush was, what, another third of a mile, maybe more like half a mile. So now: for Stanley to cover one mile at 4½ miles an hour would take—well, 5 miles an hour would be 12 minutes; 4 miles an hour would be 15 minutes; round the 4½ mile an hour pace off to say 13 minutes; then the other one third to one half mile would take somewhere around 6 minutes, wouldn't it be? So, 13 and 6, 19 minutes. Then 19 times 60 (60 seconds to the minute), and that was, was, was . . . 1100-something. And divide that by the five seconds it took to say each—

Never mind, I decided. This hunching down in a toilet hole was all getting dismal enough without me trying to figure out how many *a-mile-from-here-to-there*s there are in 1100-something. Besides, I had no idea how much time I had already spent in the calculating.

Besides again, numbers weren't really what needed thinking on. The point to ponder was, why was I hiding anyway? Why had I plunked myself into this situation? Why didn't I want to face Stanley? Why had I let the sight of him hoodoo me like this? Some gab about the weather, inquire as to how his hand was getting along, say I had to get back to digging, and that would have been that. But no, here I was, playing tur-tle to the bottom of an outhouse pit. Sometimes there's nobody stranger in this world than ourselves.

So I squatted and mulled. There is this for sure about doing those two together, they fairly soon convince you that you can think better standing up. Hell with it, I eventually told myself. If I had to pop up and face Stanley with my face all pie, so be it.

I unkinked and came upright with some elaborate arm-stretching, as if I'd just had a nice break from work down there. Then treated myself to a casual yawn and began eyeing around over the rim of the pit to determine which direction I had to face embarrassment from.

And found nobody.

No Stanley. No Bubbles. Nothing alive anywhere around, except one fourteen-year-old fool.

"So," my mother inquired upon return from her ladies' club, "everything peaceful around here?"

"Downright lonesome," I said back.

Now let me tell of my mother's contribution to that week.

It ensued around midday on Thursday. First thing that morning Isidor Pronovost showed up and I spent the front of the day working as cargodier for him, helping make up packs of supplies to take up to the fire lookouts.

"Balance," Isidor sermoned as he always did. "We got to balance the buggers, Jick. That's every secret of it." Harking back to my Bubbles experience I thought to myself, Don't I know it.

Then Isidor was not much more than out of sight with his packstring when here came my mother's brother, Pete Reese. English Creek was getting about as busy as Broadway.

Pete had driven into town from his ranch on Noon Creek on one errand or another, and now was looping home by way of English Creek to drop off our mail and see how we were faring. He stepped over and admired my progress on the outhouse hole. "Everybody on the creek'll be wanting to patronize it. You thought of charging admission?" Then handed me the few letters and that week's *Gleaner*. His doing so reminded me I was the temporary host of the place and I hurriedly invited, "Come on over to the house."

We no sooner were through the door than my mother was saying to Pete, "You're staying for dinner, aren't you," more as declaration than question. So Pete shed his hat and offered that he supposed he could, "if it's going to be something edible." Pete got away with more with my mother than just about anyone else could, including my father. "Park your tongue then," she simply retorted, and went to work on the meal while Pete and I chinned about the green year.

That topic naturally was staying near the front of everybody's mind. By now the weather service was declaring this the coolest June in Montana since 1916 and the wettest in almost as long, news which was more than welcome. In Montana too much rain is just about enough. All the while the country had been greening and greening, the crop and livestock forecasts were flourishing, too. Pete imparted that Morrel Loomis, the biggest wool buyer operating in the Two country, had come up from Great Falls for a look at the Reese and Hahn and Withrow bands, and that Pete and Fritz and Dode all decided to go ahead and consign their wool to Loomis on his offer of twenty-one and a half cents a pound. "Enough to keep me floating toward bankruptcy," Dode had been heard to say, which meant that even he was pretty well pleased with the price.

"Beats last year by a couple of cents, doesn't it?" I savvily asked Pete.

"Uh huh, and it's damn well time. Montana has got to be the champion next-year country of the entire damn world."

"How soon did you say you'd be haying?" my mother interrogated without looking around from her meal work at the stove. I wish now that she had in fact been facing around toward Pete and me, for I am sure my gratitude for that question was painted all over my face. Whenever haying began I was to drive the scatter rake for Pete, as I had done the summer before and Alec had for the few summers before that. But getting a rancher to estimate a date when he figured his hay crop would be ready was like getting him to confess to black magic. The hemming and hawing did have the basis that hay never was really ready to mow until the day you went out and looked at it and felt it and cocked an eye at the weather and decided this was as good a time as any. But I also think ranchers cherished haying as the one elastic part of their year. The calendar told them when lambing or calving would begin, and shipping time loomed as another constant, so when they had a chance to be vague—even Pete, of the same straightforward lineage as my mother, now was pussyfooting to the effect that "all this rain, hay's going to be kind of late this year"—they clung to it.

"Before the Fourth?" my mother narrowed the specification.

"No, I don't suppose." It was interesting to see comments go back and forth between this pair; like studying drawings of the same face done by two different artists. Pete had what might be called the kernel of my mother's good looks. Same neat nose, apple cheeks, attractive Reese chin, but proportioned smaller, thriftier.

"The week after?"

"Could be," Pete allowed. "Were you going to feed us sometime today or what?"

Messages come in capsules as well as bottles. The content of "Could be" was that no hay would be made by Pete Reese until after the Fourth of July, and until then I was loose in the world.

There during dinner, it turned out that Pete now was on the question end of the conversation:

"Alec been around lately?"

"Alec," my mother reported in obituary tones, "is busy Riding the Range."

"Day and night?"

"At least. Our only hope of seeing him is if he ever needs a clean shirt."

My personal theory is that a lot of misunderstanding followed my mother around just because of her way of saying. Lisabeth Reese McCaskill could give you the time of day and make you wonder why you had dared to ask. I recall once when I was about eleven that we were visited for the morning by Louise Bowen, wife of the young ranger at the Indian Head district to the south of us. Cliff Bowen was newly assigned onto the Two, having held down an office job at Region headquarters in Missoula all the time before, and Louise was telling my mother how worried she was that her year-old, Donny, accustomed to town and a fenced yard, would wander off from the station, maybe fall into the Teton River. I was in the other room, more or less reading a *Collier's* and minding my own business, but I can still hear how my mother's response suddenly seemed to fill the whole house:

"Bell him."

There was a stretch of silence then, until Louise finally kind of peeped: "Beg pardon? I don't quite—"

"Put a bell on him. The only way to keep track of a wandering child is to hear him."

Louise left not all too long after that, and that was the extent of our visits from her. But I did notice, when my father drove down to borrow

a saw set from Cliff a month or so later and I rode along, that Donny
Bowen was toddling around with a lamb bell on him.

Pete was continuing on the topic of Alec. "Well, he's at that age—"
"Pete," she headed him off, "I know what age my own son is."
"So you do, Bet. But the number isn't all of it. You might try and
keep that in mind."
My mother reached to pass Pete some more fried spuds. "I'll try,"
she allowed. "I Will Try."

When we'd eaten and Pete declared, "It's time I wasn't here" and headed
home to Noon Creek, my mother immediately began drowning dirty
dishes and I meanwhile remembered the mail I'd been handed, and
fetched it from the sideboard where I'd put it down. There was a letter
to my mother from Mr. Vennaman, the Gros Ventre school superintendent—even though Alec and I were gone from the English Creek
school my mother still was president of its board and so had occasional
dealings with the education muckymucks in Gros Ventre and Conrad—and a couple of Forest Service things for my father, probably the
latest kelleygrams. But what I was after was the *Gleaner*, thinking I'd let
my dinner settle a little while I read.
As usual, I opened to page 5. The newspaper was always eight pages
and page 5 was always the At Random page, carrying the editor Bill
Reinking's own comments, and syndicated features about famous people or events, and local history, and even poetry or quotations if Bill felt
like it. Random definitely was the right word for it, yet every week that
page was a magnet for a mind like mine.
I'd been literary for maybe three minutes when I saw the names.
"Mom? You and Pete are in the paper."
She turned from where she was washing dishes and gave me her
look that said, you had now better produce some fast truth.
I pinned down the newsprint evidence with my finger: "See, here."

25 YEARS AGO IN THE GLEANER
*Anna Reese and children Lisabeth and Peter visited Isaac
Reese at St. Mary Lake for three days last week. Isaac is pro-*

> *viding the workhorses for the task of building the roadbed
> from St. Mary to Babb. Isaac sends word through Anna that
> the summer's work on this and other Glacier National Park
> roads and trails is progressing satisfactorily.*

As she read over my shoulder I thought about the journey that
would have been in those days. Undoubtedly by democrat wagon, from
the Reese place on Noon Creek all the way north almost to Chief
Mountain, the last peak on that horizon. I of course had been over that
total route with my father, but only a piece at a time, on various riding
trips and by pickup to the northernmost part. But to do the whole journey at once, by hoof and iron wheel, a woman and two kids, struck me
as a notable expedition.

"Sounds like a long time in a wagon," I prompted cannily. "You
never told me about that."

"Didn't I." And she turned and went back to her dishpan.

Well, sometimes you could prompt my mother, and sometimes you
might as well try conversing with the stove poker.

I retreated into my hole, so to speak. Yet, you know how it is when
you're doing something your body can take care of by itself. Your mind
is going to sneak off somewhere on its own. As the rest of me dug, mine
was on that wagon journey with my mother and Pete and their mother.

There wouldn't have been the paved highway north to Browning
and the Park then, just the old road as the wheels of the freight wagons
had rutted it into the prairie. Some homesteads must have still existed
between Gros Ventre and the Blackfeet Reservation boundary at Birch
Creek, but probably not many. Those were the years when the Valier
irrigation project was new and anybody who knew grain grew on a stem
was over there around Lake Frances trying to be a farmer. Mostly empty
country, then, except for livestock, all the way to Birch Creek and its
ribbon line of cottonwoods. Empty again from there north to Badger
Creek, where I supposed some of the same Blackfeet families lived then
as now. There near Badger the Reese wagon would have passed just west
of the place where, a century and some before, Meriwether Lewis and
the Blackfeet clashed. That piece of reservation country to us was simply grass, until my father deduced from reading in a book of the Lewis
and Clark journals that somewhere off in there near where Badger flows

into the Two Medicine River was the place Lewis and his men killed a couple of Blackfeet over a stealing incident and began the long prairie war between whites and Indians. Passing that area in a pickup on paved highway never made that history seem real to me. I would bet it was more believable from a wagon. Then up from Badger, the high benches to where the Two Medicine trenched deep through the landscape. Maybe another couple of days of travel beyond that, through Browning and west and then north across Cut Bank Creek and through that up and down country above it, and over the divide to St. Mary, and there at the end of it all the road camp, its crews and tents and workhorses. In my imagination I saw it as somewhat like a traveling circus, but with go-devils and scrapers and other road machines instead of circus wagons. And its ringmaster, my grandfather, Isaac Reese. He was the only one of my grandparents yet alive when I became old enough to remember and I could just glimpse him in a corner of my mind. A gray-mustached man at the head of the table whenever we had Sunday dinner at the Reeses', using his knife to load his fork with food in a way which would have caused my mother to give Alec or me absolute hell if we had dared try it. I gather, though, that Isaac Reese got away with considerably more than that in life—I suppose any horse dealer worth his reputation did—and it was a thriving Reese ranch there on Noon Creek that Pete took over after the old man's death.

This Reese side of the family wandered into the conversation whenever someone would learn that my mother, although she was married to a man only a generation or so away from kilts, herself was just half Scottish. "The other half," my father would claim when he judged that she was in a good enough mood he could get away with it, "seems to be something like porcupine." Actually, that lineage was Danish. Isak Riis left Denmark aboard the ship *King Carl* sometime in the 1880s, and the pen of an immigration official greeted him onto American soil as Isaac Reese. In that everybody-head-west-and-grab-some-land period, counting was more vital than spelling anyway. By dint of what his eyes told him on the journey west, Isaac arrived to North Dakota determined on a living from workhorses. The Great Northern railroad was pushing across the top of the western United States—this was when Jim Hill was promising to cobweb Dakota and Montana with railroad iron—and Isaac began as a teamster on the roadbed. His ways with horses and projects proved to be as sure as his new language was shaky. My father claimed to have been on hand the famous time, years later, when Isaac couldn't find the words "wagon tongue" and ended up calling it "de Godtamn handle to de Godtamn vagon."

Within days after sizing up the railroad situation "the old boy was borrowing money right and left from anybody who'd take his note, to buy horses and more horses"—my father was always a ready source on Isaac, I guess greatly grateful to have had a father-in-law he both admired and got entertainment from—and soon Isaac had his own teams and drivers working on contract for the Great Northern.

When construction reached the east face of the Rockies, the mountains held Isaac. Why, nobody in the family ever could figure out. Certainly in Denmark he must never have seen anything higher than a barnyard manure pile. And unlike some other parts of Montana, this one had no settlement of Danes. (Though, as my father pointed out, maybe those *were* Isaac's reasons.) In any case, while his horses and men worked on west through Marias Pass as the railroad proceeded toward the coast, Isaac stayed and looked around. In a week or so he horsebacked south along the mountains toward Gros Ventre, and out of that journey bought a homestead relinquishment which became the start of the eventual Reese ranch.

Isaac Reese was either shrewd as hell or lucky as hell. Even at my stage of life I am not entirely clear whether there is any appreciable difference between the two. By whichever guidance he lit here in a region of Montana where a couple of decades of projects were standing in line waiting for a man with a herd of workhorses. The many miles of irrigation canals of the water schemes at Valier and Bynum and Choteau and Fairfield. Ranch reservoirs ("ressavoys" to Isaac). The roadbed when the branch railroad was built north from Choteau to Pendroy. Street grading when Valier was built onto the prairie. All those Glacier Park roads and trails. As each appurtenance was put onto the Two country and its neighboring areas, Isaac was on hand to realize money from it.

"And married a Scotchwoman to hang on to the dollars for him," my father always injected at this point. She was Anna Ramsay, teacher at the Noon Creek school. Her I knew next to nothing about. Just that she died in the influenza epidemic during the war, and that in the wedding picture of her and Isaac that hung in my parents' bedroom she was the one standing and looking in charge, while Isaac sat beside her with his mustache drooping whimsically. Neither my mother nor my father ever said much about Anna Ramsay Reese; which helped sharpen my present curiosity, thinking about her trundling off to St. Mary in that wagon. Like my McCaskill grandparents she simply was an absent figure back there, cast all the more into shadow by my father's supply of stories about Isaac.

In a sense, the first of those Isaac tales was the genesis of our family. The night my father, the young association rider, was going to catch Isaac by ambush and request my mother in marriage, Isaac greeted him at the door and before they were even properly sat down, had launched into a whole evening of horse topics, Clydesdales and Belgians and Morgans and fetlocks and withers and hocks. Never tell me a Scandinavian harbors no sense of humor.

When my father at last managed to wedge the question in, Isaac tried to look taken aback, eyed him hard and repeated as if he was making sure: "Marriage?" Or as my father said Isaac pronounced it: "Mare itch?"

Then Isaac looked at my father harder yet and asked: "Tell me dis. Do you ever took a drink?"

My father figured honesty was the best answer in the face of public knowledge. "Now and then, yes, I do."

Isaac weighed that. Then he got to his feet and loomed over my father. "Ve'll took one now, den." And with Mason jar moonshine reached down from the cupboard, the pairing that began Alec and me was toasted.

When I considered that I'd done an afternoon's excavating, physically and mentally, I climbed out and had a look at the progress of my sanitation engineering. By now the pile of dirt and gravel stood high and broad, the darker tone on its top showing today's fresh shovel work and the drier faded-out stuff the previous days'. With a little imagination I thought I could even discern a gradation, like layers on a cake, of each stint of my shovelfuls of the Two country, Monday's, Tuesday's, Wednesday's, and now today's light-chocolate top. Damn interesting, the ingredients of this earth.

More to the immediate point, I was pleased with myself that I'd estimated the work into the right daily dabs. Tomorrow afternoon was going to cost some effort, because I was getting down so deep the soil would need to be bucketed out. But the hole looked definitely finishable.

I must have been more giddy with myself than I realized, because when I went over to the chopping block to split wood for the kitchen woodbox, I found myself using the ax in rhythm with a song of Stanley's about the gal named Lou and what she was able to do with her wingwangwoo.

When I came into the kitchen with the armload, my mother was looking at me oddly.

"Since when did you take up singing?" she inquired.

"Oh, just feeling good, I guess," I said and dumped my cargo into the woodbox loud enough to try prove it.

"What was that tune, anyway?"

" 'Pretty Redwing,'" I hazarded. "I think."

That brought a further look from her.

"While I'm at it I might as well fill the water bucket," I proposed, and got out of there.

After supper, lack of anything better to do made me tackle my mother on that long ago wagon trip again. That is, I was doing something but it didn't exactly strain the brain. Since hearing Stanley tell about having done that winter of hairwork a million years ago in Kansas, I had gotten mildly interested and was braiding myself a horsehair hackamore. I was discovering, though, that in terms of entertainment, braiding is pretty much like chewing gum with your fingers. So:

"Where'd you sleep?"

She was going through the *Gleaner.* "Sleep when?"

"That time. When you all went up to St. Mary." I kept on with my braiding just as if we'd been having this continuing conversation every evening of our lives.

She glanced over at me, then said: "Under the wagon."

"Really? You?" Which drew me more of her attention than I was bargaining for. "Uh, how many nights?"

I got quite a little braiding done in the silence that answered that, and when I finally figured I had to glance up, I realized that she was truly studying me. Not just taking apart with a look: studying. Her voice wasn't at all sharp when she asked: "Jick, what's got your curiosity bump up?"

"I'm just interested, is all." Even to me that didn't sound like an overly profound explanation, so I tried to go on. "When I was with Stanley, those days camptending, he told me a lot about the Two. About when he was the ranger. It got me interested in, uh, old times."

"What did he say about being ranger?"

"That he was the one here before Dad. And that he set up the Two as a national forest." It occurred to me to try her on a piece of chronology I had been attempting to work out ever since that night of my cabin binge. "What, was Dad the ranger at Indian Head while Stanley still was the ranger here?"

"For a while."

"Is that where I remember Stanley from?"

"I suppose."

"Did you and Dad neighbor back and forth with him a lot?"

"Some. What does any of that have to do with how many nights I slept under a wagon twenty-five years ago?"

She had a reasonable enough question there. Yet it somehow seemed to me that a connection did exist, that any history of a Two country person was alloyed with the history of any other Two country person. That some given sum of each life had to be added into every other, to find the total. But none of which sounded sane to say. All I did finally manage was: "I just would like to know something about things then. Like when you were around my age."

No doubt there was a response she had to bite her tongue to keep from making: that she wasn't sure she'd ever been this age I seemed to be at just now. Instead came:

"All right. That wagon trip to St. Mary. What is it you want to know about it?"

"Well, just—why was it you went?"

"Mother took the notion. My father had been away, up there, for some weeks. He often was, contracting horses somewhere." She rustled the *Gleaner* as she turned a page. "About like being married to a ranger," she added, but lightly enough to show it was her version of a joke.

"How long did that trip take then?" Now, in a car, it was a matter of a couple or three hours.

She had to think about that. After a minute: "Three and a half days. *Three* nights," she underscored for my benefit, "under the wagon. One at Badger Creek and one on the flat outside Browning and one at Cut Bank Creek."

"How come outside Browning? Why not in town?"

"My mother held the opinion that the prairie was a more civilized place than Browning."

"What did you do for food?"

"We ate out of a chuck box. That old one from chuckwagon days, with all the cattle brands on it. Mother and I cooked up what was necessary, before we left."

"Were you the only ones on the road?"

"Pretty much, yes. The mail stage still was running then. Somewhere along the way I guess we met it."

She could nail questions shut faster than I could think them up. Not deliberately, I see now. That was just the way she was. A person who put no particular importance on having made a prairie trek and seen a stagecoach in the process.

My mother seemed to realize that this wasn't exactly flowering into the epic tale I was hoping for. "Jick, that's all I know about it. We went, and stayed a few days, and came back."

Went, stayed, came. The facts were there but the feel of them wasn't.

"What about the road camp?" I resorted to next. "What do you remember about that?" The St. Mary area is one of the most beautiful ones, with the mountains of Glacier National Park sheering up beyond the lake. The world looks to be all stone and ice and water there. Even my mother might have noticed some of that glory.

Here she found a small smile, one of her surprise sidelong ones. "Just that when we pulled in, Pete began helloing all the horses."

She saw that didn't register with me.

"Calling out hello to the workhorses in the various teams," she explained. "He hadn't seen them for a while, after all. 'Hello, Woodrow!' 'Hello, Sneezer!' Moses. Runt. Copenhagen. Mother let him go on with it until he came to a big gray mare called Second Wife. She never thought the name of that one was as funny as Father did."

There is this about history, you never know which particular ember of it is going to glow to life. As she told this I could all but hear Pete helloing those horses, his dry voice making a chant which sang across that road camp. And the look on my mother told me she could, too.

Not to be too obvious, I braided a moment more. Then decided to try the other part of that St. Mary scene. "Your own mother. What was she like?"

"That father of yours has been heard to say I'm a second serving of her."

Well, this at least informed me that old Isaac Reese hadn't gotten away with nearly as much in life as I'd originally thought. But now, how to keep this line of talk going—

"Was she an April Fool too?"

"No," my mother outright laughed. "No, I seem to be the family's only one of that variety."

Probably our best single piece of family lore was that my mother, our unlikeliest candidate for any kind of foolery, was born on the first of April of 1900. "Maybe you could get the calendar changed," I recall that my father joked this particular year, when he and Alec and I were spoofing her a little, careful not to make it too much, about the coincidence of her birthday. "Trade dates with Groundhog Day, maybe." She retorted, "I don't need the calendar changed, just slowed down." It sobers me to realize that when she made that plaint about the speed of time, she was not yet two thirds of the age I am now.

—"Why did I What?" The *Gleaner* was forgotten in front of her now, her gaze was on me: not her look that could skin a rock, just a highly surprised once-over.

I swear that what I'd had framed in mind was only further inquiry about my grandparents, how Anna Ramsay and Isaac Reese first happened to meet and when they'd decided to get married and so on. But somewhere a cog slipped, and what had fallen out of my mouth instead was "Why'd you marry Dad?"

"Well, you know," I now floundered, searching for any possible shore, "what I mean, kids wonder about something like that. How we got here." Another perilous direction, that one. "I don't mean, uh, *how*, exactly. More like why. Didn't you ever wonder yourself? Why your own mother and father decided to get married? I mean, how would any of us be here if those people back then hadn't decided the way they did? And I just thought, since we're talking about all this anyway, you could fill me in on some of it. Out of your own experience, sort of."

My mother looked at me for an eternity more, then shook her head. "One of them goes head over heels after anything blond, the other one wants to know the history of the world. Alec and you. Where did I get you two?"

I figured I had nothing further to lose by taking the chance: "That's sort of what I was asking, isn't it?"

"All right." She still looked skeptical of the possibility of common sense in me, but her eyes let up on me a little. "All right, Mr. Inquisitive. You want to know the makings of this family, is that it?"

I nodded vigorously.

She thought. Then: "Jick, a person hardly knows how to start on this. But you know, don't you, I taught most of that—that one year at the Noon Creek school?"

I did know this chapter. That when my mother's mother died in the flu epidemic of 1918, my mother came back from what was to have been her second year in college and became, in her mother's stead, the Noon Creek teacher.

"If it hadn't been for that, who knows what would have happened," she went on. "But that did bring me back from college, about the same time a redheaded galoot named Varick McCaskill came back from the army. His folks still were in here up the North Fork. Scotch Heaven. So Mac was back in the country and the two of us had known each other, oh, all our lives, really. Though mostly by sight. Our families didn't always get along. But that's neither here nor there. That spring when this Mac character was hired as association rider—"

"Didn't get along?"

I ought to have known better. My interruption sharpened her right up again. "That's another story. There's such a thing as a one-track mind, but honestly, Jick, you McCaskill men sometimes have no-track minds. Now. Do you want to Hear This, Or—"

"You were doing just fine. Real good. Dad got to be the association rider and then what?"

"All right then. He got to be the association rider and—well, he got to paying attention to me. I suppose it could be said I paid some back."

Right then I yearned for the impossible. To have watched that double-sided admiration. My mother had turned nineteen the first of April of that teaching year; a little older than Alec was now, though not a whole hell of a lot. Given what a good-looker she was even now, she must have been extra special then. And my father the cowboy—hard to imagine that—would have been in his early twenties, a rangy redhead who'd been out in the world all the way to Camp Lewis, Washington. Varick and Lisabeth, progressing to Mac and Bet. And then to some secret territory of love language that I couldn't even guess at. They are beyond our knowing, those once young people who become our parents, which to me has always made them that much more fascinating.

—"There was a dance, that spring. In my own schoolhouse, so your father ever since has been telling me I have nobody to blame but myself." She again had a glow to her, as when she'd told me about Pete helloing the horses. "Mac was on hand. By then he'd been hired by the Noon Creek ranchers and was around helping them brand calves and so on. That dance"—she shrugged, as if an impossible question had been asked—"that dance I suppose did it, though neither of us knew it right then. I'd been determined I was never going to marry into a ranch life. Let alone to a cow chouser who didn't own much more than his chaps and hat. And later I found out from your father that he'd vowed never to get interested in a schoolmarm. Too uppity to bother with, he always thought. So much for intentions. Anyway, now here he was, in my own schoolroom. I'd never seen a man take so much pleasure in dancing. Most of it with me, need I say. Oh, and there was this. I hadn't been around him or those other Scotch Heaveners while I was away at college, and I'd lost the knack of listening to that burr of theirs. About the third time that night he said something I couldn't catch, I asked him: 'Do you always talk through your nose?' And then he put on a *real* burr and said back, 'Lass, it saves wearrr and tearrr on my lips. They'rrre in prrrime condition, if you'rrre everrr currrious.'"

My father the flirt. Or flirrrt. I must have openly gaped over this, for my mother reddened a bit and stirred in her chair and declared, "Well, you don't need full details. Now then. Is that enough family history?"

Not really. "You mean, the two of you decided to get married because you liked how Dad danced?"

"You would be surprised how large a part something like that plays. But no, there's more to it than that. Jick, when people fall in love the way we did, it's—I don't mean this like it sounds, but it's like being sick. Sick in a wonderful way, if you can imagine that. The feeling is in you just all the time, is what I mean. It takes you over. No matter what you do, what you try to think about, the other person is there in your head. Or your blood, however you want to say it. It's"—she shrugged at the impossible again—"there's no describing it beyond that. And so we knew. A summer of that—a summer when we didn't even see each other that much, because your father was up in the Two tending the association cattle most of the time—we just knew. That fall, we were married." Here she sprung a slight smile at me. "And I let myself in for all these questions."

There was one, though, that hovered. I was trying to determine whether to open my yap and voice it when she took it on herself. "My guess is, you're thinking about Alec and Leona, aren't you."

"Yeah, sort of."

"Lord knows, they imagine they're in a downright epidemic of love," my mother acknowledged. "Alec maybe is. He's always been all

go and no whoa. But Leona isn't. She can't be. She's too young and"—
my mother scouted for aptness—"flibberty. Leona is in love with the
idea of men, not one man. And that's enough on that subject." She
looked across at me in a way that made my fingers quit even pretend-
ing they were manufacturing a horsehair hackamore. "Now I have one
for you. Jick, you worry me a little."

"Huh? I do?"

"You do. All this interest of yours in the way things were. I just hope
you don't go through life paying attention to the past at the expense of
the future. That you don't pass up chances because they're new and
unexpected." She said this next softly, yet also more strongly than anything else I'd ever heard her say. "Jick, there isn't any law that says a
McCaskill can't be as forward-looking as anybody else. Just because
your father and your brother, each in his own way, looks to the past to
find life, you needn't. They are both good men. I love the two of
them—the three of you—in the exact way I told you about, when your
father and I started all this. But, Jick, be ready for your life ahead. It
can't all be read behind you."

I looked back at her. I wouldn't have bet I had it in me to say this.
But it did come out: "Mom, I know it all can't. But some?"

That next afternoon, Friday, was the homestretch of my digging. It
needed to be, with my father due home sometime the next morning. And
so once more unto the bowels of the earth, so to speak, taking down with
me into the outhouse pit an old short-handled lady shovel Toussaint Rennie had given my father and a bucket to pack the dirt out with.

My mood was first-rate. My mother's discourse from the evening
before still occupied my thinking. The other portion of me by now was
accustomed to the pit work, muscles making no complaint whatsoever,
and in me that feeling of bottomless stamina you have when you are
young, that you can keep laboring on and on and on, forever if need be.
The lady shovel I was using was perfect for this finishing-off work of
dabbing dirt into the bucket. To make it handy in his ditch-riding Toussaint always shortened the handle and then ground off about four
inches of the shovel blade, cutting it down into a light implement about
two thirds of a normal shovel but which still, he proclaimed, "carries all
the dirt I want to." And working as I had been for a while each day
without gloves to get some good calluses started, now I had full benefit

of the smooth old shovel handle in my bare hands. To me, calluses have always been one of the marks of true summer.

How long I lost myself to the rhythm of the lady shovel and the bucket I don't know. But definitely I was closing in on the last of my project, bottoming the pit out nice and even, when I stepped toward my ladder to heft up a pailful of dirt and found myself looking into the face of a horse. And above that, a hat and grin which belonged to Alec.

"Going down to visit the Chinamen, huh?"

Why did that get under my skin? I can run that remark of Alec's through my ears a dozen times now and find no particular reason for it to be rilesome. In my brother's lofty position I'd likely have commented in similar fashion. But there must be something about being come upon in the bottom of an outhouse hole that will unhinge me, for I snapped right back to Alec:

"Yeah, we can't all spend our time roosting on top of a horse and looking wise."

Alec let up on his grinning at that. "You're a little bit owly there, Jicker. You maybe got a touch of shovelitis."

I continued to squint up at him and had it framed in my mind to retort "Is that anything like wingwangwoo fever?" when it dawned on me that Alec was paying only about half attention to our conversation anyway. His gaze was wandering around the station buildings as if he hadn't seen them for a decade or so, yet also as if he wasn't quite seeing them now either. Abstracted, might be the twenty-five-cent word for it. A fellow with a lot on his mind, most of it blond and warm.

One thing did occur to me to find out:

"How much is 19 times 60?"

"1140," replied Alec, still looking absent. "Why?"

"Nothing." Damned if I was going to bat remarks back and forth with somebody whose heart wasn't in it, so I simply asked, "What brings you in off the lone prairie?" propped an arm against the side of my pit and waited.

Alec finally recalled that I was down there and maybe was owed some explanation for the favor of his presence, so he announced: "I just came by for that town shirt of mine. Need it for rodeo day."

Christamighty. The powers of mothers. Barely a full day had passed since Mom forecast to Pete that it would take the dire necessity of a shirt to draw Alec into our vicinity, and here he was, shirt-chaser incarnate.

It seemed to me too good a topic to let him have for free. "What, are you entering the pretty shirt contest this year?"

Now Alec took a squint down at me from the summit of the horse, as if I only then really registered on him. "No, wisemouth, the calf roping." Hoohoo. Here was going to be another Alec maneuver just popular as all hell with our parents, spending money on the entry fee for calf-roping.

"I guess that color of shirt does make calves run slower," I dead-panned. The garment in question was dark purplish, about the shade of chokecherry juice. Distinctive, to put it politely. "It's in the bottom drawer there in our—the porch bedroom." Then I figured since I was being helpful anyway, I might as well clarify the terrain for Alec. "Dad's in Missoula. But maybe you'd already heard that, huh?"

But Alec was glancing around in that absent-minded way again, which was nettling me a little more every time he did it. I mean, you don't particularly like to have a person choosing when to phase in and out on you. We had been brothers for about fourteen and five-sixths years, so a few seconds of consecutive attention didn't strike me as too awful much to expect of Alec.

Evidently so, though. He had reined his horse's head around to start toward the house before he thought to ask: "How's Mom's mood?"

"Sweet as pie. How's yours?"

I got nothing back from that. Alec simply passed from sight, his horse's tail giving a last little waft as if wiping clean the field of vision which the pit framed over me.

As I was reaching down to resume with my bucket of earth, though, I heard the hooves stop and the saddle creak.

"Jicker?" Alec's voice came.

"Yeah?"

"I hear you been running the mountains with Stanley Meixell."

While I knew you couldn't have a nosebleed in the English Creek valley without everybody offering you a hanky for a week afterward, it had never occurred to me that I too was automatically part of this public pageant. I was so surprised by Alec knowing of my Stanley sojourn that I could only send forth another "Yeah?"

"You want to be a little more choosy about your company, is all."

"Why?" I asked earnestly of the gape of the pit over me. Two days ago I was hiding out from Stanley in this very hole like a bashful badger, and now I sounded like he was my patron saint. "What the hell have you got against Stanley?"

No answer floated down, and it began to seem to me that this brother of mine was getting awful damn cowboyish indeed if he looked down on a person for tending sheep camp. I opened my mouth to tell him something along that line, but what leaped out instead was: "Why's Stanley got everybody in this damn family so spooked?"

Still nothing from above, until I heard the saddle leather and hooves again, moving off toward the house.

The peace of the pit was gone. Echoes of my questions to Alec drove it out. In its stead came a frame of mind that I was penned down here, seven feet below the world in a future outhouse site, while two members of this damn McCaskill family were resting their bones inside the house and the other one was gallivanting off in Missoula. To each his own and all that, but this situation had gotten considerably out of proportion.

The more I steamed, the more a dipper of water and a handful of gingersnaps seemed necessary to damper me down. And so I climbed out with the bucket of dirt, flung it on the pile as if burying something smelly, and headed into the house.

"Your mind is still set," my mother was saying as I came through the doorway into the kitchen.

"Still is," agreed Alec, but warily. Neither of them paid me any particular attention as I dippered a drink from the water bucket. That told me plenty about how hot and heavy the conversation was in here.

"A year, Alec." So she was tackling him along that angle again. Delay and live to fight again another day. "Try college for a year and decide then. Right now you and Leona think the world begins and ends in each other. But it's too soon to say, after just these few months."

"It's long enough."

"That's what Earl Zane likely thought, the day before Leona dropped him for you." That seemed to me to credit Earl Zane with more thought capacity than he'd ever shown. Earl was a year or so older than Alec, and his brother Arlee was a year ahead of me in school, and so far as I could see the Zane boys were living verifications that the human head is mostly bone.

"That's past history," Alec was maintaining.

I punctuated that for him by popping the lid off the Karo can the gingersnaps were kept in. Then there was the sort of scrabbling sound as I dug out a handful. And after that the little sharp crunch as I took a first bite. All of which Alec waited out with the too patient annoyance of somebody held up while a train goes by. Then declared: "Leona and I ain't—aren't skim milk kids. We know what we're doing."

My mother took a breath which probably used up half the air in the kitchen. "Alec. What you're doing is rushing into trouble. You can't get ahead on ranch wages. And just because Leona is horse happy at the moment doesn't mean she's going to stay content with a ranch hand for a husband."

"We'll get by. Besides, Wendell says he'll boost my wages after we're married."

This stopped even my mother, though not for long. "Wendell Williamson," she said levelly, "has nobody's interest at heart but his own. Alec, you know as well as anybody the Double W has been the ruin of that Noon Creek country. Any cattle ranch he hasn't bought outright he has sewed up with a lease from the bank—"

"If Wendell hadn't got those places somebody else would have," Alec recited.

"Yes," my mother surprised him, "maybe somebody like you. Somebody who doesn't already have more money than he can count. Somebody who'd run one of those ranches properly, instead of gobbling it up just for the sake of having it. Alec, Wendell Williamson is using you the way he uses a handkerchief to blow his nose. Once he's gotten a few years of work out of you"—another kitchen-clearing breath here—"and evidently gotten you married off to Leona, so you'll have that obligation to carry around in life, too—once he's made enough use of you and you start thinking in terms of a real raise in wages, down the road you'll go and he'll hire some other youngster—"

"Youngster? Now wait one damn min—"

"—with his head full of cowboy notions. Alec, staying on at the Double W is a dead end in life."

While Alec was bringing up his forces against all this, I crunched into another gingersnap.

My brother and my mother sent me looks from their opposite sides of the room, a convergence about as taut as being roped with two lassos simultaneously. She suggested: "Aren't you supposed to be shoveling instead of demolishing cookies?"

"I guess. See you around, Alec."

"Yeah. Around."

Supper that night was about as lively as dancing to a dead march.

Alec had ridden off toward town, Leona-ward, evidently altered not one whit from when he arrived, except for gaining himself the rodeo shirt. My mother was working out her mood on the cooking utensils. I was a little surprised the food didn't look pulverized when it arrived to the table. So far as I could see, I was the only person on the place who'd made any true progress that day, finishing the outhouse hole. When I came in to wash up I considered announcing cheerfully "Open for business out there" but took a look at my mother's stance there at the stove and decided against.

So the two of us just ate, which if you're going to be silent is probably the best thing to be doing anyway. I was doubly glad I had coaxed as much conversation out of her last night as I had. I sometimes wonder if life is anything but an averaging out. One kind of day and then its opposite.

Likely, though, the mother of Alec McCaskill would not have agreed just then that life has its own simple average. For by the time my mother washed the supper dishes and I was drying them, I began to realize she wasn't merely in a maternal snit. She was thinking hard about something. And if I may give myself credit, it occurred to me that her thinking deserved my absence. Any new idea anybody in the McCaskill family could come up with deserved all encouragement.

"Need me any more?" I asked as I hung the dish towel. "I thought I might ride up to check on Walter's and fish my way home till toward dark." The year's longest day was just past; twilight would go on for a couple or three hours yet.

"No. No, go ahead." Her cook's instinct roused her to add: "Your father will be home tomorrow, so catch us a big mess." In those times a person could; the legal limit was twenty-five fish a day.

And then she was back into the thinking.

Nothing was amiss at Walter Kyle's place. As I closed the door on that tidy sparse room, I wondered if Walter didn't have the right idea. Live alone and let everybody else knock bruises on one another.

The fishing was as close to a cinch as fishing can ever be. Since I was using an honest-to-God pole and reel and it was a feeding time of evening, the trout in those North Fork beaver dams all but volunteered. Do I even need to say out loud that I limited? One more time I didn't owe my father a theoretical milkshake, and there still was evening left when the gill of that twenty-fifth trout was threaded onto my willow stringer and I went to collect Pony from the tall meadow grass where she was grazing.

My mother still was in her big think when I came back into the ranger station toward the last of dusk. I reported that the mess of cleaned fish was in a pan of water in the spring house, then stretched myself in an obvious sort of way, kissed her goodnight, and headed for the north porch and my bed. I honestly didn't want to be around any more heavy cogitation that day.

The north porch, a screened-in affair, had been built to take advantage of the summer shade on that side of the English Creek ranger station house, but in late spring Alec and I always moved out there to use it as our bedroom. Now that he was bunking at the Double W, I of course had the room to myself, and I have to testify here that gaining a private bedroom goes far toward alleviating the absence of a brother.

Not just the privacy did I treasure, though. It seemed to me at the time, and still does, that a person could not ask for a better site than that one for day's end. The north porch made a sort of copperwire bubble into the night world. Moths would bat and bat against the screening, especially if I'd brought a coal oil lamp out with me. Mosquitoes, in the couple of weeks in early June when they are fiercest, would alight out there and try to needle their way in, and there's a real reward to lying there knowing that those little whining bastards can't get at you. Occasional scutterings and whishes in the grass brought news of an owl or skunk working on the field mouse population, out there beyond the lampshine. Many an evening, though, I would not even light the lamp, just use the moon when I went out to bed. Any bright night filled the width of that porch with the shaggy wall of English Creek's cottonwoods and aspen, and atop them like a parapet the blunt black line of the benchland on the other side of the water. Out the west end of the porch a swatch of the mountains stood: Roman Reef, and the peaks of Rooster Mountain and Phantom Woman behind it. With Alec's cot folded away I had room to move mine longways into the east end of the room, so that I could lie looking at the mountains, and enjoy the bonus too that, with my head there below the east sill, the sunrise would over-shoot me instead of beaming into my face.

I recall that this was a lampless night, that I was flopping into bed without even any thought of reading for a while, more tired from the day than I'd realized, when I heard my mother at the telephone starting a call.

"Max? This is Beth McCaskill. Can't you think of anybody better to do that?" A short space of silence, then she announced: "All right then. I'll do it. I still think your common sense has dried up and blown away. But I'll Do It." And whanged down the receiver as if her words might sneak back out of the telephone wire.

What that was about I had no clue. Max? The only Max I could conjure up was Max Devlin, the assistant supervisor at the Two Medi-cine forest headquarters down in Great Falls, and why she would be calling him up this time of night just to doubt his common sense I couldn't figure. But maybe the go-round with Alec had put her into her mood to deliver the Forest Service a little of what she considered it gen-erally deserved. I definitely was not going back out there to inquire. Sleep was safer.

My father arrived home from Missoula full of sass and vinegar. He always came away from a Region headquarters session avid to get back to the real planet again.

Even the fact that it was Saturday and he had a blank week of diary entries to catch up on didn't dent his spirits. "Easy enough after one of these Mazoola schools. Let's see: Monday, snored. Tuesday, tossed and turned. Wednesday, another restless day of sleep. . . ."

As for my handiwork out back, he was duly impressed. "The entire Fort Peck dam crew couldn't have dug better."

What ought I to tell about the days between then and the Fourth of July? The outhouse got moved in good order, fitting over my pit like a hen onto a fresh nest, and I put in another shovel day of tossing the dirt into the old hole. My father combed the Two up, down, and sideways, checking on the fire lookouts and patrolling the allotments to see how the range was looking and siccing Paul Eliason and the CCC crews onto trail and road work and any other improvements that could be thought up. Shearing time came and went; I helped wrangle Dode Withrow's sheep in the pens the shearers set up at the foot of the South Fork trail to handle the Withrow and Hahn and Kyle bands, then Pete came and took me up to the Blackfeet Reservation for a couple more days' wrangling when his were sheared out there on the open prairie north of the Two Medicine River. Nothing more was seen of Alec at English Creek. My mother no doubt posted my father about the going-over she had given Alec when he came by for the shirt, although a reaming like that has to be seen and heard to be entirely appreciated.

Beyond that, I suppose the main news by the morning of the Fourth when the three of us began to ready to go to town for the holiday was that we *were* going. For my father didn't always get the Fourth of July off; it depended on fire danger in the forest. I in fact was getting a little nervous about this year. The cool summer turned itself around in the last week of June. Each day, a little hotter and stickier. Down in Great Falls they had first a dust storm—people trying to drive in from Helena reported hundreds of tumbleweeds rolling across the highway on Gore Hill—and after that about fifteen minutes of thunderstorm with rain coming down as if from faucets. But then, the Falls receives a lot of bastardly weather we don't. Particularly in summer, its site out there on the plains gives storms a chance to build and build before they strike the city. The mountain weather was our concern, and so much of May and June had been cool and damp that even this hot start of July wasn't really a threat, yet.

Final persuasion came from the holiday itself. That Fourth morning arrived as a good moderate one, promising a day warm enough to be comfortable but nowhere near sweltering, and my father said his decision as we sat down to breakfast. It came complete with a sizable grin, and the words of it were: "Watch out, Gros Ventre. Here we come."

I had a particular stake in a trouble-free Fourth and parental good humor. By dint of recent clean living and some careful asking, and I suppose the example of son-in-rebellion provided to my parents by Alec, I had won permission to make a horseback sojourn into town in order to stay overnight with my best friend from school, Ray Heaney.

As I cagily pointed out, "Then the morning after the Fourth, I can just ride back out here and save you a trip into town to get me."

"Strange I didn't see the logic of all this before," commented my mother. "You'll be saving us a trip we wouldn't have to make if you didn't stay in there in the first place, am I right?" But it turned out that was just her keeping in practice.

Of course, receiving permission from your parents is not the same as being able to hang on to it, and I was stepping pretty lightly that morning to keep from inspiring any second thoughts on their part. In particular, as much as possible I was avoiding the kitchen and my mother's culinary orbit. Which was sound Fourth of July policy in any case. A reasoning person would have thought she was getting ready to lay siege to Gros Ventre, instead of only going in there on a picnic.

My father ventured through for a cup of coffee and I overheard my mother say "Why I said I'd do this I'll never know" and him respond "Uh huh, you're certainly downright famous for bashfulness" and then her response in turn, but with a little laugh, "And you're notorious for sympathy."

As I was trying to dope that out—my mother bashful about a creek picnic?—my father poked his head into where I was and asked: "How about tracking down the ice creamer and putting it in the pickup?"

I did so, meanwhile trying to calculate how soon I could decently propose that I start my ride to town. I didn't want to seem antsy about it. On the other hand I sure desired to get the Fourth of July under way.

But here came my father out and over to me at the pickup. Then commemorated himself with me forever by saying, "Here. Better carry some weight in your pocket so you don't blow away." With which I was handed a half dollar.

I must have looked my startlement. Other Fourth of Julys, if there was any spending money bestowed on Alec and me it was more on the order of ten cents. If there was any.

"Call it shovel wages." My father stuck his hands in his hip pockets and studied the road to town as if he'd never noticed it before. "You might as well head on in. We'll see you there at the park." Then, as if in afterthought: "Why don't you ride Mouse, he can stand the exercise."

When you are fourteen you take a step up in life whenever you can find it and meanwhile try to keep a mien somewhere between "At last!" and "Do you really mean that?" I stayed adult and stately until I was behind the barn and into the horse pasture; then gave in to a grin the dimension of a jack-o-lantern's. A by God full-scale horse, mine for the holiday. In the corner of the pasture where Pony was grazing she lifted her head to watch me but I called out, "Forget it, midget," and went on over and bridled Mouse.

—

Mouse and I scooted right along that road toward Gros Ventre. He was a fast walker, besides elevating me and my spirits more than I'd been used to on Pony. The morning—mid-morning and past, by now—was full of sun, but enough breeze was following along English Creek for a person to ride in pure comfort. The country still looked just glorious. All the valley of English Creek was fresh with hay. Nobody was mowing quite yet, except for the one damp green swath around Ed Van Bebber's lower field where he had tried it a week too early as he did every year.

I was more than ready for the Fourth. A lot seemed to have happened since that evening back at the start of June when I looked up and saw Alec and Leona parading down the rise to join us for a family supper. One whole hell of a lot. No longer was I even sure that we four McCaskills quite were a family. It was time we all had something else on our minds besides ruckus. Alec plainly already did, the way he intended to trig up on behalf of Leona and a calf. And given how my mother was whaling into the picnic preparation and my father was grinning like a Chessy cat about getting the day off from rangering and I was strutting atop this tall horse with coinage heavy in my pocket, the Fourth was promising to do the job for the other three of us.

It is no new thought to say that life goes on. Yet that's where it does go.

In maybe an hour and a half, better time than I would have thought possible for that ride in from the English Creek station, Mouse and I were topping the little rise near the turnoff to Charlie Finletter's place, the last ranch before town.

From there a mile or so outside, Gros Ventre looked like a green cloudbank: cottonwood trees billowing so thick that it took some inspection to find traces of houses among them. Gros Ventre's neighborhoods were planted double with cottonwoods, a line of trees along the front yards and another between sidewalk and street. Then the same colonnade again on the other side of the street. All of this of course had been done fifty or more years before, a period of time that grows you a hell of a big cottonwood. Together with the original groves that already rose old and tall along English Creek before Gros Ventre was ever thought of, the streetside plantation produced almost a roof over the town. This cottonwood canopy was particularly wonderful just before a rain, when the leaves began to shiver, rattle in their papery way. The whole town seemed to tingle then, and the sound picked up when a gust of wind from the west ushered in the rain, and next the air was filled with the seethe of water onto all that foliage. In Gros Ventre even a dust-settler sounded like a real weather event.

The English Creek road entered town past the high school, one of those tan-brick two-story crates that seemed to be the only way they knew how to build high schools in those days, and I nudged Mouse into an even quicker pace so as not to dwell on that topic any longer than necessary. We were aiming ourselves across town, to the northeast end where the Heaneys' house stood.

Mouse and I met Main Street at the bank corner, alongside the First National, and here I can't help but pause for a look around Gros Ventre of that Fourth of July day, just as I did then before reining Mouse north along the street.

Helwig's grocery and merc, with its old-style wooden square front and the Eddy's bread sign in its window.

The Toggery clothing store, terra cotta along its top like cake frosting.

Musgreave's drugstore, with the mirror behind the soda fountain so that a person could sit there over a milkshake—assuming a person had the price of a milkshake, not always the case in those times—and keep track of the town traffic.

Grady Tilton's garage.

Dale Quint's saddlery and leather repair shop. Maybe a decent description of Gros Ventre of that time was that it still had a leather man but not yet a dentist. A person went to Conrad for tooth work.

Saloons, the Pastime and Spenger's, although Dolph Spenger was a dozen or more years dead.

The Odeon movie theater, the one place in town with its name in neon script. The other modern touch lent by the Odeon was its recent policy of showing the movie twice on Saturday night; first at seven-thirty, then the "owl show" at nine.

The post office, the only new building in Gros Ventre since I was old enough to remember. A New Deal project, this had been, complete with a mural of the Lewis and Clark expedition portaging around the Great Falls of the Missouri River in 1805. Lewis and Clark maybe were not news to postal customers of the Two country, but York, Clark's Negro slave standing out amid the portagers like a black panther in a snowfield, definitely was.

The little stucco-sided Carnegie library, with its flight of steps and ornamented portico as if a temple had been intended but the money gave out.

Across from the library the town's smallest storefront, where Gene Ladurie had his tailor shop until his eyes went bad; now the WPA sewing room was situated there.

The Lunchery, run by Mae Sennett. The occasional times when I would be with my father when he was on Forest Service meal money, the Lunchery was our place and oyster stew our order. It of course came from a can, but I see that bowl yet, the milk yellowing from the blob of butter melting in the middle of it, and if Mae Sennett was doing the serving herself she always warned, "Watch out for any oysterberries," by which she meant those tiny pearls that sometimes show up. I have to say, I still am not truly comfortable eating in any establishment that doesn't have that tired ivory look to its walls that the Lunchery did. A proof that the place has been in business longer than overnight and at least has sold decent enough food that people keep coming back.

Doc Spence's office. Across the empty lot from Doc's, the office of the lawyer, Eli Kinder. Who, strange to say, was a regular figure in the sheep traffic through this street, when the bands flowed through town on their way to the summer grass of the Blackfeet Reservation. Eli was a before-dawn riser and often would arrive downtown just as a band of sheep did. It was odd to see him, in his suit and tie, helping those wool-lies along Main Street, but Eli had been raised on a ranch down in the Highwood Mountains and knew what he was doing.

The sidestreet businesses, Tracy's creamery and Ed Heaney's lumber yard and hardware and Adam Kerz's coal and trucking enterprise.

The set of bank buildings, marking what might be called the down of downtown: the First National Bank of Gros Ventre in tan brick, and cattycorner from it the red brick of what had been the English Creek Valley Stockmen's Bank. The Valley Stockmen's went under in the early 1920s when half of all the banks in Montana failed, and the site now was inhabited, if not exactly occupied, by Sandy Staub's one-chair barber shop. The style in banks in those times was to have a fancy doorway set into the corner nearest the street intersection—Gros Ventre's pair of bank buildings stared down each other's throats in exactly this fash-ion—and when Sandy took over the Valley Stockmen's building he simply painted barber-pole stripes on one of the fat granite pillars sup-porting the doorway.

What have I missed? Of course; also there on the Valley Stockmen's block the newspaper office, proclaiming on a plate-glass window in the same typeface as its masthead: GLEANER. Next to that a more recent enterprise, Pauline Shaw's Moderne Beauty Shoppe. The story was that when Bill Reinking first saw his new neighboring sign, he stuck his head in the shop to ask Pauline if she was sure she hadn't left an "e" off Beauty.

I heard somebody say once that the business section of every Western town he'd ever seen looked as if it originated by falling out the back end of a truck. Not so with Gros Ventre. During those Depression years Gros Ventre did look roadworn. Weathered by all it had been through. But to me the town also held a sense of being what it ought to be. Of aptness, maybe is the term. Not fancy, not shacky. Steady. Settlement here dated back to when some weary freight wagoneer pulled in for the night at the nice creekside sheltered by cottonwoods. As the freighters' trail between Fort Shaw on the Sun River and southern Alberta developed, this site became a regular waystop, nicknamed The Middle since it was about midway between Fort Shaw and Canada—although some of us also suspect that to those early-day wagoneers the place seemed like the middle of nowhere. Gros Ventre grew to about a thousand people when the homesteaders began arriving to Montana in droves in the first decade of this century—my mother could remember in her childhood coming to town and seeing wagon after wagon of immigrants heading out onto the prairie, a white rag tied on one spoke of a wagonwheel so the revolutions could be counted to measure the bounds of the claimed land—and that population total never afterward varied more than a hundred either way.

This south to north route Mouse and I were taking through Gros Ventre, I now have to say, saved for the last what to me was the best of the town: a pair of buildings at the far end of Main Street, last outposts before the street/highway made its curve and zoomed from Gros Ventre over the bridge across English Creek.

The night during our campjacking trip when I was baptizing my interior with alcohol and Stanley Meixell was telling me the history of the Two Medicine National Forest from day one, a surprise chapter of that tale was about the hostelry that held the most prominent site in Gros Ventre. Stanley's arrival to town when he first came here to the Two was along the route Mouse and I had just done, from the south, and as Stanley rode along the length of Main Street, here at the far end a broad false-front with a veranda beneath it was proclaiming:

BEER   LIQUORS   CIGARS

MEALS AT ALL   **NORTHERN HOTEL**   LUNCHES
HOURS   PUT UP

C. E. SEDGWICK, PROP.

"Looks like it could kind of use a prop, all right," Stanley observed to a bib-overalled idler leaning against one of the porch posts. Who turned out to be the exact wrong person to make that joke to: C. E. Sedgwick himself.

"If my enterprise don't suit you," Sedge huffed, "you can always bunk down there in the diamond willows," indicating the brush at the bend of English Creek.

"How about," Stanley offered, "me being a little more careful with my mouth, and you giving me a second chance as a customer?"

Sedge hung his thumbs into his bib straps and considered. Then decided: "Go mute and I might adopt you into the family. Bring your gear on in."

The Northern burned in the dry summer of 1910. Although, according to old-timers, "burned" doesn't begin to say it. Incinerated, maybe, or conflagrated. For the Northern blaze took the rest of the block with it and threatened that whole end of town; if there had been a whisper of wind, half of Gros Ventre would have become ash and a memory. Sedge being Sedge, people weren't surprised when he decided to rebuild. After all, he went around in those overalls because what he really liked about being a hotelier was the opportunity to be his own maintenance man. But what Sedge erected still sat, this Fourth when I was atop Mouse, across the end of Main Street as a kind of civic astonishment. A three-story fandango in stone, quarried from the gray cliffs near where English Creek joins the Two Medicine River; half a block square, this reborn Sedgwick hostelry, with round towers at each corner and a swooping pointed ornament in the middle, rather like the spike on those German soldiers' helmets. Even yet, strangers who don't know that the Pondera County courthouse is twenty-two miles east in Conrad assume that Sedge's hotel is it. Sedge in fact contributed to the civic illusion by this time not daubing a sign all across the front of the place. Instead only an inset of chiseled letters rainbowing over the entranceway:

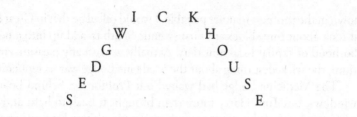

Sedge sold out in 1928, to a family from Seattle who seemed to somehow eke a living out of that big gray elephant of a hotel even after hard times hit. About 1931 Sedge died of pleurisy, and almost as if she'd been waiting just offstage, his widow emerged as one of Gros Ventre's most well-to-do citizens and certainly the looniest. Lila Sedgwick was a tall bony woman. Her build always reminded me of Abraham Lincoln. Almost any day she could be seen downtown three or four times, some days six or eight, for she no sooner would get home than she would forget about having just gone for the mail or on some other errand and would go for it again. In her long old-style dresses with those Lincoln arms and elbows poking out she inevitably was a figure of fun, although the one and only time I said something smart about her my mother's frown closed me down in a hurry.

"Lila Sedge is not to be laughed at," she said, not in her whetstoned voice but just sort of instructively. "The clouds have settled on her mind."

I don't know where my mother got that, but always after when I would see Lila Sedge, creeping along this street for the third time in an hour or gandering up at a cottonwood tree as if she'd never encountered one before, I would wonder about how it was to have a clouded mind. Somewhere in there, I supposed, a bruise-colored thunderhead that was Sedge's death. Maybe mares' tails high away in the past where she was a girl. Fluffs which carried faces—aunts, uncles, schoolmates, any of us she happened to meet on the street—in and out of her recognition. Until my mother's words about Lila Sedge I had never thought of the weather of the brain, but more and more I have come to believe in it.

But enough on that. The Sedgwicks and their namesake hotel provided Gros Ventre its one titanic building and its roving human landmark. The enterprise across the street from the Sedgwick House ministered to the town internally.

The Medicine Lodge saloon gave Gros Ventre its "rough" section of town in the thriftiest manner possible. I would calculate that in Great Falls it took about three blocks of First Avenue South to add up into a neighborhood of similar local notoriety. Actually, as with any pleasure emporium, the wickedest thing about the Medicine Lodge was its reputation.

The Medicine Lodge had waited out Prohibition behind boarded windows, but Tom Harry more than brought it back to light and life. Also, maybe after those dry years the town was thirsty for a saloon with a bit of flair. Tom Harry had come over from running a bar, and some said a taxi dance joint as well, at the Fort Peck dam project. Supposedly all he brought with him was a wad of cash and the picture of Franklin Delano Roosevelt which had adorned the wall of his Fort Peck enterprise. Be that as it may, in the Medicine Lodge FDR was promptly joined on the wall by a minor menagerie of stuffed animal heads Tom Harry acquired from somewhere. Several buck deer and an antelope and a mountain sheep and a bobcat snarling about the company he was in, not to mention the six-point elk head which set off arguments every hunting season about how much his absent body would weigh.

As matters proved out, along with Tom Harry also came a set of invisible rules of saloon behavior which every so often somebody would stray across. I think of the night when my father and I were entering the Medicine Lodge and met a stranger with a cigar in his mouth being forcibly propelled into the street. It turned out that although Tom Harry himself went around under a blue cigarette haze—tailormades; no Fort Peck bartender ever had time to roll his own—he would not tolerate cigar smoke.

In itself, the taxidermy herd populated the Medicine Lodge considerably. But the place also held a constant legion of the living, more or less. These setters, as my father called the six or eight guys who sat around in there—he was not above stepping in for a beer after our Lunchery meal, and if nobody official-looking was on hand Tom Harry didn't seem to mind my being with him—the setters always occupied the stools at the far end of the bar, and anybody who entered got long gazes from them as if they were cataloguing the human race.

Decapitated animals and owlish geezers do not, I realize, sound like much of a decor. And yet the Medicine Lodge did three times as much business as Spenger's or the Pastime, both much more "respectable" places back downtown. I suppose it is and ever will be the habit of the race: people gravitate to a certain place to do their drinking, and logic will never veer them. At least one night a week in the Medicine Lodge, gravitation amounted to something more like an avalanche. Saturday night, thirsts converged from everywhere in the Two country. Hay hands who had come in for a bath and haircut at Shorty Staub's but decided instead to wash down the inside of themselves. Shearing crews one time of year, lamb lickers (as guys who worked in lambing sheds were known) another. Any season, a sheepherder in from the mountains or the reservation to inaugurate a two-week spree. Government men from reclamation projects. Likely a few Double W cowpokes. Definitely the customary setters, who had been building up the calluses on their elbows all week just for this. Always a sufficient cast of characters for loud dialogues, occasional shoving matches, and eventual passing-outs. Maybe you couldn't get away with cigar smoke in the Medicine Lodge, but you could with what counted.

Turning east past the Sedgwick House and the Medicine Lodge, Mouse and I now were into the Heaneys' side of town. An early priest had persuaded the Catholic landowner who platted this particular neighborhood to name the streets after the first missions in Montana, which in turn bore the names of saints. This created what the current Gros Ventre postmaster, Chick Jennings, called "the repeater part of town," with mailing addresses such as St. Mary St., St. Peter St., and St. Ignatius St. It was at the end of St. Ignatius St. that the Heaney house stood, a white two-story one with sills of robin's egg blue. Ed Heaney owned the lumber yard, and so was the one person in town in those Depression years with some access to paint. The robin's egg blue had been a shipping mistake by the manufacturer; it is a shade pretty delicate to put up against the weather of Montana; and Ed lugged the can home and made the best of it.

The place looked empty as I rode up, which was as I expected. Rather than the creek picnic, the Heaneys always went out to a family shindig at Genevieve's parents' farm, quite a ways east of Gros Ventre on the Conrad road. So with Ray out there I wouldn't link up with him until the rodeo, and I simply slung my warbag inside the Heaneys' back porch and got on Mouse again, and went picnicking.

Cars and pickups and trucks were parked so thick that they all but swamped the creekside part of town. It is nice about a horse, that you can park him handily while Henry Ford still would be circling the block and cussing. I chose a stand of high grass between the creek bank and the big cottonwoods just west of the picnic and pastured Mouse on a tie of rope short enough that he couldn't tangle it around anything and long enough for him to graze a little. Then gave him a final proud pat, and headed off to enlist with the picnickers.

Some writer or another put down that in the history of Montana, the only definite example of civic uplift was when the Virginia City vigilantes hung the Henry Plummer gang in 1864. I think that overstates, a bit. You can arrive into the most scruffy of Montana towns and delve around a few minutes and in all likelihood find a public park, of some sort. In Gros Ventre's instance the park was a half circle of maybe an acre, fronting on English Creek just west of Main Street and the highway bridge, one last oasis before the road arrowed north into the plains and benchlands. In recent years WPA crews had made it a lot more of a park than it had been, clearing out the willows which were taking over the creek bank and then laying in some riprap to keep the spring runoff out. And someone during that WPA work came up with an idea I've not seen before or since. There near the creek where a big crippled cottonwood leaned—a windstorm had ripped off its main branches—a crew sawed the tree off low to the ground, leaving a broad stump about two feet high, then atop the stump was built a speaker's pulpit, a slatted round affair somewhat on the order of a ship's crow's nest. The one and only time I saw Senator Burton K. Wheeler, who some people thought might become president if Roosevelt ever stopped being, we were let out of school to hear him give a speech from this speaking stump.

From where I had left Mouse I emerged into the creekside corner of the park where the stump pulpit stood, and I stopped beside it to have a look around.

A true Two country Fourth of July. The trees were snowing.

Fat old cottonwoods stood all along the arc between the park and the neighborhood, while younger trees were spotted here and there across the rest of the expanse, as if they had been sent out to be shade-bearers. The day was providing just enough breeze into the treetops to rattle them a little and make them shed their cotton wisps out through the air like slow snow.

Through the cottonfall the spike of tower atop the Sedgwick House stuck up above one cottonwood at the far side of the park. As if that tree had on a party hat.

As for people, the park this day was a bunch of islands of them. I literally mean islands. The summer thus far had stayed cool enough that even a just warm day like this one was putting people into the shade of the cottonwoods, each gathering of family and friends on their specific piece of dappled shade like those cartoons of castaways on a desert isle with a single palm tree.

I had to traipse around somewhat, helloing people and being helloed, before I spotted my mother and my father, sharing shade and a spread blanket with Pete and Marie Reese and Toussaint Rennie near the back of the park.

Among the greetings, my father's predominated: "Thank goodness you're here. Pete's been looking for somebody to challenge to an ice-cream-making contest." So before I even got sat down I was off on that tangent. "Come on, Jick," Pete said as he reached for their ice-cream freezer and I picked up ours, "anybody who cranks gets a double dish."

We took our freezers over near the coffee and lemonade table where everybody else's was. This year, I should explain, was the turn of English Creek and Noon Creek to provide the picnic with ice cream and beverage. Bill Reinking, who despite being a newspaperman had some fairly practical ideas, was the one to suggest the system; that instead of everybody and his brother showing up at the Fourth armed with ice creamers and coffeepots and jugs of lemonade, each part of the community take a turn in providing for all. Now one year the families west of Main Street in Gros Ventre did the ice cream, coffee and ade, the next year the families east of Main Street, the one after that those of us from English Creek and Noon Creek, and then after us what was called "the rest of Creation," the farm families from east and south and north of town and anybody else who didn't fit some other category.

So for the next while Pete and I took turns with the other ice-cream manufacturers, cranking and cranking. Lots of elbow grease, and jokes about where all that fancy wrist work had been learned. Marie shortly came over on coffee duty—she was going to do the making, my mother would serve after everybody'd eaten—and brought along a message from my father and Toussaint: "They say, a little faster if you can stand it." Pete doffed his Stetson to them in mock gratitude. The holiday definitely was tuning up. And even yet I can think of no better way to begin a Fourth of July than there among virtually all of our English Creek neighbors. Not Walter Kyle, up on the mountain with his sheep; and not the Hebners, who never showed themselves at these creek picnics; and not the Withrows, who must have been delayed some way. But everybody else. The South Fork folks other than the Withrows: Fritz and Greta Hahn, Ed and Alice Van Bebber. Then the population of the main creek, those who merely migrated downstream here to the park, so to speak. Preston and Peg Rozier. Charlie and Dora Finletter. Ken and Janet Busby, and Bob and Arleta Busby; I had half wondered whether Stanley Meixell might show up with the Busbys, and was relieved that he hadn't. Don and Charity Frew. The Hills arrived last, while I was still inventorying the crowd; J.L. leaning shakily on his wife Nan. "Set her down, J.L.," somebody called, referring to the ice creamer the Hills had brought with them, "we'll do the twirling." "I get to shivering much more than this," J.L. responded, "and I can just hold the goddamn thing in my hands and make ice cream." In truth, J.L.'s tremble was constant and almost ague-like by now. It is terrible to see, an ailment fastened onto a person and riding him day and night. I hope not to end up that way, life over and done with before existence is.

But that was not the thought for this day. If a sense of life, of the blood racing beneath your skin, is not with you at a Fourth of July creek picnic, then it is never going to be.

When Pete and I finished ice-cream duty and returned to the blanket, my father had Toussaint on the topic of what the Fourth of July was like when Gros Ventre and he were young.

"Phony Nose Gorman," Toussaint was telling. "Is he one you remember?"

My father shook his head: "Before my time." Much of Toussaint's lore was before anyone's time.

"Tim Gorman," Toussaint elaborated, "Cox and Floweree's foreman awhile. Down on Sun River. Froze his nose in that '86 winter. Some doctor at Fort Shaw fixed him up. Grafted skin on. I saw him after, the surgery was good. But Phony Nose Gorman he was called. He was the one the flagpole broke with. There across from the Medicine Lodge, where that garage is now. He was climbing it to put Deaf Smith Mitchell's hat on top. On a bet. Those times, they bet on the sun coming up."

Toussaint Rennie this day looked maybe sixty-five years old, yet had to be at least a dozen beyond that. He was one of those chuckling men you meet rarely, able to stave off time by perpetually staying in such high humor that the years didn't want to interrupt him. From that little current of laugh always purling in him Toussaint's face had crinkled everywhere it could. Tan and wrinkled deep, that face, like a gigantic walnut. The rest of Toussaint was the general build of a potbelly stove. Girth and age and all, he still was riding the ditches of the Blackfeet Reservation's Two Medicine irrigation project, his short-handled shovel sticking out of a rifle scabbard as his horse plodded the canal banks. Allotting a foot-and-a-half head of water to each farm ditch; plugging gopher holes or muskrat tunnels in the canal bank with gunny sacks of dirt; keeping culverts from clogging; in a land of scarce water a ditch rider's job was vital above most others, and Toussaint apparently was going to hold his until death made it drop from his hand.

In about the way that shovel was carried in that scabbard, the history of the Two country rested there in Toussaint's memory, handy to employ. And sharpened by steady use. It never was clear to me how Toussaint, isolated way to hell and gone—he bached out there a few miles west of where the highway crossed the Two Medicine River, about fifteen miles from Browning and a good thirty from Gros Ventre—could know news from anywhere in the Two country as fast as it happened. Whatever the network was (my father called it moccasin telegraph) Toussaint was its most durable conductor. He came to the Two in the time of the buffalo, a boy eight or so years old when his family roved in from somewhere in the Dakotas. The Rennies were part French; my father thought they might have started off as Reynauds. But mostly tribal haze. Of their Indian background Toussaint himself was only ever definite in declaring himself *not* a Blackfeet, which had to do with the point that the Two Medicine woman he married, Mary Rides Proud, *was* one. The usual assumption was that the Rennie lineage was Métis, for other Métis families had ended up in this general region of Montana after the Riel rebellion in Canada was put down in 1885. But count back across the decades and you found that Toussaint already had grown to manhood here in the Two country by the time the Canadians were hanging Louis Riel and scattering his followers. Toussaint himself was worse than no help on this matter of origin, for all he would say was to claim pedigree from the Lewis and Clark expedition: "I come down from William Clark himself. My grandfather had red hair."

Thinking back on it now, I suspect the murk of Toussaint's lineage was carefully maintained. For the one thing unmistakable about the

Rennie family line was its knack for ending up on the side of the winners in any given contest of the Montana frontier. "The prairie was so black with buffalo it looked burnt. I was with the Assiniboines, we came down on the buffalo from the Sweetgrass Hills," one Toussaint tale would relate, and the next, "The trader Joe Kipp hired me to take cattle he was selling to the Army at Fort Benton. He knew I kept Indians from stealing them." Able to straddle that way, Toussaint had a view into almost anything that happened in the early Two country. He was with the bull teams that brought the building materials for the original Blackfeet Reservation agency north of Choteau, before there was a Choteau or a Gros Ventre. "Ben Short was the wagon boss. He was a good cusser." After the winter of '86, Toussaint freighted cowhides off the prairie by the thousands. "That was what was left in this country by spring. More cowhides than cows." He saw young Lieutenant John J. Pershing and his Negro soldiers ride through Gros Ventre in 1896, herding a few hundred woebegone Crees north to push them back over the line into Canada. "Each creek those soldiers crossed, English Creek and Birch Creek and Badger Creek and all of them, some more Crees leaked away into the brush." He saw the canals come to the prairie, the eighty-thousand-acre irrigation project that built Valier from scratch in 1909 and drew in trainloads of homesteaders. "Pretty quick they wondered about this country. Dust blew through Valier there, plates were turned facedown on the table until you turned them up to eat off of. One tree, the town had. Mrs. Guardipee watered it from her wash tubs." And the Two Medicine canal he himself had patrolled for almost a quarter century, the ditch rider job he held and held in spite of being not a Blackfeet: "It stops them being jealous of each other. With me in the job, none of them is." The first blats of sheep into this part of Montana were heard by Toussaint. "I think, 1879. People called Lyons, down on the Teton. Other sheepmen came fast. Charlie Scoffin, Charlie McDonald, Oliver Goldsmith Cooper." The first survey crews he watched make their sightings. "1902, men with telescopes and Jacob's staffs."

—"The first Fourth of July you ever saw here," my father was prompting. "When was that, do you think?"

Toussaint could date it without thinking. "Custer's year. '76. We heard just before the Fourth. All dead at the Little Bighorn. Everybody. Gros Ventre was just only a hotel and saloon then. Men took turns, coming out of the saloon to stand sentry. To look north." Here Toussaint leaned toward Pete's wife Marie and said in mock reproach: "For Blackfeet."

All of us echoed his chuckle. The tease to Marie was a standard one from Toussaint. Married to Pete, she of course was my aunt, and if I'd had a thousand aunts instead of just her she still would have been my favorite. More to the point here, though, Marie was Toussaint's granddaughter, and the only soul anywhere in that family who could get along with him. Most of Toussaint's sons wouldn't even speak to him, his daughters had all married out of his orbit as rapidly as they could, and down through the decades any number of his Rides Proud in-laws had threatened to shoot him. (Toussaint claimed he had a foolproof antidote to such threats: "I tell them bullets can fly more than one direction.") I myself remember that the last few years of her life, Toussaint and his wife Mary didn't even live under the same roof; whenever my father and I stopped by their place, Toussaint was to be found in residence in the bunkhouse. Thus all the evidence said that if you were a remove or two from him Toussaint could be a prince of the earth toward you, but anybody sharing the same blood with him he begrudged. Except Marie. Marie was thin and not particularly dark—her father was Irish, an office man at the agency in Browning—and only her black hair, which she wore shoulder-long, brought out the Blackfeet ancestry and whatever farther east Indian heredity it was that Toussaint transmitted. So her resemblance to Toussaint really was only a similar music in her voice, and the same running chuckle at the back of her throat when she was pleased. Yet be around the two of them together for only a minute and you knew without mistake that here were not merely natural allies but blood kin. There just was something unmistakably alike in how each of them regarded life. As if they had seen it all before and shared the amusement that things were no better this time around.

But Toussaint's story of the first Fourth wasn't quite done. "I took a turn at sentry. I was in there drinking with them. In the saloon. Already an old man, me. Fifteen."

"Ancient as Jick," Marie murmured with a smile in my direction. If she but knew. Maybe my toot with Stanley that night in the cabin didn't break any saloon records, but it was spree enough for a starter.

"Jick has a few months to go yet," my mother corrected Marie's observation.

"I'm getting there as fast as I can," I defended, drawing a laugh from our assemblage.

As you can see, an all but perfect Fourth of July picnic so far. I say all but, because the year before, Alec had been with us instead of off sparking Leona. The only awareness of him this year was the way people took some care not to mention him to my parents.

My mother turned to Marie and asked: "Do you suppose these scenery inspectors have earned any food?"

"We'll take pity on them," Marie agreed, and the picnic provisions began to emerge from the pair of grub boxes.

The blanket became like a raftload of food, except that such a cargo of eating likely would have sunk any raft.

There were the chickens my mother spent part of the morning frying. Delectable young spring fries with drumsticks about the thickness of your thumb. This very morning, too, Toussaint had caught a batch of trout in the Two Medicine and now here they beckoned, fried up by Marie. Blue enamel broilers of fish and fowl, side by side. The gateposts of heaven.

Marie's special three bean salad, the pinnacle of how good beans can taste. My mother's famous potato salad with little new green onions cut so fine they were like sparks of flavor.

New radishes, sweet and about the size of a marble, first of Marie's garden vegetables. A dozen and a half deviled eggs arrayed by my mother.

A jar of home-canned pickled beets, a strong point of my mother's. A companion jar of crabapple pickles, a distinction of Marie's.

A plate of my mother's corn muffins. A loaf of Marie's saffron bread. Between the two, a moon of Reese home-churned butter.

An angelfood cake by Marie. A chocolate sour cream cake from my mother.

My eyes feasted while the rest of me readied to. My father urged, "Dive in, Toussaint," and the passing of dishes got under way.

"Been a while since breakfast," Pete proclaimed when he had his plate loaded. "I'm so excited to see food again I'm not sure I'll be able to eat."

"Too bad about you," Marie said in that soft yet take-it-or-leave-it way so like Toussaint's. And my mother didn't overlook the chance to put in: "Wait, we'll sell tickets. People will line up to see Pete Reese not eat."

"Come on now, Bet," came the protest from Pete. "I have never eaten more than I could hold."

As they should do at a picnic, the conversing and the consuming cantered along together in this fashion. I think it was at the start of the second plateload, when we were all letting out-dubious hmmms about having another helping of this or that but then going ahead and having it, that Pete asked my father if fire school in Missoula had made him any smarter than he was before.

"Airplanes," my father announced. "Airplanes are the firefighting apparatus of the future, at least according to this one hoosier we heard from over there."

"The hell. How's that gonna work?"

"I didn't say it was going to work. I just said what the hoosier told us. They're going to try parachutists—like these guys at fairs?"

"Say on," urged Toussaint, squinting through a mask of eager puzzlement. Toussaint always was avid to hear developments of this sort, as if they confirmed for him the humorous traits of the human race. "That radio stuff," he had declared during the worst of the drought and the dust storms, "it monkeys with the air. Dries it out, all that electric up there."

"They're just now getting ready to test all this out," my father continued his report of latest up-in-the-air science. "Send an airplane with a couple of these parachutists over a mountain smoke and see if they can jump down there and tromp it out before it grows to a real fire. That's the cheery theory, anyhow."

Pete shook his head. "They couldn't pay me enough to jump out of one of those."

"Hell, Pete, the jumping would be easy money. The landing is the only drawback." My father readied to plow into another of Toussaint's trout, but first offered as if in afterthought: "Fact is, I told them I'd volunteer"—my mother's full skepticism sighted in on him now, waiting to see if there was any color of seriousness in this—"if the parachute was going to be big enough for my saddle horse and packstring too."

The vision of my father and assorted horses drifting down from the sky the way the cottonwood fluffs were floating around us set everybody to laughing like loonies.

Next it was Toussaint's inning again. The mention of horses reminded him of a long ago Fourth of July in Gros Ventre when everybody caught horse race fever. "How it happened, first they matched every saddle horse against every other saddle horse. Ran out of those by middle of the afternoon. Still plenty of beer and daylight left. Then somebody got the notion. Down to the stable, everybody. Brought out the stagecoach horses. Bridled them, put boys on them bareback. Raced them against each other the length of Main Street." The Toussaint chuckle. "It was hard to know. To bet on the horse, or how high the boy would bounce."

Which tickled us all again. Difficult to eat on account of laughing, and to laugh on account of eating. Give me that dilemma anytime.

All this horse talk did remind me about Mouse, and I excused myself to go picket him onto another patch of grass. Truth to tell, getting myself up and into motion also would shake down some of the food in me and make room for more.

Thinking back on that scene as I wended my way to the edge of the park where Mouse was tethered, I have wished someone among us then had the talent to paint the portrait of that picnic. A group scene that would have preserved those faces from English Creek and Noon Creek and Gros Ventre and the out-east farming country and, yes, Toussaint's from the Two Medicine. That would convey every one of those people at once and yet also their separateness. Their *selves,* I guess the word should be. I don't mean one of those phony-baloney gilt concoctions such as that one of Custer and all his embattled and doomed troopers there at the Little Bighorn, which hangs in three fourths of the saloons I have ever been in and disgusts me every single time. (To my mind, Custer can be done justice only if shown wearing a tall white dunce cap.) But once I saw in a magazine, *Look* or *Life* or one of those old every-week ones, what one painter tried in this respect of showing selves. He first painted little pictures of tropical flowers, in pink and other pastels; wild roses I guess would be our closest comparison flower here in the Two country. Some several hundred of those, he painted. Then when all these were hung together in the right order on the wall, the flower colors fit together from picture to picture to create the outline of a tremendously huge snake. In any picture by itself you could not see a hint of that snake. But look at them together and he lay kinked across the entire wall mightier than the mightiest python.

That is the kind of portrait I mean of the creek picnic. Not that very many of those people there in the park could be called the human equivalent of flowers, nor that the sum of them amounted to a colossal civic snake. But just the point that there, that day, they seemed to me all distinctly themselves and yet added up together too.

I have inquired, though, and so far as I can find, nobody ever even thought to take a photograph of that day.

When I came back from retethering Mouse, my parents and Pete and Marie were in a four-way conversation about something or other, and Toussaint was spearing himself another trout out of the broiler. His seemed to me the more sensible endeavor, so I dropped down next to him to inflict myself on the chicken supply. I was just beginning to do good work on my favorite piece of white meat, a breastbone, when Toussaint turned his head toward me. The potato salad had come to rest nearest my end of the blanket and I reached toward it, expecting that he was going to ask me to pass it to him. Instead Toussaint stated quietly: "You are a campjack these days."

Probably I went red as an apple. I mean, good Christamighty. Toussaint's words signaled what I had never dreamt of: moccasin telegraph had the story of my sashay with Stanley.

Everything that coursed through me in those moments I would need Methuselah's years to sort out.

Questions of source and quantity maybe hogged in first. How the hell did Toussaint know? And what exactly did he know? My dimwitted approach to a barbwire fence in an electrical storm? My tussle with Bubbles? My alcoholic evening in the cabin? No, he couldn't know any of those in detail. Could he?

The unnerving possibility of Toussaint having dropped some mention of that last and biggest matter, my night of imbibing, into the general conversation while I was off tending Mouse made me peer toward my mother.

No real reassurance there. Her mood plainly had declined since the parade of the food onto the blanket, she now was half listening to my father and Pete and half gazing off toward the ripples of English Creek. Whatever was occupying her mind, I could only send up prayers that it wasn't identical to the topic on mine.

Geography next. How far had the tale of Jick and Stanley spread?

Was I traveling on tongues throughout the whole damn Two country? "Hear about that McCaskill kid? Yeah, green as frog feathers, ain't he? You wonder how they let him out of the house by himself."

And beyond that, philosophy. If I was a Toussaint topic, just what did that constitute? The mix of apprehension and surmise was all through me. Plus a flavor of something which seemed surprisingly like pride. Better or worse, part of me now was in Toussaint's knowledge, his running history of the Two. In there with Phony Nose Gorman and the last buffalo hunt and the first sheep and the winter of '86 and Lieutenant Black Jack Pershing and the herded Crees and—and what did that mean? Being a part of history, at the age of fourteen years and ten months: why had that responsibility picked me out?

They say when a cat walks over the ground that will be your grave, a shiver goes through you. As I sat there that fine July noon with a breastbone forgotten in my hand, Toussaint again busy eating his trout after leaving the track of those six soft words across my life—"You are a campjack these days"—yes, I shivered.

My father's voice broke my trance. "If Toussaint and Jick ever would get done eating for winter, we could move along to the delicacy part of the meal. Some fancy handle-turning went into the making of that ice cream, you know. Or at least so I hear by rumor."

My mother was up, declaring she'd bring the cups of coffee if a certain son of hers would see to the dessert. Toussaint chuckled. And put up a restraining hand as I started to clamber to my feet, ready to bolt off to fetch dishes of ice cream, bolt off anywhere to get a minute of thinking space to myself.

"Do you know, Beth," Toussaint began, stopping her and my heart at the same time, "do you know—your potato salad was good."

A picnic always slides into final contentment on ice cream. All around us as each batch of people finished dessert and coffee, men flopped onto their backs or sides while the women sat up and chatted with one another.

I, though; I wasn't doing any sliding or flopping, just sitting there bolt upright trying to think things through. My head was as gorged as my stomach, which was saying a lot.

My father, though, acted as if he didn't have a thing in the world on his mind. To my surprise, he scootched around until he had room to lie flat, then sank back with his head in my mother's lap and his hat over his face.

"Pretty close to perfect," he said. "Now if I only had an obedient wife who'd relieve me of these dress shoes."

"If I take them off you," my mother vowed, "you'll be chasing after them as they float down the creek."

"This is what I have to put up with all the time, Toussaint," came his voice from under the hat. "She's as independent as the moon." My mother answered that by sticking out a thumb and jabbing it between a couple of his ribs, which brought a *whuw!* out of him.

Down at creekside, the school superintendent Mr. Vennaman was stepping up into the stump rostrum. Time for the program, evidently. I tried to contain at the back of my mind the cyclone of thoughts about Toussaint and moccasin telegraph and myself.

"—always a day of pleasure," Mr. Vennaman's voice began to reach those of us at the back of the park. "This is a holiday particularly American. Sometimes, if the person on the stump such as I am at this moment doesn't watch his enthusiasm, it can become a little too much so. I am always reminded of the mock speech which Mose Skinner, a Will Rogers of his day, proposed for this nation's one hundredth birthday in 1876: 'Any person who insinuates in the remotest degree that America isn't the biggest and best country in the world, and far ahead of every other country in everything, will be filled with gunpowder and touched off.'"

When the laughing at that died down, Mr. Vennaman went on: "We don't have to be quite that ardent about it, I think. But this is a day we can simply be thankful to be with our other countrymen. A day for neighbors and friends and family.

"Some of those neighbors, in fact, are here with a gift of song for us." Mr. Vennaman peered over toward the nearest big cottonwood. "Nola, can the music commence?"

This was interesting. For under that towering tree sat a piano. Who came up with the idea I never did know, but some of the Gros Ventre men had hauled the instrument—of course it was one of those old upright ones—out of Nola Atkins's front room, and now here it was on the bank of English Creek, and Nola on the piano bench readying to play. I'd like to say Nola looked right at home, but actually she was kept busy shooing cottonwood fluff off the keys and every so often there'd be a *plink* as she brushed away a particularly stubborn puff.

Nonetheless, Nola bobbed yes, she was set.

I think it has to be said that the singing at events such as this is usually a pretty dubious proposition, and that's more than likely why some out-of-town group was invited to perform at each of these Fourth picnics. That way, nobody local had anything to live down. This year's songsters, the Valier Men's Chorus, now were gathering themselves beside Nola and the piano. Odd to see them up there in that role, farmers and water company men, in white dress shirts and with the pale summits of their foreheads where hats customarily sat.

Their voices proved to be better than you might expect. The program, though, inadvertently hit our funny bones as much as it did our ears, because the chorus's first selection was "I Cannot Sing the Songs of Long Ago," and then, as if they hadn't heard their own advice, they wobbled into "Love's Old Sweet Song." The picnic crowd blossomed with grins over that, and I believe I discerned even a trace of one on Nola Atkins at the piano.

Mr. Vennaman came back up on the stump, thanking the Valierians "for that memorable rendition" and introducing "yet another neighbor, our guest of honor this day." Emil Thorsen, the sheepman and state senator from down at Choteau, rose and declared in a voice that could have been heard all the way downtown that in early times when he was first running for office and it was all one county through here from Fort Benton to Babb instead of being broken up into several as it is now, he'd have happily taken up our time; "but since I can't whinny any votes out of you folks any more, I'll just say I'm glad to be here among so many friends, and compliment you on feeding as good as you ever did, and shut myself up and sit down." And did.

Mr. Vennaman popped to his feet again, leading the hand-clapping and then saying: "Our next speaker actually needs no introduction. I'm going to take a lesson from Senator Thorsen and not bother to fashion one." Two traits always marked Mr. Vennaman as an educator: the bow tie he perpetually wore and the way, even saying hello on the street, he seemed to be looking from the front of a classroom at you. Now he peered and even went up on his tiptoes a bit, as if calling on someone in the back row of that classroom, and sang out: "Beth McCaskill?"

I knew I hadn't heard that quite right.

Yet here she was, getting up from beside my father and smoothing her dress down and setting off toward the speaker's stump, with folded sheets of paper clutched in her business hand. No doubt about it, I was the most surprised person in the state of Montana right then. But Pete and Marie were not far behind and even Toussaint's face was squinched with curiosity.

"What—?" I floundered to my father. "Did you know—?"

"She's been sitting up nights writing this," he told me with a cream-eating grin. "Your mother, the Eleanor Roosevelt of English Creek."

She was on the stump now, smoothing the papers onto the little stand, being careful the creek breeze didn't snatch them. She looked like she had an appointment to fight panthers, but her voice began steady and clear.

"My being up here is anybody's suggestion but my own. It was argued to me that if I did not make this talk, it would not get made. That might have been the better idea.

"But Maxwell Vennaman, not to mention a certain Varick McCaskill, has the art of persuasion. I have been known to tell that husband of mine that he has a memory so long he has to tie knots in it to carry it around with him. We'll all now see just how much my own remembering is made up of slip knots."

Chuckles among the crowd at that. A couple of hundred people being entertained by my mother: a minute before, I would have bet the world against it.

"But I do say this. I can see yet, as clearly as if he was standing in long outline against one of these cottonwoods, the man I have been asked to recall. Ben English. Many others of you were acquainted with Ben and the English family. Sat up to a dinner or supper Mary put on the table in that very house across there." Heads turned, nodded. The English place was directly before us, across the creek from the park. One of the Depression's countless vacant remnants, with a walked-away look to it. If you were driving north out of Gros Ventre the English place came so quick, set in there just past the highway bridge, that chances were you wouldn't recognize it as a ranch rather than a part of the town. But from the park, the empty buildings across there seemed to call their facts over to us. The Englishes all dead or moved away. The family after them felled by the Depression. Now the land leased by Wendell Williamson. One more place which had supported people, now populated by Double W cows.

"Or," my mother was continuing, "or dealt with Ben for horses or cattle or barley or hay. But acquaintance doesn't always etch deep, and so at Max Vennaman's request I have put together what is known of Ben English.

"His is a history which begins where that of all settlers of the West of America has to: elsewhere. Benson English was born in 1865 at Cobourg, in Ontario in Canada. He liked to tell that as he and his brothers one by one left home, their mother provided each of them with a Bible, a razor, whatever money she could, and some knitted underwear." My mother here looked as if she entirely approved of Ben English's mother. "Ben English was seventeen when he followed his brother Robert into Montana, to Augusta where Robert had taken up a homestead. Ben found a job driving freight wagon for the Sun River Sheep Company from the supply point at Craig on the Missouri River to their range in the mountains. He put in a year at that, and then, at eighteen, he was able to move up to driving the stage between Craig and Augusta." She lifted a page, went right on as if she'd been giving Fourth of July speeches every day of her life. "Atop there with four horses surging beneath him seemed to be young Ben English's place in the world. Soon, with his wages of forty dollars a month, he was buying his own horses. With a broke team in the lead and his green ones in the other traces, he nonetheless somehow kept his reputation as a driver you could set your clock by." Here she looked up from her sheets of paper to glance over to Senator Thorsen. "Ben later liked to tell that a bonus of stage driving was its civic opportunities. On election day he was able to vote when the stage made its stop at the Halfway House. Then again when it reached Craig. Then a third time when he got home to Augusta."

When the laughter of that was done, my mother focused back down to her pages. "There was a saying that any man who had been a stage-coach driver was qualified to handle the reins of heaven or hell, either one. But Ben English, as so many of our parents did, made the choice halfway between those two. He homesteaded. In the spring of 1893 he filed his claim southwest of here at the head of what is now called Ben English Coulee. The particulars of the English homestead on Ben's papers of proof may sound scant, yet many of us here today came from just such beginnings in this country: 'A dwelling house, stable, corrals, two and a half miles of wire fences, thirty acres of hay cut each season—total value, eight hundred dollars.'

"Around the time of his homesteading Ben English married Mary Manix of Augusta, and they moved here, to the place across the creek, in 1896. Their only child, Mary, was born there in 1901."

Here my mother paused, her look fastened over the heads of all of us on the park grass, toward the trunk of one of the big cottonwoods farthest back. As if, in the way she'd said earlier, someone was standing in outline against the gray bark. "A lot of you can remember the look of Ben English. A rangy man, standing well over six feet, and always wearing a black Stetson, always with a middle crimp. He sometimes grew a winter beard, and in his last years he wore a mustache that made him look like the unfoolable horse dealer he was. Across thirty-some years my father, Isaac Reese, and Ben English knew each other and liked each other and tried to best each other. Put the pair of them together, my mother used to say of their visits, and they would examine a horse until there was nothing left of it but a hank of tail hair and a dab of glue. Once when my father bought a horse with an odd stripe in its face, Ben told him he was glad to see a man of his age taking up a new occupation: raising zebras. My father got his turn back when Ben bought a dark bay Clydesdale that stood twenty-one hands high at the shoulder, very likely the hugest horse there ever has been in this valley, and, upon asking what the horse's name was, discovered it was Benson. Whenever my father saw Ben and the Benson horse together he called out, 'Benson andt Benson, but t'ank Godt vun of t'em vears a hadt.'"

Of all the crowd, I am sure my father laughed loudest at this Isaac Reese tale, and Pete was nodding in confirmation of that accent he and my mother had grown up under. Our speaker of the day, though, was sweeping onward. "Anyone who knew Ben English more than passingly will recall his knack for nicknames. For those of you old enough to remember them around town, Glacier Gus Swenson and Three Day Thurlow both were christened that way by Ben English." Chuckles of recognition spattered amid the audience. Glacier Gus was an idler so slow that it was said he wore spurs to keep his shadow from treading on his heels. Three Day Thurlow had an everlasting local reputation as a passable worker his first day on a job, a complainer on his second, and gone sometime during his third. "Ben's nicknaming had no thought of malice behind it, however. He did it for the pleasure it gave his tongue. In any event, in their pauper's graves Glacier Gus and Three Day each lie buried in a suit given by Ben English."

She put the page she had just finished beneath the others, and the next page she met with a little bob of her head, as if it was the one she'd been looking for all this time. "So it is a justice of language that a namer himself lives on in an extra name. Originally this flow of water was simply called Gros Ventre Creek, to go with the townsite. But it came to be a saying, as the sheepmen and other travelers would pass through here, that they would stop for noon or the night when they reached English's Creek. An apostrophe is not the easiest thing in the world to keep track of, and so we know this as English Creek."

She paused again and I brought my hands up ready to clap, that sounding to me like the probable extent of the Ben English history. But no, she was resuming. Do I never learn? My mother had her own yard-stick as to when she was done with a topic.

"I have a particular memory of Ben English myself. I can see him yet, riding past our ranch on Noon Creek on his way to his cattle range in the mountains, leading a string of cayuse pack horses carrying block salt. On his way back he would ride into our yard and pass the time of day with my father while still sitting in his saddle, but hardly ever would he climb down and come in. His customary explanation was that he had to get home and move the water. He seemed to feel that if he stayed in the saddle, he indeed was on his way to that irrigating task."

My father had his head cocked in a fashion as if what she was reciting was new to him. I figured that was just his pride in her performance, but yet . . .

"And that memory leads to the next, of Ben English in his fields across from us here, moving the water. Guiding the water, it might be better said. For Ben English used the water of his namesake creek as a weaver uses wool. With care. With respect. With patience. Persuading it to become a product greater than itself." Once more she smoothed the page she was reading from. "Greater than itself. As Ben English himself became, greater than himself. From the drudgery of a freight wagon to the hell deck of a stagecoach to a dry-land homestead to a ranch of green water-fed meadows that nicely supported a family, that was the Montana path of Ben English. Following his ability, trusting in it to lead him past the blind alleys of life. This is the day to remember a man who did it that way."

Was I the only one to have the thought brim up in me then? That suddenly, somehow, Alec McCaskill and the Double W had joined Ben English in this speech?

Whether or not, my mother had returned to the irrigation theme.

"Bill Reinking has been kind enough to find for me in the *Gleaner* files something which says this better than I can. It is a piece that I remembered was published when the first water flowed into the ditches of the Valier irrigation project. Who wrote it is not known. It is signed simply 'Homesteader.' Among the hundreds, no, thousands who were homesteading this country then, maybe 'Homesteader' isn't quite as anonymous as 'Anonymous.' But awfully close. It is titled 'The Lord of the Field.'" She drew a deep breath. "It reads:

" 'The irrigator is the lone lord of his field. A shovel is his musket, gumboots are his garb of office, shank's mare is his steed. To him through the curving laterals the water arrives mysteriously, without sign of origin or destination. But his canvas dam, placed with cunning, causes the flood to hesitate, seek; and with an eager whisper, pour over the ditch bank and onto the grateful land. The man with the shovel hears the parched earth drink. He sees its face of dusty brown gladden to glistening black. He smells the odor of life as the land's plants take the water in green embrace. He feels like a god, exalted by this power of his hand and brain to create manmade rain—yet humble as even a god must be under the burden of such power.' "

I honestly believe the only breath which could be discerned in that crowd after that was the one my mother let out. Now she locked her attention to her written sheets, and the words it gave her next were:

"Ben English is gone from us. He died in the summer of 1927, of a strained heart. Died, to say it plainly, of the work he put into this country, as so many have. My own father followed Ben English to the grave within three years. Some say that not a horse in the Two country has had a good looking-over since their passing." Which was one of the more barbed things she could have said to this audience, full as it was of guys who considered themselves pretty fancy horsemen. But she of course said it anyway and sailed on.

"Ben English is gone, and the English place stands empty across there, except for the echoes of the auctioneer's hammer." A comment with bigger barbs yet. Ted Muntz, whose First National Bank had foreclosed on the English place from the people Mrs. English sold it to, without doubt was somewhere in this audience. And all out among the picnic crowd I saw people shift restlessly, as if the memory of the foreclosure auctions, the Depression's hammer sales, was a sudden chafe.

My father by now was listening so hard he seemed to be frozen, an ice statue wearing the clothing of a man, which confirmed to me that not even he knew how far my mother was headed with this talk.

"English Creek is my second home," she was stating now as if someone was arguing the point with her, "for you all know that Noon Creek is where I was born and grew up. Two creeks, two valleys, two claims on my heart. Yet the pair are also day and night to me, as examples of what has happened to this country in my lifetime. Noon Creek now is all but empty of the families I knew there. Yes, there is still the Reese name on a Noon Creek ranch, I am proud as anything to say. And the Egan name, for it would be easier to dislodge the Rocky Mountains than Dill Egan. But the others, all the ranches down Noon Creek but one—all those are a roll call of the gone. The Torrance place: sold out at a loss, the family gone from here. The Emrich place: foreclosed on, the family gone from here. The Chute place: sold out at a loss, the family gone from here. Thad Wainwright's place, Thad one of the first cattlemen anywhere in this country: sold out at a loss, Thad passed away within a year. The Fain place: foreclosed on, the family gone from here. The Eiseley place: sold out at a loss, the family gone from here. The Nansen place." Here she paused, shook her head a little as if again disavowing Alec's news that this was where he and Leona would set up a household. "The Nansen place: foreclosed on, Carl dead by his own hand, Sigrid and the children gone from here to her parents in Minnesota."

What she was achieving was a feat I hadn't known could be done. While her words were expressing outright the fate of those Noon Creek ranching families, she was telling an equally strong tale with the unsaid. "All the ranches down Noon Creek but one" had been her phrase of indictment. Everybody in this park this day knew what "but one" meant; knew who ended up holding the land, by outright buy or by lease from the First National Bank of Gros Ventre, after each and every of those sales and foreclosures. A silent echo I suppose sounds like a contradiction in terms, yet I swear this was what my mother was ringing into the air: after every "sold—foreclosed—gone from here," the reverberating unspoken fact of that family ranch swallowed by the Double W.

"English Creek," she was going on, "thankfully has been spared the Noon Creek history, except once." We knew the next of her litany; it stared us in the face. "The English place. After Ben's death, sold to the Wyngard family who weren't able to make a go of it against the Depression. Foreclosed on, the Wyngards gone from here.

"A little bit ago, Max Vennaman said this is a day for friends and neighbors and families. So it is. And so too we must remember these friends and neighbors and families who are not among us today because they were done in by the times." This said with a skepticism that suggested the times had familiar human faces behind them.

"But an auction hammer can shatter only a household, not the gifts of the earth itself. While it may hurt the heart to see such places as the home of Ben English occupied only by time and the wind, English Creek is still the bloodstream of our valley. It flows its honest way"—the least little pause here, just enough to seed the distinction from those who prosper by the auction hammer—"while we try to find ours."

She looked up now, and out across us, all the islands of people. Either she had this last part by heart or was making it up as she went, because never once did she glance down at her sheaf of pages as she said it.

"There is much wrong with the world, and I suppose I am not known to be especially bashful about my list of those things. But I think it could not be more right that we honor in this valley a man who savvied the land and its livelihood, who honored the earth instead of merely coveting it. It could not be more right that tall Ben English in his black hat amid his green fields, coaxing a head of water to make itself into hay, is the one whose name this creek carries."

She folded her sheaf of papers once, then again, stuck them in the pocket of her dress and stepped down from the stump.

Everybody applauded, although a few a lot more lukewarmly than others. Under our tree we were all clapping hard and my father hardest of all, but I also saw him swallow in a large way. And when he realized I was watching him, he canted himself in my direction and murmured so that only I could hear: "That mother of yours."

Then she was back with us, taking compliments briskly. Pete studied her and said: "Decided to give the big boys some particular hell, didn't you?" Even Toussaint told her: "That was good, about the irrigating." But of us all, it was only to my father that she said, in what would have been a demand if there hadn't been the tint of anxiousness in it: "Well? What did you think?"

My father reached and with his forefinger traced back into place a banner of her hair that the creek breeze had lifted and lain across her ear.

"I think," he said, "I think that being married to you is worth all the risk."

I lead the world in respect for picnics, but I do have to say that one was enough to last me for a while.

Toussaint's murmur to me, my mother's speech to the universe. A person's thought can kite back and forth between those almost forever.

It was just lucky I now had specific matters to put myself to, fetching Mouse from where he was tethered and riding through the dispersing picnickers and heading on across the English Creek bridge to the rodeo grounds.

I was to meet Ray Heaney on the corral alongside the bucking chutes, the best seats in the arena if you didn't mind perching on a fence pole. Again this year my father drilled home to me his one point of rodeo etiquette. "Just so you stay up on that fence," he stipulated. "I don't want to see you down in there with the chute society." By which he meant the clump of fifteen or twenty hangers-on who always clustered around the gates of the bucking chutes, visiting and gossiping and looking generally important, and who regularly were cleared out of there two or three times every rodeo by rampaging broncs. When that happened, up onto anything climbable they all would scoot to roost, like hens with a weasel in their midst, and a minute or so after the bronc's passage they'd be right back in front of the chutes, preening and yakking again. I suppose the chute society offended my father's precept that a horse was nothing to be careless around. In any case, during the housecleanings when a bronc sent them scrambling for the fence it was my father's habit to cheer loudly for the bronc.

No Ray yet, at our fence perch. So I stayed atop Mouse and watched the world. In the pens behind the chutes the usual kind of before-rodeo confusion was going on, guys hassling broncs here and calves there, the air full to capacity with dust and bawling and whinnying. Out front, about half the chute society was already planted in place, tag-ends of their conversations mingling. "That SOB is so tight he wouldn't give ten cents to see Christ ride a bicycle backwards. . . . Oh hell yes, I'll take a quarter horse over a Morgan horse any time. Them Morgans are so damn hot-blooded. . . . With haying coming and one thing and another, I don't see how I'm ever going to catch up with myself. . . ."

I saw my mother and father and Pete and Marie and Toussaint— and Midge Withrow had joined them, though Dode wasn't yet in evidence—settling themselves at the far end of the grandstand, farthest from the dust the bucking horses would kick up.

Other people were streaming by, up into the grandstand or to sit on car fenders or the ground along the outside of the arena fence. I am here to recommend the top of a horse as an advantageous site to view mankind. Everybody below sees mostly the horse, not you.

Definitely I was ready for a recess from attention. From trying to judge whether people going by were nudging each other and whispering sideways, "That's him. That's the one. Got lit up like a ship in a storm, out there with that Stanley Meixell."

Keen as I could be, I caught nobody at it, at least for sure, and began to relax somewhat. Oh, I did get a couple of lookings-over. Lila Sedge drifted past in her moony way, spied Mouse and me, and circled us suspiciously a few times. And the priest Father Morrisseau knew me by sight from my stays with the Heaneys, and bestowed me a salutation. But both those I considered routine inspections, so to speak.

People kept accumulating, I kept watching. A Gros Ventre rodeo always is slower to get under way than the Second Coming.

Then I happened to remember. Not only was I royally mounted, I also was carrying wealth.

I nudged Mouse into action, to go do something about that four-bit piece my father had bestowed. Fifty whole cents. Maybe the Depression *was* on the run.

The journey wasn't far, just forty yards or so over to where, since Prohibition went home with Hoover, the Gros Ventre Rotary Club operated its beer booth. I swung down from Mouse and stepped to the plank counter. Behind it, they had several washtubs full of icewater and bottles of Kessler and Great Falls Select stashed down into the slush until only the brown necks were showing. And off to one side a little, my interest at the moment, the tub of soda pop.

One of the unresolved questions of my life at that age was whether I liked orange soda or grape soda better. It can be more of a dilemma than is generally realized: unlike, say, those picnic options of trout or fried chicken, you can't just dive in and have both. Anyway, I voted grape and was taking my first gulp when somebody inquired at my shoulder, "Jick, how's the world treating you?"

The inquirer was Dode Withrow, and his condition answered as to why he wasn't up in the grandstand with Midge and my folks and the others. As the expression goes, Dode had fallen off the wagon and was still bouncing. He was trigged out in a black sateen shirt and nice gray gabardine pants and his dress stockman Stetson, so he looked like a million. But he also had breath like the downwind side of a brewery.

"'Lo, Dode. You looking for Midge and the folks? They're down at the far end."

Dode shook his head as if he had water in his ears. "That wife of mine isn't exactly looking for me." So. It was one of the Withrow family jangles that Dode and Midge built up to about once a year. During them was the only time Dode seriously drank. Tomorrow there was going to be a lot of frost in the air between Midge and Dode, then the situation would thaw back to normal. It seemed to me a funny way to run a marriage; I always wondered what the three Withrow daughters, Bea and Marcella and Valerie, did with themselves during the annual temper contest between their parents. But this summer was showing that I had everything to learn about the ways of man and woman.

"Charlie, give me a couple Kesslers," Dode was directing across the beer counter. "Jick, you want one?"

"Uh, no thanks," dumbly holding up my grape soda the way a toddler would show off a lollipop.

"That stuff'll rot your teeth," advised Dode. "Give you goiter. St. Vitus' dance."

"Did you say two, Dode?" Charlie Hooper called from one of the beer tubs.

"I got two hands, don't I?"

While Dode paid and took a swig from one bottle while holding the other in reserve, I tried to calculate how far along he was toward being really drunk. Always tricky arithmetic. About all that could be said for sure was that of all the rodeo-goers who were going to get a skinful today, at this rate Dode was going to be among the earliest.

Dode tipped the Kessler down from his mouth and looked straight at me. Into me, it almost seemed. And offered: "Trade you."

I at first thought he meant his bottle of beer for my grape pop, and that befuddled me, for plainly Dode was in no mood for pop. But no, he had something other in mind, he still was gazing straight into my eyes. What he came out with next clarified his message, but did not ease my bafflement. "My years for yours, Jick. I'll go back where you are in life, you come up where I am. Trade, straight across. No, wait, I'll toss in Midge to boot." He laughed, but with no actual humor in it. Then shook his head again in that way as if he'd just come out from swimming. "That's in no way fair. Midge is okay. It's me—" he broke that off with a quick swig of Kessler.

What seemed needed was a change of topic, and I asked: "Where you watching the rodeo from, Dode? Ray and I are going to grab a fence place up there by the booth. Whyn't you sit with us?"

"Many thanks, Jick." He made it sound as if I had offered him knighthood. "But I'm going to hang around the pens awhile. Want to watch the broncs. All I'm good for any more. Watching." And off he swayed, beer bottle in each hand as if they were levers he was steering himself by. I hated to see Dode in such a mood, but at least he always mended quick. Tomorrow he would be himself, and probably more so, again.

Still no Ray on the fence. The Heaneys were taking their sweet time at the family shindig. When Ray ever showed up I would have to compare menus in detail with him, to see how the Heaneys could possibly outeat what we had gone through at the creek picnic.

By now my pop had been transferred from its bottle into me, and with time still to kill and figuring that as long as I had Mouse I might as well be making use of him, I got back up in the saddle.

I sometimes wonder: is the corner of the eye the keenest portion of the body? A sort of special sense, operating beyond the basic ones? For the corner of my right eye now registered, across the arena and above the filing crowd and top pole of the fence, a chokecherry-colored shirt; and atop that, a head and set of shoulders so erect they could not be mistaken.

I nudged Mouse into motion and rode around to Alec's side of the rodeo grounds.

When I got there Alec was off the horse, a big alert deep-chested blood bay, and was fussing with the loop of his lariat in that picky way that calf ropers do. All this was taking place out away from the arena fence and the parked cars, in some open space which Alec and the bay and the lariat seemed to claim as their own.

I dismounted too. And started things off with: "I overheard some calves talking, there in the pens. They were saying how much they admired anybody who'd rope them in a shirt like that."

"Jicker!" he greeted me back. "What do you know for sure?" Alec's words were about what they ever would have been, yet there hung that tone of absent-mindedness behind them again. I wanted to write it off to the fact that this brother of mine had calf roping on his mind just then. But I couldn't quite convince myself that was all there was to the matter.

It did occur to me to check whether Alec was wearing a bandanna this year, and he wasn't. Evidently my father at least had teased that off him permanently.

"Think you got a chance to win?" I asked, just to further the conversation.

"Strictly no problem," Alec assured me. All the fuss he was giving that rope said something else, however.

"How about Bruno Martin?" He was the young rancher from Augusta who had won the calf-roping the previous year.

"I can catch a cold faster than Bruno Martin can a calf."

"Vern Crosby, then?" Another quick-as-a-cat roper, who I had noticed warming up behind the chute pens.

"What, you taking a census or something?" Alec swooshed his lariat overhead, that expectant whir in the air, and cast a little practice throw.

I explored for some topic more congenial to him. "Where'd you get the highpowered horse?"

"Cal Petrie lent him to me." Cal Petrie was foreman of the Double W. Evidently Alec's ropeslinging had attracted some attention.

I lightly laid fingertips to the bay's foreshoulder. The feel of a horse is one of the best touches I know. "You missed the creek picnic. Mom spoke a speech."

Alec frowned at his rope. "Yeah. I had to put the sides on Cal's pickup and haul this horse in here. A speech? What about? How to sleep with a college book under your pillow and let it run uphill into your ear?"

"No. About Ben English."

"Ancient history, huh? Dad must have converted her." Alec looked like he intended to say more, but didn't.

There wasn't any logical reason why this should have been on my mind just then, but I asked: "Did you know he had a horse with the same name as himself?"

"Who? Had a what?"

"Ben English. Our granddad would say 'T'ank Godt vun of t'em vears a—'"

"Look, Jicker, I got to walk this horse loose. How about you doing me a big hairy favor?"

Something told me to be a little leery. "Ray's going to be waiting for me over on the—"

"Only take a couple minutes of your valuable time. All it is, I want you to go visit Leona for me while I get this horse ready."

"Leona? Where is she?"

"Down toward the end of the arena there, by her folks' car."

As indeed she was, when I turned to see. About a hundred feet from us, spectating this brotherly tableau. Leona in a clover-green blouse, that gold hair above like daybreak over a lush meadow.

"Yeah, well, what do you mean by visit?"

"Just go on over there and entertain her for me, huh?"

"Entert—?"

"Dance a jig, tell a joke." Alec swung into the saddle atop the bay. "Easy, hoss." I stepped back a bit and Mouse looked admiring as the bay did a little prance to try Alec out. Alec reined him under control and leaned toward me. "I mean it, about you keeping Leona company for me. Come get me if Earl Zane shows up. I don't want that jughead hanging around her."

Uh huh. Revelation, all twenty-two chapters of it.

"Aw, the hell, Alec. I—" was about to declare that I had other things in life to do than fetch him whenever one of Leona's ex-boyfriends came sniffing around. But that declaration melted somewhere before I could get it out, for here my way came one of those Leona smiles that would burn down a barn. Simultaneously she patted the car fender beside her.

While I still was molten in the middle of all that, Alec touched the bay roping horse into a fast walk toward some open country beyond the calf pens. So I figured there was nothing for it but go on over and face fate.

"'Lo, Leona."

"Hello, John Angus." Which tangled me right at the start. I mean, think about it. The only possible way in this world she could know about my high-toned name was from Alec. Which meant that I had been a topic of conversation between them. Which implied—I didn't know what. Damn it all to hell anyway. First Toussaint, now this. I merely was trying to have a standard summer, not provide word fodder for the entire damn Two country.

"Yeah, well. Great day for the race," I cracked to recoup.

Leona smiled yet another of her dazzlers. And said nothing. Didn't even inquire "What race?" so I could impart "The human race" and thereby break the ice and—

"You all by your lonesome?" I substituted. As shrewd as it was desperate, this. Not only did it fill the air space for a moment, I would truthfully tell Alec I had been vigilant about checking on whether or not Earl Zane was hanging around.

She shook her head. Try it sometime, while attempting to keep a full smile in place on your face. Leona could do it and come out with more smile than she started with. When she had accomplished this facial miracle she leaned my way a little and nodded her head conspiratorially toward the other side of the car.

Holy Jesus. Was Earl Zane over there? Earl Zane was Alec's size and built as if he'd been put together out of railroad ties. Alec hadn't defined to me this possibility, of Earl Zane already being on hand. What was I supposed to do, tip my hat to him and merrily say "Hi there, Earl, just stand where you are, I'll go get my brother so he can come beat the living daylights out of you"? Or better from the standpoint of my own health, climb back on Mouse and retreat to my original side of the arena?

For information's sake, I leaned around Leona and peered over the hood of the car. And was met by startled stares from Ted and Thelma Tracy—Leona's parents—and another couple with whom they were seated on a blanket and carrying on a conversation.

"Your folks are looking real good," I mumbled as I pulled my head back to normal. "Nice to see them so."

Leona, though, had shifted attention from me to the specimen of horseflesh at the other end of the reins I was holding. "Riding in style, aren't you?" she admired.

"His name is Mouse," I confided. "Though if he was mine, I'd call him, uh, Chief Joseph."

Leona slowly revolved her look from the horse to me, the way the beam of a lighthouse makes its sweep. Then asked: "Why not Crazy Horse?"

From Leona that was tiptop humor, and I yukked about six times as much as I ordinarily would have. And in the meantime was readying myself. After all, that brother of mine had written the prescription he wanted from me: entertain her.

"Boy, I'll have to remember that. And you know, that reminds me of one. Did you ever hear the joke about the Chinaman and the Scotchman in a rowboat on the Sea of Galilee?"

Leona shook her head. Luck was with me. This was my father's favorite joke, one I had heard him tell to other Forest Service guys twenty times; the heaviest artillery I could bring to bear.

"Well, see, there was a Chinaman and a Scotchman together in a rowboat on the Sea of Galilee. Fishing away, there. And after a while the Chinaman puts down his fishing pole and he leans over and nudges the

Scotchman and says, 'Jock, tell me. Is is true what they say about Occidental women?' And the Scotchman says, 'Occidental, hell. I'm cerrtain as anything that they behave the way they do on purrpose!'"

I absolutely believed I had done a royal job of telling, even burring the R's just right. But a little crimp of puzzlement now punctuated Leona's smiling face, right between her eyes. She asked: "The Sea of Galilee?"

I cast a wide look around for Alec. Or even Earl Zane, whom I would rather fight with one hand in my pocket than try to explain a joke to somebody who didn't get it. "Yeah. But you see, that isn't—"

Just then, Mouse got into the act. Why he could not have waited another two minutes until I had found a way to dispatch myself from Leona; why it didn't come into his horse brain any other time of the day up until that very moment; why—but no why about it, he was proceeding, directly in front of where Leona and I were sharing the fender, to take his leak.

The hose on a horse is no small sight anyway during this process. But with Leona there six feet away spectating, Mouse's seemed to poke down, down, down.

I cleared my throat and examined the poles of the arena fence and then the posts that supported the poles and then the sky over the posts and then crossed and uncrossed my arms a few times, and still the downpour continued. A wild impulse raised in me: Mouse's everlasting whiz reminded me of Dode Withrow spraddled atop that boulder the second day of this unprecedented summer, and I clamped my jaw to keep from blurting to Leona that scene and the handhold joke. That would be about like you, John Angus McCaskill. Celebrate disaster with a dose of social suicide. Do it up right.

Meanwhile Leona continued to serenely view the spectacle as if it was the fountains of Rome.

"I'll take over now, Jicker." Alec's voice came from behind us; he had circled outside of the arena on the bay horse. Peals of angel song could not have come more welcome. "How'd he do as company, Leona?"

Leona shined around at Alec, then turned back to bestow me a final glint. And answered: "He's a wonder."

I mounted up and cleared out of there; Alec and Leona all too soon would be mooning over each other like I didn't exist anyway; and as promptly as I was out of eyeshot behind the catch pen at the far end of the arena I gave Mouse a jab in the ribs that made him woof in surprise. Chief Joseph, my rosy hind end.

But I suppose my actual target was life. This situation of being old enough to be on the edge of everything and too young to get to the middle of any of it.

"Hi," Ray Heaney greeted as I climbed onto the arena fence beside him. The grin-cuts were deep into his face and the big front teeth were out on parade. Ray could make you feel that your arrival was the central event in his recent life. "What've you been up to?"

"Oh"—summary seemed so far out of the question, I chose neutrality—"about the usual. You?"

"Pilot again." So saying, Ray held up his hands to show his calluses. One hard oblong bump across the base of each finger, like sets of knuckles on his palms. I nodded in commendation. My shovel calluses were mosquito bites in comparison. This made the second summer Ray was stacking lumber in his father's lumber yard—the "pile it here, pile it there" nature of that job was what produced the "pilot" joke—and his hands and forearms were gaining real heft.

Now Ray thrust his right mitt across to within reach of mine. "Shake the hand that shook the hand?" he challenged. It was a term we had picked up from his father—Ray could even rumble it just like Ed Heaney's bass-drum voice—who remembered it from his own boyhood in Butte when guys still went around saying "Shake the hand that shook the hand of John L. Sullivan," the heavyweight boxing champ of then.

I took Ray up on the hand duel, even though I pretty well knew how this contest of ours was going to turn out from now on. We made a careful fit of the handshake grip; then Ray chanted the start, "One, two, *three.*"

After about a minute of mutual grunted squeezing, I admitted: "Okay. I'm out-squoze."

"You'll get me next time," Ray said. "Didn't I see Alec riding around acting like a calf roper?"

Some years before, Ed Heaney had driven out from Gros Ventre to the ranger station one summer Saturday to talk forest business with my father. And with him, to my surprise and no little consternation, came his son my age, Ray. I could see perfectly damn well what was intended here, and that's the way it did happen. Off up the South Fork our fathers rode to eyeball a stand of timber which interested Ed for buck-rake teeth he could sell at his lumber yard, and Ray and I were left to entertain one another.

Living out there at English Creek I always was stumped about what of my existence would interest any other boy in the world. There was the knoll with the view all the way to the Sweetgrass Hills, but some-how I felt that might not hold the fascination for others that it did for me. Ordinarily horses would have been on hand to ride, the best solu-tion to the situation, but the day before, Isidor Pronovost and some CCC guys had taken all the spare ones in a big packstring to set up a spike camp for a tree-planting crew. Alec was nowhere in the picture as a possible ally; this was haying time and he was driving the scatter rake for Pete Reese. The ranger station itself was no refuge; the sun was out and my mother would never let us get away with lolling around inside, even if I could think up a reasonable loll. Matters were not at all improved by the fact that, since I still was going to the South Fork grade school and Ray went in Gross Ventre, we only knew each other by sight.

He was a haunting kid to look at. His eyes were within long deep-set arcs, as if always squinched the way you do to thread a needle. And curved over with eyebrows which wouldn't need to have been much thicker to make a couple of respectable blond mustaches. And then a flattish nose which, wide as it was, barely accommodated all the freck-les assigned to it. When Ray really grinned—I didn't see that this first day, although I was to see it thousands of times in the years ahead—deep slice-lines cut his cheeks, out opposite the corners of his mouth. Like a big set of parentheses around the grin. His lower lip was so full that it too had a slice-line under it. This kid looked more as if he'd been carved out of a pumpkin than born. Also, even more so than a lot of us at that age, his front teeth were far ahead of the rest of him in size. In any schoolyard there always were a lot of traded jibes of "Beaver tooth!" but Ray's frontals really did seem as if they'd been made for toppling willows.

As I say, haunting. I have seen grown men, guys who ordinarily wouldn't so much as spend a glance at a boy on the street, stop and study that face of Ray's. And here he was, thank you a whole hell of a lot, my guest for this day at English Creek.

So we were afoot with one another and not knowing what to do about it, and ended up wandering the creek bank north of the ranger station, with boredom building up pretty fast in both of us. Finally, I got the idea of showing him the pool a little ways downstream in English Creek where brook trout always could be seen, hanging there dark in the clear water. In fact, I asked Ray if he felt like fishing, but for some reason he looked at me a little suspiciously and mumbled, "Huh uh."

We viewed the pool, which took no time at all, and then thrashed on along in the creek brush for awhile, just to be doing anything. It was semi-swampy going, so at least we could concentrate on jumping across the wet holes. Ray was dressed in what I suppose his mother thought were old enough clothes to go into the country with, but his old clothes were so noticeably ritzier than my everyday ones that he maybe was embarrassed about that. Anyway, for whatever reason, he put up with this brushwhacking venture of mine.

Whacked was what he got. My mind was on something else, likely how much of the day still gaped ahead of us, and without thinking I let a willow spring back as I pushed past it. It whipped Ray across the left side of his face and drew a real yelp from him. Also a comment to me:

"Watch out with those, beetle brain."

"Didn't mean to," I apologized. Which most likely would have buried the issue, except for what I felt honor bound to add next: "Sparrow head."

You wonder afterwards how two reasonably sane people descend into a slanging match like that.

"Slobberguts," Ray upped the ante with.

"Booger eater," I promptly gave him back.

"Pus gut."

"Turd bird."

As I remember it, I held myself in admirable rein until Ray came out with "turkey dink."

For some reason that one did it. I swung on Ray and caught him just in front of the left ear. Unluckily, not quite hard enough to knock him down.

He popped me back, alongside the neck. We each got in a few more swings, then the fisticuffs degenerated into a wrestle. More accurately, a mud wallow.

We each were strong enough, and outraged enough, to be able to tip the other, so neither one of us ended up permanently on top. Simply, at some point we wore out on wanting to maul one another any further, and got to our feet. Ray's clothes looked as if he'd been rolled the length of a pig pen. Mine I guess weren't much better, but they hadn't started off as fancy and so I figured my muss didn't matter as much.

Of course, try convince my mother of that. Come noon we had to straggle in to get any dinner, and when she laid eyes on us, we were in for a scouring in more ways than one. Ray she made change into a set of my clothes—funny, how improved he looked when he was out of that town gear—and sat us at opposite ends of the table while we ate, then immediately afterward she issued two decrees: "Jick, I believe you would like To Read in the Other Room. Ray, I think you would like To Put Together the Jigsaw Puzzle I Am Going to Put Here on the Table for You."

When I started high school in Gros Ventre, Ray came over to me at noon hour the first day. He planted himself just out of arm's reach from me and offered: "Horse apple."

I balled up both my fists, and my tongue got ready the words which would fan our creekside battle to life again: "Beaver tooth." Yet the direction of Ray's remark caught my notice. "Horse apple" was pretty far back down the scale from "turkey dink."

For once in my life I latched on to a possibility. I held my stance and tendered back to Ray: "Mud minnow."

It started a grin on him while he thought up: "Slough rat."

"Gumbo gopher," I provided, barely managing to get it out before we were both laughing.

Within the week I was asking my mother whether I could stay in town overnight with Ray, and after that I made many a stay-over at the Heaneys' throughout the school year. Not only did I gain the value of Ray and me being the best of friends; it was always interesting to me that the Heaneys were a family as different from ours as crochet from oil cloth. For one thing they were Catholic, although they really didn't display it all that much. Just through a grace before every meal and a saint here and there on the wall and eating fish on Friday, which eventually occurred to me as the reason Ray had looked at me suspiciously there at the creek when I asked him about fishing. For another, in almost every imaginable way the Heaney family was as tidy as spats on a rooster. (The "almost" was this: Ray and his sister Mary Ellen, three years younger, were allowed liberties with their food that I'd never dreamt of. Take hotcakes as an example. Ray and Mary Ellen poured some syrup on, then rolled each hotcake up, then syruped the outside and began eating. A kind of maple syrup tamale, I now know enough to realize. When I first began overnighting with them they urged me to try mine that way, but the thought of my mother's response to something like that made me figure I might as well not get converted. At other meals too Ray and Mary Ellen squooged their food around in remarkable ways and ate only as much of it as they felt like. I tell you, it shocked me: people my own age leaving plates that looked more as if they'd been walked through than eaten from.) Ray's mother, Genevieve, kept that big two-story house dusted and doilied to a faretheewell. Mary Ellen already had her mind set on being a nurse—she was a kind of starchy kid anyway, so it was a good enough idea—and you couldn't scratch a finger around there without her wanting to daub it with Mercurochrome and wrap you up like a mummy.

Then there was Ray's father, Ed. You could hang your hat on Ed Heaney's habits. Every evening he clicked the lock on the door of the lumber yard office as if it was the final stroke needed to complete six o'clock, and if he wasn't walking in the kitchen door at five minutes after six, Genevieve started peering out the kitchen window to see what had happened to him. Another five minutes, Ed washing up and toweling down, and supper began. As soon as supper was over Ed sat at the kitchen table going through the Falls *Leader* and visiting with Genevieve while she did the dishes, his deep voice and her twinkly one, back and forth, back and forth. Then at seven straight up, Ed strode into the living room, planted himself in his rocking chair and clicked on the big Silvertone floor radio. He listened straight through until ten o'clock— if somebody spouting Abyssinian had come on the air, Ed would have sat there and listened—and then went up to bed. Thus everything in the Heaney household in the evening was done against the backdrop of Ed's Silvertone, and Genevieve and Ray and Mary Ellen had become so used to tuning out sound that you often had to say something to them a couple of times to make it register. In Ray, there was an opposite kind of consequence, too. Ray had heard so much radio he could mimic just about any of it, Eddie Cantor and Walter Winchell and Kaltenborn giving the news and all those.

But Ed, I was telling about. You couldn't know it to look at Ed Heaney, because the lumber yard life had put a middle on him, and he was bald as a jug, but he served in France during the war. In fact spent I don't know how much time in the trenches. Enough that he didn't want to squander one further minute of his life talking about it, evidently. Just once did I ever manage to get him going on that topic. That Ed won some medals over there I knew because Ray once sneaked them out of a dresser drawer in Ed and Genevieve's bedroom and showed them to me. You wouldn't expect medal-winning about Ed either. In any case, though, one Heaney suppertime when I was in to stay with Ray some topic came up that emboldened me to outright ask Ed what he remembered most about being in the war. Figuring, of course, I might hear tales that led to the medals.

"Shaving."

After a while Ed glanced up from his eating and realized that Ray and Mary Ellen and Genevieve and I were all regarding him in a stymied way.

"We had to shave every day," he elaborated. "Wherever we were. Belleau Wood, we only got a canteen of water per man per day. But we still used some of it to shave. The gas masks they gave us were a French kind. Sort of a sack that went over your face like this." Ed ran a hand around his chinline. "If you had whiskers it didn't fit tight enough. Gas would get in. You'd be a goner."

Ed began to take another bite of his supper, but instead repeated: "Belleau Wood. About midday there we'd be in our foxholes—graves, we called them—all of us shaving, or holding our shirts up to read them for lice. Thousands of us, all doing one or the other."

The other four of us waited, dumbstruck, to see where this sudden hallway of Ed's memory led.

But all he said more was "Pass the stringbeans, please."

Now that we were established atop the arena corral, I reported to Ray my chin session with Dode Withrow at the beer booth. Ray took what might be called a spectator interest in the Withrow family. He never came right out and said so, but his eye was on the middle Withrow girl, Marcella, who was in the same high school class we were. Marcella was trim in figure like Midge and had a world-by-the-tail grin like Dode's usual one. So far Ray's approach to Marcella was distant admiration, but I had the feeling he was trying to figure out how to narrow the distance.

Maybe the day would come when I was more interested in a Leona or a Marcella than in perching up there above general humanity, but right then I doubted it. I considered that the top-pole perch Ray and I had there next to the bucking chutes was the prime site of the whole rodeo grounds. We had clear view of every inch of the arena, the dirt oval like a small dry lake bed before us. And all the event action would originate right beside us, where even now the broncs for the first section of bareback riding were being hazed into the chutes alongside my corral spot. The particular Gros Ventre bucking chute setup was that as six broncs at a time were hazed in for their set of riders, pole panels were retracted between each chute, leaving what had been the half-dozen chutes as one long narrow pen. Then as the horses crowded in a single file, the panels were shoved in place behind them one by one, penning each bronc into the chute it would buck into the arena from. As slick a system as there is for handling rodeo broncs, I suppose. But what is memorable to me about it is the instant before the pole panels were shoved into place to serve as chute dividers: when the horses came swarming into the open chute pen, flanks heaving, heads up and eyes glittering. From my perch, it was like looking down through a transom into a long hallway suddenly filled with big perplexed animals. Not many sights are its equal.

Above and to the left of Ray and me was the announcing booth and its inhabitants, a nice proximity which added to the feeling that we were part of the inside happenings of the rodeo. To look at, the booth resembled a little woodshed up on stilts, situated there above and just in back of the middle of the bucking chutes. It held elbow room for maybe six people, although only three of the booth crowd did any actual rodeo work. Tollie Zane, if you could call his announcing work. Tollie evidently was in residence at the far end of the booth, angled out of view from us but a large round microphone like a waffle iron standing on end indicated his site. Then nearest to us was the scorekeeper, Bill Reinking, editor of the *Gleaner*, prominent with his ginger mustache and silver-wire eyeglasses. I suppose he did the scorekeeping on the principle that the only sure way for the *Gleaner* to get any accuracy on the rodeo results was for him to originate the arithmetic. Between Bill and Tollie was the space for the timekeeper, who ran the stopwatch to time the events and blew the whistle to signal when a bronc rider had lasted eight seconds atop a bareback or ten in a saddle ride. The timekeeper's spot in the booth was empty, but this was about to be remedied.

"Wup wup wup," some Paul Revere among the chute society cried. "Here she comes, boys! Just starting up the ladder!"

Heads swiveled like weathervanes hit by a tornado. And yes, Ray and I also sent our eyes around to the little ladder along the side of the announcing booth and the hypnotizing progress up it of Velma Simms.

"Tighter than last year, I swear to God," someone below us was contending.

"Like the paper fits the wall," testified another.

And yet another, "But I still need to know, how the hell does she get herself into those britches?"

Velma Simms came of Eastern money. Plumbing equipment I believe was its source; I have seen her family name, Croake, on hot-and-cold spigots. And in a community and era which considered divorce usually more grievous than manslaughter, she had been through three husbands. That we knew of. Only the first was local, the lawyer Paul Bogan. They met in Helena when he got himself elected to the legislature, and if my count is right, it was at the end of his second term when Velma arrived back to Gros Ventre and Paul stayed over there at the capital in some kind of state job. Her next husband was a fellow named Sutter, who'd had an automobile agency in Spokane. In Gros Ventre he was like a trout out of water, and quickly went. After him came Simms, an actor Velma happened across in some summer performance at one of the Glacier Park lodges. By February of his first Two country winter Simms was hightailing his way to California, although he eventually did show up back in Gros Ventre, so to speak, as one of the cattle rustlers in a Gene Autry movie at the Odeon. Lately Velma seemed to have given up marrying and instead emerged each Fourth with a current beau tagging along. They tended to be like the scissorbill following her up the ladder now, in a gabardine stockman's suit and a too clean cream Stetson, probably a bank officer from Great Falls. I cite all this because Paul Bogan, the first in the genealogy, always had served as rodeo timekeeper, and the next Fourth of July after his change of residence, here Velma presented herself, bold as new paint, to take up his stopwatch and whistle. It was her only instance of what might be called civic participation, and quite why she did it nobody had a clue. But Velma's ascension to the booth now was part of every Gros Ventre rodeo. Particularly for the male portion of the audience. For as you may have gathered, Velma on her Fourth appearances was encased in annual new slacks of stunning snugness. One of the theoreticians in the chute society just now was postulating a fresh concept, that maybe Velma heated them with an iron, put them on hot, and let them shrink down on her like the rim onto a wagon wheel.

I saw once, in recent years at the Gros Ventre rodeo, a young bronc rider and his ladyfriend watching the action through the pole arena gate. They each held a can of beer in one hand, and the rider's other hand was around the girl's shoulders. *Her* other hand, though, was down resting lightly on his rump, the tips of her fingers just touching the inseam of his Levis back there. I'll admit to you, it made my heart turn around and face north. That the women now can and will do such a thing seems to me an advance like radio. My awe of it is tempered only by the regret that I am not that young man, or any other. But let that go. My point here is just that in the earlier time, only rare self-advertised rumps such as that of Velma Simms were targets of public interest, and then only by what my father and the other rangers called ocular examination.

It registered on me there had been a comment from Ray's direction. "Come again?" I apologized.

"No hitch in Velma's gitalong," Ray offered one more time.

I said something equally bright in agreement, but I was surprised at Ray making an open evaluation of Velma Simms, even so tame a one as that. The matter of Marcella maybe was on his mind more than I figured.

Just then an ungodly noise somewhere between a howl and a yowl issued above us. A sort of high HHHRUNGHHH like a cat was being skinned alive. I was startled as hell, but Ray knew its source. "You see Tollie's loudspeaking getup?" he inquired with a nod toward the top of the announcer's booth. I couldn't help but have noticed such a rig. The contraption was a pyramid of rods, which held at its peak a half-dozen big metal cones like those morning-glory horns on old phonographs, pointing to various points of the compass. Just in case those didn't cover the territory, there was a second set of four more 'glory horns a couple of feet beneath. "He sent off to Billings for it," informed Ray, who had overheard this information when Tollie came to the lumber yard for a number of two-by-fours to help brace the contraption into place. "The guy who makes them down there told him it's the real deal to announce with."

We were not the only ones contemplating Tollie's new announcing machinery. "What the goddamn hell's Tollie going to do," I heard somebody say below us, "tell them all about it in Choteau?" Choteau was thirty-three miles down the highway.

"WELCOME!" crackled a thunderblast of voice over our heads. "To the Gros Ventre rodeo! Our fifteenth annual show! You folks are wise as hooty owls to roost with us here today. Yes sir! Some of everything is liable to happen here today and—" Tollie Zane, father of the famous Earl, held the job of announcing the Gros Ventre rodeo on the basis by which a lot of positions of authority seem to get filled: nobody else would be caught dead doing it. But before this year, all that the announcing amounted to was shouting through a megaphone the name of each bucking horse and its rider. The shiny new 'glory horns evidently had gone to Tollie's head, or at least his tonsils. "The Fourth of July is called the cowboys' Christmas and our festivities here today will get under way in just—"

"Called what?" somebody yelled from the chute society. "That's Tollie for you, sweat running down his face and he thinks it's snowflakes."

"Santy Claus must have brought him that goddamn talking contraption," guessed somebody else.

"Naw, you guys, lay off now," a third one put in. "Tollie's maybe right. It'd explain why he's as full of shit as a Christmas goose."

Everybody below us hee-heeed at that while Tollie roared on about the splendiferous tradition of rodeo and what heart-stopping excitement we were going to view in this arena today. Tollie was a kind of plodding talker anyway, and now with him slowed down either out of respect for the new sound system or because he was translating his remarks from paper—this July Christmas stuff was originating from somewhere; had a kit come with the 'glory horns and microphone?—you could about soft-boil an egg between parts of his sentences.

"Anybody here from Great Falls?"

Quite a number of people yelled and waved their hands.

"Welcome to America!"

Out in the crowd there were laughs and groans. And most likely some flinching in the Rotary beer booth; a real boon to business, Tollie cracking wise at the expense of people who'd had ninety miles of driving time to wonder whether this rodeo was worth coming to.

But this seemed to be a day when Tollie, armed with amplification, was ready to take on the world. "How about North Dakota? Who's here from North Dakota?"

Of course, no response. Tourists were a lot scarcer in those days, and the chances that anybody would venture from North Dakota just to see the Gros Ventre rodeo were zero and none.

"That's right!" blared Tollie. "If I was you I wouldn't admit it neither!"

Tollie spieled on for a while, actually drawing boos from the Choteau folks in the crowd when he proclaimed that Choteau was known as a town without a single bedbug: "No sir they are all married and have big families!" At last, though, the handling crew was through messing with the chute alongside Ray and me, and Tollie was declaring "We are just about to get the pumpkin rolling. Bareback riding will be our first event."

"Pumpkin?" questioned whoever it was in the chute society that was keeping tab of Tollie's excursions through the calendar. "Judy H. Christ! Now the whistledick thinks it's Halloween."

About all that is worth mentioning of the early part of the rodeo is that its events, a section of bareback riding and after that some steer-wrestling or mauling or whatever you want to call it, passed fairly mercifully. Ray and I continued to divide our time snorting laughs over something either Tollie or the chute society provided. Plus our own wiseacre efforts, of course. Ray nearly fell off the corral from cackling when I speculated whether this much time sitting on a fence pole mightn't leave a person with the crack in his behind running crosswise instead of up and down. You know how that is: humor is totally contagious when two persons are in the same light mood. And a good thing, too, for by my estimation the actual events of a rodeo can always use all the help they can get. Although like anybody out here I have seen many and many a rodeo, to me the arena events are never anything to write home special about. It's true that bareback riding has its interesting moments, but basically the ride is over and done with about as it's getting started. I don't know, a guy flopping around on the naked back of a horse just seems to me more of a stunt than a sport. As for steer-wrestling, that is an absolutely phony deal, never done except there in front of a rodeo crowd. Leaping onto a running steer has about as much to do with actual cattle ranching as wearing turquoise belt buckles does. And that calf-roping. Calf-roping I nominate as an event the spectators ought to be paid for sitting through. I mean, here'll come one yayhoo out after the calf swinging a community loop an elephant could trot through, and the next guy will pitch a loop so teeny that it bounces off the back of the calf's neck like a spitwad. Whiff whiff whiff, and then a burst of cussing as the rope-flinger's throw misses its mark: there is the essence of rodeo calf-roping. If I ran the world there'd be standards, such as making any calf-roping entrant dab onto a fencepost twenty feet away, just to prove he knows how to build a decent loop.

"Alec's bringing his horse in," Ray reported from his sphere of the arena. "Guess he's roping in this section."

"So's everybody else in the world, it looks like." Horsemen and hemp, hemp and horsemen. It was a wonder the combined swishing of the ropes of all the would-be calf ropers now assembling didn't lift the rodeo arena off the ground like an autogyro. As you maybe can tell, my emotions about having a brother forthcoming into this event were strictly mixed. Naturally I was pulling for Alec to win. Brotherly blood is at least that thick. Yet a corner of me was shadowed with doubt as to whether victory was really such a good idea for Alec. Did he need any more confirming in his cowboy mode? Especially in this dubious talent of hanging rope necklaces onto slobbering calves?

This first section of the calf-roping now proceeded about as I could have foretold, a lot of air fanned with rope but damn few calves collared. One surprise was produced, though. After a fast catch Bruno Martin of Augusta missed his tie, the calf kicking free before its required six seconds flat on the ground were up. If words could be seen in the air, some blue dandies accompanied Martin out of the arena.

The other strong roper, Vern Crosby, snagged his calf neatly, suffered a little trouble throwing him down for the tie, but then niftily gathered the calf's legs and wrapped the pigging string around them, as Tollie spelled out for us, "faster   than   Houdini   can   tie his   shoe   laces!"

So when the moment came for Alec to guide the blood bay roping horse into the break-out area beside the calf chute, the situation was as evident as Tollie's voice bleating from that tin bouquet of 'glory horns:

"Nineteen   seconds   by Vern   Crosby   is still the time   to beat.   It'll take   some fancy   twirling by this   next   young   buckaroo.   One of   the hands   out at   the Double   W   he's getting   hisself   squared away   and   will be   ready   in just—"

The calf chute and the break-out area where each roper and his horse burst out after the creature were at the far end of the bucking chutes from us. Ray cupped his hands and called across to there: "Wrap him up pretty, Alec!"

Across there, Alec appeared a little nervous, dandling his rope around more than was necessary as he and the bay horse waited for their calf to emerge. But then I discovered I was half nervous myself, jiggling my foot on its corral pole, and I had no excuse whatsoever. You wouldn't catch me out there trying to snare a two-hundred-pound animal running full tilt.

The starter's little red flag whipped down, and the calf catapulted from the chute into the expanse of the arena.

Alec's luck. Sometimes you had to think he held the patent on four-leaf clovers and rabbit's feet. The calf he drew was a straight runner instead of a dodger. Up the middle of the arena that calf galloped as if he was on rails, the big horse gaining ground on him for Alec every hoofbeat. And I believe that if you could have pulled the truth from my father and mother right then, even they would have said that Alec looked the way a calf roper ought to. Leaning forward but still as firm in his stirrups as if socketed into them, swinging the loop of the lariat around and around his head strongly enough to give it a good fling but not overdoing it. Evidently there had been much practice performed on Double W calves as Alec rode the coulees these past weeks.

"Dab it on him!" I heard loudly, and realized the yell had been by me.

Quicker than it can be told Alec made his catch. A good one, where all the significant actions erupt together: the rope straightening into a tan line in the air, the calf gargling out a *bleahh* as the loop choked its neck and yanked it backward, Alec evacuating from the stirrups in his dismount. Within a blink he was in front of the tall bay horse and scampering beside the stripe of rope the bay was holding taut as fish-line, and now Alec was upending the calf into the arena dust and now gathering calf legs and now whipping the pigging string around them and now done.

"The time   for Alec   McCaskill"—I thought I could hear gloom inside the tinny blare of Tollie's voice, and so knew the report was going to be good—"seventeen   and   a half   seconds."

The crowd whooped and clapped. Over at the far fence Leona was beaming as if she might ignite, and down at the end of the grandstand my parents were glumly accepting congratulations on Alec. Beside me Ray was as surprised as I was by Alec's first-rate showing, and his delight didn't have the conditions attached that mine did.

"How much is up?" he wondered. I wasn't sure of the roping prize myself, so I asked the question to the booth, and Bill Reinking leaned out and informed us, "Thirty dollars, and supper for two at the Sedgwick House."

"Pretty slick," Ray admired. I had to think so myself. Performance is performance, whatever my opinion of Alec's venue of it. Later in the afternoon there would be one more section of calf ropers, but with the main guys, Bruno Martin and Vern Crosby, already behind him, Alec's leading time looked good enough to take to the bank.

Tollie was bleating onward. "Now we turn to some prairie sailors and the hurricane deck," which translated to the first go-round of saddle bronc riding. I will say for saddle bronc riding that it seems to me the one rodeo event that comes close to legitimate. Staying on a mount that is trying to unstay you is a historic procedure of the livestock business. "The boys are hazing the ponies into the chutes and when we commence and get started the first man out will be Bill Semmler on a horse called Conniption. In this meanwhile though did you hear the one about the fellow who goes into the barber shop and—"

I never did get to hear Tollie's tonsorial tale, for I happened to glance down to my left into the bucking chutes and see disaster in a spotted horsehide charging full tilt at me.

"Hang on!" I yelled to Ray and simultaneously flipflopped myself rightward and dropped down the fence so that I had my arms clamped around both the top corral pole and Ray's hips.

Ray glommed tight to the pole with his hands. WHOMP! and a clatter. The impact of the pinto bucking horse slamming into the chute end where our section of corral cornered into it went shuddering through the pair of us, as if a giant sledgehammer had hit the wood; but our double gripping kept us from being flung off the top of the fence.

"Jesus!" Ray let out, rare for him. "There's a goosy one!"

Our narrow brush did not escape microphone treatment. "This little Coffee Nerves pinto down at chute six has a couple of fence squatters hugging the wood pretty good!" Tollie was alerting the world. "We'll see whether they go ahead and kiss it!"

"Numbnuts," I muttered in the direction of the Zane end of the announcing booth. Or possibly more than muttered, for when I managed to glower directly up there, Bill Reinking was delivering me a certifying wink and Velma Simms was puckered the way a person does to hold in a laugh.

Ray had it right, the pinto was truly riled and then some, as I could confirm while cautiously climbing back onto my perch and locking a firm arm around the corner post between chute and corral. No way was I going to take a chance on being dislodged down into the company of this Coffee Nerves bronc. The drawback of this flood-the-chutes-with-horses system was that the first horse in was the last to come out, from this end chute next to me. While the initial five horses were being bucked out Coffee Nerves was going to be cayusing around in chute six and trying to raise general hell.

The pinto looked more than capable. Coffee Nerves had close-set pointy ears; what are called pin ears, and indicate orneriness in a horse. Worse, he was hog-eyed. Had small darty eyes that shot looks at the nearest threat all the time. Which, given my position on the fence, happened to be me. I had not been the target of so much eyeball since the tussle to get that Bubbles pack horse up the side of the mountain.

Ray was peering behind me to study Coffee Nerves, so he was the one who noticed. "Huh! Look who must've drew him."

There in back of chute six, Earl Zane was helping the handlers try to saddle the pinto.

My session of watchdogging Leona for Alec of course whetted my interest in the matter of Earl Zane, whom I ordinarily wouldn't bat an eye to look at. Now here he loomed, not ten feet away from Ray and me, at the rear of Coffee Nerves' chute amid the cussing crew of handlers trying to contend with the pinto and the saddle that was theoretically supposed to go on its back. Earl Zane had one of those faces that could be read at a glance: as clear as the label on a maple sugar jug it proclaimed SAP. I suppose he was semi-goodlooking in a sulky kind of way. But my belief was that Earl Zane's one known ability, handling horses, derived from the fact that he possessed the identical amount of brain as the average horse did and they thus felt affinity with him. Though whether Coffee Nerves, who was whanging a series of kicks to the chute lumber that I could feel arrive up through the corral pole I was seated in, was going to simmer down enough to accommodate Earl Zane or anybody else remained an open question.

In any case, I was transfixed by what was brewing here. Alec looked likely to win the calf-roping. Coffee Nerves gave every sign of being the buckingest saddle bronc, if Earl could stay on him. Two winners, one Leona. The arithmetic of that was something to contemplate.

Various geezers of the chute society were peering in at Coffee Nerves and chiming "Whoa, hoss" and "Here now, knothead, settle down," which was doing nothing to improve the pinto's disposition. After all, would it yours?

Distracted by the geezer antics and the Earl-Alec equation, I didn't notice the next arrival until Ray pointed out, "Second one of the litter."

Indeed, Earl Zane had been joined in the volunteer saddling crew by his brother Arlee, the one a year ahead of Ray and me in school. Another horse fancier with brain to match. And full to overflowing with the Zane family swagger, for Arlee Zane was a big pink specimen: about what you'd get if you could coax a hog to strut around on its hind legs wearing blue jeans and a rodeo shirt. Eventually maybe Arlee would duplicate Earl, brawny instead of overstuffed. But at present there just was too much of all of him, up to and including his mouth. At the moment, for instance, Arlee had strutted around to the far side of the announcing booth and was yelping up to his sire: "Tell them to count out the prize money! Old Earl is going to set his horse on fire!" God, those Zanes did think they were the ding-dong of the world's bell.

"How about a bottle of something?" I proposed to Ray. The mental strain of being around three Zanes at once must have been making me thirsty. "I'm big rich, I'll buy."

"Ace high," Ray thought this sounded, and added that he'd hold our seats. Down I climbed, and away to the beer booth again. The tubs weren't showing many Kessler and Select necks by now. I half expected to coincide with Dode again, but didn't. But by the time I returned to Ray with our two bottles of grape, I was able to more or less offhand-edly report that I had seen Marcella and the other Withrow daughters, in the shade under the grandstand with a bunch more of the girls we went to school with. Leona on one side of the arena, Marcella and the school multitude on the other, Velma Simms in the air behind us; I did have to admit, lately the world was more full of females than I had ever previously noticed.

"Under way   again." Tollie was issuing forth. "A   local buckaroo   coming out   of chute   number   one—"

Bill Semmler made his ride but to not much total, his bronc a straight bucker who crowhopped down the middle of the arena in no particu-larly inspired way until the ten seconds were up and the whistle blew.

"Exercise," commented Ray, meaning that was all Semmler was going to get out of such a rocking-horse ride.

At that, though, exercise was more than what was produced by the next rider, an out-of-town guy whose name I didn't recognize. Would-be rider, I ought to say, for a horse called Ham What Am sailed him onto the earth almost before the pair of them issued all the way out the gate of chute two. Ham What Am then continued his circuit of the arena, kicking dirt twenty feet into the air with every buck, while the ostensible rider knelt and tried to get any breath back into himself.

"Let's give   this   hard luck   cowboy   a—big hand!" Tollie advocated. "He sure   split a   long crack   in the air   that time."

"You guys see any crack out there in the air?" somebody below us inquired. "Where the hell is Tollie getting that stuff?"

"Monkey Ward," it was suggested. "From the same page featuring toilet paper."

But then one of the Rides Proud brothers from up at Browning, one or another of Toussaint's army of grand-nephews he wasn't on speaking terms with, lived up to his name and made a nice point total atop a chunky roan called Snuffy. Sunfishing was Snuffy's tactic, squirming his hind quarters to one side and then the other with each jump, and if the rider manages to stay in tune with all that hula wiggling it yields a pretty ride. This performance was plenty good enough to win the event, unless Earl Zane could do something wonderful on top of Coffee Nerves.

Following the Rides Proud achievement, the crowd laughed as they did each year when a little buckskin mare with a flossy mane was announced as Shirley Temple, and laughed further when the mare piled the contestant, some guy from Shelby, with its third jump.

"That Shirley   for a little   gal   she's got   a mind of her   own," bayed Tollie, evidently under the impression he was providing high humor. Then, sooner than it seemed possible for him to have drawn sufficient breath for it, he was giving us the next loud-speaker   dose.   "Now here   is a rider   I have   some acquaintance with.   Getting set   in chute   number five on Dust Storm   Earl Zane.   Show them   how   Earl!"

So much for assuming the obvious. Earl had not drawn the pinto; his and Arlee's participation in saddling it was only the Zane trait of sticking a nose into anything available.

The fact remained, though, that Alec's rival was about to bounce out into the arena aboard a bucking animal. I craned my neck trying to get a look at Leona, but she was turned in earnest conversation with a certain calf roper wearing a chokecherry shirt and I could only see a golden floss. Quite a wash of disappointment went through me. Somehow I felt I was missing the most interesting scene of the entire rodeo, Leona's face, just then.

"And here   he comes   a cowboying   sonofagun   and a son   of   yours truly—"

In fairness, I will say Earl Zane got a bad exit from the chute, the cinnamon-colored bronc he was on taking a little hop into the arena and stopping to gaze around at the world just as Earl was all primed for him to buck. Then as it sank in on Earl that the horse wasn't bucking and he altered the rhythm of his spurring to fit that situation, Dust Storm began to whirl. A spin to the left. Then one to the right. It was worth the admission to see, Earl's thought process clanking one direction and the horse's the other, then each reversing and passing one another in the opposite direction, like two drunks trying to find each other in a revolving door. The cinnamon bronc, though, was always one phase ahead of Earl, and his third whirl, which included a sort of sideways dip, caused Earl to lurch and lose the opposite stirrup. It was all over then, merely a matter of how promptly Earl would keep his appointment with the arena dirt.

"Blew a stirrup" came from the chute society as Earl picked himself up off the planet and the whistle was heard. "Ought've filled those stirrups with chewing gum before he climbed on that merry-go-round."

Tollie, however, considered that we had seen a shining feat. "Almost made it   to the   whistle   on that   rough one!   You can   still show   your face   around home,   Earl!"

Possibly the pinto's general irritation with the world rather than the diet of Tollie's voice produced it, but either way, Coffee Nerves now went into his biggest eruption yet. Below me in the chute he began to writhe and kick, whinnying awfully, and I redoubled my life grip on the corner post as the *thunk! thunk!* of his hooves tattooing the wood of the chute reverberated through the seat of my pants.

"Careful," Ray warned, and I suppose sense would have been to trade my perch for a more distant site. Yet how often does a person get to see at close range a horse in combat with mankind. Not just see, but feel, in the continuing *thunks*; and hear, the pinto's whinny a sawblade of sound ripping the air; and smell, sweat and manure and animal anger in one mingled unforgettable odor.

Coffee Nerves' hammerwork with his hooves built up to a crash, a splay of splinters which sent the handlers tumbling away from the back of the chute, and then comparative silence. Just the velocity of air through the pinto bronc's nostrils.

"The sonofabitch is hung up," somebody reported.

In truth, Coffee Nerves was standing with his rear right leg up behind him, the way a horse does for a blacksmith to shoe him. Except that instead of any human having hold of that wicked rear hoof, it was jammed between a solid chute pole and the splintered one above it.

As the handling crew gingerly moved in to see what could be done about extrication, Tollie enlightened the crowd:

"This little   pinto pony   down in   six   is still proving   kind of   recaltrisant.   The chute boys   are doing   some   persuading   and   our show   will resume   in just   a jiffy.   In the   meantime   since this is the   cowboys'   Christmas   so to say that reminds   me of a   little   story."

"Jesus, he's back on to Christmas" issued from the chute society. "Will somebody go get Tollie a goddamn calendar?"

"Dumb as he is," it was pointed out, "it'll take two of us to read it to him."

"There was   this   little boy   who wanted   a pony for   Christmas." Somebody had gone for a prybar to loosen the imprisoning poles and free the renegade pony of chute six, but in the meantime there was nothing to do but let Tollie wax forth. Even at normal, Tollie's voice sounded as if his adenoids had gotten twined with his vocal cords. With the boost from the address system, his steady drone now was a real ear-cleaner. "Well   you see   this   little boy kept   telling   the other kids   in   the family   that he had it   all   fixed up   with Santa Claus.   Santa Claus   was going   to bring him   a pony   certain sure. So   when   Christmas Eve   came   they all   of them hung   their stockings   by the   fireplace there."

"If I hang a woolsack alongside my stove," somebody in front of the chutes pined, "suppose I'd get Velma Simms in it?"

"And the   other kids   thought   they'd teach   this little boy   a lesson.   So after   everybody   had gone to bed they got back up again and went on out to the barn and got some ladies, excuse my language, horse manure."

"Quick, mark that down," somebody advised up to Bill Reinking. "That's the first time Tollie's ever apologized for spouting horse shit."

"And filled his stocking with it. So the next morning they're all gathered to look and see what Santa Claus left each one of them. Little Susie says 'Look, he left me a dollie here in my stocking.' And little Tommy says And look he left me apples and oranges in mine.' And they turned to the little boy and asked 'Well, Johnny what did Santa leave *you*?' And Johnny looked in his stocking and said 'He left me my pony but he got away!'"

There was that sickly laughter a crowd gives out because it's embarrassed not to, and then one of the chute men called up to the booth that they had the goddamn bronc freed, get the rider on him before he raised any more hell.

BACK TO BUSINESS!" Tollie blared as if he was calling elephants, before Bill Reinking managed to lean across and shove the microphone a little farther from Tollie's mouth. "Back to business. The bronc in chute six has consented to rejoin us. Next man up last one in this go-round on a horse called Coffee Nerves will be Dode Withrow."

I yanked my head around to see for sure. 11s. Dode was up top the back of chute six, gazing at the specimen of exasperated horse below. Dode did look a little soberer than when I met up with him by the beer booth. He wasn't any bargain of temperance yet, though. His face looked hot and his Stetson sat toward the back of his head in a dude way I had never seen him wear it.

Ray was saying, "I never knew Dode to enter the bucking before." Which coincided with what was going through my mind, that Dode was the age of my father and Ray's. That his bronc-stomping had taken place long years ago. That I knew for a certainty Dode did not even break horses for his own use anymore but bought them saddle ready from Tollie Zane.

"No," I answered Ray, "not in our time."

I had a clear view down into the chute as the bronc crew tried to keep Coffee Nerves settled long enough for Dode to ease into the saddle. The pinto went through another symphony of commotion, kicking and slamming sideways and whinnying that sawtoothed sound; but then hunched up motionless for a moment in a kind of sitting squat, contemplating what next to pull from its repertoire. In that moment Dode simply said "Good enough" and slid into the saddle.

As if those words of Dode's were a curfew, the gapers and gawkers of the chute society evaporated from the vicinity where Coffee Nerves would emerge into the arena, some of them even seeking a safe nest up on the corral.

"One of   our friends   and   neighbors   Dode   is. Rode   many   a bad one in   his time.   He'll be dancing out   on this   little pinto   in just   one minute."

It honestly occurred no more than a handful of seconds from then. Dode had the grip he wanted on the bucking rope and his arm was in the air as if ready to wave and he said in that same simple tone, "Open."

The gate swung, and Coffee Nerves vaulted into the arena.

I saw Dode suck in a fast breath, then heard it go out of him in a *huhhh* as the horse lit stiff-legged with its forefeet and kicked the sky with its hind, from both directions ramming the surprise of its force up through the stirrups into Dode. Dode's hat left him and bounced once on the pinto splotch across Coffee Nerves' rump and then toppled into the dust of the arena. But Dode himself didn't shake loose at all, which was a fortunate thing because Coffee Nerves already was uncorking another maneuver, this time swapping ends before crashing down in all stiff-legged style. Dode still sat deep in the saddle, although another *huhhh* reamed its way out of him. Maybe imagine you have just jumped from a porch roof to the ground twice in about five seconds, to give yourself some idea of the impact Dode was absorbing. He must have been getting Coffee Nerves' respect, for now the bronc exactly reversed the end-swapping he had just done, a trick almost guaranteed to catch the rider leaning wrong. Yet Dode still was up there astride the pinto.

I remember tasting dust. My mouth was open to call encouragement to Dode, but there was nothing that seemed good enough to call out for this ride he was making.

Now Coffee Nerves launched into the jump he had been saving up for, a real cloud-chaser, Dode at the same instant raking the horse's shoulders with his spurs, both those actions fitting together exactly as if animal and man were in rhythm to a signal none of the rest of us could hear, up and up the horse twisting into the air and the rider's free left arm high above that, Coffee Nerves and Dode soaring together while the crowd's urging cry seemed to help hold them there, a wave of sound suspending the pair above the arena earth so that we all could have time to fix the sight into memory everlastingly.

Somewhere amid it all the whistle blew. That is, off some far wall of my awareness echoed that news of Dode having ridden Coffee Nerves, but the din that followed flooded over it. I still believe that if Coffee Nerves had lit straight, as any sane horse would do descending from a moon visit like that, Dode would not have blown that left stirrup. But somehow Coffee Nerves skewed himself half sideways about the time he hit the ground—imagine now that the ground yanks itself to one side as you plummet off that porch—and Dode, who evidently did not hear the timer's whistle or was ignoring it, stayed firm in the right stirrup, nicely braced as he was, but the pinto's slewfoot maneuver jolted his boot from the left one. And now when Coffee Nerves writhed into his next buck, cattywampus to the left, he simply sailed away from under Dode, who dropped off him back first, falling like a man given a surprise shove into a creek.

Not water, however, but dust flew up around the form which thumped to the arena surface.

The next developments smudged together. I do know that now I was shouting out "Dode! Dode!" and that I lit running in the arena direct from the top of the corral, never even resorted to any of the poles as rungs to get down, and that Ray landed right behind me. As to what we thought we were going to accomplish I am not at all clear; simply could not see Dode sprawled out there by himself, I suppose.

The pickup man Dill Egan was spurring his horse between Dode and Coffee Nerves, and having to swat the pinto in the face with his hat to keep him off Dode. Before it seemed possible my father and Pete were out there too, and a half dozen other men from out of the grandstand and Alec and a couple of others from the far side of the arena, their hats thwacking at Coffee Nerves as well, and through all the commotion I could hear my father's particular roar of "HYAH! HYAH!" again and again before the bronc finally veered off.

"Fell off   the rainbow   on that one   right enough," Tollie was blaring. So that registered on me, and the point that the chute society, this once when they could have been useful out here in the arena, were dangling from various fence perches or peering from behind the calf chute. But the sprint Ray and I made through the loose arena dirt is marked in me only by the sound that reached us just as we reached Dode. The noise hit our ears from the far end of the arena: a tingling *crack!* like a tree breaking off and then crashing and thudding as it came down.

For a confused instant I truly thought a cottonwood had fallen. My mind tried to put together that with all else happening in this over-crowded space of time. But no, Coffee Nerves had slammed head-on into the gate of the catch pen, toppling not just the gate but the hefty gatepost, which crunched the hood of a parked car as it fell over. People who had been spectating along the fence were scattering from the prospect of having Coffee Nerves out among them.

The bronc however had rebounded into the arena. Piling into that gatepost finally had knocked some of the spunk out of Coffee Nerves. He now looked a little groggy and was wobbling somewhat, which gave Dill Egan time to lasso him and dally the rope around a corral post.

This was the scene as I will ever see it. Dode Withrow lying out there with the toes of his boots pointing up and Coffee Nerves woozy but defiant at the end of the lasso tether.

Quite a crowd encircled Dode, although Ray and I hung back at its outer edge; exactly what was not needed was any more people in the way. Doc Spence forged his way through, and I managed to see in past the arms and legs of all the men around him and Dode. And saw happen what I so desperately wanted to. When Doc held something under Dode's nose, Dode's head twitched.

Before long I heard Dode give a long *mmmm,* as if he was terrifically tired. After that his eyes came open and he showed that he was able to move, in fact would have tried to sit up if Doc Spence hadn't stopped him. Doc told Dode to just take it easy, damn it, while he examined Dode's right leg.

By now Midge and the Withrow girls had scurried out and Midge was down beside Dode demanding, "You ninny, are you all right?"

Dode fastened his look on her and made an *mmmm* again. Then burst out loud and clear, "Goddamn that stirrup anyway," which lightened the mood of all of us around him, even Midge looking less warpath-like after that. I could just hear the razzing Dode was going to take from his herder Pat Hoy about this forced landing of his: "Didn't know I was working for an apprentice bronc stomper, Dode. Want me to saddle up one of these big ewes, so's you can practice staying on?"

Relief was all over my father as he went over to the grandstand fence to report to my mother and Marie and Toussaint. Ray and I tagged along, so we heard it as quick as anybody. "Doc thinks it's a simple leg break," my father relayed. "Could have been a hell of a lot worse. Doc's going to take him to Conrad for overnight just to make sure."

My mother at once called out to Midge an offer to ride with her to the hospital in Conrad. Midge, though, shook her head. "No, I'll be all right. The girls'll be with me, no sense in you coming."

Then I noticed. Toussaint was paying no attention to any of this conversation, nor to the process of Dode being put on a stretcher over his protestations that he could walk or even foot-race if he had to, nor to Coffee Nerves being tugged into exit through what little was left of the catch pen gate. Instead he, Toussaint, was standing there gazing into the exact center of the arena, as if the extravaganza that Coffee Nerves and Dode had put on still was continuing out there. The walnut crinkles deepened in his face, his chuckle rippled out, and then the declaration: "That one. That one was a ride."

There of course was more on the schedule of events beyond that. Tollie inevitably thought to proclaim, "Well, folks   the show   goes on." But the only way for it to go after that performance by Coffee Nerves and Dode was downhill, and Ray and I retained our fence perch just through the next section of calf-roping to see whether Alec's seventeen and a half seconds would hold up. Contestant after contestant rampaged out, flailed some air with a lariat, and came nowhere close to Alec's time.

It had been a rodeo. English Creek had won both the saddle bronc riding and the calf-roping.

While the rodeo grounds emptied of crowd Ray and I stretched our attendance as long as we could. We watched the wrangling crew unpen the broncs and steers and calves. Listened to as much of the chute society's post mortem as we could stand. Had ourselves another bottle of pop apiece before the beer booth closed. Then I proposed that we might as well take a horse tour of Gros Ventre. Ray thought that sounded dandy enough, so I fetched Mouse and swung into the saddle, and Ray climbed on behind.

We had sightseen most of the town before wandering back past the Medicine Lodge, which by now had its front door propped open with a beer keg, probably so the accumulating fume of cigarette smoke and alcoholic breath wouldn't pop the windows out of the place. As Dode Withrow would have said, it sounded like hell changing shifts in there. The jabber and laughter and sheer concentration of humanity beyond that saloon doorway of course had Ray and me gazing in as we rode past, and that gaze was what made me abruptly halt Mouse.

Ray didn't ask anything, but I could feel his curiosity as to why we were stalled in the middle of the street. Nor was it anything I could put into words for him. Instead I offered: "How about you riding Mouse down to your place? I'll be along in a little. There's somebody I got to go see."

Ray's look toward the Medicine Lodge wondered "In there?" but his voice only conveyed, "Sure, glad to," and he lifted himself ahead into the saddle after I climbed down. Best of both worlds for him. Chance to be an unquestioning friend and get a horse to ride as well.

I went into the blue air of the saloon and stopped by the figure sitting on the second bar stool inside the doorway. The Medicine Lodge was getting itself uncorked for the night ahead. Above the general jabber somebody toward the middle of the bar was relating in a semishout: "So I told that sonofabitch he just better watch his step around me or there's gonna be a new face in hell for breakfast." My interest, though, was entirely here at the seated figure.

The brown hat moved around as he became aware of me.

"'Lo, Stanley," I began, still not knowing where I was going next with any of this.

"Well, there, Jick." The crowfoot lines clutched deeper at the corners of Stanley Meixell's eyes as he focused on me. He didn't look really tanked up, but on the other hand couldn't be called church-sober either. Someplace in between, as he'd been so much of our time together on the mountain. "Haven't seen you," he continued in all pleasantness, "since you started living aboveground."

Good Christ, Stanley had noticed my ducking act that day I was digging the outhouse hole and he rode by. Was my every moment visible to people anymore, like a planet being perpetually studied by one of those California telescopes?

"Yeah, well. How you been?"

"Fine as snoose. And yourself?"

"What I mean, how's your hand doing?"

Stanley looked down at it as if I was the first to ever point out its existence. He still had some doozies of scabs and major bruises there on the injury site, but Stanley didn't seem to regard this as anything but ordinary health. "It ain't bad." He picked up the bottle of beer from the counter before him. "Works good enough for the basics, anyway." And tipped down the last of that particular beer. "Can I buy you a snort?"

"No, no thanks."

"On the wagon, huh? I've clumb on it some times myself. All else considered, though, I'd just as soon be down off."

It occurred to me that since I was in this place anyway it didn't cost any more to be cordial. The stool between Stanley and the doorway was vacant—an empty mixed-drink glass testified that its occupant had traveled on—so I straddled the seat and amended: "Actually I would take a bottle of orange, though."

Stanley indicated his empty beer bottle to Tom Harry, the nearest of the three bartenders trying to cope with the crowd's liquid wants. "When you get time, professor. And a sunjuice for my nurse, here."

Tom Harry studied me. "He with you?" he asked Stanley.

"Closer than kin, him and me," Stanley solemnly vouched to the barman. "We have rode millions of miles together."

"None of it aged him that much," Tom Harry observed, nonetheless setting up a bottle of orange in front of me and a fresh beer for Stanley.

"Stanley," I started again. He was pushing coins out of a little pile, to pay for the latest round. Fishing up a five-cent piece, he held it toward me between his thumb and forefinger. "Know what this is?"

"Sure, a nickel."

"Naw, it's a dollar a Scotchman's been squeezing." The fresh beer got a gulp of attention. For the sake of the conversation I intended I'd like to have known how many predecessors that bottle had had, but of course Tom Harry's style of bartending was to swoop empties out of sight so no such incriminating count could be taken.

I didn't have long to dwell on Stanley's possible intake, for some out-of-town guy wearing a panama hat zigged when he meant to zag on his way toward the door and lurched into the pair of us. Abruptly the guy was being gripped just above the elbow by Stanley—his right hand evidently had recuperated enough from Bubbles for this, too—and was retargeted toward the door with advice from Stanley: "Step easy, buddy, so you don't get yourself hurt. In this county there's a five-dollar fine for drawing blood on a fool."

Mr. Panama Hat hastily left our company, and Stanley's handling of the incident reminded me to ask something. "How you getting along with Canada Dan these days?"

"Better," Stanley allowed. "Yeah, just a whole lot better." He paid recognition to his beer bottle again. "Last I heard, Dan was up in Cut Bank. Doing some town herding."

Cut Bank? Town herding? "What, did the Busby boys can him?"

"I got them to give Dan a kind of vacation." Then, in afterthought: "Permanent."

I considered this. Up there in the Two with Stanley those weeks ago, I would not have bet a pin that he was capable of rousing himself to do justice to Canada Dan. Yet he had.

"Stanley—"

"I can tell you got something on your mind, Jick. Might as well unload it."

If I could grapple it into position, that was exactly what I intended. To ask: what was that all about, when we first met you there on the mountain, the skittishness between you and my father? Why, when I ask anyone in this family of mine about Stanley Meixell, is there never a straight answer? Just who are you to us? How did you cross paths with the McCaskills in the past, and why are you back crisscrossing with us again?

Somebody just beyond Stanley let out a whoop, then started in on a twangy rendition of the song that goes: *I'm a calico dog, I'm a razor-back hog, I'm a cowboy on the loose! I can drink towns dry, I can all but fly, I flavor my beans with snoose!* In an instant Tom Harry was there leaning over the bar and categorically informing the songster that he didn't care if the guy hooted, howled, or for that matter blew smoke rings out his butt, but no singing.

This, Stanley shook his head over. "What's the world coming to when a man can't offer up a tune? They ruin everything these days."

First Dode, now Stanley. It seemed my mission in life this Fourth of July to steer morose beer drinkers away from even deeper gloom. At least I knew which direction I wanted to point Stanley: back into history.

"I been trying to figure something out," I undertook honestly enough, one more time. "Stanley, why was it you quit rangering on the Two?"

Stanley did some more demolition on his beer, then cast a visiting glance around the walls at Franklin Delano Roosevelt and the stuffed herd, and eventually had to look at me and ask as if verifying:

"Me?"

"Uh huh, you."

"No special reason."

"Run it by me anyway."

"Naw, you'd be bored fast."

"Why'n't you let me judge that."

"You got better use for your ears."

"Jesus, Stanley—"

All this while I was attempting to pry sense out of Stanley, the tail of my eye was trying to tell me something again. Someone had come up behind me. Which wasn't particular news in the Medicine Lodge throng, except this someone evidently had no other site in mind; his presence stayed steadily there, close enough to make me edgy about it, sitting half braced as I was in case this guy too was going to crash in our direction.

I turned on the bar stool to cope with the interloper and gazed full into the face, not all that many inches away, of Velma Simms.

I must tell you, it was like opening a kitchen drawer to reach in for a jelly spoon and finding instead the crown jewels of England. For I had never been close enough, head-on, to Velma to learn that her eyes were gray. Gray! Like mine! Possibly our four were the world's only. And to garner further that her lipstick, on the very lips that ruled the rodeo whistle, was the beautiful dark-beyond-red of ripe cherries. And that she was wearing tiny pearl earrings, below the chestnut hair, as if her ears could be unbuttoned to further secrets even there. And that while the male population of northern Montana was focusing on the backside of Velma's renowned slacks, they were missing important announcements up front. Sure, there could be found a few lines at the corners of her eyes and across her forehead. But to me right then, they simply seemed to be affidavits of how imaginative a life this lady had led.

Unbelievable but so. Out of all the crowded flesh in the Medicine Lodge just then, solely onto me was fixed this attention of Velma Simms.

She just stood there eyeing me while I gaped, until the point of her attention finally prodded through to me.

"Oh. Oh, hello, Mrs.—uh, Velma. Have I got your seat?" I scrambled off the bar stool as if it was suddenly red-hot.

"Now that you mention it," she replied, and even just saying that, her words were one promissory note after another. Velma floated past me and snuggled onto the stool. A little extra of that snuggle went in Stanley's direction.

"Saw you there at the announcing booth," I reminisced brightly.

"Did you," said she.

I may be a slow starter, but eventually I catch up with the situation. My quick gawp around the saloon confirmed what had been trying to dawn on me. This year's beau in the gabardine suit was nowhere.

"Yeah, well," I began to extricate myself. "I got to be getting."

"Don't feel you need to rush off," said Stanley. As if God's gift to the male race wasn't enthroned right there beside him. "The night's still a pup."

"Uh huh. That's true, but—"

"When you got to go," put in Velma, twirling the empty mixed-drink glass to catch Tom Harry's attention for a refill, "you got to go."

"Right," I affirmed. "And like I say, I, uh, got to go."

What made me add to the total of my footprints already in my mouth I can't truly account for. Maybe the blockade I had hit again in wanting to ask all the questions of Stanley. In any case, the parting I now blurted out was:

"You two in a dancing mood tonight? What I mean, see you at the dance, will I?"

Stanley simply passed that inquiry to Velma with a look. In theory, Velma then spoke her answer to me, although she didn't unlock her gaze from him at all as she said it: "Stanley and I will have to see whether we have any spare time."

So. One more topic clambering aboard my already bent-over brain. Stanley Meixell and Velma Croake Bogan Sutter Simms.

"Ray? What kind of a summer are you having?"

We were up in the double window of his bedroom, each of us propped within the sill. A nice breeze came in on us there, the leaves of the big cottonwood in the Heaneys' front yard seeming to flutter the air our way.

Downstairs the radio had just been turned on by Ed Heaney, so it was seven o'clock. The dance wouldn't get under way for an hour or so yet, and as long as Ray and I were going to be window sitting anyway for the next while, I figured I'd broach to him some of all that was on my mind.

"Didn't I tell you? Pilot."

"No, I don't mean that. What it is, do things seem to you kind of unsettled?"

"How?"

"Well, Christ, I don't know. Just in general. People behaving like they don't know whether to include you in or out of things."

"What kind of things?"

"Things that went on years ago. Say there was an argument or a fight or something, people fell out over it. Why can't they just say, here's what it was about, it's over and done with? Get it out of their systems?"

"That's just grownups. They're not going to let a kid in on anything, until they figure it's too late to do him any good."

"But why is that? What is it that's so goddamn important back there that they have to keep it to themselves?"

"Jick, sometimes—"

"What?"

"Sometimes maybe you think too much."

I thought that over briefly. "What am I supposed to do about that? Christ, Ray, it's not like poking your finger up your nose in public, some kind of habit you can remind yourself not to do. Thinking is thinking. It happens in spite of a person."

"Yeah, but you maybe encourage it more than it needs."

"I what?"

"See, maybe it's like this." Ray's eyes squinched more than ever as he worked on his notion, and the big front teeth nipped his lower lip in concentration. Then: "Maybe, let's say maybe a thought comes into your head, it's only about what you're going to do next. Saddle up Mouse and take a ride, say. That's all the thought it really needs. Then put on the saddle and climb on. But the mood you're in, Jick, you'd stop first and think some more. 'But if I go for a ride, where am I going to go?'" Ray here went into one of his radio voices, the words coming clippity-clippity like old Kaltenborn's. "'What is it I'll see when I get there? Did anybody else ever see it? And if anybody did, is it going to look the same to me as it did to them? And old Mouse here, is it going to look the same to Mouse as it does to me?'"

Raymond Edmund Heaney von Kaltenborn broke off, and it was just Ray again. "On and on that way, Jick. If you think too much, you make it into a whole dictionary of going for a ride. Instead of just going. See what I'm saying?"

"Goddamn it now, Ray, what I mean is more important than god-damn riding a horse."

"It's the same with anything. It'll get to you if you think about it too much, Jick."

"But what I'm telling you is, I don't have any choice. This stuff I'm talking about is on my mind whether or not I want it to be."

Ray took a look at me as if I had some sort of brain fever that might be read in my face. Then in another of his radio voices intoned: "Have you tried Vicks VapoRub? It sooooothes as it wooooorks."

There it lay. Even Ray had no more idea than the man in the moon about my perplexity. This house where we sat tucked in blue-painted sills, above its broad lawned yard and under its high cottonwoods, this almost second home of mine: it ticked to an entirely different time than the summer that was coursing through me. The Heaney family was in place in the world. Ed was going to go on exiting the door of his lumber yard at six every evening and picking up his supper fork at ten after six and clicking on that Silvertone radio at seven, on into eternity. Genevieve would go on keeping this house shining and discovering new sites for doilies. Mary Ellen would grow up and learn nursing at the Columbus Hospital in Great Falls. Ray would grow up and take a year of business college at Missoula and then join his father in the lumber yard. Life under this roof had the rhythm of the begattings in the Bible. The Heaneys were not the McCaskills, not even anywhere similar, and I lacked the language to talk about any of the difference, even to my closest friend.

> "Swing, swing, and swing 'em high!
> Allemande left and allemande aye!
> Ingo, bingo, six penny high!
> Big pig, little pig, root hog or die!"

The dance was under way, but only just, when Ray and I wandered down there to the Sedgwick House to it. Which is to say the hall—I suppose old C. E. Sedgwick or maybe even Lila Sedge conceived of it as a ballroom, but everybody else considered it the dance hall—was crammed to an extent that made the Medicine Lodge look downright lonely across the street, but not all that many people were dancing yet. Visiting, circulating, gathering an eyeful of everybody else, joking, trying to pry out of a neighbor how many bushels an acre his wheat looked like or what his lambs weighed by now, but only one square of actual dancers out there footing it to Jerome Satterlee's calling. Partly, everybody knew it took Jerome a little while (translate that to a few drinks) to get his tonsils limbered up. And then he could call dances until your shoes fell off your feet.

"A little thin out here on the floor, it looks to me like," Jerome was now declaring, preparatory to the next dance. "You know what I mean? Let's get one more square going here, make it look like we mean business. Adam, Sal, step on out here, you can stand around and grab any time. How about all you Busbys, you're half a square yourselves. Good, good. Come on now, one more couple. Nola plays this piano twice as good when we got two squares on the floor." At the upright, Nola Atkins sat planted as if they'd simply picked up the piano bench from the creek picnic with her on it and set them both down here on the band platform. Beside her, Jeff Swan had his fiddle tucked under his chin and his bow down at his side as if it was a sword he was ready to draw. "One more couple. Do I have to telephone to Valier and ask them to send over four left feet? Whup, here they come now, straight from supper, dancers if I ever saw any. Leona Tracy and Alec McCaskill, step right in there. Alec, you checked your horse and rope at the door, I hope? Now, this is somewhat more like—"

Stepping in from the Sedgwick House dining room, rodeo prize money in his pocket and free supper under his belt and a grin everywhere on his face there was any space for it, Alec looked like a young king coming home from his crowning ceremony.

Even so, to notice this glorious brother of mine you had to deliberately steer your eyes past Leona. Talk about an effort of will.

Leona took the shine in any crowd, even a dance hall full. The day's green blouse was missing. I mean, she had changed out of it. Now she wore a white taffeta dress, full and flouncy at the hem. In square dancing a lot of swirling goes on, and Leona was going to be a swirl worth seeing.

I shot a glance around the dance hall. My parents had missed this grand entry. They'd gone out to J. L. and Nan Hill's ranch, a couple of miles up English Creek, for supper and to change clothes, and were taking their own sweet time about getting back in. And Pete and Marie were driving Toussaint home to the Two Medicine, so they'd be even later arriving. I was the sole family representative, so to speak, to record the future Mr. and Mrs. Alec McCaskill come swanking in.

"Ready out there? Sure you are. You'll get to liking this so much, before the night is out you'll want to trade your bed for a lantern." Jerome, when he got to going good, put a lot of motion into his calling, using both arms to direct the traffic of dancers; kind of like a man constantly hanging things here and there in a closet. His gestures even now said he was entering into the spirit of the night. "All right, sonnies and honeys. Nola, Jeff, let's make 'em prance. Everybody, here we go:

> *"First four forward. Back to your places.*
> *Second four follow. Shuffle on back.*
> *Now you're getting down to cases,*
> *Swing each other till the floorbeams crack!"*

Here in the time I am now it seems hard to credit that this Fourth of July dance was the first I ever went to on my own. That is, was in company with somebody like Ray instead of being alone as baggage with my parents. Of course, without fully acknowledging it Ray and I also were well on our way to another tremendous night, the one when each of us would step through this dance hall doorway with a person neither parent nor male alongside. But that lay await yet. My point just now is that where I was in life this particular Fourth night, closing in on fifteen years of age, I had been attending dances since the first few months of that total. And Alec, the all-winning rodeo-shirted sashayer out there on the floor right now, the same before me. Each a McCaskill baby bundled in blankets and cradled in chairs beside the dance floor. Imbibe music along with mother's milk: that was the experience of a lot of us of Two country upbringing. Successors to Alec's and my floorside infancy were here in the Sedgwick House hall this very night: Charity Frew's half-year-old daughter, and another new Helwig baby, and a couple of other fresh ones belonging to farm folks east of town, a swaddled quartet with chairs fenced around them in the farthest corner of the dance hall.

> *"Salute your ladies, all together.*
> *Ladies, to the gents do the same.*

> *Hit the lumber with your leather.*
> *Balance all, and swing your dame!"*

It might be said that the McCaskill dancing history was such that it was the portion of lineage that came purest into Alec and me. Definitely into Alec. Out there now with that white taffeta back and forth to him like a wave of the sea, he looked like he could romp on forever. What little I knew of my father's father, the first McCaskill to caper on America's soil instead of Scotland's, included the information that he could dance down the house. Schottisches and Scotch reels in particular, but he also adopted any Western square dances. In his twinkling steps, so to speak, followed my mother and father. Dances held in ranch houses, my mother-to-be arriving on horseback with her party dress tied on behind the saddle, my father-to-be performing the Scotch Heaven ritual of scattering a little oatmeal on the floor for better gliding. Schoolhouse dances. In the face of the Depression even a hard times dance, the women costumed in gunnysack dresses and the men in tattered work clothes. And now Alec the latest McCaskill dancer, and me beginning to realize I was on my way.

> *"Bunch the ladies, there in the middle.*
> *Circle, you gents, and dosie doe.*
> *Pay attention to old Jeff's fiddle.*
> *Swing her around and away you go!"*

Can it be that all kinds of music speak to one another? For what I always end up thinking of in this dancing respect is a hymn. To me it is the one hymn that has ever seemed to make much sense:

> *"Dance, dance, wherever you may be,*
> *I am the Lord of the dance," said he,*
> *"And I'll lead you all, wherever you may be,*
> *And I'll lead you all in the dance," said he.*

I almost wish I had never come across those words and their tune, for they make one of those chants that slip into your mind every time you meet up with the circumstances they suggest. It was so then, even as Ray nudged me to point out the Busby brothers going through a fancy twirl with each other instead of with their wives and I joined Ray and everybody else in laughing, and it is so now. Within all else those musical words, a kind of beautiful haunting. But I suppose that is what musical words, and for that matter dances and dancers, are for.

> *"Gents to the center, ladies round them.*
> *Form a circle, balance all.*
> *Whirl your girls to where you found them.*
> *Promenade all, around the hall!"*

This concluding promenade brought Alec and Leona over toward where Ray and I were onlooking, and spying us they trooped right up. Leona in the flush of the pleasure of dancing was nearly more than the eyes could stand. I know Ray shifted a little nervously beside me, and maybe I did too.

"Mister Jick again," she greeted me. At least it wasn't "Hello, John Angus." "And Raymond Edmund Heaney," she bestowed on Ray, which really *did* set Ray to shifting around.

So high in flight was Alec tonight, though, that nobody else had to expend much effort. A lank of his rich red hair was down across his forehead from the dancing, and the touch of muss just made him look handsomer.

"Here's a pair of wall guards," he observed of Ray and me while he grinned mightily. "You guys better think about getting yourselves one of these things," giving Leona a waist squeeze.

Yeah, sure, right. As if Leonas were as plenty as blackberries. (I have wondered often. If Marcella Withrow had been on hand that night instead of at the Conrad hospital with her father, would Ray have nerved himself up and squired her out onto the floor?) But if you can't carry on conversation with your own brother, who can you? So to keep mouth matters in motion, I asked: "How was it?"

Alec peered at me and he let up on that Leona squeezing. "How was what?"

"Supper. The supper you won for handcuffing that poor little calf."

"Dandy," he reported, "just dandy." And now Leona awarded *him* a squeeze, in confirmation.

"What'd you have, veal?" Ray put in, which I thought was pretty good. But Alec and Leona were so busy handling each other's waists they didn't catch it, and Alec said, "Naw, steaks. Dancing fuel." He looked down at his armful of Leona. "Speaking of which—"

"TIMBERRR!"

I was not the only one whose ears almost dropped off in surprise. That cry was a famous one at any dance such as this. It dated back to Prohibition days, and what it signaled back then, whenever somebody stuck his head in through the dance hall doorway and cut loose the call, was the availability of Mason jar moonshine for anybody who cared to step outside for a sip.

So my surprise was double. That the cry resounded through the hall this night and that the timber crier there in the doorway, when I spun around to see, proved to be my father, with my mother on his arm.

He wore his brown pinstripe suit coat, a white shirt, and his newest Levis. She was in her blue cornflower frock with the slight V neckline; it was pretty tame by today's standards, but did display enough of throat and breastbone to draw second glances. Togged out that way, Varick and Lisabeth McCaskill made a prime pair, as rangers and wives often did.

Calls and claps greeted my father's solo.

"You'd be the one to know about timber, Mac!"

"Hoot mon, Scotch Heaven has come to town!"

"Beth, tell us fair and square: has he been up in the Two practicing that?"

Even Alec wagged his head in—admiration? consternation? both and more?—before declaiming to Leona, "There's dancing to be done. Let's get at it before the rowdy element cuts loose with something more."

Ray and I sifted over to my parents' side of the hall. My father was joshing Fritz Hahn that if Dode could still ride a bronc like that, it was Fritz's turn next Fourth to uphold the South Fork reputation. Greta and my mother were trading laughter over something, too. Didn't I tell you a dance is the McCaskill version of bliss?

"Here they are, the future of the race," my father greeted Ray and me. "Ray, how're you summering?"

"Real good," Ray responded, along with his parenthetical grin. "Quite a rodeo, wasn't it."

"Quite a one," my father agreed, with a little shake of his head which I knew had to do with the outcome of the calf-roping. But at once he was launched back into more visiting with Fritz and Ray, and I just parked myself and inventoried him and my mother. It was plain my father had timbered a couple of drinks; his left eyelid was down a little, as if listening to a nightlong joke. But no serious amount. My mother, though. My mother too looked bright as a butterfly, and as she and my father traded grab with the Hahns and other people who happened by to say good words about her Ben English speech or his timber whoop, both her and him unable to keep from glancing at the back-and-forth of the dancers more than at their conversationalists, a suspicion seeded in me. Maybe, more than maybe, my mother had a drink or two in her, too.

here you guys been?" I voiced when I got the chance.

And received what I deserved. "Places," stated my mother, then laughed.

Well, I'd had one escape this day. Getting in and out of the Medicine Lodge without coinciding with my own parents there.

Out on the floor, the swirl was dissolving as it does after the call and music have hit their climax, and Jerome was enlisting everybody within earshot for the next variety of allemande and dosie doe. "Now I can't call dances to an empty floor, can I? Let's up the ante here. Four squares this time, let's make it. Plenty of territory, we don't even have to push out the walls yet."

"The man needs our help," my father suggested to my mother and the Hahns, and off they all went, to take up places in the fourth square of dancers forming up.

The dance wove the night to a pattern all its own, as dances do. I remember the standard happenings. Supper hour was announced for midnight, both the Sedgwick House dining room and the Lunchery were going to close at one A.M. Ray and I had agreed that supper hour—or rather, an invitation to oyster stew at the Lunchery, as my parents were certain to provide—would be our personal curfew. Jerome at one point sang out, "Next one is ladies' choice!" and it was interesting to see some of the selections they made, Alice Van Bebber snagging the lawyer Eli Kinder and immediately beginning to talk him dizzy, pretty Arleta Busby putting out her hand to that big pile of guff Ed Van Bebber, of all damn people. My parents too made South Fork pairings, my mother going over to Fritz Hahn, Greta Hahn coupling onto my father's arm. Then after one particularly rousing floor session, Jerome announced that if anyone cared to pass a hat he and the musicians could manage to look the other way, and collection was taken to pay him and Nola and Jeff.

As I say, all this was standard enough, and mingled with it were some particularities of this night. The arrival of Good Help and Florene Hebner, magically a minute or so after the hat had been passed. Florene still was a presentable-looking woman, despite a dress that had been washed to half its original color. Good Help's notion of dressing up was to top off his overalls with a flat cap. My mother once commented, "A poor-boy cap and less under it." The departure of the grocery store family, the Helwigs, with Luther Helwig wobbling under the load of booze he had been taking on and his wife Erna beside him with the bawling baby plucked from the far end chair corral. In such a case you always have to wonder: was a strategic motherly pinch delivered to that baby? And my eventual inspiration for Ray and me to kill off the last of my fifty-cent stake with a bottle of pop apiece. "How about stepping across for something wet?" was the way I proposed it to Ray. He took on a worried look and began, "I don't know that my folks want me going in that—" "Christ, not the Medicine Lodge," I relieved him, "I meant the Lunchery." Through it all, dance after dance after dance, my tall redheaded father and my white-throated mother in the musical swim at one end of the hall, my tall redheaded brother and Leona starring at the other end.

It was in fact when Ray and I returned from our pop stop that we found a lull in the dancing and made our way over to my parents again, to be as convenient as possible for an oyster stew invite.

"I suppose you two could eat if you had to?" my father at once settled that issue, while my mother drew deep breaths and cast a look around the hallful.

"Having fun?" I asked her, just to be asking something, while my father was joshing Ray about being girl-less on such a night.

"A ton," she confirmed.

Just then Jerome Satterlee appeared in our midst, startling us all a little to see him up close instead of on the platform. "What, did you come down for air, Jerome?" my father kidded.

"Now don't give an old man a hard time," responded Jerome. "Call this next one, how about, Mac. Then we can turn 'em loose for midnight supper. Myself, I got to go see a man about a dog."

My father was not at all a square dance caller of Jerome's breadth. But he was known to be good at—well, I will have to call it a sort of Scotch cadence, a beat of the kind that a bagpipe and drum band puts out. Certainly you danced smoother to Jerome's calling, but my father's could bring out stamping and clapping and other general exuberation.

I think it is not too much to say that with my eyes closed and ears stuffed, I could have stood there in the Sedgwick House and told you whether it was Jerome or my father calling the dance, just by the feel of how feet were thumping the hall floor.

To make sure their smooth terms could stand his absence, my father looked the question at my mother, and she told him by a nod that he ought to go do the call. She even added, "Why don't you do the Dude and Belle? This time of night, everybody can stand some perking up."

He climbed onto the band platform. "'Lo, Nola, Jeff. This isn't any idea of mine, understand."

"Been saving you the best strings of this fiddle, Mac," Jeff answered. "When you're ready."

Nola nodded, echoed: "When you're ready."

"All right, then. Try to make me look like I know what I'm doing." My father tipped his left shoulder down, pumped a rhythm with his heel a number of times to get a feel of the platform. Then made a loud hollow clap with his hands which brought everybody's attention, and called out over the hall: "Jerome is taking a minute to recuperate. He said he hates to turn things over to anybody with a Scotch notion of music, but saw no choice. So you're in for it."

"What one we gonna do, Mac, the Two Medicine two-step?" some wit yelled out.

"No sir. I've got orders to send you to midnight supper in style. Time to do the Dude and Belle. And let's really do it, six squares' worth." My father was thinking big. Six squares of dancers in this hall would swash from wall to wall and end to end, and onlookers already were moving themselves into the doorway or alongside the band platform to grant space. "All right. You all know how it starts. Join hands and circle left."

Even yet I am surprised that I propelled myself into doing it. I stepped away from Ray, soldiered myself in front of my mother, and said:

"Mrs. McCaskill, I don't talk through my nose as pretty as the guy you usually gallivant around with. But suppose I could have this dance with you anyway?"

Her face underwent that rinse of surprise that my father sometimes showed about her. She cast a look toward the top of my head as if just realizing my height. Then came her sidelong smile, and her announcement:

"I never could resist you McCaskill galoots."

Arm in arm, my mother and I took a place in the nearest square. People were marshalling everywhere in the hall, it looked like a major parade forming up. Another thunderclap from my father's hands, Nola and Jim opened up with the music, and my father chanted us into action.

> *First gent, swing the lady so fair.*
> *Now the one right over there.*
> *Now the one with the sorrel hair.*
> *Now the belle of the ballroom.*
> *Swirl and twirl And promenade all.*
>
> *Second gent, swing the lady first-rate."*

Besides my mother and me, our square was Bob and Arleta Busby, and the Musgreaves who ran the drugstore, and luck of luck, Pete and Marie, back from returning Toussaint to the Two Medicine and dancing hard the past hour or so to make up for time lost. All of them but me probably had done the Dude and Belle five hundred times in their lives, but it's a basic enough dance that I knew the ropes. You begin with everybody joining hands—my mother's firm feel at the end of one of my arms, Arleta's small cool hand at my other extreme—and circling left, a wheel of eight of us spinning to the music. Now to my father's call of "You've done the track, now circle back" the round chain of us goes into reverse, prancing back to where we started. Swing your partner, my mother's cornflower frock a blue whirlwind around the pair of us. Now the lady on the left, which in my instance meant hooking arms with Arleta, another first in my life. Now return to partner, all couples do some sashaying right and left, and the "gent" of this round steps forth and begins swinging the ladies in turn until he's back to his own partner. And with all gusto, swings her as the Belle of the Ballroom.

> *"Third gent, swing the lady in blue."*

What I would give to have seen all this through my father's eyes. Presiding up there on the platform, pumping rhythm with his heel and feeling it multiplied back to him by the forty-eight feet traveling the dance floor. Probably if you climbed the helmet spike of the Sedgwick

House, the rhythm of those six squares of dancers would have come quivering up to you like spasms through a tuning fork. Figure within figure within figure, from my father's outlook over us, the kaleidoscope of six simultaneous dance patterns and inside each the hinged couple of the instant and comprising those couples friends, neighbors, sons, wife with flashing throat. The lord of the dance, leading us all.

> *"Fourth gent, swing the lady so sweet."*

The fourth gent was me. I stepped to the center of our square, again made the fit of arms with Arleta Busby, and swung her.

> *"Now the one who looks so neat."*

Marie glided forth, solemnly winked at me, and spun about me light as a ghost.

> *"Now the one with dainty feet."*

Grace Musgreave, plump as a partridge, didn't exactly fit the prescription, but again I managed, sending her puffing out of our fast swirl.

> *"Now the belle of the ballroom."*

The blue beauty, my mother. *"Swirl and twirl."* Didn't we though. *"Now promenade all."* Around we went, all the couples, and now it was the women's turn to court their dudes.

> *"First lady, swing the gent who's got sore toes.*
> *Now the one with the great big nose.*
> *Now the one who wears store clothes.*
> *Now the dude of the ballroom.*
>
> *Second lady, swing the gent in size thirteens.*
> *Now the one that ate the beans.*
> *Now the one in brand new jeans.*
> *Now the dude of the ballroom.*

> *Third lady, swing the gent with the lantern jaw.*
> *Now the one from Arkansas.*
> *Now the one that yells, 'Ah, hah!'*
> *Now the dude of the ballroom."*

So it went. In succession I was the one in store clothes, the one full of beans, and the lantern-jawed one—thankful there not to be the one who yells "Ah hah!" which Pete performed for our square with a dandy of a whoop.

> *"Fourth lady, swing the gent whose nose is blue."*

My mother and Bob Busby, two of the very best dancers in the whole hall.

> *"Now the one that spilled the glue."*

Reese reflections dancing with each other, my mother and Pete.

> *"Now the one who's stuck on you."*

My mother and sallow Hugh Musgreave.

> *"Now the dude of the ballroom."*

She came for me, eyes on mine. I was the proxy of all that had begun at another dance, at the Noon Creek schoolhouse twenty years before. My father's voice: *"Swirl him and twirl him."* My moment of dudehood was an almighty whirl, as if my mother had been getting up the momentum all night.

> *"All join hands and circle to the left,*
> *Before the fiddler starts to swear.*
> *Dudes and belles, you've done your best.*
> *Now promenade, to you know where."*

"Didn't know you were a lightfoot," Ray greeted me at the edge of the throng heading through the doorway to supper hour.

"Me neither," I responded, blowing a little. My mother was with Pete and Marie right behind me; we all would have to wait for my father to make his way from the band platform. "Let's let them catch up with us outside. I can use some air."

Ray and I squirmed along between the crowd and the lobby wall, weaseling our way until we popped out the front entry of the Sedgwick House.

I was about to say here that the next historic event of this Fourth of July, Gros Ventre category, was under way as the two of us emerged into the night, well ahead of my parents and the Reeses. But given that midnight had just happened I'd better call this the first occurrence of July 5.

The person most immediately obvious of course was Leona, white and gold in the frame of light cast onto the street by the Sedgwick House's big lobby window. And then Arlee Zane, also there on that raft of light; Arlee, ignorance shining from every pore.

Beyond them, a bigger two with the reflected light cutting a line across their chests; face to face in the dimness above that, as if they were carrying on the nicest of private chats. Except that the beam-frame build of one and the chokecherry shirt of the other showed them to be Earl Zane and Alec and therefore they were not chatting.

"Surprised to see you without a skim milk calf on the end of a string," Earl was offering up as Ray and I sidled over beside Leona and Arlee so as not to miss anything. Inspiring Arlee to laugh big as if Earl's remark deserved it.

"What, are you out here in the night looking for that cinnamon pony?" I give Alec credit for the easy way he said this, tossing it out as a joke. "He went thataway, Earl."

Earl proved not to be in the market for humor just now, however.

"I suppose you could have forked him any better?" You could all but hear the thick gears move in Earl's head to produce the next remark. "You likely had a lot of riding practice recently."

"Earl, you lardbrain," this drew from Leona.

But Alec chose to cash Earl's remark at face value. "Some of us do get paid to stay on horses instead of bailing off of them. Come on, Leona, let's go refuel before the dancing starts again."

Earl now had another brain movement. "Surprised you can dance at all these days, what with marriage on your mind." He leaned a little toward Alec to deliver the final part: "Tell me this, McCaskill. Has it ever climbed out the top of your pants yet?"

That one I figured was going to be bingo. After all, anybody who has grown up in Montana has seen Scotch lawsuits get under way for a lot less commentary than that. At dances the situation was common enough almost to be a regular feature. One guy with a few too many drinks in him calls some other guy a name none too fond, and that party responds with a fist. Of course the commotion was generally harsher than the combat, but black eyes and bent noses could result.

"Earl, you jugheaded—" Leona was responding, but to my considerable disappointment Alec interrupted her by simply telling Earl, "Stash it, sparrowhead. Come on, Leona, we got business elsewhere."

"I bet you got business all right," Earl adventured on. "Leona business. Snatch a kiss, kiss a snatch, all the same to you, McCaskill, ain't it?"

I can't truly say I saw it happen. Not in any way of following a sequence: this and then this and then this. No, the event simply arrived into my mind, complete, intact, engraved before its realization could make itself felt. Versions of anything of this sort are naturally suspect, of course. Like that time Dempsey fought Gibbons up at Shelby for the heavyweight championship. About ten thousand people were there, and afterward about a quarter million could provide you an eyewitness account. But I will relate just as much of this Earl and Alec episode as I can vouch for. One instant Earl was standing there, admiring the manufacture of his last comment, and then in the next instant was bent in half, giving a nasty tossing-up noise, *auheughhh*, that made my own stomach turn over.

What can have inspired Alec, given that the time-honored McCaskill procedure after loss of temper was to resort to a roundhouse right, to deliver Earl that short straight jab to the solar plexus?

That economical punch of Alec's produced plenty, though. Every bit of this I can see as if it were happening over again right now. Earl now in full light, doubled down as he was, Alec stepping around him to collect Leona, and the supper crowd in its long file out of the Sedgwick House stopping and gawking.

"God DAMN!" exploded between Ray and me, Arlee pushing through and combining his oath with the start of a haymaker targeted on Alec's passing jaw.

Targeted but undelivered. On the far side of Arlee's girth from me Ray reached up, almost casually it seemed, and latched onto Arlee's wrist. The intended swing went nowhere after that, Ray hanging on to the would-be swingster as if he'd just caught him with that hand in the cookie jar, and by the time Arlee squared around and managed to begin to tussle in earnest with Ray—thank heaven for the clomping quality of the Zane brain—I had awarded Arlee a bit of a shove to worry him from my side.

Where the ruckus would have progressed beyond that I have ever been curious about. In hindsight, that is. For if Arlee had managed to shake out of Ray's grip, he was elephant enough to provide us both some pounding.

But by now my father was on hand, and Pete and two or three other men soldiered out of the crowd to help sort us into order, and somebody was fetching Tollie Zane out of the Medicine Lodge on Earl's behalf.

"Jick, that's enough," my father instructed. "Turn him loose, Ray. It's over."

This too I am clear about. Those sentences to Ray and me were the full sum of what was said by any McCaskill here in this aftermath. What traveled to Alec from my father was a stare, a studying one there in the frame of hotel light as if my father was trying to be sure this was the person he thought it was.

And got back from Alec one of the identical caliber.

Then Leona was in the grasp of my brother, and my mother stepped out alongside my father, and each couple turned and went.

"Ray?"

"What?"

We were side by side in bed, in the dark of his room. Outside the open twin windows a breeze could be heard teasing its way through the leaves of the giant cottonwood.

"You helped a lot, there at the dance."

"That's okay."

"You'll want to watch out Arlee doesn't try get it back on you."

"Yeah."

There was silence then, and the dark, until Ray startled me with something between a giggle and a laugh. What the hell now? I couldn't see what he was doing, but as soon as words started issuing from him, I knew. He was pinching his nose closed.

"He wants   to watch out   around   me" came droning out in exact imitation of Tollie's rodeo announcing, "or I'll   cut his heart out   and drink   his blood."

That got me into the act. With a good grasp on my nose, I proposed in the same tinny tone:

"Yank off   his arm   and make him   shake hands with it."

Ray giggled and offered:

"Grab him   by the   epiglommis   until   his eyes pooch out."

"Sharpen   the point   on his   head"—I paused for my own giggles—"and   pound him   in   like a post."

"Kickenough   crap   out of   him   to daub   a log barn," Ray envisioned. "Goddamn   booger   eater   him anyhow."

With each atrocity on Arlee our laughing multiplied, until the bed was shaking and we tried to tone things down before Ray's folks woke up and wondered just what was going on.

But every time we got ourselves nearly under control, one or the other of us erupted again—"thump   old Arlee   as far   into hell"—on and on, laughing anew, snorting it out in spite of ourselves— "as a bird   can fly   in a   lifetime"—sides shaking and throats rollicking until we were almost sick, and then of course we had to laugh at the ridiculousness of that.

Nor, when Ray finally did play out and conked off to sleep, did that fever of humor entirely leave me. I would doze for a while and then be aware I was grinning open-eyed into the darkness about one or another moment of that immense day, that never-can-be-forgotten Fourth. Here I rest, world, as happy as if I had good sense and the patent on remembrance. My mother on the park stump giving her Ben English speech and Dode at the top of that leap by Coffee Nerves and my father calling out the Dude and Belle to the dancing crowd and my brother one-punching Earl Zane and Ray pitching in on Arlee and, you bet, Stanley Meixell collecting Velma Simms. Scene by scene they fell into place in me, smooth as kidskin and exact as chapter and verse, every one a perfect piece of that day and now of the night; a set of hours worth the price of the rest of the life.

THREE

The sun shines, hay is being made. All along English Creek and Noon Creek, mowing and raking and stacking are the order of the day. As to how this year's cutting compares with those of recent years—have you seen any rancher lately who wasn't grinning like a Christian holding four aces?

—*GROS VENTRE WEEKLY GLEANER, JULY 20*

"Hand me a half-inch, would you, Jick."

"Here you go." I passed the open-end wrench of that size to Pete beneath the power buckrake. There was a grunt of exertion, a flash of metal as the wrench flew and clattered off the chassis, and the news from Pete:

"Sonofabitch must be a three-eighths."

I had been here before. "Did you hit your knuckles?"

"Sure did."

"Did you round the head off the bolt?"

"Sure did."

"Are you sure you want to put up hay again this year?"

"Guess what, nephew. The next rusted-up sonofabitch of a bolt under here has got your name on it."

At noon of that first day of preparing Pete's haying machinery, when he and I came in to wash up for dinner Marie took one look at the barked knuckles and skin scrapes and blood blisters on the both of us and inquired: "Did you two count your fingers before you started all this?"

—

Despite what it took out of a person's hide I still look back on that as topnotch employment, my job of haying for Pete.

The Reese ranch was a beauty for hay. Pete inherited not only my grandfather Isaac Reese's acreage there along Noon Creek but old Isaac's realization that nurturing more than one source of income is as good an idea as you can have in Montana. Pete was continuing with the sheep Isaac had turned to after the crash of cattle prices and also was improving the ranch's hayfields, running ditches into the bottomland meadows of wild hay to irrigate them from Noon Creek. Even in the Depression's driest years, Pete always had hay to sell during the winter. This year it looked as if he would have a world of the stuff. Those wild meadows of timothy and wiregrass lay one after another along the creek like green pouches on a thong. Then there was the big field atop the Noon Creek–English Creek divide which grew dry-land alfalfa. In a wet year like this one, the alfalfa was soaring up more than knee high and that wide benchland field looked as green as they say the Amazon is.

Those first days after the Fourth of July, the hay was very nearly ready for us and I was more than ready for it. Ready to have the McCaskill family situation off my mind for the main part of each day, at least. It did not take a great deal of original thinking to realize that the deadlock between my parents and Alec now was stouter than it had been before. If Alec ever needed any confirming in his rooting tooting cowboy notion of himself, his rodeo day calf-roping and pugilistic triumph had more than done so. Both of those and Leona too. Alec's feet might not even touch the ground until about August. Anyway, I had spent so much thought on the Alec matter already that summer that my mind was looking around for a new direction. My father, my mother, my brother: let them do the sorting out of Alec's future. I now had an imminent one haying at Noon Creek—all my own.

I might have known. "The summer when," I have said my mother ever after called this one. For me, the summer when not even haying turned out as expected. The summer when I began to wonder if anything ever does.

To be quite honest, on a task like those first few days of readying the equipment for haying I provided Pete more company than help. I mean, I can fix machinery when I have to but I'd rather be doing anything else. My point of view is that I would be more enthusiastic about the machine era if the stuff healed itself instead of requiring all the damn repair it does. And Pete was much the same as me where wrench work was involved.

But I still maintain, companionship is no small thing to create. Amid all that damn bolting, unbolting, rebolting, bushing, shimming, washering, greasing, oiling, banging, sharpening, straightening, wouldn't you welcome a little conversation? And the farther removed from the mechanical chore at hand the better? At least my uncle and I thought so. I recall Pete, just right out of the blue, telling me about the Noon Creek Kee-Kee bird. "You never heard of the Kee-Kee bird we got around here? Jick, I am surprised at you. The Kee-Kee bird shows up the first real day of winter every year. Lands on top of the lambing shed over there and takes a look all around. Then he says, 'Kee-Kee-Keerist All Mighty, this is c-c-cold c-c-country!' and heads for California." I in return favored Pete with a few of the songs from Stanley's repertoire, starting with the one about the lady who was wild and wooly and full of fleas and never had been curried above her knees. He looked a little surprised at my musical knowledge, but was interested enough.

This sticks with me, too: how startling it was to hear, from a face so reminiscent of my mother's, the kind of language Pete unloosed on the haying equipment during those repair days. It also was kind of refreshing.

All in all, then, Pete and I got along like hand and glove. And I have already recited Marie's glories, back there at the Fourth of July picnic. If anybody in the Two country could cook in the same league as my mother, it was Marie. So my ears and the rest of me both were well nourished, that couple of days as Pete and I by main strength and awkwardness got the haying gear into running order. It never occurred to me at the time, but I suppose Pete welcomed having me around—and Alec in the earlier summers when he was in the raking job—because he and Marie were childless. Their son died at birth, and Marie very nearly died with him. Her health in fact had never been strong since. So for a limited time, at least, someone my age was a privileged character with the Reeses.

Even so, I held off until Pete and I were finishing up the last piece of equipment, replacing broken guards on the mowing machine, before I tried him on this:

"Pete, you know Stanley Meixell, don't you?"

"Used to. Why?"

"I'm just sort of curious. My folks don't say much about him."

"He's been a long time gone from this country. Old history."

"Were you around him when he was the English Creek ranger?"

"Some. When anybody on Noon Creek who could spell K-O-W was running cattle up there on the forest. During the war and just after, that was."

"How was he as a ranger?"

"How was he?"

"Well, yeah. I mean, did Stanley go about things pretty much the way Dad does? Fuss over the forest like he was its mother hen, sort of?"

"Stanley always struck me as more of a rooster than a mother hen." That, I didn't get. Stanley hadn't seemed to me particularly strutty in the way he went about life. "But I will say this," Pete went on. "Stanley Meixell and your father know these mountains of the Two better than anybody else alive. They're a pair of a kind, on that."

"They are?" That the bunged-up whiskey-sloshing camptender I had squired around up there in the Two was as much a master of the mountains as my father—all due respect to Pete, but I couldn't credit it.

Figuring maybe Pete's specific knowledge of Stanley was better than his general, I asked: "Well, after he was the English Creek ranger, where was his ticket to?"

"His ticket?"

"That's the saying Forest Service guys have about being transferred. After here, where'd Stanley get transferred to?"

"The Forest Service isn't my ball of string, Jick. How do you feel about sharpening some mower sickles? There's a couple against the wall of the shop somewhere."

"How's she going, Jick?"

The third morning I rode over to Pete and Marie's, the mower man Bud Dolson greeted me there at breakfast. Pete had gone into Gros Ventre to fetch him the night before, Bud having come up on the bus all the way from Anaconda. Ordinarily he was on the bull gang at the smelter there, a kind of roustabout's job as I understood it. "Good to get out in the real air for a change," Bud claimed was his reason for coming to mow hay for Pete summer after summer. Smelter fumes would be sufficient propulsion to anywhere, yes. But I have a sneaking hunch that the job as mower man, a month of being out here by himself with just a team of horses and a mowing machine and the waiting hay, meant a lot in itself to somebody as quiet as Bud.

The first genuine scorching day of summer arrived with Bud, and by about nine o'clock the dew was off the hay and he was cutting the first swath of the nearest of the Noon Creek meadows, a path of fallen green beside the standing green.

"How do, Jick."

While I was saddling Pony to go home to English Creek at the end of that afternoon, Perry Fox came riding in from Gros Ventre.

You still could find Perry's species in a lot of Montana towns then, old Texas punchers who rode north on a trail drive somewhere before the turn of the century and for this reason or that never found their way back to Texas. Much of the time when I was growing up, Gros Ventre had as many as three of them: Andy Cratt, Deaf Smith Mitchell, and Perry Fox. They had all been hands for the old Seven Block ranch when it was the cattle kingdom of this part of Montana, then afterward hung on by helping out the various small ranchers at branding time and when the calves were shipped, and in between, breaking a horse for somebody now and again. Perry Fox was the last of them alive yet. Into his seventies, I guess he had to be, for Toussaint Rennie told my father he could remember seeing both Perry and Deaf Smith Mitchell in the roundup of 1882, skinny youngsters aboard big Texican saddles. Now too stove-up for a regular ranch job, Perry spent his winters in Dale Quigg's saddle store helping out with harnessmending and other leather work and his summer job was on the dump rake for Pete.

As I responded to Perry's nod and drawl of greeting and watched him undo his bedroll and warbag from behind his saddle—like Bud, Perry would put up in the bunkhouse here at Pete's now until haying was done—I couldn't help but notice that he had a short piece of rope stretched snug beneath his horse's belly and knotted into each stirrup. This was a new one on me, stirrups tied like that. That night I asked my father about it.

"Come to that, has he," my father said. "Riding with hobbled stirrups."

I still didn't savvy.

"At his age Perry can't afford to get thrown any more," my father spelled it out for me. "He's too brittle to mend. So with the stirrups tied down that way, he can keep himself clamped into them if his horse starts to buck."

"Maybe he just ought to quit riding horseback," I said, without thinking it through.

My father set me straight on that, too. "Guys like Perry, if they can't ride you might as well take them out and shoot them. Perry has never learned to drive a car. The minute he can't climb onto a horse and keep himself there, he's done for."

The fourth morning, Pete had me harness up my team of horses and take my rake to the mowed field to help Perry get the dump-raking under way.

Truth be told, that day I was the one who did the majority of the dump-raking—scooping the hay into windrows, that was—while Perry tinkered and tinkered with his rake teeth and his dump lever and his horses' harness and so on. Right then I fully subscribed to what Pete said about his custom of hiring Perry haying after haying: "He's slow as the wrath of Christ, but he is steady." I suppose if my behind was as aged and bony as Perry's, I wouldn't have been in any hurry either to apply it to a rake seat for the coming four or five weeks.

At the end of that day of windrowing, when Perry and I had unhitched our teams and Pete was helping us look them over for any harness sores, up the road to the ranch buildings came the Forest Service pickup and in it my father and my mother as well. They'd been to Great Falls on a headquarters trip my father had to make and before starting home they swung by First Avenue South to chauffeur the last of the haying crew to Pete.

He tumbled out of the back of the pickup now. The stackman, Wisdom Johnson.

"Hey, Pete!" cried Wisdom. Even after the two-hour ride from Great Falls in the open breezes Wisdom was not what could be called even approximately sober. On the other hand he wasn't so swacked he had fallen out of the pickup on the way to the job, which was the hiring standard that counted. "Hey, Perry!" the greeting process went on. "Hey, Jick!" If the entire population of Montana had been there in the

Reese yard, Wisdom would have greeted every one of them identically. Wisdom Johnson's mind may not have been one of the world's broadest, but it liked to practice whatever it knew.

"As I savvy it, Wisdom," acknowledged Pete, "that's what you're here for all right. Hay."

"Pete, I'm ready for it," Wisdom testified earnestly. "If you want to start stacking right now, I am ready. You bet I am. How about it, ready to go?" Wisdom squinted around like Lewis and Clark must have. "Where's the field?"

"Wisdom, it's suppertime," Pete pointed out. "Morning will be soon enough to start stacking. You feel like having some grub?"

Wisdom considered. "No. No, I don't." He swallowed to get rid of the idea of food. "What I need to do is sort of sit down for a while."

Perry stepped forward. "I'll herd him to the bunkhouse. Right this way, Wisdom. Where'd you winter?"

"Out on the coast," reported Wisdom as he unsteadily accompanied Perry. "Logging camp, up north of Grays Harbor. Rain! Perry, do you know it'd sometimes rain a week steady? I just did not know it could rain that much."

Chin in hand and elbow propped on the doorframe, my mother skeptically watched all this out the rolled-down window of the pickup. Now she opened the door and stepped out. Not surprisingly, she looked about two-thirds riled. I don't know of any Montana woman who has never gritted her teeth, one time or another, over that process of prying men off bar stools and getting them launched toward whatever they're supposed to be doing in life. "I'll go in and visit Marie," she announced, which my father and Pete and I all were glad enough to have happen.

Pete made sure my mother was out of earshot, then inquired: "He in Sheba's place, was he?"

"No, in the Mint, though he did have Bouncing Betty with him. She wasn't about to turn loose of him as long as he had a nickel to his name." Upon study, my father looked somewhat peevish, too. Wisdom Johnson must have taken considerable persuading to part with Bouncing Betty. "So at least I didn't have to shake him directly out of a whore's bed. But that's about the best I can say for your caliber of employee, brother-in-law."

Pete broke a grin at my father and razzed: "I wouldn't be so damn hard up for crew if you'd paid attention to the example of Good Help Hebner and raised anything besides an occasional scatter raker."

Somehow Pete had known what the moment needed. Pete's kidding had within it the fact that the other of the rake-driving McCaskill brothers had been Alec, and he was not a topic my father particularly cared to hear about these days. Yet here it came, the half wink of my father's left eye and the answer to Pete's crack: "Scatter rakers were as good as I could do. Whatever that says about *my* caliber."

The fifth day, we made hay.

The windrows that Perry and I had raked formed a pattern I have always liked. A meadow with ribs of hay, evenly spaced. Now Perry was dump-raking the next field down the creek and Bud was mowing the one beyond that.

Those of us in the stacking crew began our end of the matter. We sited the overshot stacker toward the high edge of the meadow, so the haystack would be up out of the deepest winter snowdrifts along Noon Creek. With the power buckrake, Pete shoved several loads of hay into place behind the stacker. Then Wisdom maneuvered and smoothed that accumulation with his pitchfork until he had the base of his stack made the way he wanted it. An island of hay almost but not quite square—eight paces wide, ten paces long—and about chest high.

"You said last night you're ready, Wisdom," called Pete. "Here it comes." And he bucked the first load of hay onto the fork of the stacker. "Send it to heaven, Clayton."

The final man, or I should say member, of our haying crew was the stacker team driver, twelve-year-old Clayton Hebner. Pete always hired whichever Hebner boy was in the twelve-to-fourteen-year range for that stacker team job and they were pretty much interchangeable, a skinny kid with a forelock and nothing to say for himself; apparently the volume knob for that whole family was on Good Help Hebner. All that was really noticeable about Clayton was his Hebner way of always eyeing you, as if you were the latest link in evolution and he didn't want to miss the moment when you sprouted wings or fins. At Pete's words Clayton now started into motion his team of horses hitched to the cable which, through a tripod-and-pulley rig within the stacker, lifts the twin arms of the stacker and the hay-loaded fork, and the hay went up and up until—

It occurs to me: does everybody these days think that hay naturally comes in bales? That God ordained that livestock shall eat from loaves of hay tied up in twine by thirteen-thousand-dollar machinery? If so, maybe I had better describe the notion of haying as it used to be. All in the world it amounted to was gathering hay into stacks about the size of an adobe house; a well-built haystack even looks as solid and straightforward as an adobe structure, though of course stands higher and has a rounded-off top. But try it yourself sometime, this gathering of ten or twelve tons of hay into one stack, and you will see where all the equipment comes in. Various kinds of stackers were used in various areas of the West, beaver slides, Mormon derricks, two-poles, jayhawks, but Pete's preference was an overshot. An overshot stacker worked as its name suggests, tossing a load of hay up over a high wide framework which served as a sort of scaffolding for the front of the haystack. If, say, you hold your arms straight out in front of you, with your hands clutching each end of a basket with hay piled in it: now bring your arms and the basket straight up over your head with a little speed and you are tossing the hay exactly as an overshot does. In short, a kind of catapult principle is involved. But a calculated one, for it is the responsibility of the stacker team driver to pace his horses so that the overshot's arms and fork fling the hay onto whichever part of the stack the stackman wants it. Other than being in charge of the speed of the team, though, driving the stacker team is a hell of a dull job, walking back and forth behind the horses as they run the overshot up and down, all damn day long, and that's why a kid like Clayton usually got put on the task.

So hay was being sent up, and as this first haystack and the day's temperature both began to rise, Wisdom Johnson suffered. This too was part of the start of haying: Wisdom sweating the commerce of Great Falls saloons out of himself. Soaking himself sober, lathering into the summer's labor. We all knew by heart what the scene would be this initial morning, Wisdom lurching around up there atop the mound of hay as if he had a log chained to each leg. It was a little painful to watch, especially now that my camptending sojourn with Stanley Meixell had taught me what a hangover truly is.

Yet agonized as Wisdom looked, the stack was progressing prettily, as we also knew it would. The stackman, he was maestro of the haying crew. When the rest of us had done our mowing or raking or bucking or whatever, the final result of it all was the haystacks the stackman built. And Wisdom Johnson could build them, as he put it, "high and tall and straight." No question about it, Wisdom was as big and brawny as the ideal stackman ought to be; nine of him would have made a dozen. And he also just looked as if he belonged atop a haystack, for he was swarthy enough to be able to pitch hay all day up there without his shirt on, which I envied much. If I tried that I'd have burned and blistered to a pulp. Wisdom simply darkened and darkened, his suntan a litmus each summer of how far along our haying season was. As July heated up into August, more than once it occurred to me that with the sweat bathing Wisdom as he worked up there next to the sun, and his arm muscles bulging as he shoved the hay around, and that dark leathering of his skin, he was getting to look like the heavyweight fighter Joe Louis. But of course that wasn't something you said to a white person back then.

This was the second summer of Wisdom being known as Wisdom instead of his true name, Cyrus Johnson. The nickname came about because he had put up hay a number of seasons in the Big Hole Basin down in the southwestern part of the state, and according to him the Big Hole was the front parlor of heaven. The hay there was the best possible, the workhorses all but put their harnesses on themselves each morning, the pies of Big Hole ranch cooks nearly floated off into the air from the swads of meringue atop them. The list of glories ran on and on. Inasmuch as the Big Hole had a great reputation for hay even without the testimony of Cyrus Johnson, the rest of us at the Reese table tended to nod and say nothing. But then came one supper-time, early in the first summer I hayed for Pete, when Cyrus started in on a fresh Big Hole glory. "You take that Wisdom, now. There's my idea of a town. It's the friendliest, drinkingest, prettiest place—"

"Wisdom? That burg?" Ordinarily Bud Dolson was silence himself. But Anaconda where he was from was not all that far from the Big Hole town of Wisdom and Bud had been there. As Cyrus now had the misfortune of asking him.

"I think so," replied Bud. "I blinked. I might've missed most of it."

Cyrus looked hurt. "Now what do you mean by that?"

"Cy, I mean that the town of Wisdom makes the town of Gros Ventre look like London, England."

"Aw, come on, Bud. Wisdom is a hell of a nice town."

Bud shook his head in pity. "If you say so, Wisdom." And ever since, the big stackman was Wisdom Johnson to us.

———

This first stack was well under way, Pete having buckraked several windrows in to the stacker. Now began my contribution to the haying process. I went over and climbed onto my scatter rake.

If you happen never to have seen one, a scatter rake simply resembles a long axle—mine was a ten-foot type—between a set of iron wheels, high spoked ones about as big around as those you think of a stagecoach having, but not nearly so thick and heavy. The "axle," actually the chassis of the rake, carries a row of long thin curved teeth, set about a hand's width apart from each other, and it is this regiment of teeth that rakes along the ground and scrapes together any stray hay lying there. As if the hayfield was a head of hair and the scatter rake a big iron comb going over it, so to speak. Midway between the wheels a seat stuck up for the rake driver—me—to ride on, and a wooden tongue extended forward for a team of horses to be hitched to.

My team was in harness and waiting. Blanche and Fisheye. As workhorses go, they weren't too bad a pair; a light team, as you didn't need the biggest horses in the world just to pull a scatter rake, but more on the steady side than frisky. That Blanche and Fisheye were civilized at all was a relief to me, because you never know what you might get in a team of horses. One of them maybe can pull like a Percheron but is dumb, and the other one clever enough to teach geometry but so lazy he constantly lays back in the traces. Or one horse may be a kicker, and his mate so mild you could pass a porcupine under him without response. So except for Fisheye staring sideways at you in a fishy way as you harnessed him, and Blanche looking like she needed a nap all the time, this team of mine was better than the horse law of averages might suggest.

I believe I am right in saying Pete was the first rancher in the Two country to use a power buckrake: an old automobile chassis and engine with a fork mounted on it to buck the hay in from the field to the stack. Wisdom Johnson a few summers before had brought word of the invention of the power buckrake in the Big Hole: "I tell you, Pete, they got them all over that country. They move hay faster than you can see." That proved to be not quite the case, but the contraption could bring in hay as fast as two buckrakes propelled by horses. Thus the internal combustion engine roared into the Reese hayfields and speeded matters up, but it also left dabs of hay behind it, scatterings which had either blown off the buckrake fork or which it simply missed. The scatter raker was the gatherer of that leftover hay, which otherwise would be wasted. In place on my rake seat, I now clucked to Blanche and Fisheye, reined them toward the part of the meadow Pete had been bucking in loads from, and my second summer of scatter raking was begun.

I suppose I have to admit, anybody who could handle a team of workhorses could run a scatter rake. But not necessarily run it as it ought to be done. The trick was to stay on the move but at an easy pace. Keep the horses in mild motion and the rake teeth down there gathering leftover hay, instead of racing around here and yon. Roam and glean, by going freestyle over a field as a fancy skater swoops around on ice. Well, really not quite that free and fancy, for you do have to tend to business enough to dump your scatterings in some good place for the buckrake to get it, and not in a boggy spot or on top of a badger mound. But still I say, the more you could let yourself go and just follow the flow of the hayfield, so to speak—keep swooping back and forth where the power buckrake had recently been, even if there wasn't much spilled hay there—the better off you were as a scatter raker. A mind as loose as mine was about right for scatter raking.

"How did it go?" my mother asked, that first night of full haying. We were waiting supper for my father, who was somewhere up the North Fork inspecting the progress of a CCC trail crew there.

"A stack and a half," I reported offhandedly as if I had been a hayhand for centuries. "About usual, for first day."

"How did you get along with Blanche and Fisheye?"

"They're kind of a logy pair of sonsa—" I remembered in time to mend my mouth; the vocabulary I'd been using around Pete and the crew was a quick ticket to trouble here at home—"of so and sos. But they're okay."

She appraised me from where she was leaning against the kitchen sink, arms folded across her chest. Then surprised me with her smile and: "It's quiet around here, without you."

I chose to take that as a compliment. More than that, I risked ribbing her in return, a little. "Well, I guess I could call you up on the telephone every noon from Pete and Marie's, and sing you a song or tell you a joke."

"Never mind, Mister Imagination," she declined. "I'll adjust."

—

I didn't pay it sufficient mind at the time, but in truth my mother *did* have to adjust. Alec in exile. Me rationed between English Creek and the Noon Creek hayfields. My father beginning to be gone more and more as fire danger increased in the forest. The reverse of her usual situation of a houseful of male McCaskills, a genuine scarcity of us. There is another topic which occupies my mind these days. The way life sorts us into men and women, not on any basis of capability that I have ever been able to see. High on the list of questions I wish I'd had the good sense to ask, throughout that immense summer, is the one to my mother. Her view about being born as a woman into a region which featured male livelihoods.

"You finally starved out, did you," she now greeted my father's late arrival. "Wash up and sit up, you two; supper will be just a minute now."

"How'd it go today?" my father asked me, and I repeated my report of Reese haying. Through that and other supper conversation he nodded and said uh huh a lot, which signaled that he was only half listening. The symptom was annual. At this point of the summer, and hot as this one suddenly had turned, fire was forever on the mind of a forest ranger. The joke was told that when the preacher at a funeral asked if anyone wanted to memorialize the deceased, a ranger was the first one onto his feet and began: "Old Tom wasn't the worst fellow I ever knew. Now I'd like to add a few words about fire prevention."

When you think about it, my father's yearly deep mood about fire was understandable enough. He was responsible for an entire horizon. The skyline made up of peaks and reefs and timbered slopes and high grasslands: that conglomeration of nature was designated his district of the Two Medicine National Forest, and every blessed inch of it was prey to lightning storms and careless campfires and flipped cigarettes. His line of defense was a light thread of men across that mass of mountain and forest; the lookouts in the tall towers, and at this time of year, the fire guards and other smokechasers he would start hiring and stationing for quick combat against lightning strikes or smolders of any sort. My father entirely subscribed to the theory that the time to fight a forest fire was before it got going. True, the timber of the Two here on the east face of the Rockies was not as big and dense and incendiary as the forests farther west in Montana and Idaho. "But that doesn't mean they're made of goddamn asbestos either" ran the complaint of east-side rangers on the Two, the Lewis and Clark, the Custer and the Helena, against what they saw as a westward tilt in the thinking and the fire budget of Region One headquarters. It was a fact that the legendary fires occurred over there west of the Continental Divide. The Bitterroot blaze of 1910 was an absolute hurricane of flame. Into smoke went three million acres of standing trees, a lot of it the finest white pine in the world. And about half the town of Wallace, Idaho, burned. And this too: the Bitterroot fire killed eighty-five persons, eighty-four of them done in directly by the flames and the other one walked off a little from a hotshot crew on Setzer Creek and put a pistol to himself. The Forest Service, which was only a few years old at the time, was bloodied badly by the Bitterroot fire. And as recently as 1934 there had been the fiasco of the Selway fires along the Idaho-Montana line. That August, the Selway National Forest became the Alamo of Region One. Into those back-country fires the regional forester, Major Kelley, and his headquarters staff poured fifty-four hundred men, and they never did get the flames under control. The Pete King Creek fire and the McLendon Butte fire and about fifteen smaller ones all were roaring at once. The worst afternoon, ten square miles of the Selway forest were bursting into flame every hour. And when the fire at Fish Butte blew up, a couple of hundred CCC guys had to run like jackrabbits. Five fire camps eventually went up in smoke, both the Pete King and Lochsa ranger stations damn near did. Nothing the Forest Service tried on the Selway worked. Nothing could work, really. An inferno has no thermostat. The rains of late September finally slowed the Selway fires, and only weeks after that Major Kelley killed off the Selway National Forest, parceled out its land to the neighboring forests and scattered its staff like the tribes of Israel. The Selway summer sobered everybody working in Region One—that total defeat by fire and the Major's obliteration of a National Forest unit—and for damn sure no ranger wanted any similar nightmare erupting in his own district.

I stop to recount all this because of what happened now, as my father finished supper and thumbed open the day's one piece of mail, an official Forest Service envelope. "What've we got here," he wondered, "the latest kelleygram?"

His next utterance was: "Sonofabitch."

He looked as if he had been hit with a two-by-four, stunned and angry. Then, as if the words would have to change themselves when read aloud, he recited from the letter:

" 'Placement of manpower this fire season will be governed by localized fire danger measurements. An enforced lag of manning below current danger will eliminate over-manning designed to meet erratic peak loads and will achieve material decrease in FF costs over past years' expenditures. Organization on east-side forests in particular is to be held to the lowest level consistent with carefully analyzed current needs.'"

My mother oh so slightly shook her head, as if this confirmed her suspicions of brainlessness in the upper ranks of the U.S. Forest Service. My father crumpled the letter and crossed the kitchen to the window looking out on Roman Reef and Rooster Mountain and Phantom Woman peak and other of the profiles of the Two.

I asked, "What's all that mean?"

"No fire guards on our side of the Divide until things start burning," said my father without turning from the window.

Right up until the time haying started, I had been rehearsing to myself how to talk my parents into letting me live in the bunkhouse at Pete's with the rest of the hay crew. It was something I imagined I much wanted to do. Be in on the gab of Wisdom and Perry and Bud, hear all the tales of the Big Hole and First Avenue South and Texas and Anaconda and so on and so on. Gain one more rung towards being a grownup, I suppose was what was working on me. Yet when haying time arrived I did not even bring up the bunkhouse issue.

For one thing, I could anticipate my mother's enunciation about one shavetail McCaskill already living in a bunkhouse "and to judge by Alec's recent behavior One Is More Than Enough." For another, with my father on the go as much as he was this summer it seemed plain that he would prefer for me to be on hand at English Creek whenever he couldn't. But do you know, I actually made it unanimous against myself. What the matter came right down to was that I didn't want to give up the porch bedroom at English Creek for the dubious gain of bunking with hay hands.

Which is how I became a one-horsepower commuter. The one horse being Pony, whom I found I regarded with considerable more esteem ever since Mouse decided to hose down the rodeo grounds that time in front of Leona. Each morning now I got up at five, went out and caught and saddled Pony outside the barn—quite a lot of light in the sky that time of year—and the pair of us would head for the Reese ranch.

Where morning is concerned, I am my father all over again. "The day goes downhill after daybreak" was his creed. I don't suppose there are too many people now who have seen a majority of the dawns of their life, but my father did, and I have. And of my lifetime of early rising I have never known better dawns than those when I rode from English Creek to my haying job on Noon Creek.

The ford north of the ranger station Pony and I would cross; if there was enough moon the wild roses along the creek could be seen, pale crowds of them; and in a few minutes of climbing we came atop the bench of land which divides the two creek drainages. Up there, at that brink of dawn hour, the world revealed all its edges. Dark lines of the tops of buttes and benches to the north, towards the Two Medicine River and the Blackfeet Reservation. The Sweetgrass Hills bumping up far on the eastern horizon like five dunes of black sand. The timbered crest of Breed Butte standing up against the stone mountain wall of the west. What trick of light it is I can't really say, but everything looked as if drawn in heavy strokes, with the final shade of night penciled in wherever there was a gulch or coulee.

The only breaks in the stillness were Pony's hooves against the earth, and the west breeze which generally met us atop that broad benchland. I say breeze. In the Two country any wind that doesn't lift you off your horse is only a breeze. My mountain coat was on me, my hat pulled low, my hands in leather work gloves, and I was just about comfortable.

Since Pete's haying season always lasted a month or a little more, I rode right through the phases of the moon. My favorite you can guess on first try. The fat full moon, resting there as if it was an agate marble which had rolled into the western corner of the sky. During the early half of my route the mountains still drew most of their light from the moon, and I watched the reefs and other rock faces change complexion, from light gray to ever so slightly pink, as the sunrise began to touch them. Closer to me, the prairie flowers now made themselves known amid the tan grass. Irises, paintbrushes, bluebells, shooting stars, sunflowers.

Then this. The first week or so of those daybreak rides, the sun was north enough that it came up between the Sweetgrass Hills. They stand sixty or seventy miles across the prairie from where I was riding, way over towards Havre, so there was a sense that I was seeing a sunrise happening in a far land. The gap between the mounded sets of hills first filled with a kind of orange film; a haze of coming light, it might be called. Then the sun would slowly present itself, like a big glowing coal burning its way up through the horizon.

Those dawns taught me that beauty makes the eyes greedy. For even after all this, mountains and moon and earth edges and the coming of the sun, I considered that what was most worth watching for was the first shadow of the day. When the sun worked its way about half above the horizon, that shadow emerged to stretch itself off from Pony and me—horse and youngster melded, into an apparition of leftover dark a couple of hundred feet in length. Drawn out on the prairie grass in that far-reaching first shadow, Pony and I loomed like some new creature put together from the main parts of a camel and a giraffe.

Is it any wonder each of these haying-time dawns made me feel remade?

Meanwhile it continued to be the damnedest summer of weather anybody could remember. All that rain of June, and now July making a habit of ninety degrees. The poor damn farmers out east of Gros Ventre and north along the High Line were fighting a grasshopper invasion again, the hot days hatching out the 'hoppers faster than the farmers could spread poison against them. And for about five days in the middle of July an epidemic of lightning storms broke out in all the national forests of Region One. A lookout reported a plume of smoke up the South Fork of English Creek, on a heavily forested north slope of Grizzly Reef. This of course caused some excitement in the ranger station, and my father hustled his assistant ranger Paul Eliason and some trail men and a nearby CCC brush crew up there. "Paul's used to those big trees out on the coast," my father remarked to my mother. "It won't hurt him to find out that the ones here are big enough to burn." That Grizzly Reef smoke, though, turned out to be a rotten log and some other debris smoldering in a rocky area, and Paul and his crew handled it without much sweat.

That mid-July dose of lightning and his dearth of fire guards to be smokechasers put my father in what my mother called "his prowly mood." But then on the morning of the twenty-first of July we woke up to snow in the mountains. Fire was on the loose elsewhere in Montana—spot fires across the Continental Divide in the Flathead country and others up in Glacier Park, and a big blaze down in Yellowstone Park that hundreds of men were on—while my father's forest lay snoozing under a cool sheet of white.

"How did you arrange that?" my mother mock-questioned him at breakfast. "Clean living and healthy thoughts?"

"The powerrr of Scotch prrayerrr," he rumbled back at her in his preacher voice. Then with his biggest grin in weeks: "Also known as the law of averages. Tough it out long enough in this country and a snowstorm will eventually happen when you actually want it to."

As I say, putting up Pete's hay always took about a month, given some days of being rained out or broke down. This proved to be a summer when we were reasonably lucky about both moisture and breakage. So steadily that none of us on the crew said anything about it for fear of changing our luck, day on day along Noon Creek our new stacks appeared, like fresh green loaves.

My scatter-raking became automatic with me. Of course, whenever my mind doesn't have to be on what I am doing, it damn well for sure is going to be on some other matter. Actually, though, for once in my life I did a respectable job of combining my task at hand and my wayfaring thoughts. For if I had a single favorite daydream of those hayfield hours, it was to wonder why a person couldn't be a roving scatter-raker in the way that sheep shearers and harvest hands moved with their seasons. I mean, why not? The principle seems to me the same: a nomad profession. I could see myself traveling through Montana from hay country to hay country—although preferably with better steppers than Blanche and Fisheye if there was much distance involved—and hiring on, team and rake and all, at the best-looking ranch of each locale. Maybe spend a week, ten days, at the peak of haying at each. Less if the grub was mediocre, longer if a real pie maker was in the kitchen. Dwell in the bunkhouse so as to get to know everybody on a crew, for somehow every crew, every hay hand, was discernibly a little different from any other. Then once I had learned enough about that particular country and earned from the boss the invite "Be with us again next year, won't you?" on I would go, rolling on, the iron wheels and line of tines of my scatter rake like some odd over-wide chariot rumbling down the road.

An abrupt case of wanderlust, this may sound like, but then it took very little to infect me at that age. Can this be believed? Except for once when all of us at the South Fork school were taken to Helena to visit the capitol, a once-in-a-while trip with my father when he had to go to forest headquarters in Great Falls was the farthest I had ever been out of the Two country. Ninety miles; not much of a grand tour. There were places of Montana I could barely even imagine. Butte. All I knew definitely of Butte was that when you met anyone from there, even somebody as mild as Ray Heaney's father Ed, he would announce "I'm from Butte" and his chin would shoot out a couple of inches on that up-sound of *yewt*. In the midst of all this wide Montana landscape a city where shifts of men tunneled like gophers. Butte, the copper kingdom. Butte, the dark mineral pocket. Or the other thing that was always said: "Butte's a hole in the ground and so's a grave." That, I heard any number of times in the Two country. I think the truth may have been that parts of Montana like ours were apprehensive, actually a little scared, of Butte. There seemed to be something spooky about a place that lived by eating its own guts, which is the way mining sounded to us. Butte I would surely have to see someday. And the Big Hole Basin. As Wisdom Johnson told it, as haying season approached in the Big Hole the hay hands—they called them hay-diggers down there, which I also liked—began to gather about a week ahead of time. They sifted in, "jungled up" in the creekside willows at the edge of town, and visited and gossiped and just lay around until haying started. I savored the notion of that, the gathering, the waiting. Definitely the Big Hole would be on my hay rake route. And the dry Ingomar country down there in the southeastern part of the state, where Walter Kyle had done his hotel style of sheep ranching. The town water supply was a tank car, left off on the railroad siding each week. Walter told of coming back to town from sheep camp one late fall day and seeing flags of celebration flying. His immediate thought was that somebody had struck water, "but it turned out to be just the armistice ending the war." Havre and the High Line country. Fork Peck dam. Miles City. Billings, Lewistown. White Sulphur Springs. Red Lodge. Bozeman and the green Gallatin Valley. For that matter, Missoula. Montana seemed to be out there waiting for me, if I only could become old enough to get there.

But. There's always a "but" when you think about going everywhere and doing everything. But how old *was* that, when I would be advanced enough to sample Montana to the full?

North of the ears strange things will happen. Do you know who kept coming to mind, as I thought my way hither and thither from those Noon Creek hay meadows? Stanley Meixell. Stanley who had gone cowboying in Kansas when he was a hell of a lot younger than I was. Stanley who there in the cabin during our camptending journey told me of his wanders, down to Colorado and Wyoming and over into the Dakotas, in and out of jobs. Stanley who evidently so much preferred the wandering life that he gave up being a forest ranger, to pursue it. Stanley who could plop himself on a bar stool on the Fourth of July and be found by Velma Simms. But Stanley who also looked worn down, played out and overboozed, by the footloose way of life. The example of Stanley bothered me no little bit. If the wanderer's way was as alluring as it seemed from my seat on the scatter rake, how then did I account for the eroded look around Stanley Meixell's eyes?

Almost before I knew it the first few weeks of haying were behind us and we were moving the equipment onto the benchland for the ten days or so of putting up the big meadow of dry-land alfalfa there. "The alfaloofee field," as Perry Fox called it. This was another turn of the summer I looked forward to with interest, for this alfalfa haying was far enough from the Reese ranch house that we no longer went in at noon for dinner. Now began field lunches.

My stomach aside, why did I look forward to this little season of field lunches? I think the answer must be that the field lunches on the bench constituted a kind of ritual that appealed to me. Not that I would want to eat every meal of my life in the stubble of a hayfield. But for ten days or so it was like camping out or being on an expedition; possibly even a little like "jungling up" the way the Big Hole hay hands started off. Whatever, the alfaloofee field lunch routine went like this. A few minutes before noon, here came Marie in the pickup. She had with her the chuckbox, the old Reese family wooden one with cattle brands burned everywhere on its sides, and when a couple of us slid it back to the tailgate and lifted it down and opened it, in there waited two or three kinds of sandwiches wrapped in dish towels, and a bowl of potato or macaroni salad, and a gallon jar of cold tea or lemonade, and bread and butter and jam, and pickles, and radishes and new garden carrots, and a pie or cake. Each of us chose a dab of shade around the power buckrake or the pickup; my preference was to sit on the running board of the pickup, somehow it seemed more like a real meal when I sat up to eat; and then we ploughed into the lunch. Afterward, which is to say the rest of the noon hour, Pete was a napper, with his hat down over his eyes. I never was; I was afraid I might miss something. Clayton too was open-eyed, in that silent sentry way all the Hebner kids had. Perry and Bud smoked, each rolling himself a handmade. This was the cue for Wisdom to pull out his own sack of Bull Durham, pat his shirt pocket, then say to Perry or Bud, "You got a Bible on you?" One or the other would loan him the packet of cigarette papers and he'd roll himself one. Strange how he could always have tobacco but perpetually be out of papers, which were the half of smoking that cost almost nothing. But that was Wisdom for you.

The womanly presence of Marie, slim and dark, sitting in the shade of the pickup beside the chuckbox and the dozing Pete, posed the need for another ritual. As tea and lemonade caught up with kidneys, we males one after another would rise, carefully casual, and saunter around to the far side of the haystack and do our deed. Then saunter back, trying to look like we'd never been away and Marie showing no least sign that we had.

Eventually Pete would rouse himself. He not only could nap at the drop of an eyelid, he woke up just as readily. "I don't suppose you characters finished this field while I was resting my eyes, did you?" Then he was on his feet, saying the rest of the back-to-work message: "Until they invent hay that puts itself up, I guess we got to."

Our last day of haying the benchland alfalfa brought two occurrences out of the ordinary.

The first came at once, when I headed Blanche and Fisheye to the southwest corner of the field to start the morning by raking there awhile. Maybe a quarter of a mile farther from where I was lay a nice grassy coulee, at the base of that slope of Breed Butte. The ground there was part of Walter Kyle's place, and with Walter summering in the mountains with his sheep, Dode Withrow always put up the hay of this coulee for him on shares. The Withrow stacking crew had pulled in and set up the afternoon before; I could pick out Dode over there, still with a cast on his leg, and I could all but hear him on the topic of trying to run a haying crew with his leg set in cement. If I hadn't been so content with haying for Pete, Dode would have been my choice of somebody to work for.

Maybe scatter rakers are all born with similar patterns of behavior in them, but in any case, at this same time I was working the corner of our field the Withrow rake driver was doing the nearest corner of theirs. Naturally I studied how he was going about matters, and a minute or so of that showed me that he wasn't a he, but Marcella Withrow.

I had no idea what the odds must be against a coincidence like that: Marcella and me having been the only ones in our class those eight years of grade school at South Fork, and now the only English Creek ones in our particular high school class in Gros Ventre, and this moment both doing the same job, in the same hay neighborhood. It made me grin. It also caused me to peek around with care, to make sure that I wouldn't be liable for any later razzing from our crew, and when the coast looked clear I waved to Marcella. She did the same, maybe even to checking over her shoulder against the razzing possibility, and we rattled past one another and raked our separate meadows. Some news to tell Ray Heaney the next time I got to town, anyway.

The other event occurred at noon, and this one went by the name of Toussaint Rennie.

He arrived in the pickup with Marie and the chuckbox of lunch. "I came to make sure," Toussaint announced, his tan gullied face solemn as Solomon. "Whether you men build haystacks right side up."

Actually the case was that Toussaint had finished ditch-riding for a while, with everybody harvesting now instead of irrigating, and Marie had driven up to the Two Medicine to fetch him for company for the day. What conversations went on between those two blood- and soul-mates I've always wished I could have overheard.

The gab between the hay crew and Toussaint was pretty general, though, until we were done eating. Pete then retired to his nap spot, and Perry and Bud and eventually Wisdom lit up their smokes, and so on. A little time passed, then Toussaint leaned from where he was sitting and laid his hand on the chuckbox. "Perry," he called over to Perry Fox. "We ate out of this, a time before."

"That we did," agreed Perry. "But Marie's style of grub is a whole helluva lot better."

Toussaint put his finger to the large F burnt into the end of the chuckbox. "Dan Floweree."

The finger moved to the 9R brand on the box's side. "Louis Robare." To the TL beside it: "Billy Ulm."

Then to the lid, where the space had been used to burn in a big D-S. "This one you know best, Perry."

I straightened up. It had come to me: where Perry and Toussaint would have first eaten out of this chuckbox. When those cattle brands were first seared into its wood. The famous roundup of 1882, from the elbow of the Teton River to the Canadian line; the one Toussaint told my father about, the one he said was the biggest ever in this part of Montana. Nearly three hundred men, the ranchers and their cowhands and horse wranglers and night herders and cooks; forty tents it took to hold them all. Each morning the riders fanned out in half circles of about a dozen miles' ride and rounded in the cattle for sorting. Each afternoon the branding fires of the several outfits sent smoke above the prairie as the irons wrote ownership onto living cowhide. When the big sweep was over, coulees and creek bottoms searched out over an area bigger than some Eastern states, it was said a hundred thousand head of cattle were accounted for.

"Davis-Hauser-Stuart," Perry was saying of the brand on the chuckbox lid. "My outfit at the time. DHS, the Damn Hard Sittin'."

Wisdom Johnson was beginning to catch up with the conversation. "Where was this you're talking about?"

"All in through here," Perry indicated with a slow swing of his head from shoulder to shoulder. "Roundin' up cattle."

"Cattle?" Wisdom cast a look around the benchland, as if a herd might be pawing out there this very moment. "Around here?" It did seem a lot to believe, that this alfalfa field and the farmland on the horizon east of us once was a grass heaven for cows.

"Everywhere from the Teton to Canada, those old outfits had cattle," Perry confirmed. "If you could find the buggers."

Bud Dolson spoke up. "When'd all this take place?"

Toussaint told him: "A time ago. '82."

"Eighteen *eighty-two?*" queried Wisdom. "Perry, how ungodly old *are* you?"

Perry pointed a thumb at Toussaint. "Younger'n him."

Toussaint chuckled. "Everybody is."

How can pieces of time leap in and out of each other the way they do? There I sat, that noontime, listening to Toussaint and Perry speak of eating from a chuckwagon box all those years ago; and hearing myself question my mother about how she and her mother and Pete were provisioned from the same chuckbox on their St. Mary wagon trip a quarter of a century ago; and gazing on Pete, snoozing there in the shade of the pickup, simultaneously my admired uncle and the boy who helloed the horses at St. Mary.

Toussaint and the history that went everywhere with him set me to thinking. Life and people were a kind of flood around me this summer, yet for all my efforts I still was high and dry where one point of the past was concerned.

When Toussaint climbed to his feet to visit the far side of the alfalfa stack, I decided. Hell, he himself was the one who brought the topic up, back at the creek picnic on the Fourth. *You are a campjack these days.* And an outhouse engineer and a dawn rider and a hay equipment mechanic and a scatter raker, and an inquisitive almost-fifteen-year-old. I got up and followed Toussaint around the haystack.

"Jick," he acknowledged me. "You are getting tall. Mac and Beth will need a stepladder to talk to you."

"Yeah, I guess," I contributed, but my altitude was not what I wanted discussed. As Toussaint tended to his irrigation and I to mine, I asked: "Toussaint, what can you tell me about Stanley Meixell? I mean, I don't know him real well. That time up in the Two, I was only lending him a hand with his camptending, is all."

"Stanley Meixell," Toussaint intoned. "Stanley was the ranger. When the national forest was put in."

"Yeah, I know that. But more what I was wondering—did he and my folks have a run-in, sometime? I can't quite figure out what they think of Stanley."

"But you," said Toussaint. "You do thinking, too, Jick. What is it you think of Stanley?"

He had me there. "I don't just know. I've never come up against anybody like him."

Toussaint nodded. "That is Stanley," he affirmed. "You know more than you think you do."

Well, there I was as usual. No more enlightened than when I started. The chronic condition of Jick McCaskill, age fourteen and eleven twelfths years, prospects for a cure debatable.

At least the solace of scatter-raking remained to me. Or so I thought. As I say, this day I have just told about was the one that finished off the benchland alfalfa. A last stint of haying, back down on the Noon Creek meadows, awaited. Even yet I go over and over in my mind the happenings which that last spell of haying was holding in store. Talk about a chain of events. You could raise and lower the anchor of an ocean liner on the string of links that began to happen now.

Our new venue for haying was the old Ramsay homestead. The "upper place," my mother and Pete both called it by habit, because it was the part of the Reese ranch farthest up Noon Creek, farthest in toward the mountains. The meadows there were small but plentiful, tucked into the willow bends of Noon Creek the way pieces of a jigsaw puzzle clasp into one another. Pete always left the Ramsay hay until last because its twisty little fields were so hard to buckrake. In some cases he had to drive out of sight around two or three bends of the creek to brink in enough hay for a respectable stack. "You spend all your damn time here going instead of doing" was his unfond sentiment.

For me on the scatter rake, though, the upper place was just fine. Almost any direction I sent Blanche and Fisheye prancing toward, there stood Breed Butte or the mountains for me to lean my eyes on. In this close to them, the Rockies took up more than half the edge of the earth, which seemed only their fair proportion. And knowing the reefs and peaks as I did I could judge where each sheep allotment was, there along the mountain wall of my father's forest. Walter Kyle atop Roman Reef with his sheep and his telescope. Andy Gustafson with one of the Busby hands, under the middle of the reef where I had camptended him: farther south, Sanford Hebner in escape from his family name and situation. Closer toward Flume Gulch and the North Fork, whatever human improvement had replaced Canada Dan as herder of the third Busby band. Lower down, in the mix of timber and grass slopes, Pat Hoy and the Withrow sheep; and the counting vee where my father and

I talked and laughed with Dode. Already it was like going back to another time, to think about that first day of the counting trip.

The upper place, the old Ramsay place, always presented me new prospects of thought besides its horizons, though. For it was here that I was born. Alec and I both, in the Ramsay homestead house that still stands there today, although abandoned ever since my father quit as the Noon Creek association rider and embarked us into the Forest Service life. I couldn't have been but a year or so old when we moved away, yet I felt some regard for this site. An allegiance, even, for a bond of that sort will happen when you have been the last to live at a place. Or so I think. Gratitude that it offered a roof over your head for as long as it did, this may be, and remorse that only emptiness is your successor there.

Alec and I, September children, native Noon Creekers. And my mother's birthplace down the creek at the Reese ranch house itself. Odd to think that of the four of us at the English Creek ranger station all those years, the place that answered to the word "home" in each of us, only my father originated on English Creek, he alone was our link to Scotch Heaven and the Montana origins of the McCaskills. We Americans scatter fast.

And something odder yet. In a physical sense, here at the upper place I was more distant from Alec than I had been all summer. The Double W lay half the length of Noon Creek from where my rake now wheeled and glided. Mentally, though, this advent to our mutual native ground was a kind of reunion with my brother. Or at least with thoughts of him. While I held the reins of Blanche and Fisheye as they clopped along, I wondered what saddle horse Alec might be riding. When we moved the stacker from one site to the next, I thought of Alec on the move too, likely patrolling Double W fences this time of year, performing his quick mending on any barbwire or post that needed it. By this stage of haying Wisdom Johnson a time or two a day could be heard remembering the charms of Bouncing Betty, on First Avenue South in Great Falls. I wondered how many times a week Alec was managing to ride into Gros Ventre and see Leona. Leona. I wondered— well, just say I wondered.

With all this new musing to be done, the first day of haying the Ramsay meadows went calmly enough. A Monday, that was, a mild day following what had been a cool and cloudy Sunday. Wisdom Johnson, I remember, claimed we now were haying so far up into the polar regions that he might have to put his shirt on. Anyway, a Monday, a getting-under-way day.

The morning of the second Ramsay day, though, began unordinary. I started to see so as soon as Pony and I were coming down off the benchland to the Reese ranch buildings. My mind as usual at that point was on sour milk soda biscuits and fried eggs and venison sausage and other breakfast splendors as furnished by Marie, but I couldn't help watching the other rider who always approached the Reeses' at about the time I did. This of course was Clayton Hebner, for as I'd be descending from my benchland route Clayton would be riding in from the Hebner place on the North Fork, having come around the opposite end of Breed Butte from me. Always Clayton was on that same weary bay mare my father and I had seen the two smaller Hebner jockeys trying to urge into motion, at the outset of our counting trip, and always he came plodding in at the same pace and maybe even in the same hooftracks as the morning before. The first few mornings of haying I had waved to Clayton, but received no response. And I didn't deserve any. I ought to have known Hebners didn't go in for waving.

But etiquette of greeting was not what now had my attention. This particular morning, Clayton across the usual distance between us looked larger. Looked slouchy, as if he might have nodded off in the saddle. Looked somehow—well, the word that comes to mind is dormant.

I had unsaddled Pony and was turning her into the pasture beside Pete's barn when it became evident why Clayton Hebner didn't seem himself this morning. He wasn't.

"Hello there, Jick!" came the bray of Good Help Hebner. "Unchristly hour of the day to be out and about, ain't it?"

"Clayton buggered his ankle up," Good Help was explaining in a fast yelp. Even before the sire of the Hebner clan managed to unload himself from the swaybacked mare, Pete had appeared in the yard with an expression that told me ranch house walls did nothing to dim the identification of Good Help Hebner. "Sprained the goshdamn thing when him and Melvin was grab-assing around after supper last night," Good Help sped on to the two of us. "I tell you, Pete, I just don't know—"

—what's got into kids these days, I finished for Good Help in my mind before he blared it out.

Yet just about the time you think you can recite every forthcoming point of conversation from a Good Help Hebner, that's when he'll throw you for a loop. As now, when Good Help delivered himself of this:

"Ought not to leave a neighbor in the lurch, though, Pete. So I'll take the stacker-driving for you a couple days till Clayton mends up."

Pete looked as though he'd just been offered something nasty on the end of a stick.

But there just was no way around the situation. Someone to drive the stacker team was needed, and given that twelve-year-old Clayton had been performing the job, maybe an outside chance existed that Good Help could, too. Maybe.

"Dandy," uttered Pete without meaning a letter of it. "Come on in and sit up for breakfast, Garland. Then Jick can sort you out on the horses Clayton's been using."

"Kind of a racehorsey pair of bastards, ain't they?" Good Help evaluated Jocko and Pep, the stacker team.

"These? Huh uh," I reassured him. "They're the oldest tamest team on the place, Garland. That's why Pete uses them on the stacker."

"Horses," proclaimed Good Help as if he had just been invited to address Congress on the topic. "You just never can tell about horses. They can look logy as a preacher after a chicken dinner and the next thing you know they turn themselves into goshdamn mustangs. One time I—"

"Garland, these two old grandmas could pull the stacker cable in their sleep. And just about do. Come on, I'll help you get them harnessed. Then we got to go make hay."

The next development in our making of hay didn't dawn on me for quite some time.

That is, I noticed only that Wisdom Johnson today had no cause to complain of coolness. This was an August day with its furnace door open. Almost as soon as all of us got to the hayfield at the upper place, Wisdom was stripping off his shirt and gurgling a drink of water.

How Wisdom Johnson did it I'll never know, but he drank water oftener than the rest of us on the hay crew all together and yet never got heatsick from doing so. I mean, an ordinary person had to be careful about putting cool water inside a sweating body. Pete and Perry and Clayton and I rationed our visits to the burlapwrapped water jug that was kept in the shade of the haystack. But Wisdom had his own waterbag, hung on the stacker frame up there where he could reach it anytime he wanted. A hot day like this seemed to stoke both Wisdom's stacking and his liquid consumption. He'd swig, spit out the stream to rinse hay dust from his mouth. Swig again, several Adam's apple swallows this time. Then, refreshed, yell down to Pete on the buckrake: "More hay! Bring 'er on!"

Possibly, then, it was the lack of usual exhortation from Wisdom that first tickled my attention. I had been going about my scatter raking as usual, my mind here and there and the other, and only eventually did I notice the unusual silence of the hayfield. Above the brushy bend of the creek between me and the stack, though, I could see the stacker arms and fork taking load after load up, and Wisdom was there pitching hay energetically, and all seemed in order. The contrary didn't seep through to me until I felt the need for a drink of water and reined Blanche and Fisheye around the bend to go in to the stack and get it.

This haystack was distinct from any other we had put up all summer.

This one was hunched forward, leaning like a big hay-colored snowdrift against the frame of the stacker. More like a sidehill than a stack. In fact, this one so little resembled Wisdom's straight high style of haystack that I whoaed my team and sat to watch the procedure that was producing this leaning tower of Pisa.

The stacker fork with its next cargo of hay rose slowly, slowly, Good Help pacing at leisure behind the stacker team. When the arms and the fork neared the frame, he idly called, "Whoap," eased Jocko and Pep to a stop, and the hay gently plooped onto the very front of the stack, adding to the forward-leaning crest.

Wisdom gestured vigorously toward the back of the stack. You did not have to know pantomime to decipher that he wanted hay flung into that neighborhood. Then Wisdom's pitchfork flashed and he began to shove hay down from the crest, desperately parceling it toward the lower slope back there. He had made a heroic transferral of several huge pitchforkfuls when the next stacker load hovered up and plooped exactly where the prior one had.

Entrancing as Wisdom's struggle was, I stirred myself and went on in for my slug of water. Not up to me to regulate Good Help Hebner. Although it was with difficulty that I didn't make some crack when Good Help yiped to me: "Yessir, Jick, we're haying now, ain't we?"

From there on Wisdom's sidehill battle was a lost cause. When that haystack was done, or at least Wisdom called quits on it, and it was time to move the stacker to the next site, even Perry stopped dumpraking in the field next door and for once came over to help.

The day by now was without a wisp of moving air, a hot stillness growing hotter. Yet here was a haystack that gave every appearance of leaning into a ninety-mile-an-hour wind. Poles and props were going to be necessary to keep this stack upright *until* winter, let alone *into* winter.

Wisdom glistened so wet with sweat, he might have just come out of swimming. Side by side Perry and I wordlessly appraised the cattywampus haystack, a little like mourners to the fact that our raking efforts had come to such a result. Pete had climbed off the buckrake and gained his first full view and now looked like he might be coming down with a toothache.

"Pete," Wisdom started in, "I got to talk to you."

"Somehow that doesn't surprise me," said Pete. "Let's get the stacker moved then we'll gab."

After the stacker was in place at the new site and Pete bucked in some loads as the base of the next stack, he shut down the buckrake and called Wisdom over. They had a session, with considerable headshaking and arm-waving by Wisdom. Then Pete went over to Good Help, and much more discussion and gesturing ensued.

Finally Good Help shook his head, nodded, spat, squinted, scratched, and nodded again.

Pete settled for this and climbed on the buckrake.

For the next little while of stacking hay there was slightly more snap to Good Help's teamstering. He now had Jocko and Pep moving as if they were only half asleep instead of sleepwalking. Wisdom managed to get his back corners of the stack built good and high, and it began to look as if we were haying semi-respectably again.

Something told me to keep informed as I did my scatter-raking, though, and gradually the story of this new stack became clear. Once more, hay was creeping up and up in a slope against the frame of the stacker. But that was not the only slope. Due to Wisdom's determined efforts to build up the back corners, the rear also stood high. Prominent behind, low in the middle, and loftiest at the front where Good Help again was dropping the loads softly, softly. Something new again in the history of hay, a stack shaped like a gigantic saddle.

Wisdom Johnson now looked like a man standing in a coulee and trying to shovel *both* sidehills down level.

My own shirt was sopping, just from sitting on the rake. Wisdom surely was pouring sweat by the glassful. I watched as he grabbed his waterbag off the frame and took a desperate swig. It persuaded me that I needed to come in and visit the water jug again.

I disembarked from my rake just as Wisdom floundered to the exact middle of the swayback stack and jabbed his pitchfork in as if planting a battle flag.

"Drop the next frigging load right on that fork!" he shouted down to Good Help. So saying, he stalked up to the back of the haystack, folded his arms, and glowered down toward the pitchfork-target he had established for the next volley of hay.

This I had to watch. The water jug could wait. I planted myself just far enough from the stack to take in the whole drama.

Good Help squinted, scratched, spat, etcetera, which seemed to be his formula of acknowledgment. Then he twirled the ends of the reins and whapped the rumps of Jocko and Pep.

I suppose the comparison to make is this: how would you react if you had spent the past hours peacefully dozing and somebody jabbed a thumb between your ribs?

I believe even Good Help was more than a little surprised at the flying start his leather message produced from Jocko and Pep. Away the pair of horses jogged at a harness-rattling pace. Holding their reins, Good Help toddled after the team a lot more rapidly than I ever imagined he was capable of. The cable whirred snake-like through the pulleys of the stacker. And the load of hay was going up as if it was being fired from one of those Roman catapults.

I spun and ran. If the arms of the stacker hit the frame at that runaway velocity, there was going to be stacker timber flying throughout the vicinity.

Over my shoulder, though, I saw it all.

Through some combination of stumble, lurch, and skid, Good Help at last managed to rare back on the reins with all his weight and yanked the horses to a stop.

Simultaneously the stacker arms and fork popped to a halt just inches short of the frame, the whole apparatus quivering up there in the sky like a giant tuning fork.

The hay. The hay was airborne. And Wisdom was so busy glowering he didn't realize this load was arriving to him as if lobbed by Paul Bunyan. I yelled, but anything took time to sink in to Wisdom. His first hint of doom was as the hay, instead of cascading down over the pitchfork Good Help was supposed to be sighting on, kept coming and coming and coming. A quarter of a ton of timothy on a trajectory to the top of Wisdom's head.

Hindsight is always twenty-twenty. Wisdom ought to have humped up and accepted the avalanche. He'd have had to splutter hay the next several minutes, but a guy as sturdy as he was wouldn't have been hurt by the big loose wad.

But I suppose to look up and see a meteorite of hay dropping on you is enough to startle a person. Wisdom in his surprise took a couple of wading steps backward from the falling mass. And had forgotten how far back he already was on the stack. That second step carried Wisdom to the edge, at the same moment that the hayload spilled itself onto the stack. Just enough of that hay flowed against Wisdom to teeter him. The teetering slipped him over the brink. "Oh, *hell*," I heard him say as he started to slide.

Every stackman knows the danger of falling from the heights of his work. In Wisdom's situation, earth lay in wait for him twenty feet below. This lent him incentive. Powerful as he was, the desperately grunting Wisdom clawed his arms into the back of the haystack as he slid. Like a man trying to swim up a waterfall even as the water sluices him down.

"Goshdamn!" Good Help marveled somewhere behind me. "Will you look at that!"

Wisdom's armwork did slow his descent, and meanwhile a sizable cloud of hay was pulling loose from the stack and coming down with him, considerably cushioning his landing. As it turned out, except for scratched and chafed arms and chest and a faceful of hay Wisdom met the ground intact. He also arrived to earth with a full head of steam, all of which he now intended to vent on Good Help Hebner.

"You satchel-ass old son of a frigging goddamn"—Wisdom's was a rendition I have always wished I'd had time to commit to memory. An entire opera of cussing, as he emerged out of the saddle-back stack. But more than Wisdom's mouth was in action, he was trying to lay hands on Good Help. Good Help was prudently keeping the team of horses between him and the stackman. Across the horses' wide backs they eyed one another, Wisdom feinting one way and Good Help going the other, then the reverse. Since the stacker arms and fork still were in the sky, held there only by the cable hitched to the team, I moved in and grabbed the halters of Jocko and Pep so they would stand steady.

By now Pete had arrived on the buckrake, to find his stacking crew in this shambles.

"Hold everything!" he shouted, which indeed was what the situation needed.

Pete got over and talked Wisdom away from one side of the team of horses, Good Help pussyfooted away from their opposite side, and I backed Jocko and Pep toward the stack to let down the arms and fork.

Diplomacy of major proportions now was demanded of Pete. His dilemma was this: if he didn't prune Good Help from the hay crew, Wisdom Johnson was going to depart soonest. Yet Pete needed to stay on somewhat civil terms with Good Help, for the sake of hanging on to Clayton and the oncoming lineage of Hebner boys as a ready source of labor. Besides all that, it was simply sane general policy not to get crosswise with a neighbor such as Good Help, for he could just as readily substitute your livestock for those poached deer hanging in his jackpines.

Wisdom had stalked away to try to towel some of the chaff off himself with his shirt. I hung around Pete and Good Help. I wouldn't have missed this for the world.

"Garland, we seem to have a problem here," Pete began with sizable understatement. "You and Wisdom. He doesn't quite agree with the way you drive stacker team."

"Pete, I have stacked more hay than that guy has ever even seen." By which Good Help must have meant in several previous incarnations, as none of us who knew him in this lifetime had ever viewed a pitchfork in his hands. "He don't know a favor when it's done to him. If he'd let me place the loads the way they ought to be, he could do the stacking while setting in a goshdamn rocking chair up there."

"He doesn't quite see it that way."

"He don't see doodly-squat about putting up hay, that fellow. I sure don't envy you all his haystacks that are gonna tip assy-turvy before winter, Pete."

"Garland, something's got to give. Wisdom won't stack if you're going to drive."

The hint flew past Good Help by a Texas mile. "Kind of a stubborn bozo, ain't he?" he commiserated with Pete. "I was you, I'd of sent him down the road long since."

Pete gazed at Good Help as if a monumental idea had just been presented. As, indeed, one had.

"I guess you're right. I'd better go ahead and can him," Pete judiciously agreed with Good Help. I gaped at Pete. But he was going right on: "I do need to have somebody on the stack who knows what he's doing, though. Lucky as hell you're on hand, Garland. Nobody else on this crew is veteran to the stacking job like you are. What we'll do, I'll put you up on the stack and we'll make some hay around here for a change, huh?"

Good Help went as still as Lot's wife, and I swear he even turned about as white.

"Ordinarily, now"—I didn't get to hear all of the ensuing catalogue of excuse, because I had to saunter away to keep my giggles in, but—"this goshblamed back of mine"—I heard more than enough—"if it'll help you out with that stubborn bozo I can just head on home, Pete"— to know that it constituted Good Help's adieu to haying.

That night at English Creek my father and mother laughed and laughed at my retelling of the saga of Wisdom and Good Help.

"A pair of dandies, they are," my father ajudged. Recently he seemed to take particular pleasure in any evidence that jugheaded behavior wasn't a monopoly of the Forest Service.

But then a further point occurred to him, and he glanced at my mother. She looked soberly back at him. It had occurred to her, too. She in fact was the one who now asked it: "Then who's going to drive the stacker team?"

"Actually," I confessed, "I am."

So that was how I went from haying's ideal job to its goddamn dullest.

Back and forth with that stacker team. All of haying until then I had idly glanced at those little towpaths worn into the meadow, out from the side of each stack we put up, identical routes the exact length of the stacker cable. Now it registered on me how many footsteps, horse and human, it took to trudge those patterns into creation. The scenery meanwhile constant: the rear ends of Jocko and Pep looming ahead of me like a pair of circus fat ladies bending over to tie their shoelaces. Too promptly I discovered a charm of Pep's, which was to hoist his tail and take a dump as soon as we were hitched up at a new stack site, so that I had to remember to watch my step or find myself shin deep in fresh horse apples.

Nor did it help my mood that Clayton with his tender ankle was able to sit on the seat of the scatter rake and do that job. *My* scatter rake. The first long hours of driving the stacker team I spent brooding about the presence of the Hebner tribe in this world.

I will say, the stacker team job shortly cured me of too much thinking. The first time I daydreamed a bit and was slow about starting the load up onto the stack, Wisdom Johnson brought me out of it by shouting down: "Hey, Jick! Whistle or sing, or show your thing!" I was tempted to part Wisdom's hair with that particular load of hay, but I forebore.

Maybe my stacker team mood was contagious. Suppertime of the second day, when I got back to English Creek I found my mother frowning over the week's *Gleaner.* "What's up?" I asked her.

"Nothing," she said and didn't convince me. When she went to the stove to wrestle with supper and I had washed up, I zeroed in on the article she'd been making a mouth at. It was one on the Random page:

PHANTOM WOMAN:
WHEN FIRE RAN
ON THE MOUNTAIN

Editor's note: The fire season is once again upon us, and lightning needs no help from the carelessness of man. It is just 10 years ago that the Phantom Woman Mountain conflagration provided an example of what happens when fire gets loose in a big way. We reprint the story as a reminder. When in the woods, break your matches after blowing them out, crush cigarette butts, and douse all campfires.

Forest Service crews are throwing everything in the book at the fire on Phantom Woman Mountain, but so far, the roar-

*ing blaze has thrown it all back. The inferno is raging in
up-and-down country near the headwaters of the North
Fork of English Creek, about 20 miles west of Gros Ventre.
Reports from Valier and Conrad say the column of smoke
can be seen from those communities. How many acres of forest have been consumed is not known. It is certain the loss is
the worst in the Two Medicine National Forest since the
record fire season of 1910.*

*One eyewitness said the crews seemed to be bringing the
fire under control until late yesterday afternoon. Then the
upper flank of the fire broke loose "and started going across
that mountain as fast as a man can run."*

H. T. Gisborne, fire research specialist for the U.S. Forest Service at
Missoula, explained the "blowup" phenomenon: "Ordinarily the front
of a forest fire advances like troops in skirmish formation, pushing
ahead faster here, slower there, according to the timber type and fuels,
but maintaining a practically unbroken front. Even when topography,
fuels, and weather result in a crown fire, the sheet of flames leaps from
one tree crown to the next at a relatively slow rate, from one-half to one
mile an hour. But when such 'runs' throw spots of fire ahead of the
advancing front, the spots burn back to swell the main front and add
to the momentum of the rising mass of heat. Literally, a 'blowup' of the
front of the fire may then happen."

No word has been received of casualties in the Phantom Woman
fire, although reports are that some crews had to flee for their lives when
the "blowup" occurred.

When my father came in for supper, my mother liberated the
Gleaner from me and handed it to him, saying: "Mac, you might as well
see this." Meaning, you might as well see it before our son the asker
starts in on you about it.

The headline stopped him. Bill Reinking always got in touch with
him about any story having to do with the Two Medicine National Forest. "Why's this in the paper?" my father now demanded of the world
at large.

"It's been ten years, Mac," my mother told him. "Ten years ago this
week."

He read it through. His eyes were intent, his jaw was out, as if stubborn against the notion that fire could happen in the Two Medicine National Forest. When he tossed the *Gleaner* aside, though, he said only: "Doesn't time fly."

The next day, two developments.

I took some guilty pleasure at the first of these. Not long before noon, Clayton dropped one wheel of the scatter rake into a ditch that was closer than he'd noticed, and the impact broke one of the brackets that attaches the dumping mechanism to the rake frame. Clayton himself looked considerably jarred, although I don't know whether mostly by the jolt of the accident or the dread that Pete would fire him for it.

But Pete being Pete, he instead said: "These things happen, Clayton. We'll cobble it with wire until we can get a weld done on it." And once I got over my secret satisfaction about the superiority of my scatter-raking to Clayton's, I was glad Pete didn't come down hard on the boy. Being a son of Good Help Hebner seemed to me punishment enough for anybody.

Then at the end of the workday, as Pony and I came down the benchland to the ford of English Creek, I saw a second Forest Service pickup parked beside my father's outside the ranger station. I figured the visitor might be Cliff Bowen, the young ranger from the Indian Head district just south of us, and it was. When I stepped in to say hello, I learned Cliff had been to headquarters in Great Falls and had come by with some fire gear for my father. And with some rangerly gripes he was sharing as well. Normally Cliff Bowen was mild as milk, but his headquarters visit left him pretty well steamed.

"Mac, Sipe asked me how things are going." Sipe was Ken Sipe, the superintendent of the Two Medicine National Forest. "I told him, about as good as could be expected, but we're going to need more smoke-chasers." July and now August had stayed so hot and dangerous that east-of-the-Divide rangers had been permitted to hire some fire manpower, but only enough, as my father had said, "to give us a taste."

"How'd that go over with him?" my father wondered.

"About like a fart in church. He told me it's Missoula policy. Hold down on the hiring, on these east-side forests. Goddamn it, Mac, I don't know what the Major's thinking of. This forest is as dry as paper. We get one good lightning storm in the mountains and we'll have fires the whole sonofabitching length of the Two."

"Maybe the Major's got it all arranged with upstairs so there isn't going to be any lightning the rest of the summer, Cliff."

"Yeah, maybe. But if any does get loose, I hope to Christ it aims for the rivets on the Major's hip pocket."

My father couldn't help but laugh. "You think snag strikes are trouble. Figure how long the Major'd smolder."

Two developments, I said back there. Amend that to three. As I led Pony to her pasture for the night, the heat brought out sweat on me, just from that little walk. When I reached the house the thermometer in our kitchen window was catching the western sun. Ninety-two degrees, it read. The hot heavy weather was back. The kind of weather that invites lightning storms.

But all we got that night was a shower, a dab of drizzle. When I climbed out of bed in the morning I debated whether Pete's hay would be too wet to stack today. So that I wouldn't make my ride for nothing, I telephoned the Reese ranch.

"Pete thinks it'll be dry enough by middle of the morning," Marie's voice told me. "Come on for breakfast. I have sourdough hotcakes."

It turned out that the sourdough hotcakes were the only real gain of the morning for our hay crew. We took our time at the breakfast table and then did a leisurely harnessing-up of our teams and made no hurry of getting to the Ramsay place's hayfields, and still Perry and Bud and Wisdom had a lot of smoke time while Pete felt of the hay and gandered at the sky. Finally Pete said, "Hell, let's try it." We would do okay for a while, put up a dozen or so loads, then here would come a sun shower. Just enough moisture to shut us down. Then we'd hay a little more, and another sun shower would happen. For a rancher trying to put up hay, that is the most aggravating kind of day there can be. Or as Pete put it during one of these sprinkly interruptions: "Goddamn it, if you're gonna rain, *rain.*"

By about two o'clock and the fourth or fifth start-and-stop of our stacking, he had had enough. "The hell with it. Let's head for home."

I naturally anticipated an early return to English Creek, and started thinking about where I might go fishing for the rest of the afternoon. My theory is, the more rotten the weather, the better the fishing. But as I was unharnessing Jocko and Pep, Pete came out of the house and asked:

"Jick, how do you feel about a trip to town?"

Inasmuch as we were rained out anyway, he elaborated, I might just as well take the scatter rake in to Grady Tilton's garage and get the broken bracket welded, stay overnight at the Heaneys' and in the morning drive the repaired rake back here to the ranch. "I checked all this out with headquarters", meaning my mother, "and she said it'd be okay."

"Sounds good to me," I told Pete. The full fact was, after the days of trudging back and forth behind the stacker team it sounded like an expedition to Africa.

So I set off for Gros Ventre, about midafternoon. Roving scatter raker Jick McCaskill hitting the road, even if the route only was to town and back.

The first couple of miles almost flew by, for it was remarkable what a pair of steppers Blanche and Fisheye now seemed to me; speed demons in comparison to Jocko and Pep. My thoughts were nothing special. Wondering what Ray Heaney would have to report. Mulling the rest of the summer. Another week or so of haying. The start of school was—Christamighty, only thirty days away. And my fifteenth birthday, one day less than that. I ask you, how is it that after the Fourth of July each summer, time somehow speeds up.

I like to believe that even while curlicues of this sort are going on in my head, the rest of me is more or less on the job. Aiming that scatter rake down the Noon Creek road I took note of Dill Egan's haystacks, which looked to me like poor relations of those Wisdom built. Way over on the tan horizon to the northeast I could see specks that would be Double W cattle, and wondered where Alec was riding or fence-fixing today. And of course one of the things a person always does a lot of in Montana is watching other people's weather. All that sky and horizon around you, there almost always is some atmospheric event to keep track of. At the top of the country road's rise from Dill Egan's place, I studied a dark anvil cloud which was sitting over the area to the northwest of me. My father was not going to like the looks of that one, hovering along the edge of his forest. And our Ramsay hayfield is going to have itself a bath, I told myself.

In a few more minutes I glanced around again, though, and found that the cloud wasn't sitting over the Ramsay place. It was on the move. Toward Noon Creek and me. A good thing I was bright enough to bring my slicker along on the rake; the coat was going to save me from some wet.

But the next time I reconnoitered, rain was pushed off my mental agenda. The cloud was bigger, blacker, and closer. A whole hell of a lot closer. It also was rumbling now like it was the engine of the entire sky. That may sound fancy, but view it from my eyes at the time: a dark block of storm, with pulses of light coming out of it like flame winking from firebox doors. And even as I gawked at it, a jagged rod of lightning stabbed from the cloud to the earth. Pale lightning, nearer white than yellow. The kind a true electrical storm employs.

As I have told, I am not exactly in love with lightning anyway. Balling the reins in both my hands, I slapped Blanche and Fisheye some encouragement across their rumps. "Hyaah, you two! Let's go!" Which may sound drastic, but try sitting on a ten-foot expanse of metal rake with lightning approaching and then prescribe to me what you would have done.

Go we did, at a rattling pace, for the next several minutes. I did my best to count distance on the thunder, but it was that grumbling variety that lets loose another thump before you've finished hearing the one before. My eyes rather than my ears had to do the weather forecasting, and they said Blanche and Fisheye and the rake and I were not going as fast as the stormcloud was traveling or growing or whatever the hell it was doing.

The route ahead stretched on and on, for immediately after coming up out of Dill Egan's place the Noon Creek road abandons the bottomland and arrows along the benchland between Noon Creek and English Creek until it eventually hits the highway north of Gros Ventre. Miles of country as exposed as a tabletop. I tell you, a situation like that reminds a person that skin is damn thin shelter against the universe.

One thing the steady thunder and the pace of the anvil cloud did tell me was that I somehow had to abandon that road. Find a place to pull in and get myself and my horses away from this ten-foot lightning rod on wheels. The question was, where? Along the English Creek road I'd have had no problem: within any little way there, a ranch could be pulled into for shelter. But around here the Double W owned everything, and wherever there did happen to be a turnoff into one of the abandoned sets of Noon Creek ranch buildings, the Double W kept the gate padlocked against fishermen. As I verified for myself, by halting my team for a quick scan at the gate into the old Nansen place.

A lack of choices can make your mind up for you in a hurry. I whapped Blanche and Fisheye again and on down the county road we clattered, heading for a high frame of gateposts about three quarters of a mile off. The main gate into the Double W.

It took forever, but at last we pulled up at that gateframe and the Double W turnoff. From the crosspiece supported by the big gateposts—the size and height of telephone poles, they really were—hung the sign:

WW RANCH
WENDELL & MEREDICE WILLIAMSON

The sign was creaking a little, the wind starting to stir in front of the storm.

Neither the sign nor the wind I gave a whit about just then. What I had forgotten was that this turnoff into the Double W had a cattle-guard built in there between the gateposts. A pit overlaid with a grill of pipes, which vehicles could cross but hoofed creatures such as cattle couldn't. Hoofed creatures such as cattle and horses. To put Blanche and Fisheye through here, I would have to open the barbwire livestock gate beside the cattleguard.

You know what I was remembering. "GODAMIGHTY, get AWAY from that!"—Stanley's cry as I approached the wire gate at the cabin during our camptending trip. "You happen to be touching that wire and lightning hits that fence—" This coming rumblebelly of a storm made that June one look like a damp washcloth. Every time I glanced in its direction now, lightning winked back. And nowhere around this entrance to the Double W was there a stick of wood, not one sole single goddamn splinter, with which to knock the hoop off the gate stick and flip the wire gate safely aside.

Holy H. Hell. Sitting here telling this, all the distance of years between that instant and now, I can feel again the prickling that came across the backs of my hands, the sweat of dismay on its way up through my skin there. Grant me three moments which could be erased from my life, and that Double W gate scene would be one.

I wiped my hands against my pants. Blanche swished her tail, and Fisheye whinnied. They maybe were telling me what I already knew. Delay was my worst possible behavior, for that storm was growing nearer every second that I stood there and stewed. I wiped my hands again. And jumped at the gate as if in combat against it. One arm grappling around the gatepost, the other arm and hand desperately working the wire hoop up off the gatestick. Oh yes, sure, this gate was one of those snug obstinate bastards; I needed to mightily hug the stick and post together to gain enough slack for the hoop to loosen. Meanwhile everyplace my body was touching a strand of barbwire I could feel a kind of target line, ready to sizzle: as if I was trussed up in electrical wiring and somebody was about to throw the switch.

I suppose in a fraction of what it takes to tell about it, I wrestled that gate open and slung it wide. Yet it did seem an immense passage of time.

And I wasn't on easy street yet. Blanche and Fisheye, I have to say, were taking all of this better than I was, but even so they were getting a little nervous about the storm's change in the air and the loudening thunder. "Okay, here we go now, nothing to it, here we go," I soothed the team and started them through the gate. I could have stood some soothing myself, for the scatter rake was ten feet wide and this gate was only about eleven. Catch a rake wheel behind a gatepost and you have yourself a first-class hung-up mess. In my case, I then would have the rake in contact with the barbwire fence, inviting lightning right up the seat of my pants, while I backed and maneuvered the rake wheel out of its bind. Never have I aimed anything more carefully than that wide scatter rake through that just-wide-enough Double W gateway.

We squeaked through. Which left me with only one more anxious act to do. To close the gate, for there were cattle in this field. Even if they were the cattle of the damn Double W, even if it mattered nothing to me that they got out and scattered to Tibet; if you have been brought up in Montana, you close a gate behind you.

So I ran back and did the reverse of the wrestling that'd opened the gate. Still scared spitless about touching that wire. Yet maybe not quite as scared as when I'd first done it, for I was able to say to myself all the while, What in the hell have I done to deserve this dose of predicament?

Again on the rake, I broke all records of driving that Double W approach road, down from the benchland to where the ranch buildings were clustered on the north side of Noon Creek. Across the plank bridge the rake rumbled, my thunder against the storm's thunder, and I sighted refuge. The Double W barn.

In minutes I had my team unhitched—leaving the scatter rake out by a collection of old machinery, so that lightning at least would have to do some sorting to find it—and was ensconcing them in barn stalls. They were lathered enough that I unharnessed them and rubbed them dry with a gunnysack. In fact, I looked around for the granary, went over there, and brought back a hatful of Double W oats apiece to Blanche and Fisheye as their reward.

Now I could draw a breath and look around for my own benefit.

The Double W had buildings and more buildings. This barn was huge and the two-story white Williamson house across the yard could have housed the governor of Montana. You would think this was ranch enough for anybody, yet Wendell Williamson actually owned another one at least as big as this. The Deuce W—its cattle brand was 2w—down in the Highwood Mountains between Great Falls and Lewistown, a hundred or more miles from here. More distance than I'd been in my whole life, and Wendell goddamn Williamson possessed both ends of it.

Be that as it may, the Double W was now my port in the storm, and I had better make my presence known.

No one was in sight. It would take a little while for the rain to bring in Alec and the other riders and the hay crew from the range and the hayfield. But somebody was bound to be in the house, and I hurried over to there before I had to do it during the storm.

I knocked at the front door.

The door opened and Meredice Williamson was standing there smiling and saying: "Yes?"

"'Lo, Mrs. Williamson. I put Blanche and Fisheye in your barn."

That seemed to be double Dutch to her. But she smiled on and commended: "That was good of you. I'm sure Wendell will be pleased."

I sought to correct her impression that a delivery of Blanche and Fisheye was involved here. "Well, no, they'll only be there until it clears up. I mean, what it is, I was driving my scatter rake to town and the storm started coming and I had to head in here on account of lightning, so I unhitched my team and put them in the barn there, I hope that's all right?"

"I'm sure it must be," she acceded, pretty plainly because she had no idea what else to say. Meredice Williamson was a city woman—a lawyer's widow, it was said—whom Wendell met and married in California a few winters before. The unkind view of her was that she'd had too much sun on the brain down there. But I believe the case honestly was that because Meredice Williamson only came north to spend summers at the Double W, she never got clued in to the Two country; never quite caught up with its rhythms of season and livelihood and lore. At least, standing there within the weathered doorway in her yellow sun frock and with her graying hair in perfect marcelled waves, she looked much like a visitor to her own ranch house.

Yet maybe Meredice Williamson was not as vague as the general estimate of her, for she now pondered my face a moment more and then asked: "Are you Beth McCaskill's other boy?"

Which wasn't exactly my most preferred phrasing of it. But she did have genealogical fact on her side. So I bobbed yes and contributed: "Jick. Alec's brother."

"Wendell thinks highly of Alec," she confided, as if I gave a hoot in hell about Mr. Double W's opinion. So far as I could see Wendell Williamson was a main contributor to Alec's mental delinquency, encouraging him in his damn cowboy notions. The summer's sunder of my family followed a faultline which led to this doorstep. Fair is fair, though, and I couldn't really blame Meredice Williamson for Wendell's doings. Innocent as a bluebird on a manure pile, this lady seemed to be. Thus I only said back:

"Yeah. So I savvy."

Just then the leading edge of rain hit, splatting drops the size of quarters on the flagstones of the walk. Meredice Williamson peered past me in surprise at the blackening sky. "It looks like a shower," she mustered. "Wouldn't you like to step inside?"

I was half tempted. On the other hand, I figured she wouldn't have the foggiest notion of what to do with me once I was in there. Furnish me tea and ladyfingers? Ask me if I would care for a game of Chinese checkers? "No, that's okay," I replied. "I'll wait in the bunkhouse. Alec likely will show up there pretty quick. I'll shoot the hooey with him until the rain's over and then head on to town." Here Meredice Williamson's expression showed that she was unsure what hooey was or why we would shoot it. In a hurry I concluded: "Anyway, thanks for the borrow of your barn."

"You're quite welcome, Jake," she was saying as I turned and sprinted across the yard. The rain was beginning to pelt in plentiful drops now, pocking the dust. Flashes of light at the south edge of the storm and the immediate rumbles made me thankful again that I was in off the rake, even if the haven was the Double W.

Strange, to be in a bunkhouse when its residents are out on the job. Like one of those sea tales of stepping aboard a ship where everything is intact, sails set and a meal waiting on the galley stove, but the crew has vanished.

Any bunkhouse exists only to shelter a crew. There is no feel of it as a home for anybody, although even as I say that I realize many ranch hands spent their lives in a bunkhouse. Alec himself was a full-timer here, and would be until he and Leona tied their knot. Even so, a bunkhouse to me seems a place you can put up with for a season but that would be enough.

If you are unaccustomed to a bunkhouse, the roomful of beds is a medley of odors. Of tobacco in three incarnations: hand-rolled cigarettes, snoose, and chewing tobacco. The last two, in fact, had a permanent existence in the spit cans beside about half the bunks. These I took special note of, not wanting to kick one of them over. Of too many bodies and not enough baths; yet I wonder why it is that we now think we have to deodorize the smell of humanness out of existence. Of ashes and creosote; the presence of an elderly stove and stovepipe. All in all, the scent of men and what it takes them to lead the ranch hands' life.

I glanced around to try and figure out which bunk was Alec's. An easy enough mystery. The corner bunk with the snapshot of Leona on the wall above the pillow.

Naturally the picture deserved a closer look.

It showed Leona on a horse in a show ring—that would be Tollie Zane's during one of his horse sales—and wearing a lady Stetson and leather chaps. And a smile that probably fused the camera. But I managed to get past the top of Leona, to where something else was tugging my eyes. Down the length of her chaps, something was spelled out in tooled letters with silver spangles between. I moved in for a closer look yet, my nose almost onto the snapshot, and I was able to make out:

M
*
O
*
N
*
T
*
A
*
N
*
A

Well, that wasn't the message that ordinarily would come to mind from looking along Leona's leg. But it was interesting.

I could hear voices, and men began trooping in. The hay crew. And at the tail end of them Alec, who looked flabbergasted to see me sitting on his bunk.

"Jicker, what in blazes—" he started as he strode over to me. I related to him my scatter rake situation and he listened keenly, although he didn't look perceptibly happier with my presence. "As soon as the rain lets up, I'll head on to town," I assured him.

"Yeah, well. Make yourself at home, I guess." Now, to my surprise, my brother seemed short of anything more to say. He was saved from having to, by the arrival of the Double W foreman Cal Petrie and the other two riders, older guys named Thurl Everson and Joe Henty. Both had leather gloves and fencing pliers, so I imagined they were glad to be in away from barbwire for a while, too.

Cal Petrie spotted me perched on the bunk aside Alec, nodded hello, and steered over to ask: "Looking for a job?" He knew full well I wasn't, but as foreman it was his responsibility to find out just what brought me here.

Again I explained the scatter rake–lightning situation, and Cal nodded once more. "A stroke of that could light you up like a Christmas tree, all right. Make yourself to home. Alec can introduce you around." Then Cal announced generally: "After supper I got to go to town for some sickle heads for the mowers, and I can take two of you jaspers in with me in the pickup. I'll only be in there an hour or so, and you got to be ready to come home when I say. No staying in there to drink the town dry, in other words. So cut cards or Indian rassle or compare dicks or however you want to choose, but only two of you are going." And he went off into the room he had to himself at the far end of the bunkhouse.

In a hay crew such as the Double W's there were ten or a dozen guys, putting up two stacks at once, and what struck me as Alec made me known to them was that three of the crew were named Mike. A gangly one called Long Mike, and a mower man naturally called Mike the Mower, and then one who lacked either of those distinctions and so was called Plain Mike. The riders who had come in with Cal Petrie I already knew, Thurl and Joe. Likewise the choreboy, old Dolph Kuhn, one of those codgers who get to be as much a part of a ranch as its ground and grass. So I felt acquainted enough even before somebody chimed out:

"What, are you another one of the famous fist-fighting McCaskills?" Alec's flooring of Earl Zane at the Fourth of July dance was of course the natural father of that remark.

"No, I'm the cut-and-shoot type," I cracked back. "When the trouble starts, I cut through the alley and shoot for home."

You just never know. That joke had gray whiskers and leaned on a cane, but it drew a big laugh from the Double W yayhoos even so.

There followed some more comment, probably for the fortieth time, about how Alec had whopped Earl, and innumerable similar exploits performed in the past by various of this crew. You'd have thought the history of boxing had taken place in that bunkhouse. But I was careful not to contribute anything further. The main rule when you join a crew, even if it's only for the duration of a rainstorm, is to listen more than you talk.

Alec still didn't look overjoyed that I was on hand, but I couldn't help that. I didn't order up the damn electrical storm, which still was rumbling and crashing around out there.

"So," I offered as an opener, "what do you know for sure?"

"Enough to get by on," Alec allowed.

"Been doing any calf-roping?"

"No."

That seemed to take care of the topic of calf-roping. Some silence, then Alec hazarded: "How's the haying going at Pete's?"

"We've pretty close to got it. A few more days left. How're they doing here?"

"More like a couple of weeks left, I guess."

And there went the topic of haying. Alec and I just sat back and listened for a little to where the discussion had now turned, the pair of slots for town. Some grumping was going on about Cal Petrie's edict that only two of the crew were going to get to see the glories of Gros Ventre on a Saturday night. This was standard bunkhouse grouse, though. If Cal had said the whole shebang of them could go to town with him there'd have been grumbling that he hadn't offered to buy them the first round of drinks as well. No, the true issue was just beginning to come out: more than half the hay crew, six or so guys, considered themselves the logical town candidates. The variety of reasoning—the awful need for a haircut, a bet to be collected from a guy who was going to be in the Medicine Lodge only this very night, even a potential toothache that necessitated preventive remedies from the drugstore—was remarkably well rehearsed. This Double W bunch was the kind of crew, as the saying went, who began on Thursday to get ready on Friday to go to town on Saturday to spend Sunday.

Long Mike and Plain Mike and a sort of a gorilla of a guy who I figured must be one of the two stackmen of this gang were among the yearners for town. Plain Mike surprised me by being the one to propose that a game of cards settle the matter. But then, you just never know who in a crew will turn out to be the tiger rider.

The proposal itself eliminated the big stackman. "Hell with it, I ain't lost nothing in that burg anyway." At the time I thought his sporting blood was awfully anemic. It has since dawned on me that he could not read; could not tell the cards apart.

Inasmuch as Plain Mike had efficiently whittled off one contender, the other four felt more or less obliged to go along with a card game.

"We need an honest banker," Plain Mike solicited.

"You're talking contradictions," somebody called out.

"Damn, I am at that. Honest enough that we can't catch him, will do. Hey there, Alec's brother! How about you being the bank for us?"

"Well, I don't know. What are you going to play?"

"Pitch," stipulated Plain Mike. "What else is there?"

That drew me. Pitch is the most perfect of card games. It excels poker in that there can be more than one winner during each hand, and cribbage in that it doesn't take an eternity to play, and rummy and hearts in that judgment is more important than the cards you are dealt, and stuff like canasta and pinochle can't even be mentioned in the same breath with pitch.

"I guess I could," I assented. "Until the rain lets up." It still was raining like bath time on Noah's ark.

"Pull up a stump," invited Plain Mike, nodding toward a spare chair beside the stove. "We'll show you pitch as she is meant to be played."

Uh huh, at least you will, I thought to myself as I added my presence to the circle of card players. But I will say this for the Double W yayhoos, they played pitch the classic way: high, low, game, jack, jick, joker. It would just surprise you, how many people go through life under the delusion that pitch ought to be played without a joker in the deck, which is a skimpy damned way of doing it, and how many others are just as dim in wanting to play with two jokers, which is excessive and confusing.

My job of banker didn't amount to all that much. Just being in charge of the box of Diamond wooden matches and paying out to each player as many matches as he'd made points, or taking matches back if he went set. Truth be told, I could have kept score more efficiently with a pencil and sheet of paper, and Alec simply could have done it in his head. But these Double W highrollers wanted to be able to squint around the table and count for themselves how much score everybody else had.

From the very first hand, when the other players were tuning up with complaints like "Is this the best you can deal, a mess like this?" and Plain Mike simply bid three, "in them things called spades," and led with the queen, it was worth a baccalaureate degree in the game of pitch to watch Plain Mike. He bid only when he had one sure point, ace for high or deuce for low, with some other point probable among his cards, so that when he *did* bid it was as good as made. But during a hand when anybody else had the bid, he managed to run with some point, jack or jick or joker, for himself, or at least—this, a real art of pitch—he managed to sluff the point to somebody besides the bidder. I banked and admired. While the other cardsters' scores gyrated up and down, with every hand Plain Mike added a wooden match or two to his total.

Around us the rest of the crew was carrying on conversation. If you can call it that. There is no place like a bunkhouse for random yatter. One guy will grouch about how the eggs were cooked for breakfast and another will be reminded of a plate of beans he ate in Pocatello in 1922. Harness the gab gas of the average bunkhouse and you'd have an inexhaustible fuel.

I was taking it all in, eyes and mind pretty much on the card game and ears shopping around in the crew conversation, when one of the pitch players popped out with:

"Aw hell, there goes Jick."

I blinked and sat up at that. Anybody would, wouldn't he? All right, so my attention was a bit divided: so what the hell business was it of some stranger to announce it to the world? But then I saw that the guy hadn't meant me, he was just bemoaning because he'd tried to run the jick past Plain Mike and Plain Mike had nabbed it with his jack of trump.

The only one to notice my peeved reaction was Plain Mike himself, who I would say did not miss many tricks in life as well as in cards. "A jick and a Jick we got here, huh?" he said now. "Who hung that nickname on you, that battling brother of yours?"

Actually my best guess was that it'd been Dode Withrow who suggested I looked like the jick of the McCaskills, but my parents were vague about the circumstance. I mean, a person wants to know his own history insofar as possible, but if you can't, you can't. So instead of trying to go into all that before this Double W crowd I just responded: "Somebody with an imagination, I guess."

"Lucky thing he didn't imagine you resembled the queen of hearts," observed Plain Mike and turned his attention back to the pitch game.

By now Alec, looking restless and overhearing all this name stuff, had come over and joined me in watching the card game. This was certainly a more silent brother than I'd ever been around before. Maybe it had something to do with his surroundings, this hay crew he and the other riders now had to share the bunkhouse with. Between checking out the window on the progress of the rain and banking the pitch game, I started mulling what it would be like to work in this hay crew instead of Pete's. If, say, ranches were swapped under Alec and me, him up the creek at the Reese place as he'd been at my age and me here at the Gobble Gobble You. Some direct comparison of companions was possible. Wisdom Johnson was an obvious choice over the gorilla of a guy who was one of the Double W stackmen, and a rangy man called Swede who more than likely was the other one. A possible advantage I could see to the gorilla was what he might have inflicted on Good Help Hebner for trying to drown him in hay, but that was wishful thinking. Over on the conversation side of the room, Mike the Mower looked somewhat more interesting than Bud Dolson. He was paying just enough attention to the pair of stories not to seem standoffish. His bunk was the most neatly made, likely showing he had been in the army. All in all, though, Mike the Mower showed more similarity to Bud than difference. Mower men were their own nationality.

From how they had been razzing one another about quantities of hay moved, three of the five pitch players—Plain Mike and Long Mike and a heavy-shouldered guy—were the horse buck-rakers. I was pretty sure how they shaped up on the job. The heavy-shouldered guy, who looked like a horseman, was the best buckraker. Long Mike was the slowest. And Plain Mike did just enough more work than Long Mike to look better.

A couple of younger guys, around Alec's age but who looked about a fraction as bright, likely were the stacker team drivers in this outfit.

Then a slouchy elderly guy in a khaki shirt, and a one-eyed one; I suppose it doesn't say much for my own haying status that I was working down through this Double W crew, getting to the bunchrakers and whoever the scatter raker was, when the telephone jangled at the far end of the room.

The ring of that phone impressed me more than anything else about the Double W had yet. I mean, there was no stipulated reason why there couldn't be a telephone in a bunkhouse. But at the time it seemed a fairly swanky idea.

Cal Petrie stepped out of his room to answer it. When he had listened a bit and yupped an answer, he hung up and looked over toward where Alec and I were on the rim of the card game.

"Come on up for supper with us," the foreman directed at me. "Give the mud a little more chance to dry out, that way."

Cal declaimed this as if it was his own idea, but I would have bet any money as to who was on the other end of that phone line. Meredice Williamson.

Not long after, the supper bell sounded the end of the card game. The heavy-shouldered guy had the highest score, and yes, Plain Mike had the next. Now that they were the town-bound pair they received a number of imaginative suggestions of entertainment they might seek in there, as the crowd of us sloshed over to the kitchen door of the house. While everybody scraped mud off his feet and trooped on in I hung back with Alec, to see what the table lineup was going to be.

"Jick," he began, but didn't go on with whatever he had in mind. Instead, "See you after supper," he said, and stepped into the house, with me following.

The meal was in the summer room, a kind of windowed porch along the side of the house, long enough to hold a table for a crew this size. I of course did know that even at a place like the Double W, family and crew ate together. If the king of England had owned Noon Creek benchland instead of Scottish moors, probably even he would have had to go along with the ranch custom of everybody sitting down to refuel together. So I wasn't surprised to see Wendell Williamson sitting at the head of the table. Meredice sat at his right, and the old choreboy Dolph Kuhn next to her. At Wendell's left was a vacancy which I knew would be the cook's place, and next to that Cal Petrie seated himself. All five of them had chairs, then backless benches filled the rest of both sides of the table, which was about twenty feet long.

I felt vaguely let down. It was a setup about like any other ranch's, only bigger. I suppose I expected the Double W to have something special, like a throne for Wendell Williamson instead of a straightback kitchen chair.

Alec and Joe and Thurl, as ranch regulars, took their places next to the head-of-the-table elite, and the hay crew began filling in the rest of the table to the far end. In fact, *at* the far end there was a kitchen stool improvised as a seat, and Meredice Williamson's smile and nod told me it was my place.

This I had not dreamt of. Facing Wendell Williamson down the length of the Double W supper table. He now acknowledged me by saying: "Company. Nuhhuh. Quite a way to come for a free meal, young fellow."

Before thinking I said back: "Everybody says there's no cooking like the Double W's."

That caused a lot of facial expressions along the table, and I saw Alec peer at me rather firmly. But Wendell merely said "Nuhhuh" again—that "nuhhuh" of his was a habit I would think anybody with sufficient money would pay to have broken—and took a taste of his cup of coffee.

To me, Wendell Williamson always looked as if he'd been made by the sackful. Sacks of what, I won't go into. But just everything about him, girth, shoulders, arms, even his fingers, somehow seemed fuller than was natural; as if he always was slightly swollen. Wendell's head particularly stood out in this way, because his hair had retreated about halfway back and left all that face to loom out. And the other odd thing up there was, what remained of Wendell's hair was thick and curly and coal-black. A real stand of hair there at the rear of that big moonhead, like a sailor might wear a watchcap pushed way back.

The cook came in from the kitchen with a bowl of gray gravy and handed it to Wendell. She was a gaunt woman, sharp cheekbones, beak of a nose. Her physiognomy was a matter of interest and apprehension to me. The general theory is that a thin cook is a poor idea.

Plain Mike was sitting at my left, and at my right was a scowling guy who'd been one of the losers in the pitch game. As I have always liked to keep abreast of things culinary, I now asked Plain Mike in an undertone: "Is this the cook from Havre?"

"No, hell, she's long gone. This one's from up at Lethbridge."

What my mother would have commented danced to mind: "So Wendell Williamson has to import them from Canada now, does he? I'm Not Surprised."

I kept that to myself, but the scowler on my right had overheard my question and muttered: "She ain't Canadian though, kid. She's a Hungrarian."

"She is?" To me, the cook didn't look conspicuously foreign.

"You bet. She leaves you hungrier than when you came to the table."

I made a polite "heh-heh-heh" to that, and decided I'd better focus on the meal.

The first bowl to reach me contained a concoction I've never known the actual name of but in my own mind I always dub tomato smush. Canned tomatoes heated up, with little dices of bread dropped in. You sometimes get this as a side dish in cafes when the cook has run out of all other ideas about vegetables. Probably the Lunchery in Gros Ventre served it four days a week. In any case, tomato smush is a remarkable recipe, in that it manages to wreck both the tomatoes and the bread.

Out of chivalry I spooned a dab onto my plate. And next loaded up with mashed potatoes. Hard for any cook to do something drastic to mashed potatoes. The gravy, though, lacked salt and soul.

Then along came a platter of fried liver. This suited me fine, as I can dine on liver even when it is overcooked and tough, as this was. But I have observed in life that there is no middle ground about liver. When I passed the platter to the guy on my right, he mumbled something about "Lethbridge leather again," and his proved to be the majority view at the table.

There was some conversation at the head of the table, mostly between Wendell and the foreman Cal about the unfairness of being rained out at this stage of haying. In light of what followed, I see now that the rainstorm was largely responsible for Wendell's mood. Not that Wendell Williamson ever needed a specific excuse to be grumpy, so far as I could tell, but this suppertime he was smarting around his wallet. If the rain had started before noon and washed out the haying, he'd have had to pay all this hay crew for only half a day. But since the rain came in the afternoon he was laying out a full day's wages for not a full day's work. I tell you, there can be no one more morose than a rancher having to pay a hay crew to watch rain come down.

Anyway, the bleak gaze of Wendell Williamson eventually found its way down the length of the table to me. To my surprise, since I didn't think anybody's welfare mattered to him but his own, Wendell asked me: "How's your folks?"

"Real good."

"Nuhhuh." Wendell took a mouthful of coffee, casting a look at the cook as he set down his cup. Then his attention was back on me:

"I hear your mother gave quite a talk, the day of the Fourth."

Well, what the hell. If Wendell goddamn Williamson wanted to tap his toe to that tune, I was game to partner him. The McCaskills of this world maybe don't own mills and mines and all the land in sight, as some Williamson back in history had managed to grab, but we were born with tongues.

"She's sure had a lot of good comments on it," I declared with enthusiasm. Alec was stirring in his seat, trying to follow all this, but he'd missed Mom's speech by being busy with his roping horse. No, this field of engagement was mine alone. "People tell her it brought back the old days, when there were all those other ranches around here. The days of Ben English and those."

"Nuhhuh." What Wendell would have responded beyond that I will never know, for Meredice Williamson smiled down the table in my direction and then said to Wendell: "Ben English. What an interesting name, I have always thought." Mr. Double W didn't conspicuously seem to think so. But Meredice sallied right on. "Was he, do you think?"

"Was he what?" retorted Wendell.

"English. Do you suppose Mr. English was of English extraction?"

"Meredice, how in hell—" Wendell stopped himself and swigged some more sour coffee. "He might've been Swedish, for all I know."

"It would be more fitting if he were English," she persisted.

"Fitting? Fit what?"

"It would be more fitting to the memory of the man and his times." She smiled toward me again. "To those old days." Now she looked somewhere over my head, and Plain Mike's, and the heads of all of us at our end of the table, and she recited:

"Take of English earth as much
As either hand may rightly clutch.
In the taking of it breathe
Prayer for all who lie beneath."

Then Meredice Williamson dipped her fork and tried a dainty bite of tomato smush.

All around the table, though, every other fork had stopped. Even mine. I don't know, maybe Kipling out of the blue would have that effect on any group of diners, not just hay hands. But in any case, there was a mulling silence as Wendell contemplated Meredice and the rest of us contemplated the Double W boss and his wife. Not even a "nuh-huh" out of Wendell.

Finally Cal Petrie turned toward me and asked, "How's that power buckrake of Pete's working out?"

"Real good," I said. "Would somebody pass the liver, please?" And that pretty much was the story of supper at the great Double W.

Alec walked with me to the barn to help harness Blanche and Fisheye. He still wasn't saying much. Nor for that matter was I. I'd had about enough Double W and brooding brother, and was looking forward to getting to town.

Something, though—something kept at me as we started harnessing. It had been circling in the back of my mind ever since the hay crew clomped into the bunkhouse that afternoon. Alec came in with them. Cal Petrie and the riders who had been fixing fence made their appearance a few minutes after that.

I may be slow, but I usually get there. "Alec?" I asked across the horses' backs. "Alec, what have they got you doing?"

On the far side of Blanche, the sound of harnessing stopped for an instant. Then resumed.

"I said, what have they—"

"I heard you," came my brother's voice. "I'm helping out with the haying."

"I figured that. Which job?"

Silence.

"I said, which—"

"Raking."

You cannot know with what struggle I resisted popping out the next logical question: "Dump or scatter?" Yet I already knew the answer. I did indeed. The old slouchy guy in the khaki shirt and the one-eyed one, they were plodding dump rakers if I had ever seen the species. And that left just one hayfield job unaccounted for. My brother the calf-roping caballero was doing the exact same thing in life I was. Riding a scatter rake.

I did some more buckling and adjusting on Fisheye. Debating with myself. After all, Alec was my brother. If I couldn't talk straight from the shoulder with him, who could I?

"Alec, this maybe isn't any of my business, but—"

"Jick, when did that detail ever stop you? What's on your mind, besides your hat?"

"Are you sure you want to stay on here? More than this summer, I mean? This place doesn't seem to me anything so special."

"So you're lining up with Mom and Dad, are you." Alec didn't sound surprised, as if the rank of opinion against him was like one of the sides in choosing up to play softball. He also didn't sound as if any of us were going to alter his thinking. "What, is there a law that says somewhere that I've got to go to college?"

"No, it's just that you'd be good at it, and—"

"Everybody seems awful damn sure about that. Jick, I'm already doing something I'm good at, if I do say so my own self. I'm as good a hand with cattle as Thurl or Joe or anybody else they ever had here. So why doesn't that count for anything? Huh? Answer me that. Why can't I stay on here in the Two country and do a decent job of what I want to, instead of traipsing off to goddamn college?"

For the first time since he stepped into the bunkhouse and caught sight of me, Alec came alive. He stood now in front of Blanche, holding her haltered head. But looking squarely at me, as I stood in front of Fisheye. The tall and blue-eyed and flame-haired Alec of our English Creek years, the Alec who faced life as if it was always going to deal him aces.

I tried again, maybe to see if I was understanding my brother's words. "Christamighty, though, Alec. They haven't even got you doing what you want to do here. You hired on as a rider. Why're you going to let goddamn Wendell do whatever he wants with you?"

Alec shook his head. "You do sound like the folks would."

"I'm trying to sound like myself, is all. What is it about the damn life here that you think is so great?"

My brother held his look on me. Not angry, not even stubborn. And none of that abstracted glaze of earlier in the summer, as though only half seeing me. This was Alec to the full, the one who answered me now:

"That it's my own."

"Well, yeah, I guess it is" was all I could manage to respond. For it finally had struck me. This answer that had popped out of Alec as naturally as a multiplication sum, this was the future. So much did my brother want to be on his own in life, he would put up with a bad choice of his own making—endure whatever the Double W heaped on him, if it came to that—rather than give in to somebody else's better plan for him. Ever since the night of the supper argument our parents thought they were contending with Alec's cowboy phase or with Leona or the combination of the two. I now knew otherwise. What they were up against was the basic Alec.

"Jick," he was saying to me, "do me a favor about all this, okay?"

"What is it?"

"Don't say anything to the folks. About me not riding, just now." He somewhere found a grin, although a puny one. "About me following in your footsteps as a scatter raker. They have a low enough opinion of me recently." He held the grin so determinedly it began to hurt me. "So will you do that for me?"

"Yeah. I will."

"Okay." Alec let out a lot of breath. "We better get you hooked up and on your way, or you'll have to roll Grady out of bed to do the welding."

One more thing I had to find out, though. As I got up on the seat of the scatter rake, the reins to Blanche and Fisheye ready in my hand, I asked as casually as I could:

"How's Leona?"

The Alec of the Fourth of July would have cracked "Fine as frog hair" or "Dandy as a field of dandelions" or some such. This Alec just said: "She's okay." Then goodbyed me with: "See you around, Jicker."

"Ray? Does it ever seem like you can just look at a person and know something that's going to happen to them?"

"No. Why?"

"I don't mean look at them and know everything. Just something. Some one thing."

"Like what?"

"Well, like—" I gazed across the lawn at the Heaney house, high and pale white in the dark. Ed and Genevieve and Mary Ellen had gone to bed, but Ray and I won permission to sprawl on the grass under the giant cottonwood until Ray's bedroom cooled down a bit from the sultry day. The thunderstorm had missed Gros Ventre, only left it its wake of heat and charged air. "Promise not to laugh at this?"

"You couldn't pay me to."

"All right. Like when I was talking to Alec out there at the Double W after supper. I don't know, I just felt like I could tell. By the look of him."

"Tell about what?"

"That he and Leona aren't going to get married."

Ray weighed this. "You said you could tell something that's going to happen. That's something that's *not* going to happen."

"Same thing."

"Going to happen and not going to happen are the same thing? Jick, sometimes—"

"Never mind." I stretched an arm in back of my head, to rub a knuckle against the cottonwood. So wrinkled and gullied was its trunk that it was as if rivulets of rain had been running down it ever since the deluge floated Noah. I drifted in thought past the day's storm along Noon Creek, past the Double W and Alec, past the hayfields of the Ramsay place, past to where I had it tucked away to tell Ray:

"Saw Marcella a while back. From a distance."

"Yeah?" Ray responded, with what I believe is called elaborate indifference.

The next morning I returned with the rake to the Reese place, confirmed with Pete that the hay was too wet for us to try, retrieved Pony, and by noon was home at English Creek in time for Sunday dinner. During which I related to my parents my visit to the Double W.

My father, the fire season always on his mind now, grimaced and said: "Lightning. You'd think the world could operate without the damn stuff." Then he asked: "Did you see your brother?" When I said I had, he only nodded.

Given how much my mother had been on her high horse against the Double W all summer, I was set to tell her of the latest cook and the tomato smush and the weakling gravy. But before I could get started she fixed me with a thoughtful look and asked: "Is there anything new with Alec?"

"No," came flying out of me from some nest of brotherly allegiance I hadn't been aware of. Lord, what a wilderness is the thicket of family. "No, he's just riding around."

This is what I meant, earlier, about the chain of events of that last spate of haying. If Clayton Hebner had not grab-assed himself into a twisted ankle, I would not now have been the sole depository of the news of Alec's Double W situation.

The second Saturday in August, one exact month since we started haying, we sited the stacker in the last meadow along Noon Creek.

Before climbing on the power buckrake Pete cast a long gaze over the windrows, estimating. Then said what didn't surprise anybody who'd ever been in a haying crew before: "Let's see if we can get it all up in one, instead of moving the stacker another damn time."

"If you can get it up here," vowed Wisdom, "we'll find someplace to put it."

So that final haystack began to climb. Bud Dolson, now that mowing was over, was on top helping Wisdom with the stacking. Perry too was done with his part of haying, no more windrows to be made. He tied his team in some shade by the creek and in his creaky way was dabbing around the stack with a pitchfork, carrying scraps of hay to the stacker fork. Clayton, I am happy to report, had mended enough to drive the stacker team again and I had regained my scatter rake.

Of course, it was too much hay for one stack. But on a last one, that never stops a hay crew. I raked and re-raked behind Pete's swoops with his buckrake. The stack towered. The final loads wouldn't come off the stacker fork by themselves, Wisdom and Bud pulled up the hay pitchforkful by pitchforkful to the round summit of the stack.

At last every stem of hay was in that stack.

"How the hell do we get off this thing?" called down Bud from the island in the air, only half joking.

"Along about January I'll feed from this stack," Pete sent back up to him. "I'll bring out a ladder and get you then."

In actuality, the descent of Wisdom and Bud was provided by Clayton running the stacker fork up to them, so they could grab hold of the fork teeth while they climbed down onto the frame.

Marie had driven up from the main ranch to see this topping-off of the summer's haying, and brought with her cold tea and fresh-baked oatmeal cookies. We stood and looked and sipped and chewed, a crew about to scatter. Perry to head back into Gros Ventre and a winter of leather work at the saddle shop. Bud tonight onto a bus to Anaconda and his smelter job. Wisdom proclaimed he was heading straight for the redwood logging country down in California, and Pete and Bud had worked on him until they got Wisdom to agree that he would ride the bus with Bud as far as Great Falls, at least getting him and his wages past the Medicine Lodge saloon. Clayton, over the English Creek–Noon Creek divide to the North Fork and Hebner life again. Pete and Marie, to fencing the haystacks and then shipping the lambs and then trailing the Reese sheep home from the reservation, and all too soon feeding out the hay we had put up. Me, to again become a daytime dweller at English Creek instead of a nightly visitor.

"Either this weather is Out Of Control," declared my mother, "or I'm Getting Old."

It can be guessed which of those she thought was the case. This summer did not seem to be aware that with haying done, it was supposed to be thinking about departure. The wickedest weather yet settled in, a real siege of swelter. The first three days I was home at English Creek after finishing at Pete's the temperature hit the nineties and the rest of the next couple of weeks wasn't a whole lot better. Too hot. Putting up with heat while you drive a scatter rake or work some other job is one thing. But having the temperature try to toast you while you're just hanging around and existing, that somehow seems a personal insult.

Nor, for all her lament about August's runaway warmth, was my mother helping the situation any. The contrary. She was canning. And canning and canning. It started each June with rhubarb, and then would come a spurt of cooking homemade sausage and layering it in crocks with the fat over it, and next would be the first of the garden vegetables, peas, and after them beets to pickle, and then the various pickings of beans, all the while interspersed with making berry jams, and at last in late August the arrival to Helwig's merc in Gros Ventre of the flat boxes of canning peaches and pears. We ate all winter on what my mother put up, but the price of it was that during a lot of the hottest days of summer the kitchen range also was blazing away. So whenever canning was the agenda I steered clear of the house as much as I could. It was that or melt.

In the ranger station as well, life sometimes got too warm for comfort, although not just because of the temperature reading.

"How's it look?" my father asked his dispatcher Chet Barnouw first thing each morning. This time of year, this sizzling August, Chet's reports were never good. "Extreme danger" was the fire rating on the Two Medicine National Forest now, day after day. There already were fires, big ones, on forests west of the Continental Divide; the Bad Rock Canyon fire in the Flathead National Forest was just across the mountains from us.

Poor Chet. His reward for reporting all this was to have my father say, "Is that the best news you can come up with?" My father put it lightly, or tried to, but both Chet and the assistant ranger Paul Eliason knew it was the start of another touchy day. Chet and Paul were young and in their first summer on the Two, and I know my father suffered inwardly about their lack of local knowledge. Except for being wet behind the ears, they weren't a bad pair. But in a fire summer like this, that was a big except. As dispatcher Chet was in charge of the telephone setup that linked the lookout towers and the guard cabins to the ranger station, and he kept in touch with headquarters in Great Falls by the regular phone system. His main site of operation, thus, was the switchboard behind a partition at one side of my father's office. I think my mother was the one who gave that cubbyhole the name of "the belfry," from all the phone signals that chimed in there. The belfry took some getting used to, for anybody, but Chet was an unhurryable type best fitted for the job of dispatcher.

Of the two, Paul Eliason gave my father more grief than Chet did. Paul did a lot of moping. You'd have thought he was born looking glum about it. Actually the case was that the previous winter, just before he was transferred to the English Creek district as my father's assistant ranger, Paul and his wife had gotten a divorce and she'd gone home to her mother in Seattle. According to what my father heard from Paul it was one of those things. She tried for a year to put up with being a Forest Service wife, but Paul at the time was bossing CCC crews who were building trail on the Olympic National Forest out in the state of Washington, and the living quarters for the Eliasons was a backcountry one-room cabin which featured pack rats and a cookstove as temperamental as it was ancient. Perfect circumstances to make an assistant ranger–city wife marriage go flooey if it ever was going to.

"He's starting to heal up," my father assessed Paul at this point of the summer. "Lord knows, I've tried to keep him busy enough he doesn't have time to feel sorry for himself."

If I rationed myself and didn't get in the way of business, my father didn't mind that I hung around in the ranger station. But there was a limit on how much I wanted to do that, too. Whenever something was happening—the lookouts up there along the skyline of the Two calling in their reports to Chet in the belfry, my father tracing his finger over and over the map showing the pocket fires his smokechasers already had dealt with—the station was a lively enough place to be. But in between those times, rangering was not much of a spectator sport.

Each day is a room of time, it is said. In that long hot remainder of August I knew nothing to do but go from one span of sun to the next with as little of rubbing against my parents as possible. My summer's work was done, they were at the zenith of theirs.

Consequently a good deal of my leisure or at least time-killing was spent along the creek. I called it fishing, although it didn't really amount to that. Fish are not dumb; they don't exert themselves to swallow a hook during the hot part of the day. So until the trout showed any signs of biting I would shade up under a cottonwood, pull an old magazine from my hip pocket, and read.

A couple of times each week I would saddle Pony and ride up to Breed Butte to check on Walter Kyle's place, then fish the North Fork beaver dams on my way home. Walter's place was a brief hermitage for me on those visits. The way it worked was this. We and Walter were in the habit of swapping magazines, and after I had chosen several to take from the pile on his shelf, I would sit at his kitchen table and think matters over for a while before heading down to the beaver dams.

That low old ranch house of Walter Kyle's was as private a place as could be asked for. To sit there at the table looking out the window to the south, down the slope of Breed Butte to the willow thickets of the North Fork and beyond to Grizzly Reef's crooked cliffs and the line of peaks into the Teton River country, was to see the earth empty of people. Just out of sight down the North Fork was our ranger station and only over the brow of Breed Butte the other direction was the old McCaskill homestead, now Hebnerized. But all else of this long North Fork coulee was vacancy. Not wilderness, of course. Scotch Heaven left traces of itself, homestead houses still standing or at least not quite fallen down, fencelines whose prime use now was for hawks to perch on. But any other breathing soul than me, no. The sense of emptiness all around made me ponder the isolation those early people, my father's parents among them, landed themselves into here. Even when the car arrived into this corner of the Two Medicine country, mud and rutted roads made going anywhere no easy task. To say nothing of what winter could do. Some years the snow here drifted up and up until it covered the fenceposts and left you guessing its depth beyond that. No, those homesteaders of Scotch Heaven did not know what they were getting into. But once in, how many cherished this land as their own, whatever its conditions? It is one of those matters hard to balance out. Distance and isolation create a freedom of sorts. The space to move in according to your own whims and bents. Yet it was exactly this freedom, this fact that a person was a speck on the earth sea, that must have been too much for some of the settlers. From my father's stories and Toussaint Rennie's, I knew of Scotch Heaveners who retreated into the dimness of their homestead cabins, and the worse darkness of their own minds. Others who simply got out, walked away from the years of homestead effort. Still others who carried it with them into successful ranching. Then there were the least lucky who took their dilemma, a freedom of space and a toll of mind and muscle, to the grave with them.

It was Alec who had me thinking along these heavy lines. Alec and his insistence on an independent life. Was it worth the toll he was paying? I could not give an absolute affidavit either way. What I did know for sure was that Alec's situation now had me in my own kind of bind. For if my parents could learn what a fizzle Alec's Double W job was, it might give them fresh determination to persuade him out of it. At very least, it might soften the frozen mood, put them and him on speaking terms again. But I had told Alec I'd say nothing to them about his situation. And his asking of that was the one true brother-to-brother moment between us since he left English Creek.

That's next thing to hopeless, to spend your time wishing you weren't in the fix you are. And so I fished like an apostle, and read and read, and hung around the ranger station betweentimes, and eventually even came up with something else I wanted to do with myself. The magazines must have seeded the notion in me. In any case it was during those hot drifting last of August days that I proposed to my mother that I paper my porch bedroom.

She still was canning. Pole beans by now, I think. She tucked a wisp of hair back from where it had stuck to her damp forehead and informed me: "Wallpaper costs money." I never did understand why parents seem to think this is such startling news, that something a kid wants costs money. Based on my own experience as a youngster, the real news would have been if the object of desire was for free.

But this once, I was primed for that response from my mother "I'll use magazine pages," I suggested. "Out of those old *Post*s and *Collier's*. There's a ton of pictures in them, Mom."

That I had thought the matter through to this extent told her this meant something to me. She quit canning and faced me. "Even so, it would mean buying the paste. But I suppose—"

I still had my ducks in a row. "No, it won't. The Heaneys have got some left over. I heard Genevieve say." Ray's mother had climaxed her spring cleaning that year by redoing the Heaney front hall.

"All right," my mother surrendered. "It's too hot to argue. The next time anybody makes a trip to town, we'll pick up your paste."

I can be fastidious when it's worth being so. The magazine accumulation began to get a real going-over from me for illustrations worthy of gracing my sleep parlor.

I'd much like to have had Western scenes, but do you know, I could not find any that were worth a damn. A story called "Bitter Creek" showed a guy riding with a rifle across the pommel of his saddle and some pack horses behind him. The pack horses were all over the scenery instead of strung together by rope, and there was every chance that the guy would blast his leg off by not carrying that rifle in a scabbard. So much for Bitter Creek. Then there was a story which showed a couple on horseback, which drew me because the pair made me think of Alec and Leona. It turned out, though, that the setting was a dude ranch, and the line under the illustration read: "One Dude Ranch is a Good Deal Like Another. You Ride Horseback and You Overeat and You Lie in the Sun and You Fish and You Play Poker and You Have Picnics." All of which may be true enough, but I didn't think it interesting enough to deserve wall space.

No, the first piece of art I really liked was a color illustration in *Collier's* of a tramp freighter at anchor. And then I found a *Post* piece showing a guy leaning on the railing of another merchant vessel and looking across the water to a beautiful sailing ship. "As the 'Inchcliffe Castle' Crawled Along the Coast of Spain, Through the Strait of Gibraltar, the Engineer Was Prey to a Profound Preoccupation." This was more like it. A nautical decor, just what the room could use. I went ahead and snipped out whatever sea story illustrations I could find in the stack of magazines. I could see that there wasn't going to be enough of a fleet to cover the whole wall, but I came across a Mr. Moto detective series that went on practically forever and so I filled in along the top of the wall with action scenes from that, as a kind of contrasting border.

When I was well launched into my paperhanging, Mr. Moto and various villains up top there and the sea theme beginning to fill in under, I called in my mother to see my progress.

"It does change the look of the place," she granted.

The evening of the twenty-fifth of August, a Friday, an electrical storm struck across western Montana and then moved to our side of the Continental Divide. It threw firebolts beyond number. At Great Falls, radio station KFBB was knocked off the air and power lines blew out. I would like to be able to say that I awoke in the big storm, so keen a weather wizard that I sat up in bed sniffing the ozone or harking to the first distant avalanche of thunder. The fact is, I snoozed through that electrical night like Sleeping Beauty.

The next morning, more than two hundred new lightning fires were reported in the national forests of Region One.

Six were my father's. One near the head of the South Fork of English Creek. One at the base of Billygoat Peak. Two in the old Phantom Woman burn, probably snags alight. One in northwest behind Jericho Reef. And one up the North Fork at Flume Gulch.

The McCaskill household was in gear before daybreak.

"Fire school never told us they come half a dozen at a time," muttered my father and went out to establish himself in the ranger station.

I stoked away the rest of my breakfast and got up to follow him. My mother half advised and half instructed, "Don't wear out your welcome." But she knew as well as anything that it would take logchains and padlocks to keep me out of the station with all this going on.

As soon as I stepped in I saw that Chet and Paul looked braced. As if they were sinners and this was the morning after, when they had to stand accountable to a tall red-haired Scotch preacher.

My father on the other hand was less snorty than he'd been in weeks. Waiting for the bad to happen was always harder for him than trying to deal with it once it did.

"All right," was all my father said to the pair of them, "let's get the guys to chasing these smokes." Chet started his switchboard work and the log of who was sent where at what time, Paul began assessing where he ought to pitch in in person.

The day was not August's hottest, but hot enough. It was vital that all six plumes of smoke be gotten to as quickly as possible, before midday heat encouraged these smudges to become genuine fires. The job of smokechaser always seemed to me a hellish one, shuffling along a mountainside with a big pack on your back and then, when you finally sighted or sniffed out the pocket of fire, using a shovel or a pulaski to smother it to death. All the while, dry trees standing around waiting to catch any embers and go off like Roman candles.

No, where firefighting of any sort was concerned I considered myself strictly a distant witness. Alec had done some, a couple of Augusts ago on the fireline against the Biscuit Creek blaze down on Murray Tomlin's ranger district at the south end of the Two, and as with everything else he showed a knack for it. But I did not take after my brother in that flame-eating regard.

It was mostly good news I was able to repeat to my mother when I visited the house for gingersnaps just past mid-morning. In those years the official Forest Service notion for fighting forest fires was what was called the ten A.M. policy: gain control of a fire by ten the morning after it's reported; if it's still out of hand by then, aim for ten the next morning, and so on. Chet had reported to headquarters in Great Falls, "We've got ten A.M. control on four of ours"—the South Fork, Billygoat, and the two Phantom Woman situations. All four were snag strikes, lightning gashing into a dead tree trunk and leaving it slowly burning, and the nearest fire guard had been able to put out the South Fork smolder, the lookout man and the smokechaser stationed on Billygoat Peak combined to whip theirs, while the Phantom Woman pair of smokes were close enough together that the smokechaser who'd been dispatched up there managed to handle both. So those four now were history. Jericho Reef and Flume Gulch were actual blazes; small ones, but still alive and trying. A fire guard named Andy Ames and a smokechaser named Emil Kratka were on the Flume Gulch blaze. Both were new to that area of the Two, but my father thought well of them. "They'll stomp it if anybody can." Jericho Reef, so much farther back in the mountains, seemed more like trouble. Nobody wanted a backcountry fire getting under way in weather like this. Paul had nibbled on the inside of his lips for a while, then suggested that he collect the CCC crew that was repairing trail on the North Fork and go on up to the Jericho Reef situation. My father told him that sounded right, and Paul charged off up there.

"Fire season in the Forest Service," said my mother. "There is nothing like it, except maybe St. Vitus' dance."

Ours was the only comparatively good news in the Two Medicine National Forest that Saturday. At Blacktail Gulch down by Sun River, Murray Tomlin was still scooting his smokechasers here and there to tackle a dozen snag strikes. The worst of the electrical storm must have dragged through Murray's district on its way to Great Falls. And on his Indian Head district south of us Cliff Bowen had a fire away to hell and gone up in the mountains, under the Chinese Wall. He'd had to ask headquarters for a bunch of EFFs, which were emergency firefighters the Forest Service scraped together and signed up in a real pinch, from the bars and flophouses of Clore Street in Helena and Trent Avenue in Spokane and First Avenue South in Great Falls and similar fragrant neighborhoods where casual labor hung out. It was going to take Cliff most of the day just to hike his EFFs up to his fire. "Gives me a nosebleed to think about fighting one up there," my father commiserated.

"Sunday, the day of rest" was the mutter from my father as he headed to the ranger station the next morning.

Had he known, he would have uttered something stronger. It turned out to be a snake of a day. By the middle of the morning, Chet was telling Great Falls about ten A.M. control on one of our two blazes—but not the one he and my father expected. Jericho Reef was whipped; Paul and his CCs found only a quarter-acre ground fire there and promptly managed to mop it up. "Paul should have taken marshmallows," my father was moved to joke to Chet. Flume Gulch, though, had grown into something full-fledged. All day Saturday, Kratka and Ames had worked themselves blue against the patch of flame, and by nightfall they thought they had it contained. But during the night a remnant of flame crawled along an area of rock coated with pine needles. Sunday morning it surfaced, touched off a tree opposite from where Kratka and Ames were keeping an eye on matters, and the fire then took off down a slant of the gulch into a thick stand of timber. In a hurry my father yanked Paul and his CCs back from Jericho Reef to Flume Gulch, and I was killing time in the ranger station, late that morning, when Chet passed along the report Paul was phoning in from the guard cabin nearest Flume Gulch.

Thus I was on hand for those words of Paul's that became fabled in our family.

"Mac," Chet recited them, "Paul says the fire doesn't look that bad. It just keeps burning, is all."

"Is that a fact," said my father carefully, too carefully. Then it all came. "Kindly tell Mr. goddamn Eliason from me that it's his goddamn job to see to it that the goddamn fire DOESN'T keep burning, and that I—no, never mind."

My father got back his breath, and most of his temper. "Just tell Paul to keep at it, keep trying to pinch it off against a rock formation. Keep it corraled."

Monday made Sunday look good. Paul and his CC crew still could not find the handle on the Flume Gulch fire. They would get a fireline almost built, then a blazing fir tree would crash over and come sledding down the gulch, igniting the next jungle of brush and windfall and tinder-dry timber. Or sparks would shoot up from the slope, find enough air current to waft to the other steep side of the gulch, and set off a spot fire there. Ten A.M. came and went, with Paul's report substantially the same as his ones from the day before: not that much fire, but no sight of control.

My father prowled the ranger station until he about had the floor worn out. When he said something unpolite to Chet for the third time and started casting around for a fresh target, I cleared out of there.

The day was another scorcher. I went to the spring house for some cold milk, then in to the kitchen for a doughnut to accompany the milk down. And here my father was again, being poured a cup of coffee by my mother. As if he needed any more prowl fuel today.

My father mimicked Paul's voice: " 'Mac, the fire doesn't look that bad. It just keeps burning, is all.' Jesus. How am I supposed to get through a fire season with help like that, I ask you."

"The same way you do every summer," suggested my mother.

"I don't have a pair of green peas as assistant and dispatcher, every summer."

"No, only about every other summer. As soon as you get them trained, Sipe or the Major moves them on and hands you the next fresh ones."

"Yeah, well. At least these two aren't as green as they were a month ago. For whatever that's worth." He was drinking that coffee as if it was going to get away from him. It seemed to be priming him to think out loud. "I don't like it that the fire outjumped Kratka and Ames. They're a real pair of smokehounds, those guys. It takes something nasty to be too much for them. And I don't like it that Paul's CCs haven't got matters in hand up there yet either." My father looked at my mother as if she had the answer to what he was saying. "I don't like any of what I'm hearing from Flume Gulch."

"I gathered that," she said. "Do you want me to put you up a lunch?"

"I haven't said yet I'm going up there."

"You're giving a good imitation of it."

"Am I." He carried his empty coffee cup to the sink and put it in the dishpan. "Well, Lisabeth McCaskill, you are famous the world over for your lunches. I'd be crazy to pass one up, wouldn't I."

"All right then." But before starting to make his sandwiches, my mother turned to him one more time. "Mac, are you sure Paul can't handle this?" Which meant: are you sure you shouldn't *let* Paul handle this fire?

"Bet, there's nothing I'd like more. But I don't get the feeling it's being handled. Paul's been lucky on his other fires this summer, they both turned out to be weinie roasts. But this one isn't giving up." He prowled over to the window where Roman Reef and Rooster Mountain and Phantom Woman peak could be seen. "No, I'd better go up there and have a look."

I didn't even bother to ask to go along. A counting trip or something else routine, that was one thing. But the Forest Service didn't want anybody out of the ordinary around a fire. Particularly if his sum of life hadn't yet quite made it to fifteen years.

"Mom? I was wondering—" Supper was in the two of us. She had washed the dishes and I had dried. I could just as well have abandoned the heat of the house for an evening of fishing. But I had to rid myself of at least part of what had been on my mind the past weeks. "I was wondering—well, about Leona."

Here was an attention-getter. My mother lofted a look and held it on me. "And what is it you've been wondering about Leona?"

"Her and Alec, I mean."

"All right. What about them?"

I decided to go for broke. "I don't think they're going to get married. What do you think?"

"I think I have a son in this kitchen who's hard to keep up with. Why are Alec and Leona tonight's topic?"

"It's not just tonight's," I defended. "This whole summer has been different. Ever since the pair of them walked out of here, that suppertime."

"I can't argue with you on that. But where do you get the idea the marriage is off?"

I thought about how to put it. "You remember that story Dode tells about Dad? About the first time you and Dad started, uh, going together? Dad was riding over to call on you, and Dode met up with him on the road and saw Dad's clean shirt and shined boots and the big grin on him, and instead of 'Hello' Dode just asked him, 'Who is she?'"

"Yes," she said firmly. "I know that story."

"Well, Alec doesn't look that way. He did earlier in the summer. But when I saw him at the Double W that time, he looked like somebody had knocked the blossom off him. Like Leona had."

My mother was unduly slow in responding. I had been so busy deciding how much I could say, without going against my promise to Alec not to tell what a botch his Double W job was, that I hadn't realized she too was doing some deciding. Eventually her thoughts came aloud:

"You may have it right. About Leona. We're waiting to see."

She saw that I damn well wanted a definition of "we."

"Leona's parents and I. I saw Thelma Tracy the last time I was in town. She said Leona's mind still isn't made up, which way to choose."

"Choose?" I took umbrage on Alec's behalf. "What, has she been seeing some other guy, too?"

"No. To choose between marrying Alec and going on with her last year of high school is what she's deciding. Thelma thinks school is gaining fast." She reminded me, as if I needed any: "It starts in a little over a week."

"Then what—what do you think will happen after that? With Alec, I mean. Alec and you and Dad."

"We'll just have to see in September. Your father still has his mad on about Alec throwing away college. For that matter, I'm not over mine either. To think, a mind like Alec's and all he wants to do Is Prance Around Like—" She caught herself. Then got back to her tone of thinking out loud: "And knowing Alec, I imagine he's still just as huffy as we are."

"Maybe"—I had some more careful deciding than ever, how to say this so as not to bring about something which would rile Alec even more—"maybe if you and Dad sort of stopped by to see Alec. Just dropped by the Double W, sort of."

"I don't see how it would help. Not until Leona and the college question are out of the way. Another family free-for-all won't improve matters. Your father and your brother. They'll have to get their minds off their argument, before anything can be done. So."

The "so" which meant, we have now put a lid on this topic. But she added, as if it would reassure me:

"We wait and see."

Say this for the Forest Service life, it enlarges your days. Not long after my mother and I were done with breakfast the next morning, the telephone rang. Everybody in a ranger's family knows the rings of all the lookout sites and guard cabins on the line. The signal was from the fire guard Ames's cabin, the one nearest to Flume Gulch.

"Rubber that, will you, Jick," called my mother from whatever chore she was on elsewhere in the house. "Please."

I went to the wall phone and put the receiver to my ear. Rubbering, which is to say listening in, was our way of keeping track of matters without perpetually traipsing back and forth between the house and the ranger station.

"Mac says to tell Great Falls there's no chance of controlling the fire by ten today," Paul was reporting to Chet. "If you want his exact words, he says there isn't a diddling deacon's prayer of whipping it today." Even on the phone Paul's voice sounded pouty. My bet was, when my father arrived and took over as fire boss, Paul had reacted like a kicked pup.

"Approximate words will do, given the mood Mac's been in," Chet told Paul. "Anything else new, up there?"

"No" from Paul and his click of hanging up.

I relayed this, in edited form, to my mother. She didn't say anything. But with her, silence often conveyed enough.

When the same phone ring happened in late morning, I called out, "I'll rubber."

This voice was my father himself.

"It is an ornery sonofabitch," he was informing Chet. "Every time a person looks at it, it looks a little bigger. We better hit it hard. Get hold of Isidor and have him bring in a camp setup. And tell Great Falls we need fifty EFFs and a timekeeper for them."

"Say again on that EFF request, Mac," queried Chet. "Fifteen or fifty? One-five or five-oh?"

"Five-oh, Chet."

Pause.

Chet was swallowing on the figure. With crews of emergency firefighters already on the Chinese Wall fire and the fires down in the Lewis and Clark forest, Two headquarters in Great Falls was going to greet this request for fifty more like the miser meeting the tax man.

"Okay, Mac," Chet mustered. "I'll ask for them. What else can I get you?" Chet could not have realized it, but this was his introduction to the Golden Rule of a veteran ranger such as my father when confronted with a chancy fire: always ask for more help than you think you'll need.

Or as my father said he'd once heard it from a ranger of the generation before him: "While you're getting, get plenty."

"Grub," my father was going on. "Get double lunches in here for us today." Double lunches were pretty much what they sound like: about twice the quantity of sandwiches and canned fruit and so on that a working man could ordinarily consume. Firefighters needed legendary amounts of food. "And get us a real cook for the camp by tonight. The CC guy we been using could burn water. I'm going to get some use out of him by putting him on the fireline."

"Okay," said Chet again. "The double lunches I'll get out of Gros Ventre, and I'll start working on Great Falls for the fifty men and a timekeeper and a cook. Anything else?"

"Not for now," allowed my father. Then: "Jick. You there?"

I jumped, but managed: "Yeah?"

"I figured you were. How's your fishing career? Owe me a milkshake yet?"

"No, I didn't go yesterday."

"All right. I was just checking." A moment, then: "Is your mother around there?"

"She's out in the root cellar, putting away canning."

"Is she. Okay, then."

"Anything you want me to tell her?"

"Uh huh, for all the good it'll do. Tell her not to worry."

"I will if I want to," she responded to that. "Any time your father asks Great Falls for help, it's worth worrying about." She set off toward the ranger station. "At least I can go into town for the double lunches. That'll keep Chet free here. You can ride in with me."

While she was gone to apprise Chet, the Flume Creek fire and my father filled my mind. Trying to imagine what the scene must be. That campsite where my father and I, and Alec in the other summers, caught our fill of brookies and then lazed around the campfire; flames now multiplied by maybe a million. In the back of all our minds, my father's and my mother's and mine, we had known that unless the weather let up it would be a miracle not to have a fire somewhere on the Two. Montana weather, and a miracle. Neither one is anything to rest your hopes on. But why, out of all the English Creek district of the Two

Medicine National Forest, did the fire have to be there, in that extreme and beautiful country of Flume Gulch?

I heard the pickup door open and my mother call: "Jick! Let's go."

I opened the screen door and stepped from the kitchen. Then called back: "No, I think I'll just stay here."

From behind the steering wheel she sent me a look of surprise. "Do you feel all right?" That I would turn down a trip to town must be a malady of some sort, she figured.

"Yeah. But I just want to stay, and do some more papering on my room."

She hesitated. Dinnertime was not far off, her cookly conscience now was siding with her motherly one. "I thought we'd grab a bite at the Lunchery. If you stay, you'll have to fix your own."

"Yeah, well, I can manage to do that."

As I was counting on, she didn't have time to debate with me. "All right then. I'll be back as soon as I can." And the pickup was gone.

I made myself a headcheese sandwich, then had a couple of cinnamon rolls and cold milk. All the while, my mind on what I had decided, my eyes on the clock atop the sideboard.

Each day a room of time. Now each minute as slow as the finding and pasting of another page onto my bedroom wall in there.

I waited out the clock because I had to. It at last came up on the noon hour. The time to do it.

Out the kitchen door I went, sprinting to the ranger station. Just before coming around to its front, I geared myself down to what I hoped was my usual walking pace.

Chet was tipped back in a chair in the shade of the porch while he ate his lunch, as I'd counted on. Dispatchers are somewhat like gophers: they're holed up indoors so much they pop out into the air at any least chance.

"Hey there, Jick," I was greeted by Chet as I sauntered onto the porch. "What's up? It's too blasted hot to move if you don't have to."

"I came to see if it's okay if I use the town line. I forgot to tell Mom something and I want to leave word for her at the Lunchery."

"Sure thing. Nothing's going on right now, you can help yourself. You should've just rung me, Jick. I'd have gone in and switched it for you." Uh huh, and more than likely have stayed on and listened, as was a dispatcher's habit. Rubbering was something that worked both directions.

"No, that's okay, I didn't want to bother you. I won't need the line long." In I went to the switchboard and moved the toggle switch that connected the ranger station to the community telephone line.

"When you're done," Chet said as I headed off the porch past him, "just ding the dealybob and I'll switch things back to our line."

"Right. Thanks, Chet. Like I say, I won't be long." I moseyed around the corner of the station out of Chet's sight, then sped like hell back to our house.

Facing the phone, I sucked in all the breath I could, to crowd out my puffing and my nervousness about all that was riding on this idea of mine. Then I lifted the receiver, rang central in Gros Ventre, and asked to be put through to the Double W.

Onto the line came a woman's voice: "Hello?"

Perfect again: Meredice Williamson. I hadn't been sure what I was going to resort to if Wendell answered.

"'Lo, Mrs. Williamson. Can I—may I speak to Alec McCaskill in the bunkhouse, please? That is, would you ask him to go to the phone out at the bunkhouse? This is, uh, personal."

Down the line came the silence of Meredice Williamson pondering her way through the etiquette of yet another Two country situation. Maybe I would have been better off with Wendell's straightforward bluster. At last she queried: "Who is this, please?"

"This is Alec's brother Jick. I put Blanche and Fisheye in your barn that time, remember? And I'm sorry to call but I just really need to talk to—"

"Oh yes. Jack. I remember you well. But you see, Alec and the other men are at lunch—"

"Yeah, I figured that, that's why I'm calling right now."

"Could I have him return your call afterward?"

"No, that'd be too late. I need to talk to him now, it's just that it's, like I said, private. Family. A family situation has come up. Arisen."

"I see. I do hope it's nothing serious?"

"It could get that way if I don't talk to Alec. Mrs. Williamson, look, I can't explain all this. But I've got to talk to Alec, while he's alone. Without the whole damn—without everybody listening in."

"I see. Yes. I think I see. Will you hold on, Jack?" As if from a great distance, I heard her say: "Alec, you're wanted on the phone. I wonder if it might be more convenient for you to answer it in the bunkhouse?"

Now a dead stretch of time. But my mind was going like a million.

All of the summer to this minute was crowded into me. From that suppertime when Alec stomped out with Leona in tow, through all the days of my brother going his stubborn way and my parents going their stubborn one, through my times of wondering how this had come to be, how we McCaskills had so tangled our family situation, to now, when I saw just how to unknot it all. At last it was coming up right, the answer was about to dance within this telephone line.

Finally a voice from across the miles. "Jick? Is that you? What in the holy hell—"

"Alec, listen, I know this is kind of out of the ordinary."

"You're right about that."

"But just let me tell you all this, okay? There's a fire. Dad's gone up to it, at Flume Gulch—"

"The hell. None of that country's ever burned before."

"Well, it is now. And that's why I got hold of you, see. Alec, Dad's only help up there is Paul Eliason, and Paul doesn't know zero about that part of the Two."

A void at the Double W bunkhouse. The receiver offered only the sounds within my own ear, the way a seashell does. At last Alec's voice, stronger than before, demanding: "Jick, did Dad ask you to call me? If so, why in all hell couldn't he do it him—"

"No, he didn't ask me. He's up on the fire, I just told you."

"Then who—is this Mom's idea?"

"Alec, it's nobody's damn idea. I mean, it's none of theirs, you can call it mine if it's anybody's. All that's involved, Dad needs somebody up there who knows that Flume Gulch country. Somebody to help him line out the fire crew."

"That's all, huh. And you figure it ought to be me."

I wanted to shout, Why the hell else would I be on this telephone line with you? But instead carefully stayed to: "Yeah, I do. Dad needs your help." And kept unsaid too: this family needs its logjam of quarrel broken. Needs you and our father on speaking terms again. Needs this summer of separation to be over.

More of the seashell sound, the void. Then:

"Jick, no. I can't."

"Can't? Why not? Even goddamn Wendell Williamson'd let you off to fight a forest fire."

"I'm not going to ask him."

"You mean you won't ask him."

"It comes to the same. Jick, I just—"

"But why? Why won't you do this?"

"Because I can't just drop my life and come trotting home. Dad's got the whole damn Forest Service for help."

"But—then you won't do it for him."

"Jick, listen. No, I can't or won't, however you want to say it. But it's not because of Dad, it's not to get back at him or anything. It's—it's all complicated. But I got to go on with what I'm doing. I can't—" All these years later, I realize that here he very nearly said: "I can't give in." But the way Alec actually finished that sentence was: "I can't go galloping home any time there's a speck of trouble. If somebody was sick or hurt, it'd be different. But—"

"Then don't do it for Dad," I broke in on him, and I may have built up to a shout for this: "Do it because the goddamn country's burning up!"

"Jick, the fire is Dad's job, it's the Forest Service's job, it's the job of the whole crew they'll bring in there to Flume Gulch. It is not mine."

"But, Alec, you can't just—" Here I ran out of argument. The dead space on the telephone line was from my direction now.

"Jick," Alec's voice finally came, "I guess we're not getting anywhere with this."

"I guess we're not."

"Things will turn out," said my brother. "See you, Jick." And the phone connection ended.

It was too much for me. I stood there gulping back tears.

The house was empty, yet they were everywhere around me. The feel of them, I mean; the accumulation, the remembering, of how life had been when the other three of my family *were* three, instead of two against one. Or one against two, as it looked now. Alec. My mother. My father.

People. A pain you can't do without.

Eventually I remembered to ding the phone, signaling Chet that I was done with the town line. Done in, was more like it.

For the sake of something, anything, to do, I wandered to my bedroom and listlessly thumbed through magazines for any more sea scenes to put on the wall. Prey to a Profound Preoccupation, that was me.

—

At last I heard the pickup arrive. Nothing else I did seemed to be any use in the world, maybe I at least had better see if my mother needed any help with the fire lunches she was bringing.

I stepped out the kitchen door to find that help already was on hand, beside her at the tailgate of the pickup.

A brown Stetson nodded to me, and under it Stanley Meixell said: "Hullo again, Jick."

Civility was nowhere among all that crowded my brain just then. I simply blurted:

"Are you going up to the fire?"

"Thought I would, yeah. A man's got to do something to ward off frostbite."

My mother was giving Stanley her look that could peel a rock. But in an appraising way. I suppose she was having second thoughts about what she had set in motion here, by fetching Stanley from the Busby's ranch, and then third thoughts that any possible help for my father was better than no help, then fourth thoughts about Stanley's capacity to *be* any help, and on and on.

"Do you want some coffee?" she suggested to Stanley.

"I better not take time, Bet. I can get by without it." The fact was, it would take more than coffee to make a difference on him. "Who's this dispatcher we got to deal with?"

My mother told him about Chet, Stanley nodded, and she and he headed for the ranger station. Me right behind them.

"Getting those lunches up there'd be a real help, all right;" Chet agreed when my mother presented Stanley. But all the while he had been giving Stanley a going-over with his eyes, and it must be said, Stanley did look the worse for wear; looked as old and bunged up and afflicted as the night in the cabin when I was rewrapping his massacred hand. In this instance, though, the affliction was not Stanley's hand but what he had been pouring into himself with it.

Not somebody you would put on a fire crew, at least if your name was Chet Barnouw and the responsibility was directly traceable to you. So Chet now went on, "But beyond you taking those up for us, I don't see how we can use—"

"How're you fixed for a hash slinger?" Stanley asked conversationally.

Chet's eyebrows climbed. "You mean it? You can cook?"

"He's A-number-one at it," I chirped in commemoration of Stanley's breakfast the morning of my hangover.

Chet needed better vouching than my notorious appetite. He turned to my mother. If ever there was a grand authority on food, it was her. She informed Chet: "When Stanley says he can do a thing, he can."

"All right then," said Chet. "Great Falls more than likely would just dig out some wino fryhouse guy for me anyway." The dispatcher caught himself and cleared his throat. "Well, let's get you signed up here."

Stanley stepped over to the desk with him and did so. Chet looked down at the signature with interest.

"Stanley Kelley, huh? You spell it the same way the Major does."

My mouth flapped open. The look I received from my mother snapped it shut again.

All politeness, Stanley inquired: "The who?"

"Major Evan Kelley, the Regional Forester. The big sugar, over in Missoula. Kind of unusual, two E's in Kelley. You any relation?"

"None that I know of."

Chet went back in his belfry, and Stanley headed to the barn to rig up a saddle horse and Homer as the pack horse. Ordinarily I would have gone along to help him. But I was shadowing my mother, all the way back to the house.

As soon as we were in the kitchen I said it.

"Mom? I've got to go with Stanley."

The same surprise as when I'd stepped up and asked to dance the Dude and Belle with her, that distant night of the Fourth. But this request of mine was a caper in a more serious direction. "I thought you'd had enough of Stanley," she reminded me, "on that camptending episode."

"I did. But that was then." I tried, for the second time this day, to put into words more than I ever had before. "If Stanley's going to be any help to Dad, I'm going to have to be the help to Stanley. You know what he told me, after the camptending. When he said he couldn't have got along up there without me. The fire camp will be even worse for him. Paul's going to be looking down his neck the whole while and the first time he catches Stanley with a bottle he'll send him down the road." Plead is not a word I am ashamed of, in the circumstances. "Let me go with him, Mom."

She shook her head. "A fire camp is a crazyhouse, Jick. It wouldn't be just you and Stanley this time. They won't let you hang around—"

Here was my ace. "I can be Stanley's flunky. Help him with the cooking. That way I'd be right there with him all the time."

Serious as all this was, my mother couldn't stop her quick sideways grin at the notion of me around food full-time. But then she sobered. With everything in me, I yearned that she would see things my way. That she would not automatically tell me I was too young, that she would let me play a part at last, even just as chaperone, in this summer's stream of events.

Rare for Beth McCaskill, not to have an answer ready by now. By now she must have been on tenth and eleventh thoughts about the wisdom of having asked Stanley Meixell to go to Flume Gulch.

My mother faced me, and decided.

"All right. Go. But stay with Stanley or your father at all times. Do you Understand That? At All Times."

"Yes," I answered her. Any term of life as clear as that, even I could understand.

Stanley was my next obstacle.

"She said you can? C-A-N, can?"

"Yeah, she did. You can go on in and ask her." I kept on with my saddling of Pony.

"No, I'll take your word." He rubbed the back of his right hand with his left, still studying me. "Going to a fire, though—you sure you know what you're getting into?"

Canada Dan and Bubbles and Dr. Al K. Hall in a tin cup had come into my life at the elbow of this man and he could stand there and ask me that?

I shot back, "Does anybody ever?"

The squinch around Stanley's eyes let up a little. "There you got a point. Okey-doke, Jick. Let's get to getting."

Up the North Fork road the summer's second Meixell-McCaskill expedition set out, Stanley on a buckskin Forest Service gelding named Buck, leading the pack horse Homer with the load of lunches, and me behind on Pony.

—

I still don't know how Stanley managed the maneuver, but by the time we were past the Hebner place and topping the English Creek–Noon Creek divide, the smoke rising out of the canyon of the North Fork ahead of us, I was riding in the lead just as on our camptending expedition. That the reason was the same, I had no doubt. I didn't bother to look back and try to catch Stanley bugling a bottle, as that was a sight I did not want to have to think about. No, I concentrated on keeping us moving at a fast walk, at least as fast as I could urge Pony's short legs to go.

Something was different, though. This time Stanley wasn't singing. To my surprise I missed it quite a lot.

Smoke in a straight column. Then an oblong haze of it drifting south along the top of Roman Reef. The day's lone cloud, like a roll of sooty canvas on a high shelf.

A quantity of smoke is an unsettling commodity. The human being does not like to think its environs are inflammable. My mother had the memory that when she was a girl at Noon Creek the smoke from the 1910 fires brought a Bible-toting neighbor, a homesteader, to the Reese doorstep to announce: "This is the wrath of God. The end of the world is come." Daylight dimming out to a sickly green color and no distinct difference between night and day, I suppose it would make you wonder.

That same 1910 smoke never really left my father. He must have been about twelve or thirteen then, and his memory of that summer when the millions of acres burned in the Bitterroot while the Two had its own long stubborn fire was the behavior of the chickens there at the family home- stead on the North Fork. "Christamighty, Jick, by about noon they'd go in to roost for the night, it got so dark." The 1910 smoke darkness, and then the scarred mountainside of Phantom Woman as a later reminder; they stayed and stayed in my father, smears of dread.

Stanley too had undergone the 1910 smoke. In the cabin he had told me of being on that fire crew on the Two fire west of Swift Dam. "Such as we were, for a crew. Everybody and his cousin was already fighting some other sonuvabitch of a fire, Bitterroot or somewheres else. We dabbed at it here as best we could, a couple of weeks. Yeah, and we managed to lose our fire camp. The wind come up and turned a flank of that fire around and brought it right into our camp. A thing I never will forget, Jick, all the canned goods blew up. That was about all that was left when the fire got done with that camp, a bunch of exploded goddamn tin cans."

All three of them, each with a piece of memory of that awful fire summer. Of how smoke could multiply itself until it seemed to claim the world.

Now that my father had stepped in as fire boss at Flume Gulch, Paul Eliason was the camp boss. I will say, Paul was marshaling things into good order. We rode in past a couple of CCs digging a toilet trench. A couple of others were setting up the fire boss tent, each of them pounding in tent pegs with the flat of an ax. The feed ground—the kitchen area—already was built, and there we encountered Paul.

Paul still had an expression as if somebody big was standing on his foot and he was trying to figure out what to say about it, but he lost no time in sending one of the CCs off with Homer and the lunches to the fire crew. "Late is better than never," he rattled off, as if he invented that. "Thanks for delivering, Jick," he next recited, awarded Stanley a nod too, and started back to his next target of supervision.

"Paul," I managed to slow and turn him, "somebody here you got to meet. This is Stanley, uh—"

"—Kelley. Pleased to know you, ranger."

"—and, he's here to—" I finally found the inspiration I needed: "Chet signed him on as your cook." Well, as far as it went, that was true, wasn't it?

Paul studied this news. "I thought Chet told me he was going to have to get one out of Great Falls, and the chances didn't look real good even there."

"He must have had his mind changed," I speculated.

"Must have," Paul conceded. He looked Stanley over. "Have you ever cooked for a fire camp before?"

"No," responded Stanley. "But I been in a fire camp before, and I cooked before. So it adds up to the same."

Paul stared. "For crike's sake, mister. Have you got any idea what it takes to cook for a bunch of firefighters? They eat like—"

"Oh yeah," Stanley inserted, "and I almost forgot to tell you, I also've ate fire camp grub. So I been through the whole job, a little at a time."

"Uh huh" emitted from Paul, more as a sigh than an acknowledgment.

Stanley swung his gaze around the camp in interest. "Have you got some other candidate in mind for cook?"

"No, no, I sure as the devil don't. I guess you're it. So the feed ground is yours, mister." Paul waved to the area where the cookstove and a work table and the big T table to serve from had been set up. "You better get at it. You're going to have CCs coming at you from down that mountain and EFFs coming up from Great Falls. Figure supper for about seventy-five." Paul turned to me. "Jick, I appreciate you getting those lunches up here. If you start back now, you'll be home well before dark."

"Well, actually, I'm staying," I informed Paul. "I can be Stanley's flunky. My mom said it's okay."

Possibly this was the first time a member of a fire crew ever arrived with an excuse from his mother, and it sure as hell was nothing Paul Eliason had ever dealt with before. Particularly from a mother such as mine. You could all but see the thought squatting there on his mind: what next from these damn McCaskills?

But Paul only said: "You sort that out with your father. He's the fire boss." And sailed off to finish worrying the camp into being.

Stanley and I began to tour our feed ground. The muleloads of groceries and cooking gear Isidor Pronovost had brought in by packstring. An open fire pit and not far from it the stove. Both were lit and waiting, as if hinting that they ought to be in use. A long work table built of stakes and poles. And about twenty feet beyond it, the much bigger T-shaped serving table. I could see the principle: tin plates and utensils and bread and butter and so forth were to be stacked along the stem of the T so the fire crew could file through in a double line, one along each side of the stem, to the waiting food at both arms of the T. The food, though. That I could not envision: how Stanley and I were going to manage, in the next few hours, to prepare a meal for seventy-five guys.

"So," Stanley announced. "I guess—"

This I could have completed in my sleep—"we got it to do."

The Forest Service being the Forest Service and Paul being Paul, there hung a FIRE CAMP COOK BOOK on a nail at the serving table. Stanley peered over my shoulder as I thumbed to the page titled "First Supper," then ran my finger down that page to where it was decreed: "Menu—beef stew."

"Slumgullion," Stanley interpreted. "At least it ain't mutton."

Below the menu selection, instructing began in earnest: "Place large wash boiler, half full of water, on fire."

"Christamighty, Stanley, we better get to—" I began, before noticing the absence at my shoulder.

Over beside the packs of groceries, Stanley was leaning down to his saddlebags. Oh, Jesus. I could forecast the rest of that movement before it happened, his arm going in and bringing forth the whiskey bottle.

I don't know which got control of my voice, dismay or anger. But the message was coming out clear: "Goddamn it all to hell, Stanley, if you start in on that stuff—"

"Jick, you are going to worry yourself down to the bone if you keep on. Here, take yourself a swig of this."

"No, damn it. We got seventy-five men to feed. One of us has got to have enough damn brains to stay sober."

"I know how many we got to feed. Take a little of this in your mouth, just enough to wet your whistle."

When things start to skid they really do go, don't they. It wasn't enough that Stanley was about to begin a bender, he was insisting on me as company. My father would skin us both. My mother would skin whatever was left of me after my father's skinning.

"Just taste it, Jick." Stanley was holding the bottle out to me, patient as paint.

All right, all goddamn right; I had run out of thinking space, all the foreboding in the world was in me instead; I would buy time by faking a little swig of Stanley's joy juice, maybe after putting the bottle to my lips like this I could accidentally on purpose drop the—

Water.

Yet not quite *only* water. I swigged a second time to be sure of the taste. Just enough whiskey to flavor it faintly. If I'd had to estimate, perhaps a finger's worth of whiskey had been left in the bottle before Stanley filled it with water.

"It'll get me by," Stanley asserted. He looked bleak about the prospect, and said as much. "It's worse than being weaned a second time. But I done it before, a time or two when I really had to. Now we better get down to cooking, don't you figure?"

"The Forest Service must of decided everything tastes better with tin around it," observed Stanley as he dumped into the stew boiler eight cans each of tomatoes and peas.

"Sounds good to me right now," I said from where I was slicing up several dozen carrots.

"You got time to slice some bread?" Stanley inquired from where he was stirring stew.

"Yeah." I was tending a round boiler in which twelve pounds of prunes were being simmered for dessert, but figured I could dive back and forth between tasks. "How much?"

"This is the Yew Ess Forest Service, remember. How ever much it says in the book."

I went and looked again at the "First Supper" page.

Twenty loaves.

"Jick, see what it says about how much of this sand and snoose to put in the stew," Stanley requested from beside the wash boiler, a big box of salt in one hand and a fairly sizable one of pepper in the other.

"It doesn't."

"It which?"

"All the cookbook says is 'Season to taste.'"

"Aw, goddamn."

My right arm and hand felt as if they'd been slicing for years. I remembered I was supposed to set out five pounds of butter to go with the bread. Stanley now was the one at the cookbook, swearing steadily as he tried for a third time to divine the proportions of salt and pepper for a wash boiler of stew.

"What's it say to put this butter on?"

His finger explored along the page. "Pudding dishes. You got time to start the coffee after that?"

"I guess. What do I do?"

"Fill two of them halfbreed boilers in the creek. . . ."

All afternoon Paul had been going through the camp at such a pace that drinks could have been served on his shirttail. But he gave Stanley and me wide berth until he at last had to pop over to tell us the fire crew was on its way in for supper.

He couldn't help eyeing us dubiously. I was sweaty and bedraggled, Stanley was parched and bedraggled.

"Mind if I try your stew?" Paul proposed. I say proposed, because even though Paul was camp boss it was notorious that a cook coming up on mealtime had to be handled with kid gloves.

This advantage must have occurred to Stanley, because he gave Paul a flat gaze, stated, "If you're starved to death, go ahead; I got things to do," and royally strode over to the work table where I was.

We both watched over our shoulders like owls, though. Paul grabbed a spoon, advanced on the stew tub, dipped out a dab, blew on it, tasted. Then repeated. Then swung around toward us. "Mister, you weren't just woofing. You *can* cook."

Shortly the CCs streamed into camp, and Stanley and I were dishing food onto their plates at a furious rate. A day on a fire line is ash and sweat, so these CCs were not exactly fit for a beauty contest. But they were at that brink of manhood—most of them about Alec's age—where energy recovers in a hurry. In fact, their appetites recuperated instantly. Some CCs were back on line for seconds before we'd finished serving everybody a first helping.

Paul saw how swamped Stanley and I were with the serving, and sent two of his CC camp flunkies to take over from us while we fussed with reheating and replenishment. The fifty emergency firefighters from Great Falls were yet to come.

So was my father. I had seen him appear into the far end of camp, conferring with Kratka and Ames, now his fireline foremen, and head with them to the boss tent. He wore his businesslike look. Not a good sign.

I was lugging a resupply of prunes to the T table when I glanced into the grub line and met the recognition of my father, his hand in mid-reach for a tin plate.

For a moment he simply tried to register that it was me standing before him in a flour sack apron.

"Jick! What in the name of hell are you doing here?"

"'Lo, Dad. Uh, I'm being the flunky."

"You're—" That stopped not only my father's tongue but all other parts of him. He stood rooted. And when I sunk in, so to speak, he of course had to get his mind to decide who to skin alive for this, Paul or Chet.

"Mom said I could," I put in helpfully.

This announcement plainly was beyond mortal belief, so now my father had definite words to express to me. "You're going to stand there with your face hanging out and tell me your mother—" Then the figure at the stove turned around to him and he saw that behind this second flour sack apron was Stanley.

"Hullo, Mac," Stanley called out. "I hope you like slumgullion. 'Cause that's what it is."

"Jesus H.—" My father became aware of the audience of CCs piling up behind him in the grub line. "I'm coming around there, you two. You better have a story ready when I arrive."

Stanley and I retreated to the far end of the kitchen area while my father marched around the T table to join us. He arrived aiming huffy looks first to one of us and then the other, back and forth as if trying to choose between targets.

"Now," he stated. "Let's hear it."

"You're kind of on the prod, Mac," observed Stanley. "You don't care that much for slumgullion, huh?"

"Stanley, goddamn you and your slumgullion. What in the hell are the pair of you doing in this fire camp?"

Stanley was opening his mouth, and I knew that out of it was going to drop the reply, "Cooking." To head that off, I piped: "Mom figured you could use our help."

"She figured what?"

"She wouldn't have sent us"—adjusting the history of my inception into the trip with Stanley and the lunches—"if she hadn't figured that, would she? And what's the matter with our cooking?" Some CCs were back in line for third helpings; *they* didn't seem to lack appreciation of our cuisine.

I noticed something else. My father no longer was dividing huffy looks between Stanley and me. He was locked onto Stanley. My presence in this fire camp was not getting my father's main attention.

As steadily as he could, after his afternoon of drought and wholesale cookery, Stanley returned the scrutiny. "Mac," he said, in that rasped-over voice from when my father and I first met him on the trail that day of June, "you're the fire boss. You can put the run on us any time you want. But until you do, we can handle this cooking for you."

My father at last said: "I'm not putting the run on anybody. Dish me up some of your goddamn slumgullion."

It was getting dusk when the EFFs arrived into camp like a raggle-taggle army. These men were drift, straight from the saloons and flophouses of First Avenue South in Great Falls, and they more than looked it. One guy even had a beard. Supposedly a person couldn't be hired for emergency firefighting unless he owned a stout pair of shoes, but of course the same passable shoes showed up on guy after guy in the sign-up line. Most of these EFFs now were shod in weary leather, and hard-worn blue jeans if they were ranch hands, and bib pants if they were gandy dancers or out-of-work smeltermen from Black Eagle. Motley as they looked from the neck down, I paid keener attention to their head-gear. There was a legend in the Forest Service that a fire boss once told his sign-up man in Spokane: "Send me thirty men if they're wearing Stetsons or fifty if they're wearing caps." Most of these EFFs at least were hatted; they were used to outdoor work, were not city guys except for recreational purposes.

I remember that this time, Stanley and I were lugging another boiler of coffee to the T table. For I damn near dropped my end when a big guy leaned out of the back of the grub line, peered woozily toward me, then yelled in greeting:

"Hey, Jick!"

Wisdom Johnson had not advanced conspicuously far on his plan to head for the redwood country for the winter. As soon as Stanley and I got the boiler situated on the table, I hustled to the back of the grub line to shake hands with Wisdom.

"That First Avenue South," he marveled. "That's just quite a place."

Uh huh, I thought. And Bouncing Betty is quite a guide to it.

What my first night in a fire camp was like I can't really tell you. For when Stanley and I at last were done washing dishes, I entered my sleeping bag and that is the last I know.

Breakfast, though. If you have not seen what six dozen firefighters will consume for breakfast, the devastation may shock you. It did me, after I awoke to the light of a gas lantern and Stanley above it half croaking, "Picnic time again, Jick."

Whack off a hundred and fifty slices of ham for frying. Mush: two sixteen-quart round boilers of water and four pounds of oatmeal into each. Milk for the mush, fifteen tall cans of Sego mixed with the same of water. Potatoes to make fried spuds—thank the Lord, we had just enough of the canned variety so that I didn't have to start peeling. Fill two more halfbreed boilers for coffee, slice another oodle of bread, open seven cans of jam.

Enough grub to feed China, it looked to me like. But Stanley viewed matters and shook his head.

"Better dig out a half dozen of those fruitcakes, Jick, and slice them up."

I still blink to think about it, but only crumbs of those fruitcakes were left when that crew was done.

That morning my father put his firefighters to doing everything that the Forest Service said should be done in such a battle. Fireline was being dug, snags were being felled, wherever possible the flames were being pinched against Flume Gulch's rocky outcroppings. One saving grace about a fire burning its way down a north slope is that it usually comes slowly, and my father's crews were able to work close, right up against the face of the fire. On the other hand, Flume Gulch truly was a bastardly site to have to tackle. The fire had started at the uppermost end of the gulch, amid a dry tangle of windfall, and was licking its way down through jungly stands of Douglas fir and alpine fir and an understory of brush and juniper and more windfall. "Heavy fuel," as it's called. Burning back and forth on the gulch's steep sides as a falling flaming tree or a shower of sparks would ignite the opposite wall of forest. So, in a sense, in a kind of slow sloshing pattern the fire was advancing right down the trough of nature's version of a flume, aiming itself into the creekside trees along the North Fork and the high grassy slope opposite the gulch. And all the forested country waiting beyond that slope.

To even get to the fire my father's men had to climb up the face of the creek gorge into the gulch, and once there they had to labor on ground which sometimes tilted sharply ahead of them and sometimes tilted sideways but always tilted. At breakfast I had heard one of the CCs telling the EFFs that Flume Gulch was a spraddledy-ass damn place.

Besides being high and topsy-turvy the fire battleground was hot and dry, and my father designated Wisdom Johnson to be the Flume Gulch water cow. What this involved was making trips along the fireline with a five-gallon water pack on his back, so that the thirsty men could imbibe a drink from the pack's nozzle—the tit. "I thought I had done every job there was," claimed Wisdom, "but I never hit this one."

About mid-morning, when he came down from the gulch to refill, Wisdom brought into camp my father's message for Paul. Paul read it, shook his head, and hustled down the trail to phone it on to Chet at the ranger station.

"What'd it say?" I pumped Wisdom before he could start back up with his sloshing water pack.

" 'No chance ten A.M. control today,'" Wisdom quoted. Then added his own view of the situation in Flume Gulch: "Suffering Jesus, they're a thirsty bunch up there."

"A lot of Great Fall nights coming out through the pores," Stanley put in piously from the work table where he and I next were going to have make double lunches for the seventy-five firefighters. Which, the cook book enlightened us, amounted to a hundred and fifty ham sandwiches, a hundred and fifty jam sandwiches, and seventy-five cheese sandwiches.

" 'Slice the meat about four slices to the inch,'" I read in a prissy voice. " 'Slice the bread about two slices to the inch.' Christamighty, they want us to do everything by the measurement and then don't provide us any damn thing to measure with."

"Your thumb," said Stanley.

"My thumb what?"

"Your thumb's a inch wide. Close enough to it, anyhow. Go by that. The Forest Service has got a regulation for everything up to and including how to swat a mosquito with your hat. Sometimes, though, it don't hurt to swat first and read up on it later."

My thumb and I set to slicing.

At noon Paul and his pair of camp flunkies and Stanley and Wisdom and I lugged the sandwiches and canned fruit and pork and beans up to the fireline.

I had grown up hearing of forest fires. The storied fire summers, Bitterroot, Phantom Woman, Selway, this one, they amounted to a Forest Service catechism. Yet here, now, was my first close view.

Except for the smoke boiling in ugly fashion into the sky, the scene was not as awful as you might expect. Orange flames were a dancing tribe amid the trees, and the firefighters were a rippling line of shovelers and axmen and sawyers as they tried to clear anything combustible from in front of the fire. But then when you got over being transfixed by the motions of flame and men, the sense of char hit you. A smell like charcoal, the black smudge of the burned forest behind the flames. And amid the commotion of the fireline work, the sounds of char, too—flames crackling, and continual snap of branches breaking as they burned, and every so often a big roar of flame as a tree crowned out.

What told me most about the nature of a forest fire was one single tree, a low scrawny young Douglas fir. It had managed to root high up within a crack in one of the gulch's rock formations, and as I was gawking around trying to register everything, I saw that tree explode. Spontaneously burst into flames, there on its stone perch so far from any other foliage or the orange feather-edge of the fire itself.

I found my father and read his face. Serious but not grim. He came over to my pack of sandwiches and plowed into one. I glanced around to be sure Paul wasn't within hearing, then said: " 'It doesn't look that bad. It just keeps burning, is all.' "

He had to grin at that. "That's about the case. But I think there's a chance we can kick it in the pants this afternoon. Those First Avenuers are starting to get their legs under them. They'll get better at fireline work as the day goes on." He studied the sky above Roman Reef as if it would answer what he said next. "What we don't need is any wind."

To shift himself from that topic, my father turned to me.

"How about you? How you getting along?"

"Okay. I never knew people could eat so much, though."

"Uh huh. Speaking of which, pass me another sandwich, would you." Even my father, conscientiously stoking food into himself. It was as if the fire's hunger for the forest had spread an epidemic of appetite among us as well.

My father watched Stanley divvy sandwiches out to a nearby bunch of EFFs. "How about your sidekick there?"

"Stanley's doing real good." Then the further answer I knew my father was inviting: "He's staying dry."

"Is he. Well, that's news. When he does get his nose in the bottle, you let me know. Or let Paul know if I'm not around. We got to have a cook. One'll have to be fetched in here from somewhere when Stanley starts a bender."

"If he does," I agreed because of all that was involved, "I'll say so."

—

Through the afternoon I flunkied for Stanley. Hot in that base camp, I hope never to suffer a more stifling day. It was all I could do not to wish for a breath of breeze.

Stanley too was sweating, his shirt dark with it.

And he looked in semi-awful shape. Agonized around the eyes, the way he had been when Bubbles butchered his hand. What bothered me more than his appearance, though, he was swigging oftener and oftener at the bottle.

As soon as Stanley went off to visit nature I got over there to his saddle pack, yanked the bottle out, and sipped.

It still was water with a whiskey trace. Stanley's craving thirst was for the trace rather than the water, but so far he hadn't given in.

This lifted my mood. As did the continuing absence of wind. I was predicting to Stanley, "I'll bet they get the fire whipped."

"Maybe so, maybe no," he responded. "Where a forest fire is concerned, I'm no betting man. How about peeling me a tub of spuds when you get the chance."

"Stanley, I guess this isn't exactly any of my business, but—have you seen Velma? Since the Fourth?"

"Now and then."

"Yeah, well. She's quite—quite a lady, isn't she?"

"Quite a one."

"Uh huh. Well. So, how are you two getting along?"

Stanley flexed his hand a time or two, then went back to cutting bacon. Tonight's main course was a casserole—if you can do that by the tubful—of macaroni and canned corn and bacon slices. "We've had some times," he allowed.

Times with Velma Simms. Plural. The gray eyes, the pearl-buttoned ears, those famous rodeo slacks, in multiple. Sweat was already rolling off me, but this really opened the spigots. I went over to the water bucket and splashed a handful on my face and another on the back of my neck.

Even so, I couldn't help resuming the topic. "Think anything will come of it?"

"If you mean permanent, nope. Velma's gave up marrying and I never got started. We both know there's a season on our kind of entertainment." Stanley slabbed off another half dozen slices of bacon, I peeled away at a spud. "But a season's better than no calendar at all, is what I've come to think." He squinted at the stacked results of his bacon slicing. "How many more hogs does that recipe call for?"

I was still peeling when the casualty came down from the gulch.

He was one of the CCs, half carried and half supported by two others. Paul hurried across the camp toward them, calling: "How bad did he get it?"

"His cawlehbone and awm," one of the helping CCs answered. New York? Philadelphia? Lord only knew what accent any of the CC guys spoke, or at least I sure didn't.

"Get him on down to the trailhead," Paul instructed the bearers. Then summoned the timekeeper: "Tony, you'll have to drive the guy in to the doc in Gros Ventre."

A limb of a falling snag had sideswiped the injured CC. This was sobering. I knew enough fire lore to realize that if the limb had found the CC's head instead of his collarbone and arm, he might have been on his way to the undertaker rather than to Doc Spence.

As yet, no wind. Calm as the inside of an oven, and as hot. I wiped my brow and resumed peeling.

"What would you think about going for a stroll?"

This proposal from Stanley startled me. By now, late afternoon, he looked as if it took ninety-nine percent of his effort to stay on his feet, let alone put them into motion.

"Huh? To where?"

His head and Stetson indicated the grassy slope of Rooster Mountain above us, opposite the fire. "Just up there. Give us a peek at how things are going."

I hesitated. We did have our supper fixings pretty well in hand. But to simply wander off up the mountainside . . .

"Aw, we got time," Stanley told me as if he'd invented the commodity. "Our stepdaddy"—he meant Paul, who was down phoning Chet the report of the injured CC—"won't be back for a while."

"Okay, then," I assented a little nervously. "As long as we're back here in plenty of time to serve supper."

I swear he said it seriously: "Jick, you know I'd never be the one to make you miss a meal."

I thought it was hot in camp. The slope was twice so. Facing south as it did, the grassy incline had been drinking in sun all day, not to mention the heat the forest fire was putting into the air of this whole area.

"Yeah, it's a warm one," Stanley agreed. I was watching him with concern. The climb in the heat had tuckered me considerably. How Stanley could navigate this mountainside in his bent-knee fashion— more than ever he looked like a born horseman, grudging the fact of ground—was beyond me.

Except for a few scrubby pines peppered here and there, the slope was shadeless until just below its summit where the forest overflowed from this mountain's north side. Really there weren't many trees even up there because of the rocky crest, the rooster comb. And Stanley and I sure as hell weren't going that high anyway, given the heat and steepness. So it was a matter of grit and bear it.

Stanley did lean down and put a hand flat against the soil of the slope as if he intended to sit. I was not surprised when he didn't plop himself down, for this sidehill's surface was so tropical I could feel its warmth through the soles of my boots.

"Looks to me like they're holding it," I evaluated the fire scene opposite us. Inasmuch as we were about halfway up our slope, we were gazing slightly downward on Flume Gulch and the fire crew. Startling how near that scene seemed; these two sides of the North Fork vee truly were sharp. Across there in the gulch we could see the smoke pouring up, a strange rapid creation to come from anything as deliberate as this downhill fire; and close under the smoke column, the men strung out along the fireline. Even the strip of turned earth and cleared-away debris, like a long wavery stripe of garden dirt, that they were trying to pen the fire with; even that we could see. In a provident moment I had snagged a pair of binoculars from the boss tent before Stanley and I set off on our climb, and with them I could pick out individuals. I found my father and Kratka in conference near the center of the fireline. Both of them stood in that peering way men do up a sidehill, one foot advanced and the opposite arm crooking onto a hip. They looked like they could outwait any fire.

The dry grass creaked and crackled under my feet as I stepped to hand the binoculars to Stanley. He had been gandering here, there and elsewhere around our slope, so I figured he was waiting to use the glasses on the actual fire.

"Naw, that's okay, Jick. I seen enough. Kind of looks like a forest fire, don't it?" And he was turning away, starting to shuffle back down to the fire camp.

When the first firefighters slogged in for supper, my father was with them. My immediate thought was that the fire was whipped: my father's job as fire boss was done.

As soon as I could see faces, I knew otherwise. The firefighters looked done in. My father looked pained.

I told Stanley I'd be right back, and went over to my father.

"It jumped our fireline," he told me. "Three places."

"But how? There wasn't any wind."

"Like hell. What do you call that whiff about four o'clock?"

"Not down here," I maintained. "We haven't had a breath all afternoon. Ask Stanley. Ask Paul."

My father studied me. "All right. Maybe down here there wasn't any. But up there some sure as hell came from somewhere. Not much. Just enough." He told me the story. Not long after Stanley and I took our look at things from the slope, with the afternoon starting to cool away from its hottest, most dangerous time, a quick south wind came along Roman Reef and caught the fire. "The whole east flank made a run like gasoline had been poured on it. Jumped our fireline like nothing and set off a bunch of brush. We got there and corraled it. But while we were doing that, it jumped in another place. So we got to that one, got that one held. And in the meanwhile, goddamned if it didn't jump one more time." That one flared and took off, a stand of fir crowning into orange flame. "I had to pull the crew away from that flank. Too damn dangerous. So now we've got ourselves a whole new fire, marching right down the mountain. Tomorrow we're going to have to hold the son-ofabitch here at the creek. Damn it all to hell anyway."

My father did fast damage to his plateful of supper and went back up to the fire. He was keeping Kratka's crew on patrol at what was left of fireline until the cool of the evening would damper the flames.

Ames's gang of CCs and EFFs meanwhile were ready to dine. Ready and then some. "Hey, Cookie!" one among them yelled out to Stanley. "What're you going to founder us on tonight?"

"Soupa de bool-yon," Stanley enlightened him in a chefly accent of some nature. "Three buckets of water and one on-yon." Actually the lead course was vegetable soup, followed by the baconized macaroni and corn, and mashed potatoes with canned milk gravy, and rice pudding, and all of it tasted just heavenly if I do say so myself.

Dark was coming on by the time Stanley and I went to the creek to fill a boiler with water as a headstart toward breakfast.

From there at creekside the fire lay above us to the west. A few times in my life I had seen Great Falls at night from one of its hills. The forest fire reminded me of that. A city alight in the dark. A main avenue of flame, where the live edge of the fire was advancing. Neighborhoods where rock formations had isolated stubbornly burning patches. Hundreds of single spots of glow where snags and logs still blazed.

"Pretty, ain't it," Stanley remarked.

"Well, yeah, I guess. If you can call it that."

"Tomorrow it'll be just an ugly sonuvabitch of a forest fire. But tonight, it's pretty."

My father had come back into camp and was waiting for Paul to arrive with the phone report from Chet. As soon as Paul showed up, my father was asking him, "How's Ferragamo?" Joseph Ferragamo was the CC the falling snag had sideswiped.

"The doc splinted him up, then took him to the hospital in Conrad. Says he'll be okay." Paul looked wan. "A lot better off than some, anyway."

"How do you mean?" my father wanted to know.

Paul glanced around to make sure none of the fire crew were within earshot. "Mac, there've been two CCs killed, over on the west-side fires. One on the Kootenai, and one on the Kaniksu fire. Snags got both of them."

My father said nothing for a little. Then: "I appreciate the report, Paul. Round up Ames and Kratka, will you. We've got to figure out how we're going to handle this fire tomorrow."

—

My father and Paul and the pair of crew foremen took lanterns and headed up the creek to look over the situation of tomorrow morning's fireline. My father of course knew the site backwards and forwards, but the hell of it was to try to educate the others in a hurry and in the dark. I could not help but think it: if Alec . . .

At their bed ground some of the fire crew already were oblivious in their sleeping bags, but a surprising many were around campfires, sprawled and gabbing. The climate of the Two. Roast you all day in front of a forest inferno, then at dark chill you enough to make you seek out fire.

While waiting for my father, I did some wandering and exercising of my ears. I would like to say here and now that these firefighters, from eighteen-year-old CCs to the most elderly denizen among the First Avenue South EFFs, were earnestly discussing how to handle the Flume Gulch fire. I would *like* to say that, but nothing would be farther from the truth. Back at the English Creek ranger station, on the wall behind my father's desk was tacked one of those carbon copy gags that circulate among rangers:

Subjects under discussion during one summer (timed by stopwatch) by U.S. Forest Service crews, trail, fire, maintenance and otherwise.

	PERCENT OF TIME
Sexual stories, experiences and theories	37%
Personal adventures in which narrator is hero	23%
Memorable drinking jags	8%
Outrages of capitalism	8%
Acrimonious remarks about bosses, foremen and cooks	5%
Personal adventures in which someone not present is the goat	5%
Automobiles, particularly Fords	3%
Sarcastic evaluations of Wilson's war to end war	2%
Sarcastic evaluations of ex-President Coolidge	2%
Sarcastic evaluations of ex-President Hoover	2%
Sears Roebuck catalogue versus Montgomery Ward catalogue	2%
The meteorological outlook	2%
The job at hand	1%

From what I could hear, that list was just about right.

—

Stanley I had not seen for a while, and it crossed my mind that he may have had enough of the thirsty life. That he'd gone off someplace to jug up from an undiluted bottle.

But no, when I at last spied my father and his fire foremen and Paul returning to camp and then heading for the tent to continue their war council, I found Stanley in that same vicinity. Looking neither worse nor better than he had during our day of cooking.

Just to be sure, I asked him: "How you doing?"

"Feeling dusty," he admitted. "Awful dusty."

My father spotted the pair of us and called over: "Jick, you hang on out here. We got to go over the map, but it won't take too long." Into the tent he ducked with Paul, Kratka and Ames following.

"You want me to get your sipping bottle?" I offered to Stanley, referring to the one of whiskey-tinged water in his saddlebag.

"Mighty kind," replied Stanley. "But it better wait." And before I could blink, he was gone from beside me and was approaching the tent where my father's war council was going on.

Stanley stuck his head in past the flap door of the tent. I heard:

"Can I see you for part of a minute, Mac?"

"Stanley, it's going to have to wait. We're still trying to dope out our fireline for the morning."

"That fireline is what it's about, Mac."

There was a moment of silence in the tent. Then Paul's voice:

"For crying out loud! Who ever heard of a fire camp where the cook gets to put in his two bits' worth? Mister, I don't know who the devil you think you are, but—"

"All right, Paul," my father umpired. "Hold on." There was a moment of silence, which could only have been a scrutinizing one. My father began to say: "Stanley, once we get this—"

"Mac, you know how much it takes for me to ask."

A moment again. Then my father: "All right. There's plenty of night ahead. We can stand a couple of minutes for me to hear what Stanley has to say. Paul, you guys go ahead and map out how we can space the crews along the creek bottom. I won't be long." And bringing one of the gas lanterns out he came, giving Stanley a solid looking-over in the white light.

Side by side the two of them headed out of earshot of the tent. Not out of mine, though, for this I was never going to miss. They had gone maybe a dozen strides when I caught up with them.

The three of us stopped at the west end of the camp. Above us the fire had on its night face yet, bright, pretty. No hint whatsoever of the grim smoke and char it showed by day.

"Mac, I'm sorry as all hell to butt into your war council, there. I hate to say anything about procedure. Particularly to you. But—"

"But you're determined to. Stanley, what's on your mind?"

"The idea of tackling the fire down here on the creek, first thing in the morning." Stanley paused. Then: "Mac, my belief is that's not the way to go about it."

"So where would you tackle it?"

Stanley's Stetson jerked upward, indicating the slope of grass across the North Fork from us. "Up there."

Now in the lantern light it was my father's eyes that showed the hurtful squint Stanley's so often did.

The thought repelled my father. The fire doubling its area of burn: both sides of the North Fork gorge blackened instead of one. More than that—

"Stanley, if this fire gets loose over the slope and up into that next timber, it can take the whole goddamn country. It can burn for miles." My father stared up at the dim angle of the slope, but what was in his mind was 1910, Bitterroot, Selway, Phantom Woman, all the smoke ghosts that haunt a fire boss. "Christamighty," he said softly, "it could burn until snowfall."

Jerking his head around from that thought, my father said: "Stanley, don't get radical on me here. What in the hell makes you say the fire-line ought to be put up there on the mountain?"

"Mac, I know you hate like poison to see any inch of the Two go up in smoke. I hated it, too. But if you can't hold the fire at the base of the gulch, it's gonna break out onto the slope there anyway."

"The answer there is, I'm supposed to hold it."

"Supposed to is one thing. Doing it's another."

"Stanley, these days we've got what's called the ten A.M. policy. The Forest Service got religion about all this a few years ago. The Major told us, 'This approach to fire suppression will be a dividend-payer.' So the rule is, try to control any fire by ten the next morning."

"Yeah, rules are rules," agreed Stanley. Or seemed to agree, for I had heard my father any number of times invoke the second part of this ranger station catechism: "And fools are fools."

My father pulled out a much-employed handkerchief, wiped his eyes, and blew his nose. Among the aggravations of his day was smoke irritation.

"All right, Stanley," he said at last. "Run this by me again. You're saying give the fire the whole damn slope of Rooster Mountain?"

"Yeah, more or less. Use the morning to backfire in front of that rocky top." Backfiring is when you deliberately burn an area ahead of a fire, to rob its fuel. It has to be done just right, though, or you've either wasted your time or given the fire some more flame to work with. "Burn in a fireline up there that hell itself couldn't jump." Stanley saw my father was still unconverted. "Mac, it's not as nasty a place as this gorge."

"Christamighty, I can't pick places to fight a fire by whether they're nasty or not."

"Mac, you know what I mean." Stanley spelled it out for my father anyway. "That slope is dry as a torch. If you put men down in this gorge and the fire sets off that slope behind them too, you're going to be sifting piles of ashes to find their buttons."

I could see my father thinking it: nothing in the behavior of the Flume Gulch fire to date supported Stanley's picture. If anything, this slow downhill fire was almost *too* slow, staying up there in wicked terrain and burning when and where it pleased. He and his crews had been able to work right up beside the fire; it was the geography they couldn't do anything about. True, the fire's behavior could all change when it reached the gorge, but—"I can't see how the fire could set off the slope across this much distance," my father answered slowly.

"I can," Stanley said back.

Still stubborn as a government mule against the notion of voluntarily doubling the size of the Flume Gulch burn, my father eyed back up at the slope of Rooster Mountain. "Hell, what if we're up there merrily backfiring and the fire doesn't come? Goes down this gorge instead, right through this camp and around that slope? Then's when we'll have a bigger mess on our hands."

"That's a risk," admitted Stanley. "But my belief is it's a worse risk to tackle that fire down in here, Mac. Up there you'd have a bigger fireline. And rocks instead of men to help stop it."

My father considered some more. Then said: "Stanley, I'd rather take a beating than ask you this. But I got to. Are you entirely sober?"

"Sorry to say," responded Stanley, "I sure as hell am."

"He is," I chimed in.

My father continued to confront Stanley. I could see that he had more to say, more to ask.

But there I was wrong. My father only uttered, "The slope is something I'll think about," and set off back to the boss tent.

Stanley told me he was going to turn in—"This cooking is kind of a strenuous pastime"—and ordinarily I would have embraced bed myself. But none of this was ordinary. I trailed my father to the war council once more, and heard him say as soon as he was inside the tent:

"Ideas don't care who their daddies are. What would you guys say about this?" And he outlined the notion of the fireline atop the slope.

They didn't say much at all about it. Kratka and Ames already had been foxed once by the Flume Gulch fire. No need for them to stick their necks out again. After a bit my father said: "Well, I'll use it all as a pillow tonight. Let's meet here before breakfast. Meantime, everybody take a look at that slope on the map."

Paul's voice finally came. "Mac, can I see you outside?"

"Excuse us again, gents."

Out came my father and Paul. Again I made sure to catch up before the walking could turn into talking.

At the west edge of the camp Paul confronted my father. "Mac, whichever way you decide on tackling this fire, I'll never say a word against you. But the fire record will. You can't get around that. If you don't have the crew down here to take the fire by its face in the morning, Sipe is going to want to know why. And the Major—if this fire gets away down the gorge and around that slope, they'll sic a board of review on you. Mac, they'll have your hide."

My father weighed all this. And at last said: "Paul, there's another if. If we can kill this fire, Sipe and the Major aren't going to give one good goddamn how we did it."

Paul peered unhappily from the flickering crack in the night on the Flume Gulch side of us, to the dark bulk of the Rooster Mountain slope on our other. "You're the fire boss," he said.

—

I am not sure I slept at all that night. Waiting, breath held, any time I imagined I heard a rustle of wind. Waiting for the morning, for my father's fireline decision. Waiting.

"Christamighty, Stanley. Twenty loaves *again?*"

"Milk toast instead of mush to start with this morning, Jick," confirmed Stanley from the circle of lantern light where he was peering down into the cookbook. "Then after the bread, it's 'Place twenty cans of milk and the same of water in a twenty-quart half-oval boiler.'"

"Yeah, yeah, yeah. Let me get the damn slicing done first."

My father and Ames were the first ones through the breakfast line. Ames's men had come off the fireline earliest last night, so they were to be the early ones onto it this morning. Wherever that fireline was going to be.

I was so busy flunkying that it wasn't until a little break after Ames's men and before Kratka's came that I could zero in on my father. He and Ames brought their empty plates and dropped them in the dishwash tub. My father scrutinized Stanley, who was lugging a fresh heap of fried ham to the T table. Stanley set down the ham and met my father's regard with a straight gaze of his own. "Morning, Mac. Great day for the race, ain't it?"

My father nodded to Stanley, although whether in hello or agreement it couldn't be told. Then he turned to Ames. "Okay, Andy. Take your gang up there to the top and get them started digging the control line for backfiring." And next my father was coming around the serving table to where Stanley and I were, saying: "Step over here, you two. I've got something special in mind for the pair of you."

Shortly, Wisdom Johnson came yawning into the grub line. He woke up considerably when my father instructed him that the tall, tall slope of Rooster Mountain, just now looming up in the approach of dawn, was where his water duty would be today.

"But, Mac, the fire's over here, it ain't up there!"

"It's a new theory of firefighting," my father told him. "We're going to do it by mail order."

Kratka's men were soon fed. It transpired that my father himself was going to lead this group onto the slope and supervise them in lighting the strips of backfires.

First, though, he called Paul Eliason over. I heard him instruct: "Have Chet tell Great Falls the same thing as yesterday—'No chance ten A.M. control today.'"

"Mac," Paul began. "Mac, how about if I at least wait until toward that time of morning to call it in? I don't see any sense in advertising what—what's going on up here."

My father leveled him a stare that made Paul sway back a little. "Assistant ranger Eliason, do you mean to say you'd delay information to headquarters?"

Paul gulped but stood his ground. "Yeah. In this case, I would."

"Now you're talking," congratulated my father. "Send it in at five minutes to ten." My father turned and called to the crew waiting to go up the mountain with him. "Let's go see a fire."

"Stanley, this makes me feel like a coward."

"You heard the man."

It was well past noon, the sweltering heart of so hot a day. The rock formation we were perched on might as well have been a stoked stove. Pony and the buckskin saddle horse were tethered in the shade of the trees below and behind us, but they stood there drooping even so.

Stanley and I were chefs in exile. This rock observation point of ours was the crown-shaped formation above the line cabin where the two of us sheltered during our camptending shenanigan. How long ago it seemed since I was within those log walls, bandaging Stanley's hand and wishing I was anywhere else.

I had heard the man. My father, when he herded the pair of us aside there at breakfast and decreed: "I want you two out of here this afternoon. You understand?" If we did, Stanley and I weren't about to admit it. My father the fire boss spelled matters out for us: "If the wind makes up its mind to blow or that fire takes a turn for some other reason, it could come all the way down the gorge into this camp. So when you get the lunches made, clear out of here."

"Naw, Mac," Stanley dissented. "It's a good enough idea for Jick to clear out, but I—"

"Both of you," stated my father.

"Yeah, well," I started to put in, "Stanley's done his part, but I could just as well—"

"Both of you," my father reiterated. "Out of here, by noon."

The long faces on us told him he still didn't have Stanley and me convinced. "Listen, damn it. Stanley, you know what happened the last argument you and I had. This time, let's just don't argue." Then, more mild: "I need you to be with Jick, Stanley."

Stanley shifted the way he was standing. Did so again. And finally came out with a quiet "Okey-doke, Mac," and headed back to his cookstove.

My father did not have to labor the point to me. I knew, and nodded it to him, that the other half of what he had just said was that I was needed to be with Stanley. But he stopped me from turning away to my flunky tasks.

"Jick," he said as if this had been stored up in him for some time. "Jick, I can't risk you." His left eyelid came down as he forced a grin to accompany his words: "You've earned a grandstand seat this afternoon. Lean back and watch the event."

Thus here we were. Simmering in safety on this rock outlook, barbecued toes our only peril. At our angle the fire camp at the mouth of the gorge was in sight but Flume Gulch and the fire itself were just hidden, in behind the end of Roman Reef that towered over us. The cloud of smoke, though, told us the fire was having itself a big time.

The grass slope of Rooster Mountain lay within clear view. A tan broad ramp of grass. If Pat Hoy had had Dode Withrow's sheep in a scattered graze there they would have been plain to the unaided eye. In fact, at first it puzzled me that although even my father agreed this rock site was a healthy enough distance behind the fire for Stanley and me, the slope seemed so close. Eventually I figured out that the huge dark dimension of the smoke made the distance seem foreshortened.

I had snagged the binoculars again from the boss tent, and every few minutes I would squat—as with the slope yesterday at this time, our island of stone was too damn hot to sit on—and prop my elbows on my knees to steady the glasses onto the fireline work.

The brow of the slope, between its rocky top and the grass expanse stretching down to the North Fork, by now resembled a reflection of the devastation in Flume Gulch opposite it. All morning until about ten o'clock, when the day began to get too hot for safe backfiring, my father's men little by little had blackened that area. First they trenched the control line along the ridgetop, then the careful, careful burning began. Four or five feet wide at a time, a strip of grass was ignited and let to burn back uphill into the bare control line. When it had burned itself out, the next strip below it was lit. Down and down, the barrier of scorch was built that way, the dark burn scar at last inflicted across the entire upper part of the slope. And even yet at the edge of the forest atop the skyline, crews were cutting down any trees which stood too close behind the backfired fireline, other teams were hauling the combustible foliage a safe distance into the rocks and timber. My father's men were doing their utmost up there to deny the Flume Gulch fire anything to catch hold and burn when it came. If it came.

Even Stanley now and again peered through the binoculars to the fireline preparation. He wasn't saying anything, though, except his appraisal when we climbed onto the sun-cooked rock: "Hotter than dollar chili, ain't it?"

The event, as my father called it. Can you believe: it took me by total surprise. After all that waiting. All that watching, anticipating. The human being is the world's most forecasting damn creature. Yes, my imagination had the scene ready as if it were a dream I'd had twenty nights in a row, how the fire at last would cross from Flume Gulch and pull itself up out of the gorge of the North Fork onto the slope, vagrant ribbons of flame at first and then bigger fringes and at last a great ragged orange length climbing toward the fireline where my father's men waited to battle it in any way they could.

Instead, just this. Nothing seemed imminent yet, the smoke still disclosed the fire as only approaching the creek gorge. Maybe just brinking down onto the height between the gulch and the gorge, would have been my guess. I deemed that the next little while would start to show whether the fire preferred the gorge or Stanley's slope. So I did not even have the binoculars to my eyes, instead was sleeving the sweat off my forehead. When Stanley simply said: "There."

From both the gorge and the bottom of the slope the fire was throwing up smoke like the chimneys of hell. So much smudge and smear, whirling, thickening, that the slope vanished behind the billowing cloud. It scared me half to death, this smoke eclipse.

The suck of fear that went through me, the sweat popping out on the backs of my hands as I tried to see through smoke with binoculars. I can never—I *want* never—to forget what went through me then, as I realized what would be happening to my father and his fire crew if they had been in the gorge as the avalanche of fire swooped into it. The air itself must be cooked, down in there.

Then this. The smoke, all of it, rose as if a windowblind was being lifted. Sixty, eighty feet, I don't know. But the whole mass of smoke lifted that much. Stanley and I could look right into the flames, abruptly they were as bright and outlined as the blaze in a fireplace. The fire already had swarmed across the gorge and was stoking itself with the grass of the lower slope. Just as clear as anything, that aggregation of flame with the smoke curtained so obligingly above it, as much fire as a person could imagine seeing at once. And then, it awes me to even remember it, the fire crazily began to double, triple—multiply impossibly. I was told later by Wisdom Johnson: "Jick, this is the God's truth, a cool wind blew over us right then, down into that fire." A wedge of air, it must have been, hurling itself under that furiously hot smoke and flame. And that air and those flames meeting. The fire spewed up across the slope in an exploding wave, a tide. The crisp tan grass of the slope, going to orange and black. In but a minute or two, gone.

The smoke closed down again, boiled some more in a gray heavy way. But then there began to be clefts in the swirl, thinnings, actual gaps. The binoculars now brought me glimpses of men spaced along the backfired fireline and the rock summit of the slope, stomping and swatting and shoveling dirt onto flame wherever it tried to find fuel enough to catch. But more and more sentrylike watching instead of fire combat. Watching the flamestorm flash into collision with the backfired barrier or the rock comb of Rooster Mountain, and then dwindle.

These years later, I wish I could have those next minutes back to makings. Could see again that slope battle, and our fire camp that the sacrifice of the slope had saved. Could know again the rise of realization, the brimming news of my eyes, that the Flume Gulch fire steadily was quenching itself against my father's fireline, Stanley Meixell's fireline.

I couldn't speak. For some time after, even. My mouth and throat were as dry as if parched by the fire. But finally I managed:

"You knew the slope would go like that."

"I had the idea it might" was as much as Stanley would admit. "Superheated the way it was, from both the fire and the sun."

He looked drained but satisfied. I may have, too.

"So," Stanley said next. "We better go get to work on goddamn supper."

Dusk. Supper now behind us, only the dishes to finish. My father came and propped himself against the work table where Stanley and I were dishwashing. "It went the way you said it would," he said to Stanley, with a nod. Which passed for thanks in the complicated system of behavior between these two men. Then my father cleared his throat, and after a bit asked Stanley if he could stand one more day of cooking while the fire crew policed smoking snags and smolder spots tomorrow, and Stanley replied yeah, cooking wasn't all that much worse anyway than dealing with sheepherders.

I broke in:

"Tell me the argument."

Nothing, from either of these two.

I cited to my father from when he directed Stanley and me to clear out of the fire camp: "The last argument you and Stanley had, whenever the hell it was." I had searched all summer for this. "What was that about?"

My father tried to head me off. "Old history now, Jick."

"If it's that old, then why can't I hear it? You two—I need to know. I've been in the dark all damn summer, not knowing who did what to who, when, where, any of it. One time you send me off with Stanley, but then we show up here and you look at him like he's got you spooked. Damn it all to hell anyway"—I tell you, when I do get worked up there is not much limit—"what's it all about?"

Stanley over his dishwater asked my father: "You never told him, huh?" My father shrugged and didn't answer. Stanley gazed toward me. "Your folks never enlightened you on the topic of me?"

"I just told . . . No. No, they sure as hell haven't."

"McCaskills," Stanley said with a shake of his head, as if the name was a medical diagnosis. "I might of known you and Bet'd have padlocks on your tongues, Mac."

"Stanley," my father tried, "there's no need for you to go into all that."

"Yeah, I think there is." I was in Stanley's gaze again. "Phantom Woman," he began. "I let that fire get away from me. Or at least it got away. Comes to the same. A fire is the fire boss's responsibility, and I was him." Stanley turned his head to my father. Then to me again. "Your dad had come up from his Indian Head district to be a fireline foreman for me. So he was on hand when it happened. When Phantom Woman blew up across that mountainside." Stanley saw my question. "Naw, I can't really say it was the same as happened on that slope today. Timber instead of grass, different this and that. Every goddamn fire. But anyhow, up she blew, Phantom Woman. Flames everywhere, all the crew at my flank of the fireline had to run out of there like singed cats. Run for their lives. It was just a mess. And then that fire went and went and went." Stanley's throat made a dry swallow. "Burned for three weeks. So that's the history of it, Jick. The blowup happened at my flank of the fireline. It was over that that your dad and I had our"— Stanley faced my father—"disagreement."

My father looked back at Stanley until it began to be a stare. Then asked: "That's it? That's what you call the history of it?"

Stanley's turn to shrug.

My father shook his head. Then uttered:

"Jick, I turned Stanley in. For the Phantom Woman fire."

"Turned him in? How? To who?"

"To headquarters in Great Falls. Missoula. The Major. Anybody I could think of, wouldn't you say, Stanley?"

Stanley considered. "Just about. But Mac, you don't—"

"What," I persisted, "just for the fire getting away from him?"

"For that and—" My father stopped.

"The booze," Stanley completed. "As long as we're telling, tell him the whole of it, Mac."

"Jick," my father set out, "this goes back a long way. Longer than you know about. I've been around Stanley since I was, what? sixteen? seventeen?"

"Somewhere there," Stanley confirmed.

"There were a couple of years in there," my father was going on, "when I—well, when I wasn't around home much. I just up and pulled out for a while, and Stanley—"

"Why was that?" This seemed to be my main chance to see into the McCaskill past, and I wanted all the view I could get. "How come you pulled out?"

My father paused. "It's a hell of a thing to have to say, after all this with Alec. But my father and I, your grandfather—we were on the outs. Not for anything like the same reason. He did something I couldn't agree with, and it was just easier all around, for me to stay clear of the homestead and Scotch Heaven for a while. Eventually he got over it and I got over it, and that's all that needs to be said about that episode." A pause. This one, I knew, sealed whatever that distant McCaskill father-son ruckus had been. "Anyway, Stanley took me on. Started me here on the Two, giving me any seasonal job he could come up with. I spent a couple of years that way, until we went into the war. And then after, when I was the association rider and your mother and I had Alec, and then you came along—Stanley suggested I take the ranger test."

I wanted to hear history, did I. A headful was now available. Stanley had been the forest arranger, the one who set up the Two Medicine National Forest. Stanley had stood in when my father was on the outs with his father. Stanley it had been who urged this father of mine into the Forest Service. And it was Stanley whom my father had—

"It never was any secret Stanley liked to take a drink," I was hearing the elaboration now. "But when I started as ranger at Indian Head and he still was the ranger at English Creek, I started to realize the situation was getting beyond that. There were more and more days when Stanley couldn't operate without a bottle at his side. He still knew more about the Two than anybody, and in the normal course of events I could kind of keep a watch on things up here and catch any problem that got past Stanley. We went along that way for a few years. Nobody higher up noticed, or at least minded. But it's one thing to function day by day, and another to have to do it during a big fire."

"And Phantom Woman was big enough," Stanley quietly dropped into my father's telling of it all.

Something was adding up in a way I didn't want it to. "After Phantom Woman. What happened after Phantom Woman?"

Stanley took his turn first. "Major Kelley tied a can to me. 'Your employment with the U.S. Forest Service is severed,' I believe is how it was put. And I been rattling around ever since, I guess." He glanced at my father as if he had just thought of something further to tell him. "You remember the couple times I tried the cure, Mac. I tried it a couple more, since. It never took."

"But you got by okay here," I protested. "You haven't had a real drink all the time we've been cooking."

"But I'll have one the first minute I get back to the Busbys'," Stanley forecast. "And then a couple to wash that one down. Naw, Jick. I know myself. I ought to, I been around myself long enough." As if to be sure I accepted the sum of him, Stanley gave it flatly: "In a pinch I can go dry for as long as I did here. But ordinarily, no. I got a built-in thirst."

Now my father. "I never expected they'd come down on Stanley that hard. A transfer, some rocking-chair job where the drinking wouldn't matter that much. Something to get him off the English Creek district. I couldn't just stand by and see both him and the Two country go to hell." The expression on my father: I suppose here was my first inkling that a person could do what he thought was right and yet be never comfortable about it. He shook his head over what had to be said next, erasing the inquiry that had been building in me. "You know how the Major is. Put up or shut up. When he bounced Stanley, he handed me English Creek. I wanted it run right, did I? Up to me to do it." My father cast a look around the fire camp, into the night where no brightness marked either Flume Gulch or the slope. "And here I still am, trying to."

Again that night I was too stirred up for sleep. Turning and turning in the sleeping bag; the question beyond reach of questioner; the two similar figures crowding my mind, they and my new knowledge of them as awake as the night.

Up against a decision, my father had chosen the Two country over his friend, his mentor, Stanley.

Up against a decision, my brother had chosen independence over my father.

Rewrite my life into one of those other McCaskill versions and what would I have done in my father's place, or my brother's? Even yet I don't know. I do not know. It may be that there is no knowing until a person is in so hard a place.

All that next morning my father had Kratka's crew felling suspicious snags in the burnt-over gulch and creek bottom, and Ames's men on the slope to patrol for any sign of spark or smudge amid that char which had been grass. Mop-up work was all this amounted to—a couple of days of it needed to be done after a fire this size, just to be on the safe side—and at lunch my father said he was thinking about letting half of the EFFs go back to Great Falls tonight. He predicted, "The thanks I'll get is that headquarters will want to know why in holy hell I didn't get them off the payroll *last* night."

Stanley and I recuperated from the lunch preparation and gradually started on supper, neither of us saying anything worthwhile.

When the hot part of the afternoon had passed without trouble, even my father was satisfied that the Flume Gulch fire was not going to leap from its black grave.

He came into camp early with the EFFs who were being let go. "Paul, the show is all yours," he delegated. "I'm going to head into Gros Ventre with one load of these guys, and Tony"—the timekeeper—"can haul the rest. Have Chet tell Great Falls to send a truck up and get them from there, would you. And Paul"—my father checked his assistant as Paul started off to phone the order to Chet—"Paul, it was a good camp."

I was next on my father's mental list. "Jick, you might as well come in with me. Stanley can leave Pony off on his ride home."

Plainly my father wanted my company, or at least my presence.

"Okay," I said. "Let me tell Stanley."

My father nodded. "I'll go round up Wisdom. He's somewhere over there bragging up Bouncing Betty to the CCs. Meet us down at the pickups."

The ride to town, my father driving and Wisdom and I beside him in the cab of one pickup and the other pickup load of EFFs behind us, was mostly nickel-and-dime gab. Our route was the Noon Creek one, a handier drive from the fire camp than backtracking over to English Creek. Reminiscent exclamations from Wisdom when we passed the haystacks of the Reese place. Already the stacks were turning from green to tan. Then my father eyeing around the horizon and thinking out loud that August sure as hell ought to be done with heat and lightning by now. More than that, I have no memory of. The fact may even be that I lulled off a little, in the motion of that pickup cab.

When we had goodbyed Wisdom and the other EFFs, my father and I grabbed a quick supper in the Lunchery. Oyster stew never tasted better, which is saying a lot. Before we could head home, though, my father said he had to stop by the *Gleaner* office. "Bill is going to want all the dope about the fire. It may take a little while. You want me to pick you up at Ray's after I'm done?" I did.

St. Ignatius St. was quiet, in the calm of suppertime and just after, except for one series of periodic *whirr*s. Which proved to be Ray pushing the lawn mower around and around the Heaney front yard. Behind him, Mary Ellen was collecting the cut grass with a lawn rake bigger than she was.

I stepped into the yard and propped myself against the giant cottonwood, in its shadowed side. Busy as Ray and Mary Ellen were, neither saw me. Myself, I was as tired as I have ever been, yet my mind was going like a million.

After a minute I called across the lawn to Ray: "A little faster if you can stand it."

His grin broke out, and from the far corner of the yard he came pushing the lawn mower diagonally across to me, somehow making in the back of his throat the *clackaclackaclackaclacka* sound of a horse-drawn haymower.

"Ray-AY!" protested Mary Ellen at his untidy shortcut across the lawn. But then here she came raking up after him.

"What do you think?" Ray asked when he reached the tree and me. "Had I better bring this out to Pete's next summer and make hay with you?"

"Sounds good to me," I said. "But that's next summer. I want to know where this one went to." The light in the Heaney kitchen dimmed out, another one came on in the living room, then the murmur of Ed's radio. Seven P.M., you could bank on it. I thought back to my last visit to this household you could set your clock by, when I pulled in from the Double W and the session with Alec that first Saturday night of the month. "It's been a real quick August."

"Quicker than you know," advised Ray. "Today is September. School's almost here."

"The hell. I guess I lost some days somewhere." Three more days and I would be fifteen years old. Four more days and Ray and Mary Ellen and I would be back in school. It didn't seem possible. Time is the trickiest damn commodity. The sound of Ed Heaney's radio in there should have been what I was hearing the night of the Fourth of July, not almost to Labor Day. Haying and supper at the Double W and the phone call to Alec and the forest fire and the revelations from Stanley and my father, all seemed as if they should be yet to happen. But they were the past now, in my mind like all that history in Toussaint's and Stanley's.

"Can we feed you something, Jick?" Ray asked in concern. "You look kind of hard-used."

"Dad and I ate uptown," I said. "And he'll be here any minute. But I suppose I could manage to—"

Just then the front porch screen door opened and Ed Heaney was standing there. We all three looked at him in curiosity because with the screen door open that way he was letting in moths, which was major disorderly conduct for him. I will always see Ed Heaney in that doorway of light, motionless there as if he had been pushed out in front of a crowd and was trying to think of what to say. At last he did manage to bring out words, and they were these:

"Ray, Mary Ellen, you better come in the house now. They've started another war in Europe."

FOUR

"We'll be in it inside of six months," was one school of thought when Europe went to war in September of 1939, and the other refrain ran, "It's their own scrap over there, we can just keep our nose out this time." But as ever, history has had its own say and in a way not foretold—at Pearl Harbor last Sunday, in the flaming message of the Jap bombs.

—*GROS VENTRE WEEKLY GLEANER, DECEMBER 11, 1941*

ALL THE PEOPLE OF that English Creek summer of 1939—they stay on in me even though so many of them are gone from life. You know how when you open a new book for the first time, its pages linger against each other, pull apart with a reluctant little separating sound. They never quite do that again, the linger or the tiny sound. Maybe it can be said that for me, that fifteenth summer of my existence was the new book and its fresh pages. My memories of those people and times and what became of them, those are the lasting lines within the book, there to be looked on again and again.

My mother was the earliest of us to get word of Pearl Harbor on that first Sunday of December, 1941. The telephone rang, she answered it, and upon learning that the call was from Two Medicine National Forest headquarters in Great Falls she began to set them straight on the day of the week. When told the news from Hawaii she went silent and held the receiver out for my father to take.

In a sense Alec already had gone to the war by then. At least he was gone, with the war as a kind of excuse. For when the fighting started in Europe and the prospect for beef prices skyrocketed, Wendell Williamson loaded up on cattle. Wendell asked Alec to switch to the Deuce W, his ranch down in the Highwood Mountains, as a top hand there during this buildup of the herd. Just after shipping time, mid-September of 1939, Alec went. It may come as no vast surprise that he and Leona had unraveled by then. She had chosen to start her last year of high school, Alec was smarting over her decision to go that way instead of to the altar, and my belief is that he grabbed the Deuce W job as a way to put distance between him and that disappointment.

I saw Leona the day of the Gros Ventre centennial, several years ago now. She is married to a man named Wright and they run a purebred Hereford ranch down in the Crazy Mountains country. The beauty still shines out of Leona. Ranch work and the riding she does have kept her in shape, I couldn't help noticing. But one thing did startle me. Leona's hair now is silvery as frost.

She smiled at my surprise and said: "Gold to silver, Jick. You've seen time cut my value."

Left to my own devices, I would not tell any further about Alec. Yet my brother, his decisions, the consequences life dealt him, always are under that summer and its aftermath like the paper on which a calendar is printed.

Before he enlisted in the army the week after Pearl Harbor, Alec did come back to Gros Ventre to see our parents. Whether reconciliation is the right amount of word for that visit I don't really know, for I was on a basketball trip to Browning and a ground blizzard kept those of us of the Gros Ventre team there overnight. So by the time I got back, Alec had been and gone. And that last departure of his from English Creek led to a desert in Tunisia. How stark it sounds; yet it is as much as we ever knew. A Stuka finding that bivouac at dusk, swooping in and splattering twenty-millimeter shells. Of the cluster of soldiers who were around a jerry can drawing their water rations, only one man lived through the strafing. He was not Alec.

So. My last words with my brother were those on the telephone when I tried to talk him into going to the Flume Gulch fire. I do have a hard time forgiving life for that.

Ray Heaney and I went together to the induction station at Missoula in September of 1942, about a week after my eighteenth birthday. And we saw each other during basic training at Fort Lewis out in Washington. In the war itself, though, we went separate ways. Ray spent a couple of years of fighting as a rifleman in Italy and somehow came through it all. These days Ray has an insurance agency over in Idaho at Coeur d'Alene, and we keep in touch by Christmas card.

I wound up in a theater of World War Two that most people don't even know existed, the Aleutians campaign away to hell and gone out in the Northern Pacific Ocean off Alaska. Those Aleutian islands made me downgrade the wind of the Two country. There is not a lot else worth telling in my warrior career, for early in our attack on Cold Mountain I was one of those who got an Attu tattoo—a Jap bullet in my left leg, breaking the big bone not far above the ankle. Even yet on chilly days, I am reminded down there.

When the army eventually turned me loose into civilian life I used my GI bill to study forestry at the university in Missoula. Each of those college summers I worked as a smokejumper for the Forest Service, parachuting out of more airplanes onto more damn forest fires than now seems sane to me. And in the last of those smokejumping summers I began going with a classmate of mine at the university, a young woman from there in the Bitterroot country. The day after graduation in 1949, we were married. That marriage lasted just a year and a half, and it is not something I care to dwell on.

That same graduation summer I took and passed the Forest Service exam and was assigned onto the Custer National Forest over in eastern Montana. I suppose one of the Mazoola desk jockeys thought it scrupulous, or found it in some regulation, that most of the state of Montana should be put between me and my father on the Two. But all that eastern Montana stint accomplished—hell, even the name got me down, that dodo Custer—was to cock me into readiness to shoot out of the Forest Service when the chance came.

Pete Reese provided the click. As soon as his lambs were shipped in the fall of 1952 Pete offered me a first crack at the Noon Creek ranch. Marie's health was giving out; she lived only a few more years, dark lovely doe she was; and Pete wanted to seize an opportunity to buy a sheep outfit down in the Gallatin Valley near Bozeman, where the winters might not be quite so ungodly. I remember every exact word from Pete in that telephone call: "You're only an accidental nephew, Jick, but I suppose maybe I can give you honorary son-in-law terms to buy the place and the sheep."

I took Pete up on his offer and came back to the Two Medicine country so fast I left a tunnel in the air.

On the twenty-first of March of 1953—we kidded that going through a lambing time together would tell us in a hurry whether we could stand each other the rest of our lives—Marcella Withrow and I were married. Her first marriage, to a young dentist at Conrad, had not panned out either, and she had come back over to Gros Ventre when the job of librarian opened up. That first winter of mine on the Reese place I resorted to the library a lot, and it began to dawn on me that books were not the only attraction. I like to think Marce and I are both tuned to an echo of Dode: "Life is wide, there's room to take a new run at it."

In any event, Marce and I seem to have gotten divorce out of our systems with those early wrong guesses, and we have produced two daughters, one married to a fish-and-game man up at Sitka in Alaska, the other living at Missoula where she and her husband both work for the newspaper. We also seem to be here on Noon Creek to stay, for as every generation ends up doing on this ranch we have lately built a new house. Four such domiciles by now, if you count the Ramsay homestead where I was born. It cost a junior fortune in double-glazing and insulation, but we have windows to the mountains all along the west wall of this place. These September mornings when I sit here early at the kitchen table and watch dawn come to the skyline of the Two, coffee forgotten and cold in my cup, the view is worth any price.

The thirty-plus years of ranching that Marce and I have put in here on Noon Creek have not been easy. Tell me what is. But so far the pair of us have withstood coyotes and synthetic fabrics and Two country winters and the decline of sheepherders to persevere in the sheep business, although we have lately diversified into some Charolais cattle and several fields of that new sanfoin alfalfa. I am never going to be red-hot about being a landlord to cows. And the problem of finding decent hay hands these days makes me positively pine for Wisdom Johnson and Bud Dolson and Perry Fox. But Marce and I are agreed that we will try whatever we have to, in order to hang on to this land. I suppose even dude ranching, though I hope to Christ it never quite comes to that.

Along English Creek, the main change to me whenever I go over there is that sheep are damn few now. Cattle, a lot of new farming; those are what came up on the latest spin of the agricultural roulette wheel. About half the families, Hahns, Frews, Roziers, another generation of Busby brothers, still retain the ranches their parents brought through the Depression. The Van Bebber ranch is owned by a North Dakotan named Florin, and he rams around the place in the same slambang fashion Ed did. Maybe there is something in the water there.

And Dode Withrow's place is run by one of Dode's other son-in-laws, Bea's husband Merle Torrance. Dode though is still going strong, the old boy. Weathered as a stump, but whenever I see that father-in-law of mine he is the original Dode: "What do you know for sure, Jick? Have they found a cure yet for people in the sonofabitching sheep business?"

Anyway, except for big aluminum sheds and irrigation sprinklers slinging water over the fields, you would not find the ranches of English Creek so different from the way they were.

The Double W now is owned by a company called TriGram Resources, which bought it from the California heirs after Wendell Williamson's death. As a goddamn tax writeoff, need I say.

How can it be twenty years since my father retired from the Forest Service? Yet it is.

After this summer I have told about, the next year was awful on him, what with Alec gone from us to the Deuce W and the decision from Mazoola in the winter of 1939 to move my father's district office from English Creek into Gros Ventre. Access realignment, they called it, and showed him on paper how having the ranger station in town would put him closer by paved road to the remote north portion of the Two. He kicked against it in every way he could think of; even wrote to the Regional Forester himself, the Major: "Since when is running a forest a matter of highway miles?" Before long, though, the war and its matters were on my father's mind and the mail was bringing Forest Service posters urging "LET'S DELIVER THE WOODS: SHARPEN YOUR AX TO DOWN THE AXIS."

The way the water of a stream riffles around a rock, the Forest Service's flow of change went past my father. Major Kelley departed Missoula during the war, to California to head up the government project of growing guayule for artificial rubber. "I'd rather take a beating than admit it," my father confessed, "but I was kind of getting used to those goddamn kelleygrams." The Two supervisor Ken Sipe was tapped for a wartime job at Forest Service headquarters in Washington, D.C., and stayed on back there. Their successors in Region One and the Two Medicine forest headquarters simply left my father in place, rangering the English Creek district. I have heard of a ranger out in the state of Washington who spent a longer career on a district, but my father's record wasn't far behind.

His first winter of retirement in Gros Ventre was a gloomy and restless time for him, although my mother and I could never tell for sure how much of that was retirement and how much just his usual winter. It was a relief to us all when spring perked him up. I had a call from him the morning of the first day of fishing season:

"Bet you a beer you've forgotten how to string ten fish on a willow."

"I can't get away" I had to tell him. "I've got ewes and lambs all over creation out here. You sure you wouldn't like to take up a career as a bunch herder?"

"Brook trout," he informed me, "are the only kind of herd that interests me. You're missing a free chance at a fishing lesson."

"I'll cash that offer next Sunday, okay? You can scout the holes for me today. I want Mom to witness your count when you get home, though. It's past time I was owed a beer, and it's beginning to dawn on me that your arithmetic could be the reason."

"That'll be the day," he rose to my joshing. "When I don't bring home ten fish on a willow. As will be shown to you personally next Sunday."

When he hadn't returned by dusk of that day, my mother called me at the ranch and I then called Tom Helwig, the deputy sheriff. I drove across the divide to English Creek and just before full dark found my father's pickup parked beside the North Fork, on Walter Kyle's old place. Tom Helwig and I and the men from the English Creek ranches searched and searched, hollering in the dark, until giving up about midnight.

With first light of the next morning I was the one who came onto my father. His body, rather, stricken by a heart attack, away back in the brush atop a beaver dam he'd been fishing. Nine trout on the willow stringer at his side, the tenth still on the hook where my father had dropped his pole.

"Jick, the summer when Alec left. Could it have come out different? If your father and I hadn't kept at him, hadn't had our notions of what he should do—would it all have been different?"

My mother brought this up in the first week after my father passed away. In a time like that, the past meets you wherever you turn. The days do not use their own hours and minutes, they find ones you have lived through with the person you are missing.

Only that once, though, in all the years from then to now, did she wonder that question aloud. The other incidents of the summer of 1939 we often talk over, when I stop by to see how she is doing. She has stayed on in her own house in Gros Ventre. "I'm sufficient company for myself," this mother of mine maintains. She still grows the biggest vegetable garden in town and is perpetual president of the library board. What irks her is when people regard her, as she puts it, "as if I was Some Kind of a Monument." I had to talk hard when her eighty-fourth birthday came this April and the new young editor of the *Gleaner* wanted to interview her. GROS VENTRE WOMAN HAS 'FOOLED' THE 20TH CENTURY was the headline. You know how those stories are, though. It is hard to fit such a life into mere inches of words.

I had never told her or my father of Alec's refusal, that noon when I phoned him about the Flume Gulch fire. And I did not when she asked could it, would it all have come out different?

But what I did say to her was the one truth I could see in that distant English Creek summer.

"If you two hadn't had the notions you did, you wouldn't have been yourselves. And if Alec hadn't gone his way, he wouldn't have been Alec."

She shook her head. "Maybe if it had been other times—"

"Maybe," I said.

334 · I VAN D OIG

And Stanley Meixell.

Stanley stayed on with the Busby brothers until their lambs were shipped that fall of 1939, then said he thought he'd go have a look at Oregon—"always did like that name." Early in the war the Busbys received word that he was working in a shipyard out there at Portland. After that, nothing.

So I am left with the last scene of Stanley after the Flume Gulch fire, before my father and I headed in to Gros Ventre. I went over to where Stanley was stirring a pot of gravy.

"Yessir, Jick. Looks like this feedlot of ours is about to close down."

"Stanley," I heard myself saying, "all that about the Phantom Woman fire—I don't know who was right or wrong, or if anybody was, or what. But I'm sorry, about the way things turned out back then."

"A McCaskill who'll outright say the word sorry," replied Stanley. He tasted the gravy, then turned to me, his dark eyes steady within the weave of squint lines. "I was more right than I even knew, that time."

"What time was that?"

"When I told your folks you looked to me like the jick of the family."

ACKNOWLEDGMENTS

THIS IS A WORK of fiction, and so English Creek, the Two Medicine National Forest, and the town of Gros Ventre exist only in these pages. Some of their geography is actual—the area of Dupuyer Creek and the Rocky Mountain Front, west of the town of Dupuyer, Montana. I'm afraid, though, that anyone who attempts to sort the real from the imagined in this book is in for confusion. In general I've retained nearby existing places such as Valier, Conrad, Choteau, Heart Butte and so on, but anything within what I've stretched geography to call the "Two Medicine country" I have felt free to change or invent. Thus my town of Gros Ventre, on Dupuyer's actual site, shares with Dupuyer only its origin as a stopover for freight wagons. That, and my love for the place.

Two persons I allude to were actual: Regional Forester Evan W. Kelley and pioneer Ben English. Insofar as possible I've sketched them from contemporary accounts or historical records. Where their lives coincide with those of my own characters, I've simply tried to do what seems to me the fiction writer's job—make the stuff up as realistically as I can. My particular thanks to Mary English Lindsey for sharing with me her memories of her father, and to Jack Hayne for contributing from his lode of knowledge about the Dupuyer area's pioneers.

I could not have created my version of the Two country in the period of this novel without the newspaper files and other local historical material of several northern Montana public libraries. I'm much indebted to Choteau Public Library and librarians Maureen Strazdas and Marian

Nett; Conrad Public Library and librarians Corleen Norman and Steve Gratzer, Great Falls Public Library, librarians Sister Marita Bartholome, Howard Morris, and Susan Storey, and library director Richard Gerken; Havre Public Library and librarian Bill Lisonby; Hill County Library and Dorothy Armstrong; Valier Public Library and librarian Sue Walley. And my appreciation as well to Harriet Hayne of Dupuyer, for sharing the taped interviews done for Dupuyer's remarkable centennial volume, *By Gone Days and Modern Ways.*

The Forest History Society provided many otherwise unavailable details of the lives led by U.S. Forest Service rangers and their families. Great thanks to my friends there for being so attentive to my needs, whether I happened to be on premises or at my typewriter in Seattle: Kathy and Ron Fahl, Mary Beth Johnson, and Pete Steen.

Much of the 1930s background for this book derives from the holdings of the three principal repositories of Montana history, and I'm grateful to the staff of each. The Renne Library of Montana State University at Bozeman; librarians Minnie Paugh and Ilah Shriver of Special Collections, and archivist Jean Schmidt. The Mansfield Library of the University of Montana at Missoula; librarian Kathy Schaefer of Special Collections, and archivist Dale Johnson. The Montana Historical Society at Helena; Bob Clark, Patricia Bick, Ellen Arguimbau—with particular thanks to reference librarian Dave Walter, who unflinchingly fielded query after query in the years I worked on this book.

For their generous encouragement and for rescuing me whenever I got lost in their specific fields of expertise, my thanks too to Montana's corps of professional historians, particularly Stan Davison, Bill Farr, Harry Fritz, Duane Hampton, Mike Malone, Rex Myers, and Rich Roeder. And I know of no other state with a published heritage of such quality and quantity as that of *Montana: The Magazine of Western History;* my gratitude to *Montana'*s editor, Bill Lang, for his skills as well as his friendship.

The University of Washington Library, my home base for this and my other books, again was an invaluable resource. I owe thanks to the Northwest Collection's Carla Rickerson, Andy Johnson, Dennis Andersen, Susan Cunningham, and Marjorie Cole; to Glenda Pearson of the Newspaper and Microcopy Center; and to Barbara Gordon of the Forest Resources library.

For vital guidance into the historical holdings of the U.S. Forest Service, I'm indebted to Maggie Nybo of Lewis and Clark National Forest headquarters in Great Falls and Raymond Karr and Jud Moore of the information office at Region One headquarters in Missoula. And I owe specific and special thanks to Charles E. "Mike" Hardy of Missoula, both for loaning me his personal collection of fireline notebooks, cookbooks, etc., and for his cataloguing of the papers of Harry T. Gisborne, long-time USFS forest fire researcher, at the University of Montana archives. I emphasize that while I have drawn from the fire descriptions of Gisborne, Elers Koch, and a number of other Montana foresters of their generation, the Flume Gulch fire is my own concoction.

I benefited greatly from listening to two career Forest Service men as they "pawed over old times": the late Nevan McCullough of Enumclaw, Washington, and Dahl Kirkpatrick of Albuquerque, New Mexico. My thanks to Mike McCullough for arranging that joint interview.

Many of the details of my Gros Ventre Fourth of July rodeo are due to the diligence of Kristine Fredriksson, registrar of collections and research at the ProRodeo Hall of Champions & Museum of the American Cowboy in Colorado Springs.

Vernon Carstensen, as ever a fund of ideas, brought to my attention the Montana origins of the famous dust storm of May, 1934, which I have appropriated for my Two Medicine country, and was a valuable sounding board about the Depression and the West.

Special thanks to my first and best friend in the Dupuyer country, Tom Chadwick; his driving skills delivered Carol and me to much of the landscape of this book.

My wife, Carol, has been the first reader of all my books. This time, camera ever in hand, she also became geographer of the Two country and architect of the town of Gros Ventre. My debt to her in all my work is beyond saying.

To my agent Liz Darhansoff, and my editor, Tom Stewart—thanks for making *English Creek* possible.

One of my first memories, a few months before my sixth birthday, is of hearing my parents and their neighbors discuss the radio news of the death of President Franklin Delano Roosevelt in April, 1945. Thus it is very nearly forty years now that I have been listening to Montanans. But never with more benefit than during the writing of *English Creek*. By interview or letter or phone, and in some instances by conversation and acquaintanceship down through the years, the following Montanans have lent me lore which in one way or another contributed to this book. My deep thanks to them all. *Bozeman:* Jake and Eleanor

Mast. *Butte:* Lucy Old. *Byunum:* Ira Perkins. *Choteau:* A. B. Guthrie, Jr. *Conrad:* Albert Warner. *Corvallis:* Helen Eden. *Deer Lodge:* Frank A. Shaw. *Dupuyer:* Lil and Tom Howe. *Flaxville:* Eugene Hatfield. *Forsyth:* James H. Smith. *Frazer:* Arthur H. Fast. *Fort Benton:* Alice Klatte, C. G. Stranahan. *Great Falls:* George Engler, Ted Fosse, Geoffrey Greene, Bradley and Joy Hamlett. *Hamilton:* Billie Abbey, George M. Stewart. *Havre:* Charles M. Brill, Edward J. Cook, Elmer and Grace Gwynn, Frances Inman, Frank Lammerding, Howard Sanderson. *Helena:* John Gruar, Eric White. *Hogeland:* Adrian Olszewski. *Jackson:* Kenneth Krause. *Malta:* Fred Olson, Egil Solberg. *Missoula:* Henry J. Viche. *Peerless:* Ladon Jones. *Superior:* Wally Ringer. *Valier:* Jim Sheble. *White Sulphur Springs:* Joyce Celander, Tony Hunolt, Clifford Shearer. *Wisdom:* Mr. and Mrs. Fred Else.

My inspiration for "The Lord of the Field" in Beth McCaskill's Fourth of July speech was Montgomery M. Atwater's article "Man-Made Rain," written for the Montana Writers' Project during the WPA era. Similarly the "Subjects under discussion . . . by U.S. Forest Service crews" was inspired by the versatile Bob Marshall, "A Contribution to the Life History of the Lumberjack," *Pulp and Paper Magazine of Canada,* May 21, 1931. The observation that a forest fire at night resembles a lighted city is from Elers Koch, in *Early Days in the Forest Service, Region One.* The theological survey joke is told by Hartley A. Calkins in that same volume. The analogy of a wedge of cool air thrusting between a fire and its smoke, and other rare eyewitness descriptions of a forest fire blowup, derive from H. T. Gisborne's article on the Half-Moon fire in *The Frontier,* November 1929.

During three summer stints of research in Montana and throughout the rest of those years of delving for and writing this book, many persons provided me hospitality, information, advice, encouragement, or other aid. My appreciation to Coleen Adams, Margaret Agee, Pat Armstrong, Genise and Wayne Arnst, Robert Athearn, John Backes, Bill Bevis, Gene and Hazel Bonnet, Merrill Burlingame, Harold and Maxine Chadwick, Juliette Crump, H. J. Engles, Clifford Field, Howard and Trudy Forbes, Glen Gifford, Sam Gilluly, Madeleine Grandy, Carol Guthrie, Vicki and Chuck Hallingstad, Gary Hammond of the Nature Conservancy's Pine Butte preserve, Eileen Harrington, John James, Carol Jimenez, Melvylei Johnson, Pat Kelley, Bill Kittredge, Dr. Jim Lane, Sue Lang, Becky Lang and Joel Lang, Marc Lee, Gail Malone, Elliot Marks of the Nature Conservancy, Sue Mathews, Ann McCartney, Nancy Meiselas, Horace Morgan, Ann and Marshall Nelson, Ken Nicholson, Peggy O'Coyne, Bud and Vi Olson, Gary Olson, Judy Olson, Laura Mary Palin, Cille and Gary Payton, Dorothy Payton, Patty Payton, Dorothy and Earl Perkins, Jarold Ramsey, Bill Rappold, Marilyn Ridge, Jean and John Roden, Tom Salansky, Ripley Schemm, Ted and Jean Schwinden, Annick Smith, Gail Steen, Fay Stokes, Margaret Svec, Merlyn Talbot, Dean Vaupel; John Waldner and the other members of the New Rockport Hutterite colony; Irene Wanner, Donald K. Watkins, Lois and Jim Welch, Rosana Winterburn, Glen Gifford, Sonny Linger, Ken Twichel. And the people of Dupuyer, Montana.

A SCRIBNER
READING GROUP GUIDE

ENGLISH CREEK

DISCUSSION POINTS

1. Much of the success of *English Creek* stems from the credibility of the narrative voice. Show how Jick McCaskill's acute sensitivity and observant personality make him a prime candidate for creating a balanced narrative structure. How does Doig artistically meld Jick's psychological musings with his more historical accounts?

2. The novel is in great part about Jick's journey into maturity, into wisdom. How does Jick bridge the gap between boyhood and manhood? Who is particularly influential in his coming of age?

3. Laconicism is a common characteristic of the ranchers and mountain men in Western film and fiction. Jick inherits his father's wry wit; show how he uses it to deal with life's bitter situations.

4. Is Alec a foil to Jick? Are there key choices that Alec makes and particular events in his life that save him from being a flat character and make him, rather, someone worth serious consideration?

5. At the end of Chapter One, Jick says, "Skinning wet sheep corpses, contending with a pack horse who decides he's a mountain goat, nursing Stanley along, lightning, any number of self-cooked meals, the hangover I'd woke up with and still had more than a trace of—what sad sonofabitch wouldn't realize he was being used out of the ordinary?" Jick's pack trip with Stanley Meixell is a jolting thrust from innocence to experience. What prompts Jick to discard his first impressions of Stanley and delve deeper into the meaning of the man behind Dr. Al K. Hall?

6. Why is Beth eager to avoid looking back? Compare and contrast Jick's attitude toward the past and its stories with his mother's attitude. Do the deaths of Varick and Alec rattle Beth into retrospective musings, even regret about what might have been?

7. Discuss how the Double W embodies the characteristics of the classic villain of the West.

8. Consider Velma Simms and Leona Tracy and how Doig paints their entrance into a room full of males. Compare and contrast the adoration they receive with the more quiet acknowledgment Beth receives from the men who love her. Why is Leona so alluring to Alec, even Jick? Is her highly physical role in the novel, a role charged with sexual tension, somehow comparable to the role of Willa Cather's Lena Lingard in *My Antonia*?

9. The Fourth of July dance adds mystery and musicality to the novel. Discuss the imagery surrounding this "beautiful haunting" and how the scene helps Jick to see his parents in a way that illuminates "all that had begun at another dance, at the Noon Creek schoolhouse twenty years before."

10. Why does Varick McCaskill listen to Stanley's advice about the fire in Flume Gulch? Were Jick not "prey to a profound preoccupation," would the novel have turned out the way that it does?

11. Doig recognizes the danger of engaging in literary symbolism at the risk of adding pretense to a novel that aims to be more realistic. What literary devices does he use instead to enliven both the narrative and his characters' voices? Do you think the inclusion of these devices, particularly song lyrics, is Doig's attempt at a fusion of poetry and fiction?

BACKGROUND NOTES

THE PIECE OF THE WORLD I ADMIRE MOST

Am I Jick? People have asked me a thousand times whether the fourteen-year-old narrator of *English Creek,* in his pivotal summer of 1939, is my literary alter ego. No, not by a long shot, as Jick McCaskill himself would put it. But his homeland, the Two Medicine country of Montana and of my trilogy by that name, for an important time was mine.

English Creek and its valley are actually the Dupuyer Creek area of northern Montana, beneath the skyline of the Rocky Mountain Front. It's the region where I lived during high school and was a ranch hand and farm worker for several summers, the "Facing North" country in my memoir, *This House of Sky*, and it is big and hard and glorious—the piece of the world I admire most. It's a country of margin, of America changing, ascending from one geography to another, and of the sensation Isak Dinesen caught in *Out of Africa*: "In the highlands you woke up in the morning and thought: Here I am, where I ought to be."

Looking back on *English Creek*, the first of my fiction to be set in Montana, I see that it shares with *This House of Sky* an emphasis on landscape and weather and their effects on people's lives. In both books (all right, in all my books) I was trying to write about the grit of an America that even yet half-exists in the mountains-and-plains West: ranching, haying, fire-fighting, the Forest Service itself, all have their own techniques and lingo which make them vivid. What I deliberately made different from *This House of Sky* was the voice of this book—the narrative not as densely poetic as *Sky's*. Instead, I tried for a kind of idiomatic eloquence, a western cadence ruffled by turns of phrase. Jick, the narrator, is a man of today looking back on 1939, which gave him the angle of view I needed to hang the storyline on, and he has the love of sayings and stories that animates a lot of otherwise taciturn westerners. I remember, as I worked on the book, how Jick's voice, built as it was from my decades of file cards and notebook of dialogue and phrasing, excited me so much I hated to admit it, for fear of jinx. But that voice of his, from the opening line when he tells us "That month of June swam into the Two Medicine country," felt true to the time and country, and came more easily than the style of any of my books before or since.